Tayo Emmanuel draws inspiration from real issues she witnesses in everyday lives to tell her stories. An incurable romantic, she is continually fascinated by the interplay and unpredictability of human relationships.

Her second novel, Echoes from the Past has been adapted into a movie, titled Echoes.

A passionate speaker on relationships and family-life matters, Tayo can be found meddling with other people's love lives when she's not writing or working.

Peace in the Abyss

Tayo Emmanuel

Published in 2021 by Total Word Publishers, United Kingdom

As always, my special appreciation goes to:

My fabulous husband and daughter, who have chosen to be my number one fans - Your words of affirmation keep me going and I count myself blessed to have you in my life.
The friends and family who urge me on and play springboard - I couldn't have done this without your support.

A very big thanks to Dr Opeyemi Kuponiyi for your support and guidance on the medical parts of this story.

Special thanks to my readers and those who take time to send me mails about their views on my books. Please keep them coming. It's always a pleasure hearing from you and I look forward to meeting you some day.

To those who love even when love hurts
To those who hurt but don't know they do
To those who bleed with no cuts to show
To those who weep, yet without tears
To those who stay, hoping love conquers
To those who leave, but return to fight
To those who fight and are lucky to win
To those who find the truth, only too late

CHAPTER ONE

A single thought was always uppermost in Preye Banigo's mind. Marriage! Four decades of living will knock on her door in the not so distant future; her two younger sisters were already married; she was well settled in her business and her biological clock was ticking faster than any marriage proposal on the horizon.

It was one of those hot lazy mornings that everything seemed to move slowly, especially the traffic. As the car snaked along the road on the way to her office on Oregun Road, her eyes darted to Timi's muscular frame of their own volition. He was handsome in so many ways that she found captivating. He carried his sporty-sculptured frame gallantly like a proud Adonis with dark penetrating eyes that made her knees go weak.

The unyielding thought about her marital status trundled through her mind like a snail in a hurry to go nowhere as she searched his face to find an answer to the question she could not bring herself to ask him. His curvy thick lips, darkened by years of smoking, formed an intriguing smile on his face which was well defined, bold and deliberate with a sharp jawline and high cheekbones

The sudden blaring of an annoying honk retrieved her mind from the unanswerable question concerning her uncertain future and refocused her on the traffic they were stuck in. Still, no tangible vehicular movement, except for reckless *okada* riders manoeuvring their bikes through the bumper-to-bumper chains of cars, some edging towards the gutter as much as they could narrowly get away with. She wondered if it was the regular rush-hour traffic Lagos roads were notorious for. *But Wednesdays are usually saner,* she mused. A look ahead revealed nothing unusual and she couldn't sight any trace of onlookers who typically gathered at accident scenes. If it wasn't an accident, maybe one of those eccentric drivers who thought they had exclusive right to hurriedness had decided to face oncoming traffic to beat everyone to the race this morning.

Calculating that the rest of the journey would be less than twenty minutes if she walked, she thought about her running kit at the back seat. But she quickly perished the thought. Timi wouldn't forgive her if she ventured to leave him in the car. After all, they were stuck in the traffic because he had opted to drop her off at work every day. She didn't want to break his mood as he intermittently hummed and swayed his head to the beats of music playing on the radio.

They had been discussing the past days' events from their different perspectives since she got into the car, until they came to a near-stop. Now, it seemed like the blanket of traffic had locked their lips as they were both deep in their separate thoughts.

Some twenty minutes later, the sight of the traffic warden's uniform at the junction that led to her office gave her some relief. A silent puff escaped her lips and she glanced at the dashboard clock. She sent a text to Tobi Abass, to apologise that she'd be late for the 9.00a.m catch-up and assured him that she'd be at the office in the next fifteen minutes.

The gate barrier of her office was already lifted up by the time Timi finally drove through. It was unusual not to find an empty parking slot, but the car park was full now. With an irritated scowl forming on his face, he speculated that someone had planned a conspiracy against his itinerary today. He scoured the car park and shook his head before raising his bulky hands to stamp them on the dashboard, initiating a shift from his erstwhile jovial disposition.

'This is unbelievable,' his raspy voice hooted.

'It's okay, you don't need to park. I'll get off once you pull up in front of the lobby,' Preye suggested, glancing at the clock for the umpteenth time. She hated being late for meetings, especially when she was the convener. It reflected bad leadership and lack of respect for other people's time, notwithstanding the fact that they were her employees. Just before her last word, a car pulled out from Timi's right side.

Timi's eyes were intent on the empty space as he quickly steered towards the slot before losing it to someone else.

'I don't mind hanging around for a while so we can chat some more before you head in,' he ignored her suggestion. He didn't like being told what to do. He hadn't endured the perfidious traffic just to drop her off without their usual chit-chat.

He lived in Omole, a Lagos suburb, and usually did the twenty minutes' walk to her cosy two-bedroom apartment in Ojodu, to drive her to her office with her car, before going with the car to run his errands. He'd return in the evening to take her home.

He had introduced this arrangement two days ago when he started his one-week annual leave. He loved the opportunity to see Preye every day and the fact that his walk to her house afforded him the opportunity to exercise effortlessly. She had resisted initially, thinking it was too much trouble for him, but she was thankful now for the time it afforded them to spend together during the ride.

She shook her head. Her body twitched to head for her office, but she couldn't simply dash out of the car without appearing rude, which could unleash an avoidable tirade from him.

'What else are we chatting about? We've already talked about our plans for the day and they haven't changed in the past thirty minutes. Sitting through that traffic has stressed me out,' she said, as she pushed away some strays of hair from her face; they were escapees from her Brazilian weave. 'Tomorrow, I'll be going straight to a client's office, so you don't have to come for me in the morning. You'll have enough time for yourself.'

He shook his thick head of well-tended afro hair. 'No Mine, I won't trade the time spent with you for anything. I can take you anywhere you want and even wait in the car. You know it's not a problem for me. I can be your driver. Unless you've found someone else to hook up with that I don't know of,' he teased. 'Honestly, it gives me some peace of mind to know you're safe and that there's no mysterious person lurking around you.' His eyes sparkled with a mischievous smile. 'I'd hate to find out that you hitched a ride with one of your high-powered clients because I wasn't around.'

'You can't possibly think there's a problem with someone giving me a ride, could you? I thought it would save both of us some time, instead of you going back and forth for my sake. My schedule is unpredictable this week and I don't like the idea of you waiting around for me.' Preye smiled, clasping her hands to avoid checking her wrist watch. Timi has succeeded in making her wait for his chitchat after all. 'By the way, the other day, Lola suggested that we needed to start considering the impact of carbon emission here in Lagos, so we should start commuting economically with our cars. My next goal is to do a straight run to the office. That way, I can totally achieve my running goals and avoid traffic altogether. What do you think?'

A few wrinkles suddenly appeared on his brow. 'Really, Mine, I think you should start thinking for yourself. I don't like the influence that friend of yours exerts on you. I can tell you she doesn't care about the environment, otherwise she wouldn't have a generator at home. Or doesn't she have one?' He wore his smirk like a prize from winning a conquest. 'She's tried to keep you away from me as much as possible, from the day we met. She has all day to fill your mind with rubbish just because she works for you. That girl has an agenda and I feel concerned that you don't see through her. I'm sure she's the reason you keep insisting that we can't live together.'

Preye drew a breath and shook her head in surprise. 'Can we not make this about Lola, please? And no, she's not the reason we don't live together,' she responded. Getting into the conversation about cohabiting never ended well, and it occasioned more squabble than she could handle at the moment. She needed to put on her work hat now. 'We can talk about it again, tomorrow.'

Really, there was nothing to talk about. He already knew her stand about living together and sex before marriage, but she had to placate him. She started to open the door and he pulled her back.

'We are meeting for lunch.' It was more a statement than a question. He planted a kiss on her cheek before inspecting the birthmark on the right side of her neck. He carefully pulled up the collar of her dress and draped her silky hair over her shoulder to ensure the birthmark was well hidden. The mark was something she hadn't thought about concealing before Timi came into her life. Her mum always said it was a kiss from God.

'I already have plans with Lola for lunch, unless you want to join us. By the way, aren't you supposed to be busy today? You said you were going to Lekki,' she reminded him.

He raised his wide bulky shoulders. 'I can't ever be too busy for you. That plan with Lola is not going to work, so you'll have to make plans with her for another day. Sure, she'll be disappointed, but she'll get over it. She sees you every day anyway. Tell her to chill. I'll see you at noon, Naana's Kitchen.' He wagged a finger in her face. 'Priorities, Preye. I don't understand why you like making out that your friend is competing with me. Anyway, I have a surprise for you.'

She forced a smile over her displeasure, grabbed her black leather handbag and adjusted her fitted navy blue dress before heading for the lobby, her high heels sounding noisily as they came in contact with the tiled floor.

*

Preye Banigo was carved in gold on the name plate placed on her black desk in her fifth-floor office. She was co-owner of Beta Limited; a firm she had started seven years ago with Tobi Abass. Hard work, intelligence, tenacity, and self-confidence were the pillars on which she had built her career foundation. And she could proudly say Beta was one of the top ten public relations firms in Nigeria under the indigenous start-ups category.

Before graduating from Regent University, Tobi and Preye had both been lucky to get head-hunted by one of the top three public relations groups in the country. They had both managed the accounts of some of the best brands in Nigeria and a few African countries, running campaigns and organising events. Preye particularly liked conducting market research and creating engaging stories from potential bland or bad scenarios. She had met a lot of high-powered individuals and celebrities along her career path and had wide international exposure.

Nine years down the line, Preye and Tobi had realised they were becoming restless and decided that if they wanted to fully unleash their creativity, they needed to run the show themselves. One day, over lunch, Tobi had asked Preye if she had enough savings or investment to last her for a year, in the event that she got sacked. When Preye responded in the affirmative, Tobi had made the proposition that they became partners. To Preye, it had felt almost like a marriage proposal and her response was, 'Why did it take you this long to ask?' They had both laughed and promised to think over it for a month.

By the third month, after fruitlessly combing the streets of Lagos for a low budget office space, they had ended up in the spare room of Tobi's flat in the Mainland area of Anthony, starting out with one of his friends as their first client.

It had been a huge risk, but they had kept at it. After two years, with four other clients in their kitty and a few millions in the bank, they had both agreed it was time to expand and rent a proper office. Hiring a sharp and clever woman like Lola Bello helped. Although she didn't have as much experience as Tobi and Preye in public relations, Lola was creative, resourceful and relentless. She was also highly connected and had a few clients to her credit. Lola had attended the same university as Preye and was one of Preye's two best friends back then. But Lola had fallen on some hard times with her marriage and getting the job at Beta had given her the much needed lifeline.

What most people hadn't known back then was that Preye Banigo's education had been primarily funded through scholarships and cooperative loans. She had been admitted as one of the sprinters for the university and having won many medals, she had pushed the school into a prominent position for national racing.

She was the oldest of three children, raised by their single mother, Miriam Banigo. Her father had left when Preye got into secondary school, putting the family under financial strain. Growing up without support from her father, Preye had felt it was her duty to support her mother and had been consumed with an overwhelming desire to over-achieve and show her two sisters how things had to be done - no complaints or excuses.

The cost of living in Lagos had taken its toll on the family. By Preye's second year at secondary school, they were forced to change location from Gbagada and downsize from their three-bedroom flat to a one-bedroom apartment in Ogba. Miriam had changed the children's school and the girls had taken turns to help out at her shop after school hours.

Despite the additional household and shop chores, Preye had maintained her top grades at school and still managed to be a member of the school's athletics club. Watching her mother work tirelessly, selling provisions at the market, Preye had resolved that failure wasn't an option for her.

Although there hadn't been much interest from her former husband after a few years of separation, Miriam had made the monumental sacrifice to keep communication channels open with Harry Banigo. Preye, who was always asking after her father hadn't realised until she was an adult that her mother would have preferred not to have anything to do with Harry after he strayed away with another woman. Yet, Miriam had remained cordial with him for the sake of the children.

Sometimes, he'd send money, but only enough to cover the essentials. Preye hadn't known until her university days that she needed a lot more than the essentials. From her interaction with school friends from wealthy families, she had realised she wanted a piece of that wealth with the independence it could afford her, and she was the only person to get it for herself. She had purposely and diligently pursued success, without losing sight of her goal to have a stable family. She had resolved as soon as she became emotionally aware, that she'd do whatever it took to avoid a broken marriage like her parents'.

Preye's mobile phone rang, just as she was settling on her swivel leather chair. She already knew who it was before picking up the phone from her desk to place the call on speaker. 'Hello, Love. I made it safely up the lift to my desk.'

'I had to be sure you weren't pissed off about my comments regarding Lola. I won't get a thing done until I know things are cool between us.' Timi said in his enchanting voice. She could visualise his lips curving into a warming smile.

'You have no reason to feel threatened by Lola or any of my friends. I love you and no one can come between us or diminish the way I feel about you. That should matter to you.'

'I feel better now. I can't wait to see you at noon.'

'Do you feel good enough to have her tag along? She's planning Zara's birthday party and I promised I'd help.' Preye crossed her fingers, hoping against reason that both Timi and Lola would agree.

'I planned a surprise for you and three would be a crowd. Can we keep today between us, please?'

The quiet emission of air from her lips was like a mesh ball of disappointment, resignation and excitement. She hated to cancel plans with Lola, but she was curious about the surprise. 'Let me talk to her and see how she reacts. My *bestie* can be cool-headed sometimes. Maybe she'll understand when I tell her about the surprise.'

'I thought I was your *bestie*,' Timi sounded like a child asking for a refill of ice cream. Preye pictured him pouting.

She was always confounded anytime Timi expressed jealousy towards her friends. 'It's a term I use only for Lola and Aisha, so don't take offence. I'll see you in a few hours. I have to get to work. My desk is swamped and I need to help Tobi with a client who is giving him some hassles.' She pressed the red button before Timi could utter another word.

Like the other offices in Beta, her office had floor-to-ceiling venetian blinds on the windows overlooking the valley between Opebi and Oregun. Several industry awards sat proudly on the walls which were painted satin grey. Her desk was a modest L-shaped graphite grey wood and leather piece, with matching white pedestals and a pint-size bookshelf filled with mostly hard-cover books.

They were expanding rapidly. Preye was in charge of strategy and operations, while Tobi focused on client services and everything else. She occasionally helped out with the problematic clients or those that were thinking of jumping ship. Some clients required extra hand-holding and she liked the challenge when they leaned on her. Preye and Tobi made a good team, and having someone reliable and easy-to-work with like Lola Bello, as the Director of Projects gave them some breathing space to plan and work strategically. When Preye needed Tobi's input, he was there without reservation and it worked both ways.

A yellow post-it note with Tobi's handwriting was stuck on her desk where her laptop sat, beside a file tray stacked with magazines and marketing brief packs. Her big leather-bound notebook and a pile of papers were tucked under a heart-shaped paper weight. On the bookshelf behind her, there were two transparent vases of freshly watered plants and a silver frame with her picture in it.

Tobi's *SOS* staring at her was all she needed to set the pace of the day's workload and to remind her that she had come in late for her meeting with him.

Before she could wrench herself from her desk, Tobi showed up in her office. He was of average height, slim but muscular, with a square face sitting on his sturdy neck.

'Boss, it's me again. I know the intrusion may be a bit much for a sunny morning, but I really need you to step in with Boomers.' Tobi deliberately called her boss sometimes to tease her, and at other times, to send a message that she was equally important in the picture, especially to their male clients. 'I've got an appointment with our gubernatorial candidate today and you know that's as good as a whole day's affair. I sincerely hope I get to see him this time,' Tobi said, shaking his head as the picture of sitting idly in the client's office flashed in front of him. 'I wonder why they make life so difficult,' he finished off, grumbling.

'Better wipe that frown off your face,' she scolded him. 'Too early in the day. And we need his account, so you have to be at your best behaviour. I'll sort out Boomers. Fill me in. What's his grouse?'

Boomers was a growing record label that signed too many artistes too fast, before they were properly vetted. The recording label had a rapidly growing fan-base of children and teenagers. But their family-friendly image was getting tarnished as there had been recent outcries from parents and moral activists against some of the artistes.

Boomers needed help to fortify their brand with their sponsors and fans. They had been having series of scandals from one artiste to another, ranging from thuggery to sexual abuse. And the owner himself didn't help matters because he was naturally proud and uncouth, always speaking out of order. Apart from his nine-to-five job in information technology, Preye's ex-fiancé, Kevin had been a budding singer with one album to his credit, so she understood the business and was a good fit to help Tobi with the client.

She paced around her office in a bid to wake her body to sync with her raging mind as she brimmed with ideas on how to promote Boomers back to good stead. Tobi and Preye spent over an hour brainstorming and she called their meeting to a close when she realised she still had to talk to Lola.

'Tobi, give me some time to reflect on what we've discussed and I'll come up with a definite plan. I have some phone calls to make now. Do me a favour and write up what we've come up with. We'll go over it and I can incorporate it with the plan. I'll call the director and set up a meeting with him for Friday.'

Preye stood up on her bare feet and stretched. She usually

kicked off her heels once she has sat at her desk and she hated jamming her feet back in when she had to. At only five feet and two inches tall, heels were necessary for height's sake. She felt more confident with a couple of extra inches and as a woman dealing with mostly men all day, she needed it.

When people talked about women making strides in the workplace, she considered those people naïve. Yes, women had started making strides, but they were just a pocket-full in Nigeria. She was as good as Tobi and worked as hard, but sometimes their top-end clients made it clear they would rather deal with him, except for the ones who had some sexual intentions towards her. Some of the more traditional ones couldn't hide their shock when she was introduced as a partner or better still, boss in Beta.

'There's the Kids' Night Out at church this evening and I'm not sure I'll make it, unless I get to see His Excellency before the end of the day,' Tobi grumbled again, still unhappy about the time-wasting bit every time he needed to see their new client. But the governor-elect was paying good money and couldn't simply be discarded. 'Thanks for your help with Boomers,' he finished, as he left Preye's office.

He had gotten married about five years after school and had two kids within five years. He and Preye had a good and mutually respectful professional relationship and she always admitted she couldn't have partnered with a more diligent and dedicated person.

Preye took a deep breath as she dialled up Lola on her mobile phone, rather than using the intercom. Looking at Lola's display picture on her phone made it even harder to cancel their plans. She didn't want to face Lola in her office down the corridor because Lola would likely guess who was behind the change in plans.

'*Omo* girl. *How now?*' Preye asked in what she hoped was a cheery voice.

'I'm walking towards the building. I've gone to see the gift items Tobi has been talking about. They are quite nice, I must say. I'm not late yet, am I? Our lunch is at one, not twelve, right?' Lola asked, talking rapidly.

Lola was thirty eight years old, divorced and had a ten-year old daughter. Equipped with the gift of the gab, she was belligerent and bold. But on the inside, she was a pussycat - kind and loving and went all out to protect the ones she loved. She described herself as obese, but she was just a size sixteen with solid curves in the right places and a mocha skin that suited her well. At five feet, ten inches, she towered over Preye.

'Punish me at will, but I'm sorry, I have to cancel. Something came up and I can't swing it for lunch,' Preye apologised hesitantly. She didn't want to lie and she was counting down the seconds until Lola figured it out.

'No! Really? What kind of trick has he pulled now? This has him written all over it.'

Preye would have feigned ignorance and ask who Lola was referring to, but knowing Lola to be a human lie detector, there was no point in lying. Preye bit her upper lip. 'He has a surprise for me and we're meeting up for lunch. I can't be sure, but he might be ready to pop the question.'

'It's convenient how he always comes up with a surprise at the most inopportune times. Times when you have plans with family, friends, or anyone who isn't him. Preye, you're the smartest woman I know, except when it comes to this guy. Well, and those other guys too. Although I blame myself for those ones.' Lola paused but Preye kept quiet. Lola sat in the lobby to collect herself before going up to her office. 'Okay. I've said my piece and there's nothing more I can do. This doesn't mean I'm happy or that I'll stop being a thorn in his side if he keeps invading my space. Remember that Zara's birthday party is in three weeks and my sweet jewel will be crushed if her godmother doesn't show up. I could have used your help with planning her school party, but I'll survive. By the way, what did you get her?' Lola asked, her voice dropping to a dulcet tone without losing a beat.

'I'm not telling you because you can't keep a secret,' Preye responded gleefully, glad for the switch in tone. Lola was like that; a light bulb that could switch darkness to brightness with just a click.

'You haven't gotten her anything yet, have you?'

Preye typed in Toys Centre to bring up the page on her laptop and she located the filter to search for ten-year-old girls gifts. 'I'm on it. Have faith. We'll be there and come bearing gifts.'

'We?' Lola queried, as she got up to head for the lift.

'Yeah, is that a problem?' Preye asked. 'With the godmother's boyfriend, maybe.' She kicked herself for the use of the plural pronoun, as she tried to make light of it.

'Nope. I don't' have a problem if he doesn't. Although I can bet he won't be there.' Lola quipped flatly. 'FYI, I'm raising my index finger for you now, but you can't see it. See you later, Boss.' Her cheery photo disappeared from Preye's phone screen before Preye could protest.

Lola Bello and Aisha Hassan, Preye's second best friend, the third of the trio, had been there for her when Kevin died of lymphoma, shortly after they got engaged. Preye's devastation after Kevin's death had been edging towards depression before her two friends organised a healing trip to Spain to help her refocus and restore some sanity to her life. She had initially protested and cried half of the time, but it had proven to be a cathartic experience. Although, she had travelled a lot before then, it had been only for work and for short periods of time. The three-week Spanish holiday had opened her up to meeting new people and exploring some exotic places she had only seen in movies. She had been able to purge her negative thoughts and replace them with a fresh perspective and the resilience to reconcile herself to the transience of life. Embracing the comfort in the brightness of the skies, the calmness from the waves of the seas and the assurance that God had a purpose for her even in the depth of her sorrow, Preye had learnt to live with the pain and felt better equipped to face life anew by the time the three of them returned from Spain. She was thankful that her friends had provided her the scaffolding when she could have collapsed.

Then there had been two disastrous relationships after Kevin.

Lola, the most adventurous of the trio had expressed concern that Preye was repelling men, so she had started persuading Preye to try dating. When Preye didn't show enough inclination, Lola had set up a profile for her on an online dating site. Not long after, two men expressed interest. Preye, unconsciously longing for love, had quickly plunged into a relationship with her first date. About two months after meeting the first date, Preye had casually mentioned to her friends that he asked her for a loan. Suspicious, Lola had secretly set up a random profile of another lady on the dating site to attract him and he fell for the bait. Lola it was who had ended the relationship, by walking the man out of Preye's flat.

The second relationship had followed almost the same route when Preye's friends discovered that the man was still legally married, although briefly separated from his wife. His profile on the dating site had stated that he was divorced. Somehow, a replica of his name and details had popped up on a legal brief Aisha was reviewing for her husband's law firm, where the suitor had named his wife as joint-executor to a new investment deed. When confronted, he had confessed that he had wanted to tell

Preye that he was going through counselling to reconcile with his wife, but he hadn't known how to break up with Preye without hurting her.

Scarred by the two experiences, Preye had erected a dam to shut the flow of romantic affection from her heart, as it appeared she was doomed to attracting unsuitable men.

Now Timi Coker was in her life, and expectedly, Lola had been suspicious of him from the beginning. Preye desperately wanted this relationship to work, so she could finally settle down to being a wife and mother. As much as she was successful in her career, she subscribed to the school of thought that her success wasn't complete without marriage and a family.

She had stopped attending the fellowship for matured singles in her home church after a few meetings, because she felt out of place and couldn't identify any male as a good prospect. It was as if the eligible single guys had permanent glue on their eyes and mouths anytime they walked past her. She was tired of the snide remarks and the pitiful looks, either from her age mates who were married, or from the younger singles who thought she was too old. Preye continually disputed Lola's efforts to assure her that those remarks and looks were only in Preye's mind. She simply couldn't get used to people giving her a shocked, second look anytime she introduced herself as Miss Banigo. And some would actually venture to ask her if she wasn't married, with their eyes popping as if they wanted an outlet from their sockets every time she responded in the affirmative.

She also dreaded the cold nights when she was alone in bed, hugging one of the four pillows she ensconced herself in. *Maybe this surprise from Timi would bring her fairy tale ending within reach,* she hoped. Forty and single didn't look like an exciting status to attain in the next one year.

CHAPTER TWO

Preye's trainers bounced smoothly against the marbled floor of her office reception. She spared an involuntary smile for the receptionist seated behind the huge mahogany office desk. As she stepped out of the revolving doors, Timi tapped her on the shoulder from behind. He had waited in the car, listening to music for about ten minutes and trotted to the entrance when he noticed she had changed position on the phone application he used to track her movement.

'Timi! You scared me,' Preye halted, her eyes widening in shock and pleasure. 'I thought we were meeting at Naana's.' With her ear pods firmly in place, she had been immersed in listening to a motivational e-book on her phone.

He put his arm around her waist and aimed to kiss her, but he caught her cheek as she turned her face away from his. 'I decided to come so I can take you to the restaurant. Expecting someone else?' Timi asked, teasing with raised eyebrows.

'No, I intended to walk there, so you might have to park the car or drive down there by yourself. I've been in meetings for hours and I need to stretch my legs. It doesn't hurt to raise my heart rate any time I get the chance.'

Timi looked down and saw her trainers. 'You changed your shoes. Interesting work look.'

'It's lunch time, and you can't imagine how badly those heels hurt. They look great, but I kick them off whenever I get the chance. I didn't think you'd care,' she said, feeling awkwardly defensive.

'You know I think you're superb and more feminine in heels. You work hard to look nice for work, but ruin it with a pair of athletic shoes. It makes you look like a clown.'

She knew her trainers, paired with her black silhouette dress wouldn't win her a fashion award but she wished he didn't make a big deal out of it. He was sometimes hypercritical, almost to the point of nasty, about how she looked, which wasn't fair since she ignored the fact that he had only two suits and some colourful fun ties he wore to work every day. He was often a *fashion miss*, but she had never told him he only looked good in jeans and casual tops. His comment hung in the air, and eventually, she brushed it off. In the grand scheme of things, it wasn't a big deal.

He said he'd have loved to walk with her, but he couldn't, because it was too hot and he preferred the coolness of the car air conditioner. As they walked towards the gate, he continued to grumble and gently nudged her towards the car. Not wanting to start an argument, she got into the car, promising herself to go for her walk later.

*

Naana's Kitchen on Allen Avenue was a contemporary plush restaurant that attracted the senior working class in and around Ikeja. Long embroidered curtains were draped over big windows, with contrasting windowpanes. The red tablecloths provided some brightness for the mahogany square tables surrounded by black leather chairs.

The restaurant served as a cosy meeting place for many and especially buzzed during lunch time. When Preye and Timi arrived, the wooden tables adorned with bright flowers were almost fully taken, as suit-clad executives focused on their meals or chatted away. The couple waited for a few minutes, enjoying the ambience of the low jazz music. Soon, a waiter led them to a table and wiped it before giving them the menu, so he could take their order.

The restaurant's specialty was a range of exotic rice dishes. But twice a year, they introduced new dishes to test customers' preferences.

Naana's Kitchen was where they had their first date, although neither knew it was a date at the time. Timi had joined the Roadrunners Club, founded by Preye and she had brought him here like she usually did, with newcomers to the club – to hear their stories and share hers.

The Roadrunners had given Preye a cause to champion and carried her through the rough years after Kevin succumbed to lymphoma.

The club welcomed runners of every ability, from casual joggers to marathon runners. Preye fell in the middle of the pack, having run a couple of marathons but preferring ten-kilometre races as she reached her mid-thirties.

Although she had masked her feelings, Preye had been smitten from the moment she laid eyes on Timi Coker. As she got to know him more, it hadn't mattered that she was older than him by three years. He was tall, at about six feet two inches and muscular without being bulky. He had full lips with slim rounded nose.

He had walked in on Preye after she had just completed a five-kilometre charity run. His sweaty dark skin had glistened, with his muscles looking like they would ripple through his shirt. And his brown eyes had sparkled enough to captivate her.

The five-kilometre run was one of the Roadrunners' three-day fund-raising annual events, which included seminars and a fun games night where few people won prizes. With approval from the local government, the five kilometre run was routed to and from the Lagos State Secretariat and Oregun, close to the Ikeja end of Lagos. Preye and Aisha, dressed in their t-shirts with Roadrunners AC logo emblazoned on the front, had been in the Roadrunners' one-room office, arranging posters and addressing letters to be sent out, when Timi walked in with an aromatic cup of coffee, to join the club with his friend.

Noticing the way Preye always avoided meeting his eyes, Timi had sensed her attraction to him from that first day and he had taken her as another romantic conquest.

He had been subtle in his approach; close enough for her to rely on him, but enigmatic enough for her to want to find out more. With some prodding from Preye, he had started going to church more regularly and eventually moved to her local church. He had helped out at Roadrunners and randomly given her little gifts; small enough to seem like they were not deliberate, but meaningful enough to show he had put some thoughts into them.

The first time he asked her out, she hadn't exactly said no. Instead, she had tactfully mentioned her reservations about the fact that she was older than him and a bit more settled in her career. Taking the tacit rejection gracefully, he had brushed aside her reservations and assured her that he wasn't a culture conformist and age was just a number to him. And he had left it at that. By then, she had begun to look forward to his daily calls.

After his job offer from Morgan Bridge, through her referral, he had taken her to lunch to celebrate. She had hoped he'd ask her out again, but he hadn't been willing to take any chance of rejection again, under the guise of playing hard to get. So he waited.

About nine months after their first meeting, convinced that there was still no other man around Preye, with the way she was invested in Roadrunners, Timi had been sure she was pining for him when she always found a way to stay beside him or talk to him every time he showed up for an activity. As he had predicted, she had been unable to hide her excitement when he asked her to be his girlfriend the second time. Her acceptance had jumped out of her mouth as if she was afraid he might change his mind.

Immediately she sat down at their table which had a view of the back garden, Preye hurriedly perused the menu and smiled at the waiter.

'I'll have *ofada* rice with *dodo* and grilled fish. With water and iced tea, please.'

'Same and let's have some *sushi* for starters.' Timi sat back and smiled, feeling accomplished. The restaurant had recently introduced *sushi* which had become a favourite of Timi. Preye had decided to keep to the familiar dishes after one taste of the *sushi,* which didn't go down well with her.

The waiter shook his head. 'We stopped serving *sushi*, sir. It wasn't very popular with our customers. But we'll be introducing another delicacy soon.'

'I'm not so pleased about that,' Timi protested. 'Let your manager know.' Dismissing the waiter with a flippant wave of his hand, he turned his attention back to Preye as the curves of his lips widened.

'Why are you smiling?' Preye asked, wondering if he saw something behind her.

'I'm taking in how beautiful you are.'

Preye smiled. 'Thanks. You make me feel that way.'

'Can I give you a tip?' he asked, still smiling.

'Sure. Do you have to ask?'

'I know your dress is expensive, but it's cut too severely and a bit dark. I think you should try something more mature. A floral print would be nice and your hair ...'

'What about my hair?' Preye cut him off, his criticisms

21

getting to her. 'I thought you loved this one because it's straight and silky. It's one of the best brands I have and I like it. It doesn't take too long to tie into a doughnut.'

'Yeah, I like it, but I like to see it falling down your shoulders. If I didn't know better, I'd think you wanted people to see the birthmark on your neck, so they can ask you about it. I think it draws a lot of attention to your neck and I don't like that. I've told you where you can have it removed, but it's up to you.' He lifted his shoulders swiftly.

'I hear you. Can we move on to the surprise you have for me because I'd hate to think I cancelled lunch with Lola to be lectured.'

She got such comments from him quite often and tried to tolerate them, but sometimes they made her feel inadequate. When they started dating, they had both agreed that they would be open and sincere with each other, so she couldn't blame him. She knew all he wanted was a good relationship. Moreover, she understood that he was an only child and it seemed he had missed out on siblings' rivalry and squabbles.

He leaned in with an envelope, instead of getting down on one knee with a velvet ring box. A bit disappointed, she opened the envelope and found a compact brochure of a holiday chalet in Badagry. Maybe sixteen months was too soon to expect an engagement ring, she thought as she smiled at the holiday surprise. Once again, Timi had pulled victory from the jaws of defeat. The lunch had been edging towards a huge let-down with his criticisms, but he had been able to redeem it with the getaway surprise. It was typical of him and it worked every time.

'A weekend away. Wow! We deserve it and I'm thrilled,' she said and mouthed a kiss to him across the table. 'Thanks, Love.'

'We'll stay in an ocean view room and I plan to bring you breakfast in bed all four mornings.'

'Four mornings?' Her eyes flickered wide as her lower lip

drooped, fluctuating between the pleasure of getting away and the pain of having to realign her work schedule. 'I thought it was a weekend getaway. I can't take two work-days away and leave Tobi to cope with that foul-mouthed *money-miss-road*,' she lamented.

A lingering smile edged out from his face. 'I wrote down the days you've taken off since this year and they haven't been too many. Tobi will survive without you and Lola will be willing to pitch in. You should learn to delegate.'

'Wow,' she replied, taken aback by his knowledge of her work schedule. 'I already take several days off each year to deal with Roadrunners, which Tobi is understanding of. Then there's your job at Morgan Bridge. Are they cool with you taking so many days off? Your leave ends this Friday.'

'Let me worry about Morgan Bridge.' Timi gazed at her with his laser-focused brown eyes. Those eyes turned her insides, anytime he gazed like that. 'I would hope that by now, I take priority over your job.'

'It's my business. It's not just a job.' She knew she was spoiling his romantic overture. Maybe she should compromise by going with her laptop, so she could get some job done. 'Okay, if you're serious about breakfast in bed, I'm in.' She wanted to ask about sleeping arrangements, but she didn't want to ruin the mood. *We will cross that bridge soon enough,* she was sure.

He moved his chair next to hers, so he could give her a hug and a passionate kiss. He jammed his tongue in her mouth. He was more about public display of affection while she was conservative, and a gentle peck would have been enough for her, but she didn't push him away, even though she wanted to. When he disengaged, she released her breath. He remained next to her as they ate their meals and sipped their iced tea. After they finished, he asked if she'd settle the bill, which she gladly did, smiling at the waiter.

Preye was well established and didn't mind picking the bills sometimes and it didn't bother Timi either. She knew he was saving for something important, although he refused to tell her what it was.

In general, money wasn't a big deal between them. He had family-money and through Preye's referrals, he had started making great strides after getting an account manager's role at Morgan Bridge, one of the oldest public relations companies in Nigeria. She was generous and didn't think twice about parting with money, most especially to someone she loved. He wasn't a go-getter like she was, but he had potential, if he made work a priority. He was laid-back in some ways, but not in others. Preye felt that if Timi paid as much attention to details at work as he did to her wardrobe and schedule, he'd be a star in his workplace.

*

As they walked back to the car, some three minutes away, Timi had his arm firmly placed around Preye's waist. He was proud to be out with her because she turned heads. Her cute stature with her round face and ridged nose gave her an exotic look. Her wide hips accentuated her small waistline and if she had been a bit taller, she could have been a diva of the fashion runway. Still, her effortless gait got her some discreet second looks, even from females. Timi felt proud and accomplished, just by being her boyfriend. He often wondered how men had passed her by until he came into her life.

'I hope our getaway does not coincide with Zara's birthday party. I gave you the date weeks ago,' Preye enquired. She felt his body stiffen.

'Remind me of the date again.' He looked straight ahead, with eyes that communicated nothing.

Desperately hoping there wouldn't be a conflict, she sighed. She didn't want to risk rocking her relationship with Lola by missing Zara's special day. 'The last Saturday of the month.'

'You won't have to miss the party. It's next weekend. I'll pick you up early from work on Friday, so we can beat traffic,' he smiled and then adjusted her collar to cover her birthmark. 'If you had to cancel though, wouldn't you?'

She felt like telling him to always check with her before he fixed a date, so she could reorganise her work and assign to others. *But he wouldn't be able to arrange a surprise if he always had to check with me,* she thought. 'Cancelling isn't an issue now, since the dates don't clash.' She guessed he was fishing for a fire-stoking answer, but he wasn't going to get it. 'Would we be going out to dinner? Well, of course, we would. I need to know what to pack, which means knowing what you've got planned. Restaurant? If so, how elegant? I'll bring my running stuff, but can we rent bikes or horses? Are we taking the car? I'll bring my laptop along, so I'm able to work if…'

He cut her off. 'Relax, we have plenty of time, and I'll tell you exactly what to pack. I've started a list which will make preparing for a holiday simple.'

'You're ever so thoughtful, but I can handle packing. I know exactly the things you'd like.' Her eyes twinkled in mischief.

'I'll give you the list, anyway,' he declared as they got into the car.

On the drive back to the office, Timi peppered Preye with questions about Tobi's client. He was curious about why Tobi required so much of his girlfriend's time since he was supposed to manage his clients' accounts and not rail her into an unnecessary overlap of functions. Preye reminded Timi that the success of the company was her joint responsibility. She reiterated that Tobi was her long-standing friend and was happily married, so Timi had no legitimate reason to be worried.

Timi was jealous of everyone, including the drycleaner, the office gateman and the hairdresser. But she had come to accept that. It was nothing more than a personality trait that she'd learn to live with. Moreover, it made her feel she was highly valued and top priority on his mind.

When they got to the office complex, he walked her to her office building and gave her a tight hug. He waited and kept his eyes on her until she got into the revolving doors. She could think of it in two ways - either he was possessive or head over heels in love. She chose the latter because it gave her a better overall feeling. The pleasing smile on her face lingered as she headed for the lifts.

'Miss Banigo, you have a package,' the receptionist announced with glee as she stopped Preye.

'Really? Thank you.' Before she opened the card, Preye guessed who would have sent it. Sure enough, the gift-wrapped pack of chocolate was from Timi. The Huba chocolate was a rare brand and it reminded her of her father, Harry Banigo. It was one of the favourite brands he used to bring home when she was little.

*

Preye settled in her office, full of thoughts of her childhood.

Harry and Miriam had gotten married because Miriam became pregnant when they were both in their twenties. At the time, charming Harry was a known playboy and he had two girlfriends of which Miriam was one. Miriam had been excited about the pregnancy, until Harry asked her to get rid of it. She loved him and wasn't ready to let him go, so she had summoned the courage to tell his mother about his plan to abort the unborn child. Harry had been mad, but his mother had been glad. Miriam had been about the only decent woman Harry's mother had met as his girlfriend. As the only child, Harry had been close to his widowed mother, and she had insisted he married Miriam, so he had obliged to avoid disappointing his mother.

But marriage for Harry had been a ruse; he hadn't been ready to leave his second girlfriend, nor his drinking habit. The more his car-dealership business had expanded, the more he wandered away from home, eventually leaving Miriam with three children, one month after his mother was been buried. Miriam had been ill-prepared for the kind of marriage she had forced herself into. Even though he was hardly around, Harry had insisted she didn't need to work and she had been at a loss when he deserted them.

She had thrown herself into raising her children and protecting her sanity. The children had been too little to understand that their father was gone for good, as he was rarely at home in the first place, so it hadn't been difficult to maintain a good relationship with them from afar through telephone calls and random visits.

The children had adored him because he spoilt them any time he came, lavishing them with gifts and sweets. Miriam had thought it would be unproductive to put a barrier between father and children and she had maintained the charade until the children were grown up enough to draw their conclusions. At the time the children needed Harry the most, his business had gone downhill and he hadn't been able to put in much money towards their education. But he was gradually bouncing back and he ensured he was available anytime he was called upon to perform a fatherly role.

CHAPTER THREE

Timi's phone rang as he steered the car into the street that led to his home.

'Hello.'

'My guy, are you still coming?' Malik's drowsy voice came across. '*I wan go sleep, abeg. Work dey tomorrow.*'

'I'm around the corner now. I'll be with you in less than five minutes,' Timi responded, releasing a short restless breath.

Timi had asked Malik to help with reviewing a presentation he needed to submit to his boss. The presentation would be due immediately he returned from his get-away with Preye, but Malik was to travel over the weekend, so Timi had to prioritise it. Timi had recently been assigned to a new team and his new boss was strict with deadlines.

Malik was Timi's childhood friend. They had lived on the same street since Timi's family moved to Omole, about twenty-five years ago. Although they were about the same age, Malik was well advanced in his career as a business development manager with Emerald Bank, partly because Timi had spent eight years at different universities to get a degree. After their secondary school, Malik had gone on to study Economics at Lagos State University, while Timi was enrolled at a British university to study Law.

Timi had come back home two years after with no certificate or any inclination to return to Britain. By the start of the new session, his unrelenting father had gotten him admission into another university in Ogun State. After his first year, he had gotten expelled and handed over to the police for his involvement in cult activities. Timi's father had used his influence to secure Timi's release and avoid prosecution. Timi's friendship with Malik had waned, due to their clashing personalities and lifestyles; Timi had been mostly out drinking, partying with his friends from the other side of town and philandering with girls. Malik, however, had been mostly at school or helping out at his father's accounting firm during the holidays, so it hadn't required much effort to avoid Timi.

Timi, envious of Malik, had also opted to work at his father's dry cleaning business but it had soon become apparent to his parents that it was either Timi left the business or the entire employees left. He had ordered people around, hurled insults at them and even threatened to sack one, until his father intervened. His father had decided to salvage his business by sacking Timi instead. For over a month, Timi had sulked and refused to talk to his parents, claiming he had been humiliated in the presence of the employees.

As the only child who had survived after several miscarriages, Timi had been pampered and used to having his way. His parents had hardly refused him anything, for as long as he could remember. He had expected his mother to appease him as she used to, but he had waited in vain. His parents had finally determined that they needed to show him some tough love, to straighten him out.

In protest, Timi had moved some of his clothes from his two-bedroom apartment in his father's house to his car and turned the car into his mobile home while gallivanting around. His parents had refused to blink.

One day, his mother had told him off when he sneaked into the house to get some food from the kitchen. Storming out of the house after exchanging words with her, he had run into Malik at the gate while he was still ranting to himself in annoyance and hunger.

Malik had succeeded in calming him down and informed him that he had just finished his youth service and would be starting work the following week at a bank. Malik asked what Timi had been up to. He had simply shrugged and blamed his parents for his woes. Malik had told him he was on his way to a love feast in church and asked if Timi would like to come along. Hungry, bored and with nothing to do, Timi had gone to church for the first time in about fifteen years.

It was at that love feast that Timi had decided to turn his life around, gradually dis-engaging from his irresponsible friends and cultivating a cordial and somewhat reverent relationship with his parents. With Malik's support, he had studied to gain admission to Pinnacle University, a private university in Lagos State. And Malik had become his best friend once again. Malik had worked at Emerald Bank and started a family while Timi went back to school.

Timi had gotten a marketing job with a start-up technology company after school, but the company soon folded up and he was out of work. After four months without a job, he had started cutting back on some of his expenses, including his gym membership.

Malik had learnt about Roadrunners from someone at his church and had asked Timi to go along with him to find out how they could join the club. Timi had persuaded Malik to sign up immediately after meeting Preye, confessing that she had stirred some pleasurable feelings in him. Malik had wanted to trim his protruding belly which his wife had been complaining about and Timi had needed to substitute his exercise regime.

From the time Timi set eyes on Preye, he had decided she was the kind of woman he wanted in his life.

Unlike the several ladies Timi had dated, she was ambitious, purposeful, independent, highly connected and a Christian, who was committed to her charity cause. Once he learnt that she wasn't in a relationship, he had delved into his best-self to befriend her, until Preye trusted him. He had known she was ready before he asked her to be his girlfriend.

He loved Preye much more than he imagined he could ever love anyone. He was sure she loved him as well, but he wasn't sure she was ready for marriage because she didn't behave like she needed him in her life.

After Preye stood up to him for passing an insulting remark about her sister, he had decided he needed to be more assertive with her and mould her into the kind of wife he wanted – a wife like his sweet mother who never argued with his father. He guessed his mother knew about his father's affairs with younger ladies, but she had never allowed that to affect her devotion to her husband. And his parents had a solid thirty-seven years of marriage to prove how relationships should work, unlike Preye's parents.

Timi reasoned that Preye was self-reliant because she had been forced to step up to being a leader to her siblings, due to the absence of a father in their lives. Since she was better established than him and had helped in getting him into Morgan Bridge, he had resolved that he'd do whatever was required to prove he was in charge of the relationship. It was only a matter of time.

Timi's head was filled with these thoughts as he drove into his friend's gated compound.

'I have an early flight to catch to Abuja in the morning and I didn't expect you'd keep me up this late,' Malik, just a little bit short of Timi, pretended to be angry as he opened the door to let Timi into the house. Malik's wife and children had travelled and he was home alone.

Malik still lived in the house he had inherited as the oldest son after his parents died. It was an ancient structure that had been modernised internally with contemporary classy furniture and fittings.

Timi yawned, following Malik to the recently varnished pine dining table. 'I'm sorry. I had to make sure Preye was ready for bed.'

'For real? That girl still *dey shark* you like this? Slow down, boy.'

'Slow down how? *When I never fast reach.*' The two friends laughed and sat at the dining table. Timi brought out his laptop from his black leather backpack and powered it up.

'Then put the ring on her finger. If you miss this one, I don't know how you'll find another good one. They don't come plenty anymore. I'm sure you know that.'

'I've been thinking of proposing, I'm just afraid she'd say no. She seems to love her autonomy so much that sometimes, I don't know where she stands on marriage, because her commitment to her job and Roadrunners doesn't give her room for much else.'

'That's a lame excuse. You should count yourself lucky she has a career. Do you want a liability? Anyway, you also need to step up your game and be the guy she can look up to,' Malik paused. 'You get what I mean?'

Timi nodded reflectively, hanging on Malik's counsel. He'd ask Preye to be his wife and he'd take control of their relationship so she could look up to him. 'Sure, let's get to work.'

Malik looked at the presentation and listened as Timi talked through it. It was a bid to represent an international property management company seeking to launch in Nigeria. Timi had put together some lovely and graphic slides, but had left out important information that could highlight the agency's strong profile and promote its achievements. Malik suggested he added some of the agency's top clients with short catchphrases, to capture the positive feedback they had received from such clients.

'You should at least appreciate the effort I put into it to create this masterpiece,' Timi snapped at Malik. 'It wasn't easy, bro.'

'My guy, nobody pays you for effort in the workplace. Do you want to improve on it or not?' Malik asked.

Timi wanted to make a good impression on his boss at the office, and Malik was good at his job. So he listened to Malik, but argued over most of the suggestions. Getting exasperated, Malik kept explaining, to justify why he felt the presentation could be better. He was used to Timi's egotism and lacked the will to argue with him this time. After about an hour that they started and without making much headway, Malik glanced at the wall clock and got up.

He made a crackle with his left hand over his right knuckles. 'I'll leave you to decide how you want to update your document. I still have four items to tackle on the list of tasks my wife left for me.'

'*You be woman wrapper o*, and you want me to slow down,' Timi teased. 'Let me give you the benefit of a best friend. I'll be engaged to Preye by the time you come back from your trip. I'm going to give her the ring next weekend.'

'You are? That's what I'm talking about.' He raised his sturdy hand to give Timi a high-five. 'You need to start coming for some conjugal training.'

They both laughed as he walked Timi to the door.

*

'You aren't going to pack according to that list he gave you, are you?' Lola asked as she flipped her hand over Preye's clothes in the wardrobe.

With an offer to help Preye pack for her upcoming getaway, Lola had come back home with Preye after they returned from a client's meeting.

Of all her friends and family, Lola liked Timi the least, and his feelings for her were mutual. Preye wished Lola would start dating seriously again, so she could have someone to fuss over, but Lola seemed to be enjoying her freedom with her occasional flirts.

'I'm using it as a guide. He's put in a bit of effort to plan this and the least I can do is to dress up for him and make it worth the while. It's called dressed-to-kill, if you aren't so fixated on riling him,' Preye twittered. 'He likes floral prints and a more feminine look as opposed to the dark colours and structured look I wear to work every day.' She brought out a long flared skirt and matched it with a pink flowery top to place in her overnight bag. 'I can do with the change as well.'

Lola's mocking laughter reverberated as she grabbed the skirt from Preye. 'Are you kidding? This is what you call dressed-to-kill? Did you borrow that from one *SU* sister in your church? Where are your short skirts and shorts? Is he enrolling you into a convent? I know you don't want to tempt him with your bum shorts, but this is ridiculous. And what about that leather skirt you bought from Italy?'

'Don't be a cow, *Omo* girl. Timi likes sexy, but we're going to a resort where black leather isn't exactly appropriate,' Preye responded. She held up a red negligee to prove her point. 'I don't know if I should wear this though. I don't want to set him on fire without being able to douse it.' She giggled naughtily. 'Pyjamas might be better.'

'Please tell me something I don't know,' Lola smirked, switching to a serious look. She browsed over Timi's list with a look of disgust on her face. 'Your track record with men hasn't been great and I want to make sure you're not lowering the standards further. I speak from experience and I can tell you it pays to be hundred per cent sure before you fully commit to a man. I wanted Bode so badly that I overlooked our incompatibility. I know you'd say it was mostly my fault, but if I had waited a bit longer, I could have found someone who would have loved me for me. Don't get me wrong, I wouldn't trade Zara for anything, but being a single mum is no picnic.'

Preye's eyes widened softly as she looked doubtfully at Lola. 'Timi is not Bode and I am not you.' Preye squeezed her lips together, as she remembered the many times she and Aisha had warned Lola to treat Bode better when Lola's marriage was tipping towards the edge. "Zara wasn't even two years old before Bode left. Timi is a committed man and he wouldn't desert me like that. *Omo* girl, you're comparing pawpaw to coconut.'

'Hmm,' Lola mused with a lift of her shoulders and shook her head.

Lola's mother had died while she was in secondary school, and Lola, an otherwise amiable girl who hadn't gotten over her mother's death, had become bitter after her father re-married five years after. The fact that her stepmother had taken care of her and her two younger brothers as any mother would didn't thaw Lola's heart. Lola had mistrusted men and considered them as betrayers, until she had been swept off her feet by the rich, gentle and smooth-talking Bode Alade during her National Youth Service year. Bode was a much-sought-after prospect, but he had eyes only for Lola and he had ignored all the warning signs about their relationship. Two years later, they were married. They had started out nice and loving, until she started nagging from becoming suspicious of her husband with every step he took.

Five years later and pregnant, she had gotten even more

jealous and frustrated, especially when Bode suggested she stopped working to look after herself and the baby. Bode's quiet demeanour and Lola's erraticism couldn't cohabit in peace and Bode had started spending more time out with friends than at home with his expectant wife. It had made Lola more belligerent.

About a year after Zara was born, there had been an argument and Lola wouldn't stop running her mouth. Bode, burning in rage, had caught himself raising his hand to slap his wife, and punched the sixty-inch television instead. The following day, Bode had left the house and refused to return. Amidst tears of regret, Lola had later confessed to Aisha and Preye that she couldn't remember what the argument had been about.

After Bode left, Lola had gradually worked her way to becoming less critical, but it was too late. One year later, the rent of their Ikoyi flat expired, and with no contact from Bode, it had become obvious that he was done with the marriage and couldn't be bothered that Lola, who had resigned her job during her second trimester, was scrounging for money with their daughter, Zara and with no place to live. Her friends hadn't told her *I told you so*. Rather, Aisha Hassan, the third in the pack, had come to Lola's rescue as she and her husband opened their home to Lola until she got her feet back on the ground. Preye had also helped financially, by giving Lola the job at Beta.

Lola never forgot her friends' kindness and she felt responsible for Preye, so she wasn't afraid to tell Preye that things seemed out of place.

Preye was insistent in her defence. '*Omo* girl, I assure you my eyes are wide open. Timi has his flaws, but it's nothing we can't work through together,' she said, tossing her travel-ready toiletries into a bag.

'What are some of those flaws, if I may ask? I have an idea, but I want to hear you say them.' Lola's voice was challenging and it wearied Preye.

'Way to put me on the spot.' The conversation was getting intense, which wasn't the way Preye wanted her evening with Lola to go. 'He's possessive but doesn't mean to be. He worries about me, and I take that to be sweet. He's laid back about his career and I'm certainly not. These aren't deal-breakers, Lola. Opposites attract, remember?'

'I don't like that you defend him and making excuses for his behaviour. All I can say about Timi Coker is that he's no Kevin Murphy.'

Preye's muscles tightened as her body raged with the intensity of a wildfire. She dumped her half-packed suitcase in a dramatic gesture that was out of her otherwise deliberate character. Its neatly folded contents scattered across the floor. She breathed rapidly, exhaling more than the air she was taking in, as she paced back and forth with tingling feet. Her eyes were blurred and fiery as they settled heavily on Lola, who remained still, with her mouth agape.

After a few seconds that seemed like a decade, Preye placed her palms on her forehead. 'You've been around me for far too long not to know how hard it was for me to accept Kevin's death,' she blurted. 'Sometimes, I still cry when no one's around to see me. Then there are the anniversaries that I quietly observe, and no one else knows about … our first date, the time he first said he loved me … and … and when he started chemo to fight off the horrible blood-thirsty cancer. Timi has dragged me out of my private hell and I love him. I don't compare him to Kevin, nor should you.'

Kevin had been a different breed, going out of his way to care for people. He had a gentleness about him that endeared people to him. His honest eyes had been illuminating and his soul had radiated through his kind smile. He had written songs that were filled with positive emotions and any tune he sang into Preye's ears, the fire that danced in her body usually flamed into her head.

Lola sat on Preye's bed. 'I'm sorry, but ...'

Preye stopped her friend from speaking any further. She could almost feel the warmth of Kevin's body next to hers as her breathing gradually slowed. 'I know you're sorry, but I need you to get out of here. I love you, Lola, but at this moment, I can't stand the sight of you.'

Without another word, Lola left Preye's stylish flat, feeling terrible that she had upset Preye, but knowing she spoke the truth. Best friends fought; it was unavoidable, and soon, the two of them would pick up from where they left off.

*

After changing into her running tracksuit, Preye pulled her hair up in an elastic band to make a doughnut, before lacing up her running shoes to go for the almost four-kilometre run to her mother's house at Ogba. The vehicular traffic on the road with cars emitting fumes made the atmosphere thick and tepid, but she hardly noticed as she ran through the familiar terrain of Ijaiye Road. Two cars were parked in her mother's compound, one of which was her sister's, Erefa. With the Banigo girls, it was always the more the merrier. Preye ran up the steps without losing her breath and burst through the front door which her mother always forgot to lock. Miriam and Erefa were pleasantly surprised to see her.

'Hello, Mum.' Preye paused at the door to catch her breath. 'I was in the neighbourhood. 'Erefa, *how you dey?*'

The modest two-bedroom flat was one of a block of four flats in a high density area of Ogba. With a sparsely decorated living room which was devoid of clutter or dust, it was functional enough for Miriam, who had developed an austere approach to living, since her husband left her.

After wiping her feet, Preye stepped on the brown rug covering the entire floor on which the tartan fabric sofas were set, with a matching coffee wooden table and a dated show glass cabinet standing against the wall. The cream flowery curtains of embroidered cotton were always drawn and looked like they were fixed to the windows. In one corner of the room was a layered console on which different pictures of Miriam and her children were displayed. A television which was only occasionally switched on, hung on the cream coloured wall with a few tangled wires dangling.

Miriam still worked at her shop, selling foodstuff while Preye and her two sisters helped out considerably with the monthly rentals of her apartment and general upkeep. It was the least they could do for Miriam Banigo, who had tirelessly supported each one of them through the challenges of youth.

Miriam thought of herself as a success because all her children were alive, successfully working or in business. Two of them had already started their own families - thirty-four-year-old Erefa and the youngest, thirty-two-year-old Tonye. Ironically, it was thirty-nine-year-old Preye, the firstborn, who was still single. She had narrowly missed getting married to Kevin who died ten years ago. Everyone had agreed that both Kevin and Preye were a perfect match and they would have ended down the aisle if he had lived long enough.

Miriam prayed every day that Preye would find some joy as much as she prayed that Erefa and Tonye would bless her with grandchildren soon.

Preye had thought she'd be the first to get married and have children amongst the siblings, but with Kevin's death, that aspiration had moved to the bottom of the list. Now that Timi was in the picture, she had started seeing the hope of making that happen again. She didn't mind pushing her career aside a bit to take the back seat to being a mother.

Miriam popped up first and gave Preye a tight squeeze. 'You're sweaty. And you were not in the neighbourhood. You came to see me. Did you run from your house?'

Preye laughed. 'Yes, Mum, I'm sweaty because I ran. I wanted to clear my head and I figured coming here was perfect. We missed each other at church last Sunday. Erefa, *when you reach here* and where's your husband? You guys are always snail and shell.' Preye went to the fridge in the kitchen and grabbed a bottle of water. She sat on the two-seater sofa and stretched her legs out onto the coffee table before tipping the liquid in the bottle into her mouth.

'Nice to see you too, big sis,' Erefa teased. 'I've been hungry for native soup and Don wanted to see a friend at Pen Cinema, so I dropped him off. He'll find his way home. Unfortunately, your mother here didn't have anything that looked like soup, so she's mixing some concoction we can only hope would taste nice.' She finished with a pout to mock Miriam.

Erefa was fashionably dressed as usual, in black jeans and a crisp white linen shirt that matched her white wedge sandals. She became the richest of the Banigo girls since marrying a business executive who was born with a silver spoon firmly rammed into his mouth. Donald was down to earth and very easy to get along with, unlike some of Preye's rich clients. Sometimes, the sisters joked that Donald didn't realise how rich he was.

The Banigos had expressed some reservations when the soft-spoken and good-looking Donald started chasing Erefa because he was way out of their zone. But five years after they got married, Erefa and Donald were still waxing strong and it was obvious Donald made Erefa happy. To be fair, the Banigo sisters were protective of one another, such that whoever tried to date anyone of them was a natural suspect.

As much as Miriam prayed every day that Preye would find love and get married before her biological clock came to a full stop, she had had her misgivings when Preye introduced Timi to the family. She found his extraordinary charm forced and she felt that he was making too much effort to impress. He also seemed to know everything and often talked over Preye. However, he doted on Preye just as much as Preye doted on him, so Miriam had to brush her concerns aside. Besides, it had been over four years that Preye was in a real relationship and it would be unfair to deter her from this.

'Liar,' Miriam accused. 'You already ate my pepper-soup. Or that doesn't qualify for soup?'

Miriam was a petite, fair woman and it was easy to see where Preye and her sisters got their good looks from. In her heydays, Miriam had been a bit fashionable, but years of toiling over the children and without a man or close friends in her life had turned her into a conservative, homely woman. Preye snapped her head towards Erefa, who smiled and glowed. Preye guessed immediately that her sister had some news.

'I'm pregnant.' Erefa's squeal was infectious.

Preye clapped, giggling. 'Wow, that's fantastic news. Oh, my God! Are you thrilled? Is Donald over the moon? How far along?' She lifted Erefa out of her chair and gave her a huge embrace. A tear of joy escaped from Preye's eye as she placed her hands on her sister's belly.

'Yes, Don couldn't be happier. He wants ten kids. I'm beyond thrilled, and it's almost three months,' Erefa beamed.

They celebrated with a bottle of non-alcoholic wine from Miriam's refrigerator. A child coming into the world was a blessing, and Preye was excited for Erefa, but it intensified thoughts of her ticking clock.

Preye didn't have feelings of jealousy; it was more of a wistful sadness that grew as the days went by, along with her hope of having a natural pregnancy due to her age.

Miriam was thankful that her first grandchild was coming along, but she didn't make any comment about it, to avoid pricking Preye. She announced that the soup was simmered a bit and packed two bowls for the sisters.

Mission of soup collection accomplished, Erefa was ready to leave.

'Preye, do you want a ride home?' she asked. 'It'll be dark soon and it's not safe, with all those reckless *danfo* drivers and *okada* riders. We can brainstorm about baby names. And if no one has told you, you should stop taking unnecessary chances running at late hours,' she scolded Preye with a wry smile. 'Maybe, that self-defence classes you took years ago are deceiving you and you think you're a pro.'

Preye gave her sister a gentle slap on the back. 'Ah, I see how it's going to be. This pregnancy is now a mouth-sharpener.'

They left Miriam's flat teasing each other. Erefa drove Preye back to her flat and they talked about Erefa and Donald's growing family. Erefa was enthusiastic about the forthcoming changes to their family dynamics and the conversation effortlessly led to questions about Timi.

'Timi is good, thanks for asking. He's whisking me to Badagry for four days. He popped the surprise at lunch the other day. That's one of the things I love about him. He comes up with romantic ideas all the time. He sends flowers, takes me to lunch and springs some lovely surprises. It's difficult not to love him,' Preye gushed.

'I'm happy for you, big sis. Now I understand why you've been a bit scarce. Obviously, you're still happy with him? Is he still into you? Is there a chance for an aisle walk any time soon? Is he the one or shall we wait for another?' Erefa mimicked the bible quote about John the Baptist.

That aisle question was a constant any time Timi's name

came up, so it didn't take Preye by surprise. 'We have our ups and downs now and then, but he's wonderful. He hasn't really been specific about marriage, but it's up in the air and I'm sure it's going to happen. Someday.' Preye said the last word with an injection of confidence and carefreeness as they pulled near her flat.

Timi was waiting on the front steps. He was right on time because he knew Preye was on her way since he usually tracked her whereabouts with a phone app, which she had resisted at first. But he had assured her that the only time he used the app was when she was out running, so he could know where she was and be sure she was safe. She agreed, appreciating the fact that he cared about her safety.

'Take care. I expect to see you more often, now that I'm carrying your niece or nephew. That's selfish of me. You need to spend more time with your sweetheart.' Erefa's cheeks expanded with her smile as she waved to Timi, who returned the gesture.

'I will, and next time, I might have good news to share.'

Preye ran into Timi's waiting arms.

CHAPTER FOUR

The Breeze Resort in Badagry was as Preye had imagined - serene with a close-to-nature ambience and lots of trees that stretched along the median road, as if they were a pathway to paradise.

As they took the left turn at the end of the road, Timi explained that the resort was split into two sections - two bedrooms for families on the right side and one bedroom for couples on the left side.

Even though the sea was out of sight, it saturated the atmosphere with its sulphuric smell and the distant rhythmic sound of sea waves.

The one-bedroom bungalow chalets created a hut façade with their round shapes of brick walls, coated with sand paint and brownish thatch-roof finishing. The living room was a blend of the old and the new. A glass dining table with two brown Panton chairs coordinated well with the pair of glass and leather side tables beside the cream leather three-seater sofa bed. The floor was rustic hard wood and the smooth walls had a neutral paint finish. Small pieces of modern canvas paintings adorning the wall complemented the vintage ceramic figurines on the console.

She took in the vibrancy of the room before peeping into the kitchen. There was a small fridge loaded with an assortment of soft drinks, alcoholic wines, and dairy products of eggs, butter and milk. A collection of different brands of tea and a tin of coffee were left on the worktop beside the electric kettle and toaster.

Preye was happy she'd be spending quality time with Timi, far from the stress and chaos of Lagos Mainland. They needed some we-time, away from the demands of everyday living in the city, to fortify their relationship. She was an admitted workaholic, which she attributed to the fact that Beta was her baby and it was her responsibility to nurture it, besides the fact that she loved her job. Timi saw his job more like something he needed to do to prove he was productive. She hoped that with time and effort, they would eventually meet in the middle and they would be able to map their future together with some concrete plans.

The other question nagging her mind as they settled into the chalet was how they would survive three intimate nights together without having sex if they shared the same bed. She didn't express any concern to Timi, trusting that she could rely on him to keep to their pact. On her part, she internally braced herself to keep her hands off him as much as possible.

After cooling down with some chilled drinks from the fridge, Timi went to the reception to find out about the resort's facilities, while Preye went to the bedroom to unpack. The bedroom was a lovers' delight. It had the same neutral colour as the living room, with beautiful wall murals of couples in various sensual postures. Vibrant flowery silky bed sheets with six duck-feather pillows were layered on the six-foot bed and a wine-coloured love-seat was tucked at the right side of the room beside the tall veneer wardrobe.

She removed her wedge sandals before she stepped on the rich purple Asiatic rug which felt lush against her bare feet. As she opened the wardrobe to keep her sandals, extra pillows and beddings fell through from the top compartments. She tucked them back in and placed her sandals in the in-built shoe rack.

Sitting on the bed to feel the plush bed sheet before bouncing a couple of times like a child, she nodded as she felt the softness of the bed. She placed her travel bag on the bed and unzipped it to start setting out her clothes. Timi walked in after securing dinner reservations as she was about to hang a black linen trouser suit.

'I see you're just as organised on holiday as you are at home,' he commented, wrapping his arms around her from behind and kissing her neck. He laid a hand on the trouser suit. 'What's this?'

'It's the suit I bought last week. In case we want to go out. I pair it with this most divine tangerine camisole underneath. I like this top because of the way it's cut. It wasn't on the list, but I had you in mind in choosing it. It matches the colours you like,' she responded casually. She avoided meeting Timi's eyes, unsure where the query was leading to.

'Lola helped you pack, didn't she?' His brow creased to form some thin lines.

She was taken off-guard by his mood change. 'Lola was around to help me pack. But we had an argument and she left. I picked this out on my own. I am capable of making my own choices, Timi.'

'I don't find these figure-hugging trousers appealing, my love. I just about make do with you in track suits. You're already short and they make you look like a midget. If you don't have anything to replace it with, we can buy you something here at the resort. Perhaps one of your sisters can use the suit. Erefa would love something like that. The two of you are almost the same size.' Timi snapped it off the hanger and shoved it back into her suitcase.

She was aghast and about to argue, but he pulled her in for a kiss. He led her to the window, which had a breath-taking view of the sea from afar. He pulled his long fingers through her straightened hair and made her forget what she was angry about in the first place. A tense moment was transformed into a passionate one.

Changing the mood quickly was Timi Coker's speciality.

*

Preye and Timi dined on an evening cruise arranged by the resort. Timi's flowery shirt and blue Bermuda shorts complimented Preye's tropical halter-dress. They sat in silence, enjoying the refreshing warmth of the breeze and they watched the sun setting into pale gold on the horizon around them. The boat gently moved through coves, with the stars twinkling above. The coastline was a brilliant stretch of distant bays and cliffs which presented a picturesque scenery of calmness, against the colliding waves of the aquatic landscape.

After dinner, they strolled to the balcony of the boat to take in the scenery. It was the kind of scene that made Preye forget about the trouser suit incident and Timi's comments about Lola. After a while, Timi pulled her to himself and they watched the stars and the stretch of water around them while he encircled her in a close cuddle, trifling with her hair. He felt they could pass for models posing for a beautiful canvas painting, depicting serenity.

There were about twenty other passengers on the boat and everyone mingled freely, talking about politics and the latest gossip in town as the tour guide proudly ran a commentary of the coastal line's geography and history.

'I feel like the luckiest man alive. This is exactly what was on my mind when I booked this place. Just me and the woman I love to the highest heights,' he whispered smoothly. 'I can stay with you like this all night long.'

'I should say thank you for organising this. Sometimes I

forget to enjoy the simplicity of life.'

'Anything for you, my angel. You brought meaning to my life when I was flailing in the wind, with no real purpose. I joined Roadrunners to keep fit and after meeting you, I just wanted to spend more time with you, but never did I think we would end up here.'

Preye swallowed hard. She had a feeling where this proclamation was heading but she had been wrong before. She allowed him to continue without interrupting.

'With you by my side, I believe I can accomplish anything because I see no limits. I want that feeling to last forever.' He lifted her chin and brought the edge of her silky hair to rest on her chest. She prayed he wouldn't hear the pumping of her heart as she waited on him to finish up with the ultimate question. 'I love you, Preye Banigo.'

With the silence echoing at her, her heartbeat increased in anticipation of what he'd say next. But he had said his piece. 'I love you too.' she responded quietly, masking her disappointment.

They continued looking at the rays of light from the balcony in silence as the boat drew close to the shore. The tour guide announced that the boat would stop at the island for about thirty minutes, which was enough time for them to walk the length and breadth of Asabe Island. He advised that they could leave their shoes in the boat.

Immediately the boat docked, four female dancers in *adire* costumes trouped out to the beats of rolling drums and local *afrobeat* music, to start a traditional choreography. Timi pulled Preye towards the dancers and twirled her to the beats as some of the passengers joined the dance troupe, while the others followed the tour guide.

'Do you want to dance or explore the island?' Timi asked without releasing her hand. 'I'd rather we stayed to dance.'

She'd have preferred to see the island, but Timi's grip of her hand didn't give her that option. So she nodded and pulled close to him.

She was enjoying this trip much more than she had anticipated. It was a wonderful sight to see Timi and some of the other tourists dancing without any inhibitions. She had guessed he could dance, but not as good as the steps he was showing her now. Apart from the occasional dance steps in church, she couldn't recall the last time she had danced this way. And the feeling was refreshing. It had been a long time she saw Timi this relaxed and carefree too.

A young vendor brought drinks round for the dancing tourists to buy. Timi took two bottles of malt drink, handed one over to Preye and paid, without breaking his steps.

'Does the resort pay for this to entertain their guests or the islanders do this for every visiting boat?' Preye was intrigued.

Timi shrugged. 'I don't know. And I don't care. I just want to enjoy myself with my dancing queen.' He pulled her close from the waist and twirled her again. Preye basked in the beauty of the moment and warmed up to him.

'We should do this more often,' she told him.

'I agree,' he responded as they continued gyrating to the beats. 'If you can make the time to simply enjoy and forget about work.'

Preye only guessed it was time to go after she saw the tour guide approaching with the entourage. 'Wow, so soon.'

'Don't worry, we'll keep dancing until the boat is ready to move,' Timi quipped. The dancers waltzed towards the boat behind Preye, but the drummers stayed as the drumbeats gradually slowed down. 'Or we can spend the night here with the drummers. I promise I'll teach you one or two more dance steps,' he teased.

'Hmm,' Preye nodded. The drummers finally rolled the

drumsticks to a stop in a rushed sequence.

'Now it's time to go,' Timi sighed regrettably as he turned Preye around to the boat. 'Will you run and let's see if I can catch up with you?'

'Are you sure about that? Remember who Preye Banigo is,' she teased. He nodded to urge her on and she simply scooped up her dress, sprinting towards the boat.

As she slowed down her pace to a walk close to the boat, she wondered if the four dancers lined up in a straight line in front of the tour guide were asking for a ride back to the resort because the tour guide's hand was raised like that of a traffic warden, stopping the dancers from boarding the boat.

The tour guide's hand came down abruptly. And immediately, the dancers turned around in unison, facing Preye. Each of them raised acrylic placards with neon letters to cover their faces. The placards read, 'PLEASE MARRY ME PREYE!'

Preye clutched her chest and looked back at Timi, shocked and unsure that it was real. The drums rolled again, heralding all the passengers on the boat to troop out once more, clapping along. Timi wasn't running. He swayed to her and danced around her until the drums came to a stop when he was in front of her. He revealed a deep red velvet box and lifted the top. The diamond sparkled as he pushed the ring into Preye's well-manicured finger, in rhythmic slow motion.

'Will you be my wife?' he asked.

It took a long minute for Preye to realise that this was the answer to the thought that had pervaded her mind ever since she agreed to be Timi's girlfriend. All she could do was nod her head as she looked at the ring on her finger. A tear filtered from the corner of one eye. Timi cocked his head and widened his eyes, waiting for a verbal response.

'Yes, yes, I will marry you,' she gushed.

The onlookers and drumbeats clapped while Preye wiped her

tears as she sniffled joyfully. Timi scooped her from the floor onto the boat. Shouts of congratulations welcomed them aboard and the waiter popped a bottle of champagne and served it round.

He raised a toast before kissing her. 'To my future queen.'

She was a bit embarrassed but overwhelmed with joy and didn't know what to say. After the other passengers left them and she was alone with him, she was finally able to speak. 'You've made me the happiest woman on the planet. I will spend the rest of my life loving you. I'm stronger with you than without you and I can't wait to be your wife.'

They both floated in a love bubble in each other's arms until the boat docked and the guide told them they could disembark. When they returned to their chalet, Preye headed to the room to change. She emitted a quiet huff at the entrance of the room and placed her hands on her raised chest, turning to look at Timi who walked closely behind her. Scented candles lined the door to the bed, with rose petals scattered all over the room. Her eyes were aglow in awe and she threw her shoes to a corner of the room.

'This is way over the top.' She shook her head, admiring him with a sweep of her eyes. 'I don't know how you've managed to swing all these tonight. You're a genius.'

He did a bow. 'I try my best, my queen. Let me know if there's any other thing you want. I'm at your service.'

With a gentle whirl on the petals, she walked towards the bed. 'A thought just crossed my mind. What would you have done if I had turned down your proposal?'

A soft smile on his lips and a wink of one eye teased her. 'I'm sure one of those dancers would have gladly taken the ring. It wouldn't have gone to waste.'

Her face flashed back a smile. 'No one would have lived up to your expectations. There's only one Preye Banigo.' Sprawling on the bed, she scooped some petals, laughing. Timi joined her on the bed.

'That I know. You're everything I'll ever need.' He turned to kiss her and she responded passionately, intertwining her body to his.

They lay still in that position for some minutes, each reflecting on how far they had come and what the future held for them. While Preye's mind conjured images of home decorations and children running around, Timi's loins were threatening to burst.

Once her heart slowed down to its natural pace, the excitement of the proposal was overtaken by the reality of the moment and she propped herself up, leaning on one hand to ask Timi about the sleeping arrangements. He raised his well-trimmed eyebrows slightly and stopped short of completing a slick smile across his face.

She shook her head and wagged her finger at him. 'Now don't you try to get smart with me, boy,' she said with a twinkle.

The room was cosy, the time felt right and the proximity of her body next to Timi's suddenly sent all the juices in her body to the boil again, dangling the idea of a passionate rendezvous in front of her. In her head, she could already see the image of their bodies entangled in an electrified rhythm of intimacy and she knew if they didn't build a solid wall tonight, there was no telling what would happen before they left the resort.

Abruptly, she grabbed two pillows from the bed. 'I don't mind, I'll take the sofa.'

'Don't be dramatic,' he said. He took the pillows from her and tossed them back on the bed. 'I'll sleep on the rug here, just to make sure you don't disappear in the middle of the night.' Smiling at the absurdity of spending the night in separate rooms, the glint in his eyes were mischievous. He brought out an extra bed sheet from the wardrobe and spread it on the floor before heading for the bathroom.

As she waited for her turn to shower and change after Timi, her happy eyes were glued to the dazzling ring on her finger and she rehearsed how she'd show off her ring to doubting Lola immediately she returned to the office.

Timi's shower was quick and he was out in less than ten minutes, changed into a cotton pyjamas top and shorts. He beckoned Preye to go. She took her toilet bag and pink woollen bathrobe from the wardrobe and went into the bathroom.

After running the bath, she soaked herself in. Her reminiscence over Timi's unexpected theatrical proposal, with a conviction that it was a testament of what their married life would be kept an intoxicating radiant smile on her face and gave her the assurance that she had made the right choice. She said a silent prayer of gratitude to God.

By the time she returned to the bedroom, Timi's chest was already thumping in a slow pulse of shallow breaths. She watched him as she tiptoed, tossing her bathrobe to the other side of the bed. The features of his face were as soft and carefree as those of a child and they exuded serenity. She changed into a red nightie, gently got into the bed and led herself into a deep sleep of contentment.

*

The next morning, Timi's body clock woke him up at 6.30a.m, to the pitched cadence of Preye's nasal sounds as she snored in her sleep. He spared no ceremony to prop himself up from his floor-bed, and didn't bother changing from his pyjamas before going to the living room for his exercise routine.

After his exercise, he quietly changed into a faded denim and red t-shirt that stood his biceps out. Peeping at Preye longingly as if she were a chinaware on a display shelf, he marvelled at how he still found her ravishingly beautiful. Her skin glowed, the curve of her hour-glass hip outlined the white sheet, there was no crease on her brow, and even with her eyes shut, she radiated blissful innocence.

With a smile of pleasure swelling from inside him like a budding flower, he left for the resort's restaurant to check on breakfast to fulfil his promise, wondering how much longer he could hold out on the no-sex pact.

Preye woke up from a dream where her image had been rocking an unfamiliar crying baby. She lay still for a moment, trying to listen to the baby's cry and confirm if it was real, but she only heard the unobtrusive whining of the overhead air conditioner. Momentarily conscious of where she was and what had happened the previous day, she wiped her eyes with the back of one finger and rolled over to let her arm fall on the rug. Timi wasn't there. She sat up, and only then remembered his promise of breakfast in bed. *Maybe this post-engagement bliss could last forever,* she hoped.

Her engagement euphoria kicked in again and she decided to share her news with the ones she cared about. Without bothering to leave the bed, she picked up her phone from the pedestal and pressed speed dial buttons. She tried Lola and then her mother, but both calls went directly to voicemail.

'Aisha, we're getting married.' Having a hard time containing her excitement once Aisha answered the phone, Preye boomed and spoke loudly. The two friends exchanged squeals.

'Congratulations, *Omo* girl. Lola said you were on holiday with Timi. So that's what it was about. It's about time things worked out for you. Let's see when you get back home. I want to hear every detail. Make sure you don't tell Lola anything in the office, so we both hear all the juicy bits at the same time. Or let's have a night out. For now, give me the abridged version. Was it romantic?'

'Picture it. Sunset cruise, we're on the balcony, the stars are gazing at us. Then a musical jamboree sprang to play. Ocean breeze blowing, then pop! The question came with a beautiful diamond solitaire. We celebrated with a champagne toast. And returned to our room where flowers were strewn from the door to the bed. And it gets better from there. Right now, I'm waiting for my breakfast in bed.' Preye stopped to take a deep breath when she noticed Timi standing in the doorway. 'Hold on Aisha.' She muted the call.

'Really? You couldn't wait until we got home to reach out to your friends.' His eyes glowed like ionized air produced by electrical current of wires with different voltage levels. He had dropped the tray of breakfast on the dining table in the living room on hearing Preye's voice talking over the phone.

Preye *unmuted* her call. 'I'll call you back, Aisha. Send my love to little Ashe and Adamu.' She pulled on her robe from the other side of the bed and faced Timi. 'I'm sorry if I offended you. My heart was exploding with joy and I wanted to share the good news with my friends.'

'This weekend is about you and me. If I hadn't walked in, what more would you have told your friend? That I'm now your servant?'

'Maybe it's a girl thing. You're being silly. You weren't here before I called and now my phone is face down,' she paused. 'I only wanted to tell her how wonderful it was to wake up next to my future husband.' She smiled weakly, trying to lighten things up. 'I love you Timi, but you have to understand that girls talk about these things. And our engagement is not something I should keep away from my friends and family.'

'Were you talking to Aisha as a solicitor or as a friend?' he asked, ignoring her as if the last words she had uttered were to the wall. He sounded unconvinced, despite her explanation to calm him. 'Do you want legal advice already?'

'Are you serious? What's your problem exactly? Aisha's husband is the one that helps with my business legalities. Why am I even explaining? What legal advice do you think I'd be asking Aisha?' she asked, throwing her hands out in exasperation. His line of questioning made no sense to her.

'It took you less than twenty-four hours to call your friend and get started on our intimate moment. Or did you want her advice on a *prenup*? You know what I think about your money, and it isn't much. I make enough and my family isn't poor either. I'm sure she thought you were jumping the gun,' he grumbled.

'Prenup? You've been watching too many American movies. Since when did money become an issue between us?' She had to take another deep breath before she could continue calmly. 'Anyway, that wasn't what I was discussing with her. You can call her and ask her directly. I shouldn't have to defend myself.'

Without thinking, she sprang up to the wardrobe to scramble for her running gear and went into the bathroom to change. She returned to the room and she faced him. 'I'm going for a run to clear my head. Afterwards, I'm going to pop into the church I noticed on the way into town. You can join if you want. Otherwise, I'll see you later and we can take this matter up again with our heads cooler.' She finished off by pulling on her trainers.

Caught off guard with her decision to leave him in the room, his eyes were wide open as his face turned to shock and he opened his mouth, but he closed it immediately because he felt his brain had frozen. It took only a moment for him to recover himself and will his eyes to soften a bit before he looked Preye in the eyes. 'Mine, I didn't mean to chase you away. I wanted us to enjoy the afterglow of the engagement and I was surprised to see you chatting away. I thought I'd have you all to myself this weekend and today we can spend the entire day in bed or go to the beachside. Maybe it's that sparkler on your finger.'

Preye stretched out her hand to look at the diamond ring and a smile of admiration brightened up her features. The ring was beautiful and she had to admit that Timi had chosen well. Knowing that it must have cost him a fortune, she appreciated him more. It was the second time an engagement ring would be on her finger and she prayed it would be the last.

Her previous proposal flashed through her mind. Kevin had done it on his knees in her hospital ward after she had a fibroid surgery. And he had gone on to announce their engagement at one of his shows, in the presence of the crew. He had been intent on not getting a diamond ring because it was common. Instead, he had given her an antiquated opal he inherited from his grandmother.

She shook her head to snap herself back from thinking about the past. She loved her ring and she loved Timi, but she still needed to be alone.

'Do something with yourself while I'm out,' she said finally, as she headed for the living room, pausing at the dining table to pick an apple before rushing out of the front door.

*

After jogging for about forty minutes on the side of the untarred roads marked as pedestrian sidewalks by persistent footfall, Preye branched at the Anglican Church she had talked about. It was an ungated ancient limestone architecture, with stained glass windows and a massive baroque cross plastered on the protruding roof top. A bell tower stood gallantly by the side of the building, but Preye couldn't see a twirl rope and she wondered if the tower still had a functional bell to rouse the town as needed.

She climbed up the worn stony stairs to access the narthex, but retreated at the immovable iron-cast door. Sitting on the six-tiered staircase, she cast her eyes mindlessly on the street ahead and she started mumbling under her breath to talk to God about her engagement to Timi, her clients at Beta, her sisters and her parents. She asked for the wisdom to understand Timi better, the patience to make the relationship work and the grace to build a wonderful family filled with bubbly children.

As soon as she finished and got up, she dusted her jogging bottoms and trotted from the church grounds. On her way back to the resort, she remembered that she needed to review a report which required her e-signature as one of the executive partners. She should have returned the report yesterday, but hadn't been able to do it because of this holiday. She didn't want to be the one to throw off everyone else's schedule at Beta.

She felt refreshed when she arrived back at the resort. There was never a time that a run and time spent with God didn't help.

Timi was in the shower, so she settled down at the dining table and ate a sandwich before going to pull out her laptop, hoping to be finished with the report before lunch time.

Moments later, she felt a presence in the room and she looked up from her keyboard, to the sight of a dripping wet Timi, wrapped in the resort's branded towel. She had been consumed in her work and hadn't noticed him walk to her side by the dining table.

He didn't bother to ask any question before slamming her laptop shut. 'You weren't supposed to bring work on this short holiday. I got over your call to Aisha and now this? I can't trust my fiancée to be alone with me without deceiving me. What's it going to be like once we get married? Are you going to invite your friends and co-workers to come on our honeymoon?'

'We don't have to find out,' she snapped defiantly with her eyelids flustering. 'I'll be devastated, but if you want the ring back, you can have it now.' Her voice had a force that she didn't know she could muster. The hurt lurking in her heart was like a deep well gushing with hot water, but the water was rather trickling down her face.

Timi's mouth twisted and he looked helpless as he wished he could retract his words. He dropped on one knee and clasped Preye's hands together, caressing them. 'I'm sorry sweetheart. I would sooner stab myself in the heart than take that ring off your finger. You mean so much to me and that's why I let my anger get the best of me. I'm not used to sharing something so precious to me, but I'm learning. Be patient with me and I'll do the same regarding your outside influences. Let's make tonight one we won't forget.' He focused on her eyes from under his thick lashes as he continued stroking her hands. 'I love you, my baby and if I start with you tonight, you'll be begging me to make sweet love to you.'

Preye couldn't trust herself to respond. As if her brain had been sapped of energy, her head felt heavy and her mind was fuzzy. Gently withdrawing her hands from him, she dragged her heavy legs along to the bedroom, sniffing. She drew in a final lungful of air as she went to the bathroom to rinse her face. Glancing at herself in the mirror, she saw a strong woman who was humble enough to forgive a remorseful lover. Another deep breath helped to force a weak smile to the surface of her features.

Timi was already in the bedroom and had replaced his towel with a pair of green khaki shorts when she returned to sit on the bed. He leaned on the wardrobe with his arms folded across his chest, his eyes prodding her to talk. His stare was as stifling as the sunlight during harmattan, but she could only roll the thought of their sleeping arrangement in her head. As she spoke, it was with her head lowered, avoiding his eyes.

'I know you'd call me old-fashioned again, but I think we should work hard at abstaining from sex until our wedding night. It means a lot to me, please.' Avoiding his narrowing eyes as she spoke through her teeth, she focused on crackling her fingers.

'Seriously?' he asked. 'Even after our engagement?' He squeezed his lips together, drawing in his cheeks.

'Yes,' she responded in a low tone. 'We go to church together and you already know my stance on this.' She finally brought her eyes to search his for some mutual understanding.

His understanding nod was as rapid as that of a lizard patting itself as he sighed. 'I'll do it for you, my beautiful damsel and future wife. But you know it's not been easy. I'm fired up every time I see you. Why do you have to be this beautiful?'

She could feel her body warming up and she slowly pushed herself up to lean up on the tips of her toes and wrap her arms around his neck. 'Thank you, *olowo ori mi*. Let the anticipation begin. Our wedding night will be hot. I promise you,' she boasted.

Holding his breath as her body brushed against his frame, his head went cloudy and he stilled his body at the electric sensation of her head on his thumping chest. He brought his chin to rest on her crown and closed his eyes.

CHAPTER FIVE

'Let me see the ring,' Aisha squeaked as she entered the office used by the Roadrunners with her toddler, Ashe. It was their last planning meeting before the biggest charity fundraiser of the year - The Lymphoma Foundation 5K. 'I hate it that you and Lola work together and she gets the gist first-hand. She's seen the ring, I bet.' Pouting her lips, she darted Preye a smug look.

'If you had made Zara's party, you would have seen it too,' Preye responded and went to pull Ashe's bubbly cheeks. 'Look at him in his little Roadrunners top. He's gotten so big. My cutie precious prince.' She dangled her fingers in Aisha's face to show off her ring. 'Getting married is one prayer point off the list now, so we can move to other prayer requests. You should have seen how he pulled it off. It was awesome. Even after two weeks, I still can't get over it,' she babbled on.

'Yeah, I missed. Sorry, I haven't been able to see you since. But I've been worried that you guys may not get to the marriage line with Timi's evasiveness. Have you got a date yet?'

Towering above Preye at close to six feet in height, Aisha had a slim body and oblong Fulani face that rivalled that of a supermodel. Her husband, Adamu called her his African Queen and treated her like royalty. They were one of those couples that everyone went to for advice about how to make love last.

Aisha and Adamu had met at the university and had gone to law school together. At the time Preye was engaged to Kevin,

63

they had been a fierce foursome. Until Kevin got sick.

'It will be within the first quarter of next year, so that gives us less than six months to prepare. The date is dependent on Timi's parents and hall's availability. You know how it is. I have to get a dress, caterer, venue, and make sure my pastor is available for the blessing. Can I count on you for help? Of everyone I know, you have the best taste. And don't let that get into your head.' Preye wagged a finger at Aisha.

'Lola said Timi has been recreating your wardrobe, so will he be picking the wedding gown or will he let us do our girly thing?' Aisha asked mischievously.

Preye placed her hands on her petite hips, looking poised for a challenge. 'That Lola and her big mouth.' She shook her head. 'As a couple, Timi and I take on each other's likes and dislikes. Lola still doesn't like him and she won't back off. You know how she runs her mouth and how protective over me she can be. After my horrible experience with those stupid guys, she's had her guards up. But she needs to know when to lie low. Relationship is give and take. After all, no one is perfect. Not Timi, not me and not Lola for that matter.'

Pulling her lips in for a pout and raising her shoulders in an exaggerated shrug of nonchalance, Aisha mused. She had warned Lola several times to stop meddling in Preye's affair, since Lola first mentioned her reservations about Timi. Aisha believed Lola hadn't given Timi a chance from the beginning. Lola felt Preye was naïve about matters of the heart, believing her Christian faith made her vulnerable to men who pretended to be what they were not. Lola would rather everyone adopted a carefree attitude like she had after her failed marriage.

Aisha felt that it was probably payback time, because when Lola announced she was getting married to Bode, Aisha and Preye had vehemently kicked against it; more for Bode's sake, rather than Lola's.

'I can hardly blame her. We love you and you know how far you've come since Kevin. As far as I know, Timi is a cool guy. It's obvious he's in love with you, but we don't want you to lose yourself in this relationship. Be proud of who you are and don't be afraid to show off that rocking figure of yours,' Aisha said with a half-smile. 'Please tell me he has no problems with our coral theme.'

The three friends had agreed they would all wear coral wedding dresses. Lola and Aisha had done their part, leaving Preye to ensure she conformed.

Preye smiled and approached her friend with open arms. 'He'll be fine with coral. We haven't started on the details yet. By the way, we made that pact over ten years ago. Is it still binding on me if I want to wear white?' she teased Aisha.

Aisha gave Preye the knowing look between intimate friends. She joined Preye to open boxes containing the event's t-shirts and they chatted on.

Preye had started the annual charity run with nudging and support from Aisha two years after Roadrunners was birthed. She had wanted to raise funds and provide a medium of awareness to reach more people. She had confessed Roadrunners helped her find another purpose in her life other than work. Over one hundred participants were signed up for the event and another fifty were expected on the day of the race.

Despite her busy schedule at work, Preye always found the energy for organising the event and to fulfil her role as president of the Roadrunners Club. But she couldn't have done it without the support of her ten volunteers who themselves had lost someone to one form of cancer or another.

Timi had joined Roadrunners about two years ago, but his interest had begun to wane after they started dating. And he had recently been questioning her devotion to the cause. She had thought he'd feel differently, since they had met through the club, but he had expressed that he felt it had fulfilled its purpose. Timi believed Preye had grieved enough for the dead Kevin and that it was time to move on.

But beyond Kevin, Preye loved running and the fact that she could give back to the community and possibly influence the health policy one day. So she vowed to keep the club going as long as there was interest, which was growing every year. Only recently, the wife of the local government chairman had signed up for the 5K run.

Tobi Abass showed up and brought along a journalist who ran a column on The Human Angle in Verity Newspaper. Tobi also ran the race every year. And this year, he was pushing his one-year-old nephew, Toba in a baby jogger.

Preye greeted the journalist with a warm smile and firm handshake before she turned to Tobi. 'Thanks partner. I have some baby-sized t-shits this year. Be sure to grab one for Toba because he's also a participant.'

'Most of the staff at Beta are pitching in, why thank me?' He looked around and raised his eyes. 'Where's Timi? We need his muscles here. He should be helping you with those boxes,' Tobi suggested.

'Timi isn't feeling up to it today, but he'll be participating in the run, I'm sure,' Preye's response lacked the kind of confidence she'd have loved to exude. She wasn't exactly being truthful, because she already sensed Timi wouldn't want to run the race. He had pretty much quit Roadrunners altogether.

After the planning meeting, the others worked on sorting out the event's materials while Preye had an informal interview with the journalist. She talked about cancer and how early detection could help a lot of sufferers, urging the government and corporate organisations to invest in cancer research and free periodic diagnostic check. She also explained why the Roadrunners needed support for the annual race and the different projects they would be executing with the funds generated.

She waited to lock up after everyone had departed, before heading home. She was sure Timi would be at her place waiting. That is what he did. He liked to make sure she was home, safely in bed and alone. He'd kiss her goodnight and then he'd go back to his house. Some days when he was working, he'd let himself in to say hello and see how she was doing before he left for work.

He practically lived in her house, except that he never slept there.

*

'Love, I'm home and I can smell my favourite *dundun and akara*. How did you know I'd be ravenous?' Preye asked in a cheerful tone.

It had been a long day and she was happy to finally be home. She kicked her trainers off and found Timi in the small kitchen. Soiled sheets of paper were crumpled and scattered in the open bin. 'You didn't leave any for me?' She was confused at the sight of the bare worktop.

'It's only good if it's hot and you came back late. I tried calling, but your phone must have been switched off because I was unable to track you. I ate a bit and thrashed the remaining. I was about to come searching for you just before you breezed in.' Even though his voice was flat, Preye noticed the vein in his neck throbbing. She didn't want to start him on a temper tantrum, so she decided to mellow down.

'I'm sorry to have worried you Love.' She walked towards the refrigerator. 'I'll fix something to eat and you can tell me all about your day.'

He was furious that she didn't understand the impact of him

not knowing where she was. He reached her from behind and slammed the refrigerator door shut, firmly turning her around. The smell of the *akara* was pungent in his breath as he forcefully kissed her, with her back against the refrigerator door.

'This will make me forget all about your naughty behaviour,' he breathed into her ear as he pulled back to paw at her red Roadrunners t-shirt, ripping it about two inches down her chest. Preye gasped and pushed him back reflexively, but Timi's weight against her body gave her little success.

She shut her eyes to draw up some strength before she faked a smile and pushed him back a second time. 'We talked about waiting until we're married. I am serious about it Timi. Let's set a date tonight. I have some details to go over with you.'

This time he softened his grip on her t-shirt and pulled back, but kept her pinned to the refrigerator. He whispered in her ears. 'I know you're serious. We're in this together, but I want you so much.' He started licking her ear, weakening her resolve to push him off.

'Timi, please,' she murmured, but it was lost on him. He went on kissing her all over the face. Her protests only made him more insistent on pushing her farther than she wanted to go as he intensified rubbing his whole body against hers. Suddenly, he lifted her like he was a rescuing fireman, carried her into the bedroom and threw her to the bed even as she continued kicking her legs. 'What are you doing?'

'Quit this nonsense. I wasted my evening worrying while you ran around with your friends. I give a lot and in return, you keep pushing me off,' he growled. 'Don't you think I've earned it?' His hands were on her top again and he pushed it up forcefully to grab her breasts, while his face searched her lips to lock her in a kiss.

She shook her head continuously to avoid his lips. 'No, Timi, stop!' Scared and powerless to defend herself against the tall, muscular man, she tried to push him away. She had always liked his physique, but not at this minute.

Eventually, he succeeded in ramming his tongue into her mouth and his hand moved below to her navel as she felt his turgidity pushing against her thigh. She managed to push the hand off her taut tummy and she continued to say no. Then she started sobbing.

Her sobs got his attention, flattening out his emotions. He got off her, looking sullen.

'Mine, I'm sorry.' He hurried up to stand against the wall, rubbing his hands against each other. 'I'm sorry I got carried away.' He sat beside her and lifted her to a sitting position on the bed. 'Does this mean that much to you?' She nodded, disoriented. He shook his deflated head, letting his shoulders drop.

Crouching at the edge of the bed against the wall, she wrapped her arms around her bent legs. A few moments of thick silence passed before she reclaimed her mind to be able to communicate with him. She exhaled. 'Timi, can I say something?'

He reached out to pat her legs, but she bent them away from him. 'I …' he started, but she raised her hand to shut him up.

'You know the bible's stance on sex before marriage and that's my stand. I'm not going to compromise that. If we have to break up now, I'll miss you, but I'll be fine. If you still want me, please don't press me on sex again. Ever!' Her pause allowed her to steady her breath after the emphasis on her last word. She shook her head as a firm gesture of her seriousness. 'I understand that we're not at the same level of spirituality, but that's not an excuse, because I believe you want to be serious with your Christian faith too,' she paused again, looking at him with a questioning sign on her stern face. He didn't respond, except with a deep exhale and a nod, so she continued. 'I find you desirable too, but I haven't come this far to mess up my relationship with God.'

She was exhausted. This was the first time he'd be forceful and hopefully, it would be the last. Her body throbbed and her heart ached as she tried to make sense of what had happened. She wanted to diminish the gravity of the incident, but she couldn't think logically.

Her emotions and thoughts were pulled in opposite directions like a tug of war. She wanted to run away from him, yet she wanted him to soothe her. *Is it wrong for him to want me so much? But he should know that it's a no go area before marriage. He's also a grown man with sexual desires.* She thought she should be grateful that he found her sexually appealing. It was just a few months to their wedding, and even in her pain, the anticipation of how they would ravish each other's bodies assaulted her reasoning until her tensed body lured her to sleep, conflicted.

*

The sunlight beamed illumination into the room and crept up on Preye. She stretched in response. She was still in her ripped Roadrunners t-shirt and she was shocked to see Timi sitting beside her on the bed, gazing at her. He reached for her hand. 'Back to life, sleeping beauty. Your prince is still here.'

'What happened? I slept off?' she quizzed, propping herself up. 'What's the time? Did you sleep here?'

'Yes, my baby. And you're still intact.' Timi reminded her about the incident. 'I love you, Preye Banigo. As a gift to you, I've decided to obey the abstinence rule until after we're married. It won't be easy, but you're worth the wait. I swear, I'll be good and God will help me too,' he chuckled, licking his lower lip slowly as he raised his hand as a sign of a pledge.

She needed to get to work, but she wasn't in a hurry to get

off the bed. 'Should we talk about it?' she asked guardedly. She didn't want him working himself back up into another rage.

'It's fine, there's nothing to talk about. I already said I'm sorry. Just be sure to keep your phone charged and we won't have a problem. I think you've outgrown the Roadrunners and you've done enough. But I'll allow it to go on for another year.'

'Timi, I…'

He put his lips to hers gently, but she turned away. 'We don't have to waste energy talking about the Roadrunners now. Since it makes you happy, you can go on, but you know I'm not for it anymore. Right?' he asked, slightly raising his brows. She nodded. 'Maybe, we should wait until after we're married and we'll see how you feel about it. I love you more every day, my baby and I can't wait to make you my wife.'

He went into the shower and invited Preye to join, promising not to touch her. She declined. Immediately he shut the bathroom door, she reached for her phone and called Aisha to set up a date.

CHAPTER SIX

Aisha lived in a big, modern four-bedroom house in Ogudu with Adamu and their two-year-old son, Ashe. The modest façade of the fence made the house blend in with the other houses on the street and hid the opulence behind the sliding steel gate. Tall and well-tended green poplar trees flanked the fence line and a four-tier solar fountain at the left side pillar of the building provided a cascading rhythm of water, which resonated against the vibrating hum of the generator.

She had stepped away from her company secretary job in a bank to work as a freelance lawyer so she could focus on Ashe. She took only a few cases that interested her and helped out with reviewing documents for Adamu to keep her mind sharp. The plan was for her to resume at Adamu's firm once Ashe was old enough to be enrolled in primary school and she was ready to resume full-time working.

Aisha let Preye in at the dot of 10.30a.m, as they had scheduled. Preye wore a black top on a long *ankara* skirt and finished off the casual look with high wedge sandals. She was a stickler for time, even on personal appointments.

'I was elated when you called for this. Quality time with my *besties* is what I've been needing, I just didn't realise it,' Aisha beamed as she tucked her long legs under her on the sofa.

She was dressed in a colourful sleeveless *adire* jumpsuit. The living room décor colour palette was comprised of white shades

- eggshell, ecru, beige and ivory, even for the leather sofas. It didn't look like a baby lived in the house and Preye wondered if they would still be able to maintain the whiteness when Ashe started walking all over the house. The life-size family portrait presented a perfect contrast against the pastiness.

'I needed a place to decompress. Work, Roadrunners and wedding ideas are coming at me at the same time. I always feel better after a few days away from it all. Your place is the first spot I thought of. Thanks for asking Lola to join. It simply escaped my mind and I feel guilty now. It feels like I only think of work anytime I see her. We should have done this since,' Preye vented solemnly.

Aisha had arranged some juices, wine and champagne, and her favourite fanciful mosaic glass wares on the triple-layer extendable coffee table. She had a glass of cranberry juice on the side stool beside her couch. Preye picked one of the glass cups and admired the mosaic design before she poured herself some cranberry juice, the same as Aisha was having. Wine and cocktails would follow later in the day. If things went as they always did, Lola would knock herself out.

'Lola and I gossip about you, waiting for you to lavish yourself with a deserved treat,' Aisha joked. 'I have a piece of advice for you.'

'Hold that thought. I'm going to run to the toilet.' Preye dashed to the restroom, trying to swing her arm normally, which was a bit difficult. The scuffle with Timi a week ago had put some strains on her arm.

As she returned, Aisha gave her a questioning glance. 'What's with your gait? Did you pull a muscle or something?'

'Oh, no! I slept in an odd position last week and woke up sore in the arm.' The words came out of her mouth before she realised she was lying to cover up for Timi.

'You should pop a paracetamol or better still, let's order

some ice-cream to make you feel better,' Aisha jested. 'To my advice, I was going to tell you, since it's now in your near-future, to beware.'

'Beware?'

'Yes, of the isolation of being a new mum. The fog of loneliness is lifting now, but it was bad at the initial stage of nursing Ashe. For hours, days, weeks and months, your life will be only about this little person. Don't get me wrong, I love Ashe more every day, but I'm primarily only a mom. Everything that is not baby-related fades away. That's why I encouraged Adamu to go with Ashe to his mother's for the weekend so we can be by ourselves and throw caution to the wind. I also needed a break from those people to unwind.'

'Lola will like the throwing caution to the wind part. And she'll add some profanities in the mix. That girl...' Preye shook her head in jest over Lola's antics. 'I'm surprised Zara hasn't taken up the habit.' Preye had forgotten how relaxing it was chatting with her girlfriends. She loved being with Timi, but spending time with him couldn't make up for being with her friends. She made a mental note to create more time for their meet-ups.

'Will you be starting a family once you're married? Or you want to wait and extend the honeymoon? That won't be bad, so you guys can get to properly know each other before the baby comes to steal Timi's place. If that's your intention, just remember that's what I did. Then I couldn't get pregnant at the time I wanted to. You know we all thought pregnancy would happen just by having regular sex.' They both laughed, recalling the many times they had consoled Aisha the months her period surfaced. 'I didn't say that thing about motherhood to scare you off. One of my favourite parts of being pregnant eventually was collecting all of the cute baby stuff. I didn't like getting fat, but it's almost impossible to avoid. Thanks to Roadrunners for helping me keep in shape.' Aisha took her glass cup and downed her cranberry juice before reaching for the bottle of champagne on the coffee table. She was getting herself in the mood to party.

Preye didn't really drink alcohol, except for the occasional champagne sips anytime there was a celebration and at some official events to click glasses. She was content to continue with the cranberry juice.

About one hour later, Lola breezed in, at the same time the masseuse Preye booked arrived. The upper part of Lola's body was shrouded in a drape of short kaftan, revealing her clean-shaved straight legs. She sauntered into the living room and dropped into one of the sofas, shutting her eyes and throwing her hands out resignedly, to mock a faint.

Preye and Aisha shook their heads and sniggered before they echoed a welcome to Lola. 'No one is competing with you on late coming, so you don't need to act it out,' Preye dismissed.

'Let's hear it. What's your excuse this time?' Aisha asked, wrinkling her nose for a mock sniff.

Lola woke up and clapped her hands. 'I don't know how women with five children cope and still have a life. Just one tiny girl and she wants to kill me,' Lola whined. 'She wants a bicycle and that's the only song I hear now.' She got up and walked to the coffee table, filled her glass with some champagne and slinked back to her seat like a roving cat. 'Aisha, you spoil us. The last time I had champagne was …' she looked up as if a day would appear on the white ceiling.

'Last week,' Preye interjected.

Aisha went to show the masseuse where to set up as Preye and Lola continued their idle chatter.

Aisha announced that the masseuse was ready and the three of them went to change, to submit themselves for the deep tissue massage sessions. They all dozed off and on during the sessions and commented about how they needed to do more to loosen up. After the massage session, Aisha escorted the masseuse out of the house and they shifted to the sauna at Aisha's backyard to sweat it out.

The late morning had turned into afternoon by the time they came out of the sauna, refreshed. They agreed to take a nap by sharing the king size bed in the guestroom downstairs.

Preye woke up first and stole out from her side of the bed. She tiptoed to the living room to avoid waking the others. Alone, she yawned and stretched her body before she took advantage of the privacy to call her fiancé. She checked her phone and realised that he had already called twice.

'Hello, Timi. The baby was sleeping so I took a nap too. I left my phone in the other room,' Preye whispered apologetically.

'I know you're okay at Aisha's. I'm just checking in. It was kind of you to help out with Ashe for the weekend. You can start getting some baby tips now.'

'I'll see you for dinner tomorrow night. I'll get out of here early and we can spend time talking about wedding details. But we still need to have some serious talk.' Preye felt it was easier talking to him over the phone, rather than facing him.

'Preye Banigo, I love you and soon you'll be Mrs Coker. You spend too much time focusing on the past. It's a waste of time with our future looking so bright.'

'I love you too. I guess that's all that matters.' She conceded. The sessions with her friends made her feel better. But her mind nagged her because she had lied to Timi about watching Ashe, even though it was for the best.

'What's wrong with you?' Lola was standing in the doorway. 'Timi's voice was loud enough for me to get the gist of your conversation. You lied that you came to take care of Ashe? Why would you do that?'

'You know Timi. The less he knows, the better. We had an

issue last week and things are a bit sensitive between us at the moment. If he thinks I ran off to party with my girlfriends, he'd assume I'm trying to avoid him or something like that. This keeps the waters calm.'

'Sounds wrong to me. Sorry, but no, I'm not sorry. If you're worried about him getting annoyed every time you hang out with your friends, then what's your future going to be like? Will he not allow you to have any life outside of your marriage? *This one na nonsense* and I'm not afraid to tell you,' Lola said, unapologetically.

Aisha came in. She didn't know about the phone call with Timi. All she knew was that Lola was being Lola and the foretold profanities had started. Lola didn't have any filter and sometimes needed to be reined in. This appears to be one of those times.

'Lola!' Aisha called out, scolding her friend as if she was the judge. 'Not tonight. We've been friends for too long and we need to learn to respect one another's choices. And by the way, have you found another husband for Preye?' She poked her face at Lola. 'Let's go have some drinks, dinner and laughs. I booked a table at Emerald, the new hotel at Ikeja GRA. Let's reserve the serious talk for tomorrow, after Preye's online church service. Or maybe the sermon would do.' Aisha giggled. 'Agree?'

Preye and Lola nodded their heads as Lola threw her arms around Preye. 'Love you.'

Grateful to Aisha for easing the foreboding tension, Preye gently pushed and grabbed one of Lola's hands. 'Let's go paint the town red.'

*

Lola insisted on driving Aisha's G Wagon to Emerald Hotel. Aisha had attended the hotel's opening with Adamu and promised herself then that she'd be back soon, either for networking or simply for the treat.

It wasn't the green marble exterior of the hotel that made Aisha choose the hotel. She found the colour rather drab. It was the enormity of the rooms' sizes, the luxuriance of the Egyptian bed sheets and the sheer splendour of the bathroom, not forgetting the doughnut-shaped swimming pool by the garden bar and its inserted rubberised water fountain in the middle.

The trio strolled leisurely towards the garden bar, their shoes making gentle sounds on the marble tiles. The arrived as the live band started playing. After getting seated, they ordered *suya* and soft drinks, and Lola added two shots of 41% rum to the order.

It wasn't long before they started shaking their heads to the music from the live band while watching the flow of people going back and forth. The stream of water tumbling down the fountain wall was soothing. Most of the human noise in the garden was from a particular table filled with bottles of expensive spirits, with three men and four young ladies vying for who could speak the loudest. The three men went to the band to *spray* some foreign currencies, in response to the band singing their praises.

'Is this how the wealthy still spend their weekends?' Lola asked, looking towards Aisha, since Aisha was the richest of them. 'I think I've become rusty.'

Aisha answered. 'Yes and no. It's only some lazy wealthy people who got their fortune from inheritance. Then there are the politicians and government contractors. They're an entitled lot. But then, you have hard-working wealthy people who don't have the time to throw away money like this. And sometimes, people just want to do whatever they wish with their money, if they derive fun from it.' She flapped her hands. 'It's neither here nor there. I prefer being the way I am, with enough money to afford the occasional extravagance.'

'In my next life, I want to be the entitled type like Bode. He made me taste the luxury of wealth and pulled the rug from under me. Stupid man. *If to say na my papa get that kain money…*' Lola eyed her friends mischievously before she continued. 'You girls won't recognise me again. I'll enjoy what I want, when I want it and it'll never get tiresome. And I will choose my friends more carefully,' she ended humorously. Aisha and Preye hissed, shaking their heads.

Of the three of them, Lola was the worst with money and she had the least of it. Some of it was due to her being a stay-at-home wife before her divorce and then being a single mother. Some of it, however, was because she spent a lot on designers' fashion. To her credit, Lola was also extremely generous and hated to see others struggle. She had a list of single mothers she gave pocket money every month.

Preye had a good amount of savings and she worked hard for every last bit. She was proud of how far she had come financially, despite her family background. She was a 40% shareholder at Beta, having given 10% to Lola. Beta was worth over seventy million naira in asset and goodwill. Preye also owned a Lexus RX300 and was saving up to buy a house. She had planned to move into her own house before she turned forty, but she had put the plan on a back-burner due to her marital status. Nigerians still struggled with respecting the status of successful single women and most people would have concluded that she couldn't get a husband because she was too successful.

When she just bought her new Lexus, a handful of well-wishers, including her mother, had asked her if she was sure her status wasn't keeping men away because they were intimidated. But her friends and business partner, Tobi always told her she couldn't put her life on hold because of something she had no control over.

Now that Timi had proposed, she hoped they could work

towards achieving her dream of home-ownership. They had to start thinking of moving out from her current apartment before the wedding, as he had stated categorically that he wasn't keen on moving in with her. It occurred to her that they needed to spend time together to discuss their finances and to sign up for the counselling sessions in church.

'I don't know about you ladies, but my massage was better than most of the sex I had last year,' Lola announced, totally steering the discussion from random gossip. With the freedom earned from her divorce, she claimed she was on a mission to explore her sexuality. She was on a third boyfriend and unlike Preye, she wasn't in it for the long term.

'Sex life with Adamu is great. The massage was good, but it doesn't compare to the loving touch of my dear husband,' Aisha giggled naughtily.

'Now I'm forced to talk about Timi,' Preye tattled cautiously in response to the two heads looking in her direction. She loosened her doughnut to let her hair loose.

'I didn't mention his name, but if you want to talk, we're listening,' Lola said, winking at Aisha. 'At least we know you're not having sex. Hopefully.' Lola ogled at Preye for confirmation.

'Is something bothering you?' Aisha leaned in.

Preye inhaled and exhaled heavily. 'I'm sure you were both surprised when I suggested spending the weekend at Aisha's.' Preye's change of tone rang with concern to her captive audience. Their eyes focused on her, waiting for her to spit out whatever was eating her. 'Timi almost got physical and he was on the verge of forcing sex on me.' She left it at that.

Aisha could usually mask her feelings, but she couldn't help but look shocked. 'Timi almost raped you? This is serious.'

Preye put up her palm. 'I didn't say he almost raped me. It wasn't that bad. He pressed a bit and tried to see how far I'd go, but it's not like he battered me. Look at me, I'm fine.'

'Did you tell him to stop?' Lola asked. She wanted to run to his house and beat the man out of him, but she remained calm, so that Aisha wouldn't scold her for speaking out of turn again.

'Yes and eventually he did. Things just happened and they won't happen again. He's promised.'

'Oh, *Omo* girl, when will you wake up from this good girl nature of yours? That guy isn't safe, and your mental well-being is at risk here. Physical too, which I didn't realise before. In case you haven't noticed, he's over six feet tall and you're five feet nothing. With the kind of life he's lived as an *ogbologbo*…hmm.' Lola shook her head for the other two to fill in the blank spaces in her unfinished statement. 'That's one of the reasons I hate pet names you people use. The way Timi calls you Mine, Mine, maybe he actually thinks he owns you.' Lola was unrelenting. 'Have you considered slowing things down between the two of you?'

'Stop being dramatic about this. Don't you think it was bound to happen, with the way we smooch each other? I can be honest with you. I do feel like having sex with him too. Except that I've resolved not to. Well, we've moved on, and if it happens again, Lola I promise, I will give you the go-ahead to whip him. We can't slow things down now that he's ready for marriage. I'm hoping I'll have our first kid within a year of getting married. My eggs are ageing as we speak and I don't want to be an old mom, pushing prams at sixty. Most importantly, Timi loves me and I love him. Please don't judge me because I'm following my heart. I need your support and not your criticism. Please.' Preye almost broke down and her friends embraced her.

Let's hope he's not having sex with someone else, Lola thought.

*

Sunday ended on a cheerful note. Adamu and Ashe came back home in the morning and it was impossible to think about anything negative with the baby prancing around everyone.

The ladies said their goodbyes in the evening, after having a big lunch in Aisha's house. Preye promised to organise more time-out with her friends and agreed they needed to see Aisha more. She saw Lola at work, but they were both kept busy at the office.

Preye was waiting at the first traffic light after Aisha's house, when her phone rang through the car's speakers.

'Mine, I'm so glad you're coming home. I've missed you. I got a little taste of what life would be like without you and it sucks.'

'Get a life, Timi. I was only gone for a night,' she laughed into the phone. She expected a response but the sound from the other end quietened for some seconds. She smacked her lips.

'You're right. Are you still coming to Omole?'

'Definitely! I wouldn't miss it for anything.'

She drove straight to his family home for dinner with him and his parents.

CHAPTER SEVEN

Since spending the weekend away with her friends, Preye had noticed that Timi was calmer and more attentive to her. Timi had also noticed that Preye was more acquiescing. There had been no temper eruptions or disagreements. Preye had gotten a box of perfume delivered to Timi's office, while he had continued to turn things around with little gifts and fun outings. At home and at work, things were at peace and progressive.

They had also had two of the four required counselling sessions with their allocated marriage counsellor in church. Preye had thought Timi's engagement with the session was perfunctory. The counsellor had asked them to freely discuss any issue of concerns and Preye had expected Timi to own their altercation over sex, but he hadn't and she hadn't brought it up either, for fear of sounding unforgiving since he had apologised. So the incident seemed to be forgotten and no longer up for discussion.

He had pointed out to Preye that they were both old enough to know how to handle their relationship without any external influence. But they had to complete the counselling sessions as a pre-requisite for getting married in church.

Preye had dinner with her siblings at Erefa's house one evening, a Roadrunners meeting the next and a working dinner with colleagues.

Timi attended a client's launch, represented his manager at

an annual convention and had a late night dinner with Preye at Miriam's house.

He was mostly in high spirits because he had started getting the recognition he knew he deserved at work. His boss assigned him the task of organising a trade exhibition, which if implemented properly, could earn him a promotion, so he was generally in amiable spirits with everyone.

It was about a month after the fun weekend at Aisha's and Timi was waiting at the ground reception of Preye's office. Immediately she stepped out of the lift with some other people, he was there with his hands stretched out holding a bunch of roses.

'It's Friday and I knew you'd be exhausted, so I picked up *dundun and akara*,' he whispered in her ears.

Her soft lips parted into a glowing smile of happiness. 'You're indulging me, Timi. Why?' she asked as the tiredness she had felt earlier when she packed her bag to leave her office seeped out of her body.

'Do I need a reason?' he asked mockingly, leading her to the car. The way the corners of his lips widened out brightened his face and clad him with an irresistible charm.

'Absolutely not!'

He had parked his Toyota in his office car park and taken a taxi to Preye's office so they could ride to her place together in her car.

They intended to spend the weekend to plan the wedding and the many things they needed to get sorted on the journey to merge their lives. The only other thing Preye had planned was lunch with her sisters after church on Sunday. Erefa and Tonye were coming by her place.

Timi thought he needed to spend some time to start clearing out his closets, so he didn't end up moving junk to Preye's flat, which would soon become his new home. His friends, Martin and Malik would help him pack.

When they got to Preye's flat, she changed into a lounge suit and walked into the living room with a load of paper in her arms. After placing the paper on the coffee table, she sat beside Timi on the sofa, crossing her legs at the feet to make herself comfortable.

'Are you ready to cross some items off our to-do list?' she asked casually.

'With you dressed like you are, it'll be hard to concentrate,' he said in a playful guttural voice before switching to a rigid tone of displeasure. 'You've taken your make-up off, and with your hair pulled up, your birthmark is on full display.'

She felt a twinge in her stomach. It wasn't the kind of comment she expected from him at such a time because they hadn't been any argument about her dressing for a while. She hoped his comment wouldn't be a harbinger of things to come.

'I've had a long week and wearing comfortable clothes is what I deserve. This is relaxing and you can expect to see a lot more of it in the years to come.'

'It's your choice. I won't argue with you.' He handed her a glass of juice. 'As an early wedding gift, I have a surprise for you.'

Like clockwork, Timi switched emotions naturally.

'You know I love surprises. What do you have for me this time? Should I close my eyes?'

'No need,' he responded as he nestled in close to her on the sofa. He removed her hair clip so her locks cascaded down her shoulders and covered her birthmark. 'I've picked up a wedding form from the local government and locked down the date for when you officially become Mrs Preye Coker.' Preye's face beamed with joy, but she soon became downcast as he went on. 'I also picked up an account opening form from the bank, so we can open a joint account. All I require is your signature. I've completed the form, knowing how you dread filling forms. And

I have the form for change of name too.'

She looked down at the paperwork Timi set before her with mixed feelings. She had been pushing forward discussing the subject of taking his last name. 'I love your name, but I was hoping to retain my name,' she said demurely.

'Excuse me? You can't be serious,' he snapped. She nodded, implying that she was indeed serious. 'Don't pull that modern woman crap on me.' He stood up and paced back and forth.

'It's not exactly a new thing. I'm established professionally as Preye Banigo and it would be confusing to my clients to make the change. It would also make me less visible to new clients. It's done all the time and I mean no offence.'

'Are you placing your professional ambition ahead of your family already? That's not going to work for this family.' He planted his feet on the ground and threw his hands on his hips.

'Why don't we shelve the issue and take a break from the paperwork? Thanks for trying to sort it out. I'd be lost without you. Let's see what's on the telly.' Preye said, reaching for the TV remote control. She didn't have the energy to argue.

'We can put off discussing the name change, but I'm pretty firm on where I stand. I'll let you sleep on it and we'll take it up again tomorrow.'

'Thanks, but I am also firm on where I stand. I'll sign the account opening form now if you want, but I'll need to get my passport photographs from the office tomorrow,' she said as she tossed a crumpled up newspaper in the bin.

'Just sign. And if you want me to sign on your behalf, it's no trouble.'

'I'll sign it.' She reached for her bag and picked a pen and continued speaking as she signed the form. 'I noticed several houses for rent around Aisha's neighbourhood. Most of them are rather big and may not fit into our budget, but there are some flats too that may be financially feasible. If we live there, it would be easy to eventually get a property to buy in the area. It's a good location for work and bringing up children. And we won't be so far away from our families too.'

'I was looking a little bit to the outskirts, like Shasha. That side of town is developing into a nice neighbourhood and it's more economical. That way, we can buy our home faster rather than paying out loads of money to a Lagos landlord. I know you'll take some convincing because you want a certain sense of prestige. Shasha may not offer that yet, but it offers some serenity and security. I've never lived in a rented apartment and I don't want to deal with landlords for more than I need to. We can also live at my parents' if you don't mind, but knowing you…' He left his sentence hanging.

She was shocked at his suggestion. His parents' home should not even have been brought into the discussion and Shasha was out of her map. She'd rather continue living in her apartment than take any of his options. But this was marriage and she recognised that she'd need to make concessions. She sighed.

'It's not like I'm looking to live in the fanciest neighbourhood. But, I'd like to be close to friends and family. I'll feel isolated living at Shasha and it will increase the time I spend commuting to and from the office,' she appealed. 'Have you ever witnessed the morning traffic coming to Ikeja?' She shook her head, hoping that would be a catch. 'You don't want to go there.'

'I want what's best for us. This isn't your decision to make anymore. It's ours. Don't worry Mine, I'll make the right choice for us. You should be grateful I didn't suggest Sango Ota.' He tried to joke, but she didn't find it funny.

She always nursed an ideal vision of planning the future with her proposed husband. Her fantasy was gradually becoming a reality and she supposed it was similar to most situations. In fairness to him, she had never gotten to this point in a relationship and she shouldn't fault him for bumps on the road. With hard work, she was sure their desires would end in compromise. She looked at him as he collected the TV remote from her and started searching for a channel. He did look good in his faded jeans. Preye smiled and pulled up a pillow to support herself on the sofa.

*

Tonye was the youngest of the Banigo girls. She had gotten married two years ago and had confessed she wasn't in a hurry to have children yet. She had confided in her sisters that she'd get her eggs frozen until she was ready to start a family. Her current pre-occupation was to discover herself, as she had put it. Dapo, Tonye's husband was a successful businessman, and he was supporting her to establish a human relations and recruitment consultancy. Tonye was following Preye's steps to be an entrepreneur. Dapo was the one who pulled Tonye through a difficult stretch of her life which extended from her late teens into her early twenties. She had fallen in with the wrong crowd at the university and had become addicted to alcohol.

Tonye had met Dapo at a job interview as one of her interviewers. Unknown to her, she had appeared dishevelled to the venue of the interview. The interviewers, including Dapo had dismissed her without as much as a question. A short while later, Dapo found her at the car park where she had been crouched in a corner, crying. He had stopped to ask her how she was doing and she had poured out her life history to him. He had gotten hooked from there, enrolling her for therapy and eventually leading her to the altar.

She was smart and driven and she wanted to prove herself. She knew she had been spoilt by her family because they had always treated her like the baby of the family that could do no wrong.

'Little girl,' Preye opened the door and Tonye, who was holding a covered dish of fruit salad, walked in. The sisters hugged each other. 'You didn't have to bring anything, but I'm glad you did. I love your new look.' Preye looked her up and down, admiring her low-cut tinted hair.

Tonye fluffed her cropped hair. 'It's grown out a bit. It proves how seldom I see you. You should try it. I find this style quite liberating and cheap for maintenance too.'

'No way. Timi would have me locked away until it grew back or at best he'd get me a lovely wig.' Preye laughed, shaking her head. 'And that golden tint … it's never gonna happen.'

'Dapo knows me better than to tell me what to do with my hair. I would ask him if it's sitting on his head or mine. You know *say I no send,*' she bragged.

Soon, they were joined by Erefa. They scooped out Tonye's fruit salad and mixed it with the prawn salad Preye had made with home-grown tomatoes from Tobi Abass' garden. The sisters' banter was quite loud as they caught up with one another's lives without reservations. The only meaningful discussion was on Erefa's impending bundle of joy. She was having a girl and had decided to name her Tamara after Donald's departed mother. Erefa was filled with ideas for the baby's room and all sorts of baby details.

'Since our pretty princess here is still enjoying her honeymoon, I predict you'll be the next to provide a grandchild to the mix, Preye. Is Timi excited about starting right away?'

Timi walked in just as the question was asked and the sisters went hush at the unexpected interruption. He was holding a bouquet of fresh flowers.

'I'll answer that. Of course, I'm excited. I'd start now if we could, but as Christians, we have to wait till we're married. I'm willing to have as many children as she desires.' He handed Preye the flowers and kissed her on the forehead. 'We can finally fill my parent's den with grandchildren.'

Preye's sisters cooed a collective *ha*. They didn't know they had been that loud.

'Hope you ladies are having fun. I dropped by just to say hello to my future sisters-in-law.' Timi laughed. 'I'll be on my way now.'

'You don't have to leave,' Erefa stopped him. 'We only wanted to talk about Preye's spinster's party. It has to be soon, before my baby is born, so I can be part of it,' Erefa said. 'It will be fun to see everyone pretending to be young. I'll video the antics and think about showing you, although I'll have to edit out the naughty bits.' She winked at Timi.

'Tonye, you're the level-headed one. I know I can count on you to keep an eye on my precious fiancée,' Timi said, not quite enthused by Erefa's joke.

Preye nearly choked on the bite of salad in her mouth. Of both her sisters, Tonye liked Timi less because he had once mocked her bookish personality by referring to her as prudish, and it hadn't been received well. Tonye was sensitive and never forgot the comment. He had also taunted her past alcoholism, calling her *shayo*. No one considered that part of Tonye's life a joking matter and Preye had felt like she had betrayed her sister to Timi. Especially since Tonye had been sober for years. She had also been close to Kevin which was probably why she often gave Timi the cold treatment.

'Sweetheart, Erefa was telling me that there are a few flats in her neighbourhood to let. It's worth a look, don't you think?' Preye asked. She didn't intend to ambush Timi, but she thought her sister might gently nudge him towards her way of thinking.

Erefa was quick to add her opinion. 'As you know, our side of Opebi is quite reserved and it's excellent for families. We've made some friends and we're really happy there. It would be easy for our little ones to get together and grow up together.'

'We'll add that to our bucket list,' Timi assented. 'I hope you ladies won't mind if I pull up a chair. I'd like to hear about plans for the spinster's night. Apparently, I haven't attended one before.' He went to sit beside Preye. I hope you won't have guys there, so no one tries to steal my lovely girl.' A grin diffused over his face, revealing his teeth.

Preye welcomed Timi to join the sister's lunch and they poured out their plans to him, but Tonye clammed up. She didn't trust the man her sister was going to marry, but she simply couldn't explain what the problem was, since it was obvious he adored Preye and Preye loved him. Besides, he was the only one who had proposed to Preye since Kevin.

Yet Tonye couldn't shake off the guilty feeling from wishing that something drastic should happen to stop her sister from marrying Timi.

CHAPTER EIGHT

She joined Timi for lunch in the afternoon before leaving for her spinster's get-away. It was planned for Friday evening to Sunday afternoon at a nearby hotel where Tonye had secured a block of rooms for the gang. The Banigo sisters, Aisha, Lola and five other women were billed to attend. Preye would be sharing a suite with Aisha and Lola, which made Timi nervous because he was afraid they might corrupt her before the big day.

Preye had made him promise that he'd keep himself busy while she was away, so that he didn't spend the time worrying. He had swept aside her suggestion for him to have a bachelor's party with his friends as well.

She had told him in advance that her phone would be turned off, but she'd be sure to check in with him and he had sounded excited that she'd have a chance to enjoy herself before the wedding.

They stood beside Preye's car at Beta to say farewell for the weekend. 'Thanks for lunch and please, don't worry about me. Things have been going smoothly for us for the most part. I think this time out with my friends will be refreshing and help me loosen up a bit,' Preye said.

'I'm sure it'll be worth it. Maybe when they see how happy you are, they'll finally admit you've found your soul mate. I kind of sense they don't approve of me. And don't even try to deny that.' He quickly added as she opened her mouth to protest. He shrugged. 'What matters is that I love you.' Without breaking a breath, he switched the subject. 'What are you wearing tonight? Are you dressing up as a sexy queen of the night?' he teased.

She wasn't sure if he meant that as a joke. 'Don't worry, all my friends are straight and won't find me sexy.' She stood on her toes and kissed him on the cheek. He pulled her in tight and put his hands on her bum before opening the car door for her.

'Mmm, I can't wait to make you my wife.'

'Be good.' She started the car and blew him a kiss as she drove off.

*

Preye checked into the hotel and discovered Aisha and Lola were already in the suite they were to share. She travelled up to the twelfth-floor suite to get the party started. 'I'm here, girls,' she called out. She was wearing her official attire of dark green skirt suit, and she had her clothes for the weekend in a travel bag.

Lola, who usually dressed in smart-casuals to work was in a pair of jeans and had changed her shirt to a chiffon see-through blouse. She looked Preye up and down. 'There had better be something stunning in that bag of yours,' Lola chided, referring to Preye's suit. 'Do I have to be your wardrobe assistant as well?' She passed Preye the glass of red wine she was sipping on. 'Something chilled to cool you down.'

Preye collected the wine from Lola, smelt it for alcohol, shook her head and returned it to her. 'Where's Aisha?' she asked as she unzipped her bag to reveal the hot-red mini-skirt and black top she intended to wear. She guessed Timi would be mad if he saw it, but she couldn't care less. She raised the skirt up to Lola's face. 'Now that's something for you to talk about.' She rolled her eyes at Lola.

'That's what I'm talking about, *Omo* girl.' Lola gave her a high five in approval. 'Aisha is on the phone with Adamu, but after that, she's turning the thing off. He knows where we are if there's an emergency. I expect the same of you.'

Preye switched off her phone and threw it on the bed as she proceeded to change her clothes. 'I know the rules. Tonight is going to be about us and not some referendum on the man I have chosen to marry. I love him and nothing is going to change my mind about Timi.'

'Timi who?' Lola joked.

'You never give up, do you?'

The first night was a simple dinner at the restaurant where they all gossiped about work, business and their love lives. Some of them had some interesting stories to share about their in-laws and ex- lovers too. Each of the ladies took turns to give Preye advice about how to keep a man and make the most of marriage.

They had a late breakfast the following morning and resumed their chitchat. The married ones talked about things that went wrong or that could have gone wrong on their wedding nights, ranging from drinking too much alcohol to premature ejaculation due to over-excitement. They all had a good laugh. Preye was warned that she might be disappointed over sex on her wedding night or even the first few days, as two of the ladies shared their experiences of sex mishaps.

As they handed her beautifully-wrapped gifts, each of the ladies gave her a piece of advice or two and added some more stories behind each of their gifts. Erefa talked about how Preye had taken care of them like a mother goose when they were growing up. She said she was sure Preye would make the best wife and mother in the world.

Aisha advised Preye to make sure she kept her motivating light burning so that she could keep on lighting the paths of those following her.

On Lola's turn, she sarcastically wiped fake tears from her eyes and stood up after parting with her gift. 'I may not be the best person to give marital advice because I've only learned how not to be married.' She paused for the laughing ladies to quieten. 'But my experience has taught me a thing or two, *Omo* girl. Keep your joy! No matter what happens, and believe me, hell will happen sometimes. You will soon find out that getting married is the easy bit, the hard bit is staying married. But I know you'll succeed because you're a strong woman and you don't give up easily. In fact, you don't give up at all. One last thing, being married doesn't mean you should forget your friends. That may be the time you need us the most. I'm a living example of that. And I should thank Aisha for not shutting us out of her life *sake of say she marry better person.*' She made to sit, but shot up before she landed on the chair, raising her hand. 'Another last thing, don't lose yourself in this marriage. Be a wife, be a mother and be yourself. Remember what I said, keep your joy. And I will always love you.' She mimicked Whitney Houston's song and went to embrace Preye.

After the rounds of advice, they parted and retired to their rooms to have short naps before meeting up at the hotel's spa for some beauty treatments. Preye had the whole works of skin rejuvenation and hydro-facial therapy alongside a holistic massage.

The ladies gathered at the hotel's restaurant for dinner, during which time they laid a good base for the night's partying as they started boozing. Not everyone imbibed though. Preye abstained, Erefa was seven months pregnant and Tonye treated alcohol like poison. She hadn't touched a drop of alcohol since she got over her addiction. She used to drink as a way to loosen her inhibitions and it had gotten out of hand. With Dapo's support, she had learned to be happy with who she was and didn't have to prove to anyone that she wasn't a prude because she didn't drink. Her family was proud of how hard she had worked on herself to come this far.

'Preye, I hope you're ready to dance because we planned to go to that new hotel, Cicero. They have a Rooftop Arena and I hear they have the hottest DJ in town. If anyone famous is in this city, they'll be at Cicero.' Tonye lifted her glass of sparkling grape juice. 'Time to let loose, ladies.'

'With this protruding belly, I hope this baby won't jump out today as I *no wan carry last for the dance*.' Erefa drank her water from a champagne flute.

'If that happens, it would be a great story to tell Tamara someday,' Preye chipped in. Everybody laughed. They all felt relaxed and freely talked without any shadow of unease. Preye glanced at the time and remembered she had promised she'd call Timi. She took a moment to run back to the room to ring him up.

She sat on the edge of the bed, ready to pop up once her call was done. 'Timi, it's me and I'm checking in, which seems silly because I'm fine. We just had dinner and Tonye says she's taking us to Cicero. Do you know the place? Beta got an invite for their opening ceremony, but I haven't been there. Tonye thinks it's nice, so...' Preye shrugged without finishing the statement. 'What are you doing with yourself?'

'You sound funny. How much have you had to drink?' he asked.

'You know I don't drink. But I did take a sip of champagne this afternoon as a toast. Nothing much.' She was too much in a hurry to get back to her friends than dwell on why he asked the question. 'We're having great fun. Don't worry, sweetie, it's not like I'm twenty-two. Are you doing anything fun tonight?' She steered the conversation back to him.

'If you count missing you as fun, that's what I'm doing. What are you wearing?' he grumbled.

She wasn't going to give in to his bait. 'Nothing special. You'll probably like it. I'll see you tomorrow afternoon. Love you.'

She switched off her phone and went back to the party.

*

The atmosphere at Cicero's sixth-floor Rooftop Arena was charged with loud voices, hyped music, drinking guests and fast-paced dancing. Although the colourful led lights set on the lower part of the walls were dim, the brightness of the moon and stars beaming from the sky above provided ample light along with a sensuality to the ambience that made Preye inhale the freshness of air as she stepped into the arena. It was the first time she'd be at such a place in over ten years. The last time being when she went to watch Kevin perform.

Preye and the ladies got a dedicated table at the centre and they stayed glued to their seats, dancing with their heads as they swayed on their chairs, until Lola jumped up to hit the metallic resin-glazed dance floor, dragging Tonye along with her. Tonye showed she still had some moves.

The other ladies hit the dance floor one after the other. Aisha moved like a gazelle and Erefa showed no sign of slowing down, despite her big belly. Several heads and fingers were pointing in their direction. Preye was thrilled to be surrounded and supported by her friends. Mary from Beta and Bisi and Helen from Roadrunners were paired off with some random men on the dance floor while the other two ladies were gyrating it out with each other.

Aisha returned to meet Preye at the bar. They had to pitch their voices high to talk because of the loud music. 'Oh, my God, Preye. Don't look. Those men over by the bar have been checking you out and they're about to walk this way. Not saying you should go home with one of them, but a little flirting wouldn't hurt,' Aisha said. 'I'm happily married and I enjoy those looks sometimes. It's an ego booster.'

Preye didn't have time to respond before one of the men reached her, pretending to be dancing. 'Hello, I'm Bala. My friends told me you ladies might be celebrating. I hope it's not a spinster's eve like they guessed, and I hope you're not the bride.'

Preye wiggled her ring finger. 'Your friends are perceptive and I'm flattered. I'm Preye.' She offered her hand. Aisha was right. It did feel good to be noticed. Preye felt a tug on her elbow. She whipped around, her black hair swatting poor Bala in the face.

It was Timi, immaculately dressed in a striped pink linen shirt and black chinos, with a pleasant smile of self-assurance on his handsome face.

'I hope I'm not interrupting,' Timi said, before bringing his lips to land on Preye's mouth. Shame-faced, Bala placed his feet backwards one after the other as if he was stepping on springs, and vanished out of sight, Preye's momentary ego booster disappearing with him.

Preye's euphoria of being admired was quickly replaced with scorching heat radiating from her head to her body as she stood transfixed, wishing she could vanish. 'What in heaven's name are you doing here? I told you I'd see you tomorrow. I'm sorry, but this isn't cool. I'm here with the girls and it's my party. The implied rule is that guys aren't allowed,' Preye said bluntly. The heat in her body had simmered to a cold and she shivered slightly.

'Good to see you too, sweetheart. Can we go somewhere we can hear each other better?' He held her arm like a display of ownership. She pulled him to the hallway leading towards the toilets, running into Tonye along the way. Preye made eye contact with Tonye and shook her head, indicating that she had things covered.

'I could tell you already had a few too much when I spoke to you earlier, and I was worried.' Timi looked her up and down and shook his head in disapproval. 'It's a good thing I came. You're drunk and you might as well wear a sign around your neck that says you're available for sex. You look like a slut, Preye and if I hadn't shown up, it seems you wouldn't have minded that guy getting under your skirt.' The veins in his neck were threatening to burst forth.

She ignored the insult as she tried to steady her breathing which was threatening to get out of control. 'First of all, I'm not drunk. I told you I had a sip, and that was since afternoon. Secondly, Timi, I'm having fun with my friends ...' her body was heating up again and she drew in a deep breath to calm her flames. '... and I'm wearing what I like. It's easy to dance in and I have the right to wear what I want. You like me to dress a certain way which I do around you, to please you. I wasn't planning to see you here, so I'm not wearing a big shirt or long skirt. Why the hell would you want to marry me if you don't trust me?' She was on the verge of tears.

'I want to marry you because I love you, Mine. If I didn't care so much, I wouldn't be jealous or care how you dressed. You should save the sexy for me and not flaunt it because it might get you in trouble.'

'In trouble? How?'

'A man could easily overpower you,' he replied.

'Like you tried once, right?' She remembered how he had been on the verge of raping her. The bad memory made her wince. 'You've properly scolded me and embarrassed me enough. Are you planning to leave anytime soon or do you want to join the party?' Her fury was stoked and her eyes burned fire at him.

But he was untouched by her ire. 'I'm here and I might as

well at least say hello to the girls, then I'll take you home.'

'You're doing no such thing.' Her calm but decisive voice made her seem taller than she was beside her. 'You can say hello to my friends but I'm staying at the hotel as planned. We have breakfast plans in the morning, I'm still mad and you have to give me until tomorrow to cool off. As you can see, I am drunk enough to still talk to you right now.' She sighed, shook her head and turned her back to him to go back into the arena.

Hands in pocket, he strolled after her to join the five ladies who stood around a bar table.

Mary, in her leopard print dress, was still dancing with Helen and Bisi, and the two ladies. It was Preye's night and although some of the girls hadn't expected Timi to show up, they kept their snarky comments to themselves. He could be fun at times and Preye hoped this would be one of those times. Surprisingly, he didn't say much and he courteously explained that he came because he thought Preye had asked him to come when she called him.

'Are you leaving now, then?' Tonye asked with a straight face.

He didn't like to be challenged, least of all by Tonye. Her question flustered him, but he let it go. 'Sure. I'll see you later Mine.' He pulled Preye by the waist and whispered one final instruction into her ear. 'Call me as soon as you're back in your room and leave your phone on.'

They watched him walk away. Preye was embarrassed at the turn of events. She was stuck with a bunch of women who were mixed in opinion of whether Timi was deserving of her or not, but they were united in their thinking that he was the biggest bully on the planet for showing up at the spinster's eve.

*

'Thanks, everyone for the amazing time and all the gifts. I won't have to buy lingerie for the rest of my life.' Preye said, as she sat at breakfast with her friends and sisters. They had gotten her gifts to pump up her honeymoon.

No one talked about Timi or his sudden appearance at Cicero to crash the spinster's eve since Preye didn't broach the issue. The fact that she tolerated his behaviour was a source of concern to Lola and Tonye especially.

Lola leaned into Aisha when Preye excused herself to go to the toilet. 'This marriage has red flags all over it,' Lola whispered. 'That Timi is an arrogant fool and you can't tell me you don't agree with me this time. I don't know how much longer I can stay silent. Before he showed up yesterday, Preye was having the time of her life. He came and the light was sucked right out of her. Didn't you notice?' Lola clenched Aisha's arm.

'I agree, but they love each other. And you know the way he's devoted to her can be quite persuasive. If you don't stop this vendetta, she'll start seeing you as an enemy. And to be fair, you might be wrong about him. Couples do have their differences, Lola, and I think they are working through theirs. I don't know what else you want to do about it,' Aisha said.

'The only reason I haven't succeeded in breaking that relationship is because I'm divorced and I don't want to be accused of turning her to *dabi moseda*.' Lola shook her head regretfully. 'How I wish...'

'What's *dabi moseda?*'

'It means ...' Lola didn't finish the sentence before Preye walked back in.

Preye told them the date of the wedding and asked them to be prepared to play different roles at the ceremony. They congratulated her once again as they started saying their farewells. She asked Erefa to call her as soon as Erefa went into labour, promising to be available on short notice for the baby's delivery.

Preye was perceptive; she knew no one approved of what Timi had done and she was grateful that no one had brought it up.

She called Timi once she was in her car. 'I'll be back at my place within an hour. Love you.'

'I love you too. I'll breathe a sigh of relief when you're back home.'

CHAPTER NINE

Timi was filled with nostalgia and warm feelings as he approached the home he had shared with his parents for as long as he could remember. He pulled up in front of the freshly painted storey building. Even though the house was over twenty years old, it still projected the class of the Coker's wealthy status in the community.

The frontage was as neat as an untainted pin, with four perfectly manicured topiaries strategically placed to add glamour to the setting. Inside, there was a beautiful blend of furniture and paintings augmented with bits and pieces of natural flowers adorning various corners in the living room, which friends described as a football field. The mauve chesterfield leather sofas were rustic in style, but they had alluring puffed cushions and they shone as if they were still in the showroom. Occupying its own grand space was the mahogany dining table, which provided a base for a glass vase filled with water and stalks of orchids. A wide-screen television and a trim line external speaker were neatly hung on the wall. The living room looked so much like one of those antique houses on exhibition, it would have been a sin to move anything out of place.

The house had the signature of Ife Coker, Timi's mother, who ran a landscape supply and interior decoration company with a clientele of wealthy individuals and organisations. She was about Preye's height, with a pretty face that said she had grown up before she had time to enjoy the zest of youthfulness. She'd have looked her natural slim self if she wore pencil skirts, but Ife loved her pleats and flares and would hardly wear any blouse with no frills or a skirt that didn't have gathers. Her fashion world revolved around flowers and this was expressed in her wardrobe of mostly flowery patterns and bright colours. Sporting a mint green top and grey floral skirt with elastic band, she moved around the house at a rapid pace; it was hard to imagine her sitting still.

Wale Coker, Timi's father was lounging on a recliner with a newspaper and biting the bottom of a pencil as he struggled with a crossword puzzle. Usually garbed in long kaftans and leather sandals, he cut a picture of affluence and contentment; his eyes were present but mysterious, his smile was playful, yet it didn't quite leave his face and his voice was firm and soft at the same time. His body showed the signs of muscles lost over the years, but he stood a lanky six foot with grey afro and a well-trimmed beard. He was the older version of Timi.

The Cokers couldn't hide the fact that Timi was the centre of their world. As their only child, they had strived to give him every advantage. While he was growing up, they had indulged him with most things he craved; he could even have gotten away with murder. The turning point had come only because Timi became a threat to his father's business and Ife had agreed with her husband that they needed to stand up to Timi, otherwise he'd be without any hope of redemption. Wale Coker would have equally capitulated when Timi had threatened to move out, but surprisingly, Ife had insisted and assured her husband that Timi would come round. Their resolve paid off, as Timi had turned out much better than anyone had expected.

To Timi, his parents presented a blueprint for the perfect marriage. His father was the dominant force in the home and his mother was happy to follow his lead. It wasn't the twelve years age difference that made Ife defer to Wale. It was perhaps his uncanny mien that made someone look on another as if the person were entitled to power. Wale Coker wrote the rule book and his wife read it diligently and adhered to it.

Ife had met Wale about a few months after leaving university and they had gotten married shortly after. She had never had to work for money and it was Wale who suggested to her to make a business out of her passion for beautifying spaces.

She had started trading in interior decorations and later expanded into horticulture and landscaping. Most of her clients were introduced by her husband, and her business never interfered with her husband's plans or needs as she had built her life around her family.

Some may say their marriage followed outdated norms, but Timi didn't think so. His parents very rarely argued and they always bragged that both their families had no history or trace of divorce. Timi believed Preye would fit into his perfect idea of a marriage. He loved bringing her around to visit his parents, so she could see how well a union like his parents' worked, unlike her case where her father had deserted his duty post.

Ife was waiting at the screen door to welcome Preye and Timi for dinner. It was less than a month before their wedding celebration. 'Welcome, my daughter,' Ife enthused, lifting up part of her skirt which was almost sweeping the floor. Her hair was fully covered with a scarf and Preye couldn't remember a time that she had seen Ife without a scarf or beret, albeit beautiful ones. 'You look more beautiful every time I see you. My son has the most fabulous taste and he must be doing something right, I guess.'

'I won't argue with that Mom.' Timi responded to his mother and handed her the bottle of wine Preye brought along for the Cokers. 'I knew the minute I looked into those sparkling eyes that she had something I'd never seen before. Then she started talking and I knew I could never let her go,' he boasted.

Timi's father didn't get up from his recliner as he cleared his throat to welcome Timi and Preye. 'It's a good time for a stout,' he said. Ife started towards the kitchen, but he stopped her. 'Don't worry, I want to mix it my special way.' He went to the kitchen while Ife asked about Preye's family and work.

Wale Coker returned with a bottle of stout. The family resemblance was unmistakable, and he was often mistaken for Timi's brother. He took excellent care of himself and aged well, which was a good sign for Timi's future. 'You remind me of what I thought when I first laid eyes on your mother. It didn't hurt that we were on the beach, and well, you know.' He laughed, barging into the conversation.

'Oh.' Ife nudged her husband diffidently. 'I was almost fully clothed because my parents wouldn't have let me out of the house otherwise. I thought I stood out because of my conservative fashion style, but ironically that's what caught your attention. Men!' She turned to her husband. 'Should I get you a glass?' she asked. Wale nodded and she went to the kitchen.

Wale continued talking to Preye and Timi. 'I saw all I needed to see to help me make up my mind. I believe all those scantily-dressed ladies are usually trying to hide some self-image problem. And when your mother walked by me and smiled...' He shook his head fondly. '...that captivating smile and I fell in love.'

'That's so romantic. You have such wonderful memories.' Preye complimented.

It was the first time she'd hear about their meeting at the beach. She never imagined that the pious-looking Ife would have dared go to the beach and worn appropriate clothing for the occasion.

Timi's parents had been gracious from the moment she met them. They constantly assured her that she was the best thing to happen to him without mincing words that she was blessed to have him as well. Ife had embraced Preye and declared she was looking forward to having Preye as her daughter, with many grandchildren, when they announced their engagement,

Ife returned with a tall crystal beer glass and placed it on the side table 'I need to find you my *juju* music playlist because I intend to dance like a proud father at your wedding,' Wale told Timi. Preye chuckled.

Timi loved the smiles on his parent's faces. Their approval meant a great deal to him; in large part because he knew he had given them a lot of horrors when growing up. Wale and Ife had devoted their lives to him, so the least he could do was to please them. He had managed to keep up with his career, which made them proud, but now their focus was on his relationship. His marriage and their prospect of becoming grandparents made them extremely happy. Finally, Ife would have her wish to fill the big house with Timi's children.

Timi excused himself to fetch drinks from the kitchen for himself and Preye. He returned with three glasses, filled with chilled *zobo* made by Ife and handed one each to Preye and Ife.

Soon the conversation moved to Timi's job at Mason Bridge, and Preye's mind wandered in reflection. Wale and Ife were beyond proud of Timi as they hung on every word that came out of his mouth.

Timi's parents had been married for thirty-nine years, which seemed like a lifetime to Preye. Her parents couldn't make it past twelve years. The Cokers had it all - a healthy child, a comfortable home, thriving businesses and a splendid marriage. Preye was working towards something similar. The only difference would be the number of children; Preye wanted two. She saw how unconditionally Wale and Ife loved their son and realised that it was what Timi wanted from her. It was what Timi needed. She'd give her all to have a home as happy as the one she was sitting in. It would be worth it.

'How's your cooking coming?' Ife asked. Preye had expressed a desire to get better in the kitchen, but her busy schedule running work and the Roadrunners hadn't made that achievable.

She was about to answer when she had a horrible flashback to the night in the kitchen with Timi roughening her. Timi gently touched her arm, and she snapped out of it. 'Oh, I've been extremely busy ma. I'm embarrassed to say I can barely put together a meal.'

Timi put his arm around Preye. 'She's selling herself short. She makes great meals the few times she chooses to settle down to it. The last time we went to her mum's, she made lunch and it was divine. And that's not because my love for you has beclouded my sense of taste.' He was being generous in his comments because Preye hadn't been much of a cook.

Preye was self-conscious. She pulled her head back and spoke softly. 'Thank you.' It wasn't that she couldn't cook. She just hated cooking. She had cooked so much while growing up and taking care of her siblings that she considered it a chore she'd rather avoid and she had been able to use her busy schedule to justify dining out more and more. Timi did have his hopes high that she'd have more time to devote to domestic responsibilities after they were married.

The evening continued on a light mood of small talks, mostly about Wale and Timi. Ife served her signature dish, which was chicken and jasmine rice, made with a blend of spices that she wouldn't divulge, yet. It was a family secret that she had promised to reveal to Preye as soon as she became Timi's wife. Preye wished Timi was like he was with his parents, under all circumstances. He complimented Preye and put her high up on a pedestal. It was like he was showing off his precious possession, and she didn't mind. It did wonders for her ego.

'I hope you saved room for dessert. I have homemade banana ice cream in the freezer. We can have that with biscuits. That's a recipe I'll also share because your little will love them.' Ife said. 'Speaking of children, have the two of you discussed how soon you're planning to have babies?' she quizzed. She wasn't known to be subtle except with her husband.

'Of course we have, Mom. We plan to begin right away, unless that's changed, Mine.' He looked at Preye for confirmation. He knew that they were on the same wavelength about their desires of having children. It was something they spoke of early on in their relationship and they had both agreed that it would be unwise to wait, especially because of Preye's age.

Preye shook her head. 'You're right. We're ready to start right away and have as many as the Lord blesses us with.' She squeezed his hand as they gazed into each other's eyes.

It was his parent's idyllic relationship that Timi modelled his on. Preye wasn't sure she was up to the task, but she decided to try her best. Attempting to be like someone else while retaining her individuality was the tricky part. It was the subservience that Ife showed towards Wale that Preye didn't think was possible in a modern relationship. All the time Preye had been with the Cokers, everything revolved around Timi's father; Ife agreed with whatever he said, she laughed even when he wasn't funny, and she served him as if there was no active bone in his body. Times had changed since his parents got married, and Timi would simply have to adjust.

Wale lifted his face from his crossword. 'Have you changed your mind about moving out? I don't know what to do with that space if you go ahead. The house is already too quiet as it is. I don't see why you can't move here until you get a place.' He turned to Preye for an answer, but Timi jumped in.

'Enjoy my company while it lasts, Dad. We are starting a brand new life on our own,' Timi jested.

Preye was thankful at times like these when Timi shielded her from uncomfortable situations. Knowing how headstrong Timi was, it had been a miracle for him to agree to move in with her after the wedding, until they got a suitable place. She hoped that wouldn't take too long.

*

Timi decided it was a good time for them to get together with his friends, Malik and Martin. Martin, who owned a grocery outlet, was a friend he had met during his clubbing days from university. Preye had met Malik at Roadrunners, when he came with Timi. She had later met Martin after getting together with Timi and she got on brilliantly well with the two guys. The four of them were meeting up at a local bar near Timi's house.

Before she got out of the car, Timi arranged Preye's hair to cover her birthmark. It was almost becoming routine.

Malik and Martin had been impressed by Preye as soon as she started talking at their first meeting. They admired her for being able to match her beauty with her high level of intelligence and her dedication to building Beta and Roadrunners. Timi had dated beautiful women in the past, but none offered the full package as Preye did. They always teased him that he must be spinning some creative tales to make her stay with him.

'Here's the happy couple.' Martin approached with open arms and a broad smile. 'I tell you, if you hadn't put a ring on Preye's lovely finger on time, I would have found her a more dashing guy. Congratulations to you both.'

Martin was rarely without a lager in his hand, which was somewhat expected because he spent most of his non-working hours fraternising at bars. He was a regular at this bar too. He was just about Preye's height, with a beer belly. But looks weren't what he relied on; Martin was a loyal friend to Timi and generous to everyone. If he became wealthy, it would only last a minute because he'd give it all away.

Martin whispered in Preye's ear as he squeezed her hand. 'Consider me a brother now. I'll always be there for you, Preye.'

'You're sweet, Martin. A girl can never have too many brothers,' she responded gleefully.

Timi held Preye tight as Malik approached. He felt that for once he had out-done Malik, who always had everything working out for him. *Yes, his wife was pretty, but Preye was more beautiful and owned a successful company,* Timi thought as he often did when his feeling of sibling rivalry towards Malik was aroused.

Malik joined the group, holding four flutes inserted into one another, a bottle of champagne and a malt drink which Malik knew was Preye's favourite anytime she hanged out with them. 'I know how weddings can be and I may not get a chance to personally congratulate you at the wedding. Preye, you're the best thing that ever happened to my friend.' Malik hugged Preye before filling her glass. He looked at Timi. 'Don't mess this up, boy. A woman like her is hard to find, and I should know. I work hard at my marriage. But it's worth the effort.'

'Will someone please applaud me for discovering her in the first place and taking that bold step?' Timi made a face. 'She wasn't' really a soft nut to crack, you know. Malik, you were simply lucky Penny agreed to marry you. That would have been your last chance.' They all laughed and the friends continued to make fun of one another as Preye watched on, enjoying the banter.

'Now you have no excuse, Martin. It's your turn to find a woman that will tolerate your inadequacies.' Malik nudged Martin. 'If Timi can do it, you can do it too.'

Timi placed his hand on the small of Preye's back. He was happy for Malik, but couldn't quite get beyond comparing himself with him anytime they got together. Apart from being married to a beautiful woman, Malik was well-educated with a master's degree, he made more money and had two children. Timi wanted all that. And now, thanks to Preye, he was on the road to catching up.

'Preye,' Martin said, turning to face her directly. 'What are your plans for your flat?'

'We've been trying to get a place. The lease runs out in about four months and I won't be renewing. We should have found a place by then. We are also looking to buy a permanent home, so we can start filling the house with babies.'

'Do you have news on that front?' Martin asked. He was into his fourth bottle and couldn't measure the propriety of what he was saying.

Timi jumped into the conversation. He didn't like the fact that Martin referred to the flat as Preye's. It was exactly the reason he hadn't wanted to move in with her. 'No, no, and don't go spreading any rumours. I'm a planner and having a family is something in our future rather than putting the cart before the horse. Why are you asking about the flat? Are you looking to move?'

'It's on my mind, and Preye's place has everything I'm looking for. The size and location are just right for a single man like me. It's a central route for both Lagos and Ogun, and her estate is still a bit upscale, if you know what I mean. Keep me posted before moving. I know I can't count on Timi for anything,' Martin joked. 'Where will you be moving to?'

'We're currently looking at the options of where we'll move to. We haven't agreed on a neighbourhood yet, but it's important to me that I'm close to work, family and friends. We'll see, I suppose.' If Preye had her way, she'd stay put in her flat with Timi, but she knew they couldn't live there for too long. It was a miracle that Timi agreed that staying in his father's house wasn't ideal. Living independently and blazing her trail had been one of her worthwhile achievements and her identity. She hadn't expected to be so scared to give a piece of it up.

Timi walked up behind Preye and wrapped both arms around her. 'Martin, your time is up with my woman. *Abeg* go find a woman, if you want to talk to a fine girl like this. This one is mine,' Timi declared.

Martin looked away from Preye and signalled for another waiter but Malik pulled him to his feet and dragged him towards the bar. 'Let's leave the lovebirds alone.'

Timi smiled with an assurance of someone who had won the jackpot. 'This is just what I like. We don't spend enough time with my friends and family. Can't you see how they adore you?' It was a statement of victory.

'You know I love your family and the guys too. I can't wait to see their performances at our wedding reception. I haven't seen Malik's wife in ages and I'm curious to see if Martin would come with a plus-one.' Preye giggled. 'It's unfortunate we're not having a bridal train. I would have loved to see Martin as your best man.'

'About our house hunt, I thought we decided on Shasha,' Timi said.

'No. it was still up in the air, remember? We haven't even checked if properties in Ikeja are affordable. First things first. We need to agree on a budget.'

'I'm certain you'll be happy moving there when you see what we get for the money. You can always teleconference a couple of days per week.' Timi smiled, like the decision had been made.

'Are you joking? Beta is my company and I love being on-site with my people. I wouldn't throw all of that responsibility on Tobi,' Preye scowled.

'We'll work it out. Don't worry your pretty little head. I'll handle the details. That's my job as your husband.' Timi kissed her and pulled her hair forward to cover her birthmark. 'We'll consider getting that thing removed after the wedding.' He walked to the bar before she could respond.

Preye considered her time with Timi's family and friends a success. He liked showing her off, and sometimes she felt he was treating her like his prized object. No one else treated her that way and that was something she was going to have to accept. It was the price she was willing to pay to have a family of her own.

CHAPTER TEN

Erefa and Aisha were the last ones left in the church vestry where Preye was waiting for her father to walk her down the aisle. Aisha was her stylist and Erefa, her main attendant. Donald kept Tamara with him in a pram. Although, the infant was only a few weeks old and still relied on her mother as a food source.

Preye wore a blush coral ball-gown with a scoop-neck and three-quarter sleeves. While they were shopping for the wedding dress, Preye and Aisha had seen a simple dress in silk with a draped low-cut back that they liked. Preye had looked like a Greek goddess when she tried it on and Aisha had cried that it was so beautiful on her. By the second outing, Preye had changed her mind and chosen a short dress, but Timi had gone with her for the fitting and he had vehemently stated that he never pictured leading a bride in a short dress to the altar. After some back and forth with the designer, they had eventually settled for the ball gown dress. Preye could only insist that she wouldn't wear the dress if it was white.

Preye was happy with the coral dress. At least, she could fulfil the pact she had made with her friends about wearing non-traditional wedding dresses. Her friends and sisters agreed that she looked lovely as a bride.

'Your hair is stunning,' Aisha complimented, admiring the beautiful bride.

Preye's hair was swept up, with some tendrils left out to

cascade down her shoulders and cover her birthmark.

'Thank you, Aisha. My hair and jewellery are thanks to you. You've been wonderfully reliable. Thanks for always being there for me. I can't thank you enough. Just think, our babies will be playmates someday if I waste no time,' Preye said.

Aisha rubbed her tummy. She was newly pregnant with her second child, which wasn't a part of her master plan, but she and Adamu were thrilled anyway. 'I want the best for you, *Omo* girl. You deserve it. And I'm sure you'll be a great mum.'

'She'll have lots of practice with my little one,' Erefa walked in with Tamara over her shoulder. 'Have you seen my sister with this baby? She's a natural.' She looked Preye over and nodded in commendation. 'Are you ready to do this, sis?'

'I am. I know some of you questioned my choice about Timi, but I'm sure more than ever that marrying him is my destiny. He has his faults and so do I, but the most important thing is that I love him, and he loves me even more. What more could I ask for?'

Aisha hugged Preye and whispered in her ears. 'You'll make a good wife. This is not the time to talk about anybody's faults.'

Erefa hugged her sister and held on tight as she shed a tear. 'I love you, big sis. I'm proud of you. I am thankful that this day has finally come. It's been long overdue.'

Erefa and Aisha went to claim their seats inside the church. The chamber music Preye had arranged earlier started playing in the background and the entrance door was closed. But the door soon opened again and Preye's father, Harry Banigo walked in. Erefa pointed him to the vestry where Preye was waiting.

Tears packed at the back of Harry's eyes when he saw Preye. 'My baby, you're simply gorgeous. Now that I see you, I realise I was in no way prepared. I am not prepared at all for the emotional mess that I'm becoming,' Harry said, patting dry his brown eyes as he straightened his tie. Almost sixty-five years old,

Harry still moved with a sleek princely grace, and with dark penetrating eyes and a baritone voice that made heads turn to look for the owner. His skin was flawless and his face was so innocent, he could easily get away with mischief. 'I have cherished you from the moment you came out kicking and screaming. Now I have to give your hand to another man that I've never met. I don't remember being this way with the other girls.' His voice was a bit shaky. 'I know I've not been the best of dads, but I know you're loving and you forgive me daily with all my faults. And you believe me when I say that I love you.'

'Oh, Daddy, I'd squeeze you, but you'd get me all wet. A wet face is not the wedding look I was going for.' Preye grabbed her father's hand. Except for the height, she looked very much like her father, down to the shape of their fingers. 'When I didn't hear from you for a couple of days, I feared you weren't coming.'

Harry was taken aback and his eyes bulged. 'You thought I wouldn't come to your wedding? I wasn't around much to see you grow up. Don't you think I should try harder to catch up with the lost years?' Harry collapsed into the chair and threw his head in his hands. 'I am so ashamed the thought even entered your mind.' He had been present for Erefa and Tonye's weddings and wondered why Preye thought she was less deserving.

'Daddy, I don't doubt your love for me, but who knows where you are these days with your current wife? And I was afraid Tonye may have spoken poorly of Timi.' Harry's current wife of five years was just a couple of years older than Preye. She was a textile dealer who travelled quite a lot, and Harry followed her whenever he could.

'No, Tonye doesn't talk to me much. But should she have? Is there any reason to be concerned?' Harry asked.

Preye shook her head. 'There isn't, Dad. I just think the girls liked Kevin so much that it's hard for them to see me with anyone else,' she said, with a smile.

'I trust you, and I'd like to think you chose well. You've beaten the odds. Graduating from university with honours, surviving the loss of your fiancé, forming your own company and starting an athletics club. All those aren't for the weak and I don't think anyone can slow you down or break your spirit.'

Preye hoped her father would approve of Timi when they eventually met at the wedding. She didn't think anyone could slow her progress and break her spirit as well.

Harry Banigo had his faults, but with time, sis rough edges had smoothened. Not to his credit, the girls had all turned out well and he didn't think he was in any position to talk to his children about relationship or marriage. He was grateful for the opportunity they gave him to be part of their lives as much as feasible, and part of maintaining that unity was not to wade into their affairs unless they invited him. If any of his daughters made a wrong choice of a spouse, he'd hold himself responsible because he had failed to provide the fatherly love and guidance when they needed it. He had faith that Preye had considered marriage from every angle and he was sure she'd be fine.

'I'm going to check with one of the girls and make sure my husband-to-be has arrived. Wouldn't it be something if I got stood up at the altar?' Preye joked. Her father didn't laugh. She tip-toed into the hallway and saw Aisha and Lola leaning against the bannister as she turned the corner. Preye heard them talking in hushed tones, so she took a step back to listen without them noticing her. It wasn't like her to snoop on her friends but it seemed as if everyone was holding their tongue. She wanted to hear their thoughts.

'... Tell me why the knot in my stomach is tightening,' Lola was saying, shaking her head. 'I don't feel good at all and I don't think there's anybody in attendance from Preye's side that thinks this marriage is a good idea either.' Lola popped a gum into her mouth. She needed a sugar burst to keep a smile on her face.

'Lola,' Aisha stretched her name. 'You've done your bit. To put it mildly, you weren't subtle in your efforts, and that didn't work. I've also raised it with Preye and she seems to know what she's doing. Timi is a charming guy. Maybe he's a smooth operator and knows the right buttons to push, like the arsonist who puts out the fire and gets celebrated for it.' Aisha shrugged. 'All we can do now is support them and be there if Preye needs us.'

'That's for sure, because I can tell she'd need us. Mark my words,' Lola said as she adjusted her designer's tulle lace dress. 'If she wasn't so proud and thinks she needs to be strong, I'm sure she'd have called for help and if Timi turns out to be the asshole I think he is, you have to let me take the first shot at him. Slapping that smug grin off his face will give me great pleasure.'

Aisha smiled. 'We're going to have to flip a coin for that one. You do remember that I'm a karate black-belt. But what exactly is your grouse?'

Lola shook her head. 'Isn't that the problem? I wish I could say.'

There was a lull in the conversation, so Preye moved towards them and acted like she hadn't heard their discussion.

'My girls, it should be time to walk down the aisle with my father. Will one of you confirm if the groom has arrived?' Preye put on her best smile, but inside she was musing over Lola's relentless concerns. It cuts deep into Preye's heart that her *besties* were not fully on board with her.

'He's here and waiting,' Aisha assured.

'Shall I cue your music for entrance?' Lola asked. Erefa had gone to breast-feed and the lot fell on Lola to perform a portion of her duties.

Preye nodded her head enthusiastically and went back to

fetch her father to begin the small ceremony. She had wanted a lavish wedding with a rented limo and about five hundred guests, but they had continued reducing the numbers until they got to one hundred and fifty guests. Timi had insisted that they needed to save rabidly, as it was wiser they bought a house when they moved, rather than pay a more exorbitant rent. Preye commented they would be comfortable in the flat for a few months but that didn't work for him.

Timi had promised a surprise to be announced during his wedding reception speech. Preye couldn't think of what she wanted that Timi hadn't already given her. She hoped it wasn't too over the top because she didn't want to be embarrassed.

*

Timi's chest deflated as he finally breathed in relief once he heard, 'I now pronounce you husband and wife.' Throughout the wedding ceremony, he had thought about everything that could go wrong: an ex showing up to claim he had an unknown child; Preye deciding she was no longer interested; Preye's father claiming he wasn't good enough; or one of Preye's friends making a scene to annoy the pastor.

After the service, he grabbed his bride's hand tightly as they walked through the breezeway to the reception area. There was a warmth on his inside that made his face explode into a thousand stars and he felt light enough to walk on the clouds to gaze down at the people who had convened to witness his wedding. Like his father's, the smile didn't leave his face as he held on to Preye, whose smile glowed out from the depth of her soul – a woman of his own and a mate for the rest of his life.

Their guests waved and cheered as they arrived at the reception hall entrance which buzzed with life and excitement. When the song they had chosen started, the chatters quietened and the guests stood in ovation to herald them in.

Malik and Penny stopped the newly married couple as the danced towards slowly to their seat. 'Congratulations my man,' Malik beamed with the innocent air of a child as he slapped Timi on the back. 'Welcome to the club, I'm sure it's going to be the best decision you've ever made.'

Malik's wife, Penny nudged Timi and chuckled. 'I swear, I'm not saying this just because he's standing next to me.' She tilted her head towards Malik. 'Being a husband and father makes life more interesting and makes everything else pale in significance.'

'I know how lucky I am, Malik. Look at how beautiful my wife is. She's finally mine, and I couldn't be happier.' Timi smiled. Preye thought Timi sounded like he had been on a hunt and bagged a prized animal. She hoped she wouldn't be mounted on the living room wall one day. She knew it was just a comment and she shouldn't make a big deal of it. No one else seemed bothered.

They finally waltzed their way to the bridal sofa and sat beside a massive bouquet of pink roses. Timi patted his jacket pocket to feel for the surprise, and of course, it was there. He hoped he'd get a wonderful reaction from his new wife. Money would be temporarily tight but it would be worth it in the long run.

'Mrs Coker, you've never been more beautiful. If it were up to me, you know we'd skip the dinner and dancing and move directly to the unveiling. I want you so bad, Mine.'

Preye felt sexy and ready, but she put up a dismissive front. 'Then you wouldn't have a chance to present me with the surprise. Do I get a hint?' she asked.

Timi faked thinking about it for a moment and tapped his index finger on his temple. 'No, you get no hint. I can't wait to see the look on your face. It's a token of my love, and I hope you will be impressed.' If she wasn't instantly thrilled, Timi knew he could talk her into appreciating his surprise later on.

'You already impress me, Mr Coker. I don't need any dandy act to know you love me. I hope your surprise won't take me out of town for too long because the honeymoon already takes a big chunk of time. Work is about to get crazy as the Boomers account is up for renewal. Beta will have to show its worth,' Preye said. As soon as the words had left her mouth, she regretted them. He'd hate that she brought up work. Preye prepared for his reaction.

'Wow,' he simulated a clap. 'Even today, you can think about work. Am I going to be competing with Beta during our entire marriage?'

'No, Love. Please forget I brought it up. I'll build boundaries between home-life and work.' The conversation Preye had overheard between Aisha and Lola crept into her mind, but she didn't know what to make of it.

'Please do. That said, make sure home and marriage take priority, always,' Timi said tersely, but with the smile still glued to his face. None of the guests could guess what was transpiring between the couple.

He lifted his wrist to look at his watch and shook his head in dismay. It had been less than four hours since making her his wife and already, she was challenging him. He tried to shake off the undesirable thoughts brewing in his mind; it was way too early in the marriage. He'd be happier if Preye could be more submissive and homely. He felt slighted that she even had space in her mind to think about work, but he chose to push away negative thoughts on his wedding day. He wasn't sure where he was pushing those thoughts and hoped they would be replaced with joyful emotions, otherwise they might return in a torrential flood.

Preye smiled. 'Of course.' Inside, she felt stifled by his rules and realised that the compromises of marriage wouldn't be easy.

Could all marriages require that much compromise? she wondered.

*

Timi stood after dinner to announce his surprise in front of all their friends and family. He raised a glass and said all of the required platitude before beginning.

'As some of you know, my beautiful bride and I have been searching for a home, a place to start our lives together. Hopefully, a place where we can grow as a family.' He cleared his throat and turned to Preye. He dangled a set of keys in her face. 'Yesterday I signed the papers and everything is set for us to move in. Our new home is in Regalia Court at Festac Extension. Please wish us well as we start creating new memories for our forever after.'

Timi pulled Preye up from her chair and kissed her while their friends and family clapped, whistled and hooted. When she heard Festac, Preye froze as her heart sank. Her insides started churning as if she'd throw up. *Festac!* She had resisted going to Shasha. Now Shasha sounded like heaven compared to Festac. *How and when did Festac get into the picture? Why would Timi buy a house they would live in without any input from her?* This gift and gesture of his was a sham; a home she didn't want. He was well aware that her preferred neighbourhood was anywhere not so far from where she currently lived and worked. *Didn't he know what it meant to her or he simply didn't care?* Despite her confusion, there was no way for her to protest in front of their wedding guests and she had to keep up the appearance that she was grateful; any other lady would be ecstatic.

Timi was relieved that he no longer needed to keep a secret from his wife. He was tired of making excuses about why he couldn't spend lavishly to spoil her as he would have loved to. He had sold his car and borrowed some money from his father to raise the deposit for the house. Since Preye already had savings towards buying a house, he knew paying off his father wouldn't be a problem. Raising the deposit and securing the mortgage in good time before the wedding had been a tough task and he was proud that he had been able to pull it off, and he wouldn't have to spend more than two weeks in Preye's cosy flat. He could tell from her sweaty palms that his gift wasn't something she expected.

Timi was certain, however, that in time she'd see things his way.

CHAPTER ELEVEN

A week at Angelica Beachside Hotel in Accra was a pleasant way to start their fused lives. They had both been busy with work and pre-wedding activities and they needed the honeymoon to reconnect and enjoy their time as a couple. As their wedding gift, Beta had paid for the hotel accommodation and Timi had bought the flight tickets a week to the wedding.

Their honeymoon room overlooked the beach and there was an orange glow flooding through the white lacy curtains into the unlit room. Her heart was racy with mixed emotions and apprehensiveness as she headed for the balcony, but Timi pulled her in and landed his lips on hers.

Without taking his eyes off hers, he gently rid her body of the dress and everything underneath until she didn't have anything on. Her skin tingled as she responded to his touch with every fibre of her being. It was what she had waited for and the intensity and urgency was as she had imagined; sensual, intoxicating and physically gratifying as she breathed in every scent of Timi's being. Slowly and gently, his hands and lips moved all over her body as if he was teasing her to take the lead. In a frenzy, she started taking his clothes off and he obliged her, soaking in the hunger in her eyes.

They tumbled unto the scented white sheets, caressing each other's bodies and guiding themselves into the passionate fireworks of sexual consummation and release. They were in unison in purpose, body and soul until they drifted off to sleep, satiated.

The following morning and the days after, they joined other lodgers after breakfast to lounge on the golden sand; they sat to watch the tumbling waves of the unending flow of water, picking pebbles and tossing them back; they walked, holding hands and ran around the palm trees lining the shore on the warm damp sand; they wiggled their hands in water and built sand castles; kitted in sunglasses, they looked far into the aquatic distance and watched the splaying shades of the sun blending into the sky and the sea, to create a halo; and they mingled with other families to savour the splendour of the refreshingly warm atmosphere.

Preye resisted the urge to visit any of the markets in town since she knew Timi wasn't interested. They joined a tour organised by the hotel, to the Aburi Botanical Gardens. It was an idyllic place with a hilltop view and lined with palm trees on both sides of the road from the entrance. The whispering trees which stood regally towards the sky; the endearing butterflies playing carelessly to beautify the atmosphere and the captivating aroma emitted by the array of flowers made Timi and Preye appreciate the beauty and tranquillity of nature and they wondered and argued if living in the brick and mortar city of Lagos was worth the hype.

The highlight of Timi's days was sex, which happened daily. At times, twice a day didn't satisfy his sexual hunger and by midweek, it became clear to Preye that she had lovemaking in mind, while Timi wanted sex.

'Are you going to sleep?' she asked as he rolled over after satisfaction came his way, while she was yet to climax or even come close. The double bed they lay on in their cosy room suddenly seemed too small. The room was dimly lit with elegant but functional furniture items, all made of oak. The white curtains adorning the windows made the little pieces of native paintings splashed on the walls look understated. After the first night, the sessions of sex she had been looking forward to, had turned into mandatory chores.

'Do you have a problem with that? I'm good until sunrise, but I promise to give you one more tonight. I have a lot to make up for, after the agony you put me through.'

'You were worth the wait, Timi,' She cleared her throat and thought of a way to approach the subject carefully. 'I want you to pay more attention to detail,' she entreated. She thought if she didn't ask for what you wanted, she might not get it.

'Detail?' He was clueless.

She sat up to explain. 'I need more time to get to sexual arousal and satisfaction, like you were with me the first time. Try more foreplay and tenderness, so we both feel complete. Let's work together to find our pace,' she said softly. 'You've been pounding away, and I'm sore from making love three times a day. Can we slow down and enjoy each other…please?'

An exhausted Timi pulled her in for a kiss. 'I can't make any promises, Mine. I can't help it if you're smoking hot and I'm horny. Let's get some sleep. Otherwise, we'll need a vacation to recover from our honeymoon.'

He hadn't expected her to complain about sex on their honeymoon and not while in bed. He had been forced into celibacy before the wedding because of her religious beliefs which he was yet to fully align with, and sex with her felt pretty good. He expected her to be flattered that he couldn't get enough of her. Having to follow rules while in bed with his wife wasn't something he anticipated.

She lay awake, staring at the ceiling. The bright side was that the more times they made love, the sooner her dream to have a child would come true. She hoped she'd be one of those women fortunate enough to get pregnant on their honeymoon. It would be a pleasant surprise if she didn't have a period for the next nine months. She got up and went to sit on the veranda, looking across the ocean, to write thank-you cards.

'How about a walk on the beach, Mine?' Timi asked. He wanted to try some romance to appease her.

'Sounds great. A walk will be refreshing. It would be a bit chilly since the sun has gone down. I'll get dressed now.' She grabbed her trainers and unpacked a mini bag from the suitcase to bring out a set of jogging suits.

'What is this?' The look on his face couldn't be any different if he had discovered trash in a jewellery box. 'I asked you to pack enough appropriate tops and scarves for this trip. Can we dispense with all the athletic wear?' Timi asked. 'You're a married woman now and I don't want you looking like a college student.'

'You can't expect that I'm going to change my wardrobe overnight because I got married.' Preye had thought the constant complaining about her wardrobe would subside, but it was only intensifying.

'My parents have been married as long as they have been because my mum is willing to make minor concessions for my father. She dresses as he wishes. My mother cooks the type of food my dad likes and puts their marriage above all else. You don't see anyone like Lola getting in the way of their time together. I love you, but don't make this more difficult than it has to be.' He had thought his wife would willingly change her wardrobe to suit his taste. He believed she should want her husband to approve of the clothes she wore. It worked for his parents, why not for them?

He stormed out.

Preye stopped dead in her tracks as she took in the words uttered from her husband's mouth. He was asking her to give up her individuality for the sake of their marriage that he was modelling after his parents'. They had been mere comments all along, but it sounded like a demand now. The honeymoon wasn't over and for the first time, she felt a pang of regret.

She set the joggers aside because she didn't want to challenge him again on their honeymoon, but she vowed to make up for her passivity. She put on a lemon-coloured cotton cardigan, which she believed, made her look like a fruit. She looked best in jewel tones or dark colours, but Timi liked her in bold vibrant colours. She looked in the mirror and sighed before heading for the lobby to meet him.

She caught him checking out women as she neared the swimming pool. Yes, the women were scantily clad and gorgeous, but they were mostly teenagers or in their twenties.

Preye yanked his hand off his hip. 'What are you doing?'

He stepped back and chuckled. 'This is rich. Are you jealous of me admiring some of God's exquisite creations? You've got to admit that one is near perfection.' He continued looking at the dark and tall lady in a bikini suit. 'I missed out on you at that age, but I imagine you had it going on back then too. Don't worry, cover-ups exist to mask those little imperfections that come with age.'

'Don't you think that's rude and distasteful? I don't like it,' she charged at him.

'But I haven't changed. You're hypersensitive just because we're now married. A man doesn't stop admiring beautiful women the moment a ring is slipped on to his finger,' he replied. He smiled to make a joke out of the incident.

'I refuse to accept your behaviour as normal. I dated Kevin for years and he never came close to acting like you were just now. He was a good looking man and women threw themselves his way.' Preye stammered because she was extremely mad from bottling up her emotions. She recognised that bringing up her dead fiancé wasn't fair, but she was too angry to think rationally.

'Do you respect me at all?'

'I respect the hell out of you Preye. I'm not Kevin! He's dead. I'm Timi and I'm alive. As you may well know, men have different mechanics from women and I gain enjoyment from looking at beautiful creatures. It's not like I was groping or propositioning them. I guess this means we aren't going for a beach walk anymore. I'm heading to the gift shop to pick something up for my mom,' he pronounced as he walked away calmly.

Preye had hit him below the belt by bringing up Kevin. Comparing him to a dead man would make him look a huge monster and Kevin a saint. It was now obvious to him that she still thought of Kevin more than he realised.

From that point on, they simply went through the motions, finding solace in their outdoor activities. She hoped that things would normalise when they returned home and got into a rhythm.

She needed to get back to her normal life to get her ego and energy booster. She was itchy from her resolve not to check in with her friends or work because of Timi's reaction on their last holiday trip. Now, more than anything, she missed work and her colleagues, especially because she had practically been working half-capacity while she was preparing for the wedding. Tobi had made the sacrifice to work overtime to pick up the slack. Going back to Roadrunners would provide a release as well. Nothing helped to clear her head as much as a long run.

*

'Only one more day in paradise. I thought I'd go for a walk, maybe I can burn off some of the pounds I've gained here. Care to join?' Preye asked Timi. She wore a denim skirt and a Roadrunner t-shirt. Her hair was pulled up and her birthmark showed. Timi's mind was pre-occupied with other things than to comment on that right now.

He shook his head. 'I know it doesn't seem like something I'd do, but I have to check in at work to see how Banky has been coping with my tasks. You don't mind, I hope.'

Preye liked it when he put in extra effort at work because it was something he seldom did. 'Not at all. Have I met him?'

'I don't think so, but he knows who you are. He was an acquaintance of your Kevin. He knew Kevin from the neighbourhood he grew up in and would run into him sometimes. Well, until Kevin's illness. If you met him then, it was likely a blur.'

'Yea, I forgot a lot of things that happened when Kevin was sick. I shouldn't be more than forty-five minutes.' Preye kissed him. 'Love you.' She smiled and hoped he'd have finished with work by the time she returned.

After walking for about five minutes on the beach, she gradually picked up pace and started running before she realised it. She found it mentally and physically invigorating. Running also made her a more relaxed person to be around.

Her heart pounded each time she saw a young child as she hoped there would be a little one in her life soon. She used to feel jealous every time she passed a mother and child, but now she allowed herself to feel a kinship. She ran down a long stretch of beach that must have been close to three kilometres.

In the end, she ran back and waded in the water for a while before returning to their hotel room, feeling refreshed. She burst through the door and found a serious-looking Timi, wearing his tracksuit and staring out towards the ocean.

'Hey! You startled me,' he said. Since the day Preye mentioned Kevin, Timi had tried to get Kevin Murphy out of his mind, and he just hadn't. It was wrong for Preye to have brought him up during an argument and he had been thinking of a way to make her hurt equally as bad.

'Are you going for a run as well? I think it will do you some good and help clear out the cobwebs,' she suggested, as she took a gulp from the cold bottle of water she had taken from the fridge. 'Is something wrong? You're not usually this pensive.' She was concerned.

'There's something I need to tell you. I was going to keep it to myself, but I don't want to keep secrets. It's no way to begin a marriage. The last thing I want to do is upset you and I hope you know that.'

'You're scaring me. Has someone died?' The colour drained from her face. 'Out with it, please.'

'Kevin was cheating on you. He was with another woman on several occasions and he introduced her to Banky as his girlfriend.' Timi looked away as he spoke.

'As a singer, Kevin had a ton of friends and many of them were women. Your Banky must have been mistaken,' Preye refuted. 'He didn't have a dishonest bone in his body and would never have cheated on me.'

'Banky saw the two of them kissing several times. They were also a pair.' Timi caressed Preye's shoulders. 'I'm sorry, Mine. I can't imagine the betrayal you're feeling.'

She brushed off his touch. 'I don't know what to think.' She sat down and tears formed in her eyes as her heartbeat became laden.

'Do you want me to sit with you, or would you prefer some space?'

'Leave me alone, please. Go for your run. We can talk when you return,' she responded, holding herself back from crying.

As Timi left, Preye reminded him to take his phone and ear buds. He told her that the phone battery was low and asked that she charged it. She plugged the phone in a socket before curling up on the bed. She wasn't quite sure if she believed or doubted

Timi's revelation and that made her upset. She wondered how she could be mad at a dead person. She couldn't confront Kevin and would have to live with the pain of uncertainty that now sat in her stomach like a rock.

She heard Timi's phone ring and she picked it up without thinking. 'Hello, Timi Coker's phone. Preye speaking.'

'Ho, hello. I wanted to speak with Timi. This is Banky from the office. Congrats once again, Mrs Coker.'

'Thanks a lot. Is there anything I can help with?' Preye switched to her work mode.

'No, don't worry. I was supposed to call him earlier regarding some issues but I got tied up on another call,' Banky said.

'You didn't speak to him earlier?' Preye asked.

'No. Was he annoyed?'

'Not at all. He went for a run, and if it's not an emergency, I don't see why it can't wait until Monday.' Her heartbeats quickened. 'Hold on, before you go, how close were you to Kevin Murphy?'

Banky was silent for a moment. 'I'm sorry, Mrs Coker. That name doesn't ring a bell. Is he a friend of yours or Timi's?'

'Something like that. I won't keep you. I'll tell my husband you called.' Preye threw the phone against the wall. It didn't break but it made her feel good as she fumed. She couldn't understand why Timi had lied. Then she remembered bringing up Kevin's name when they had last argued and she concluded that she deserved being lied to. It didn't stop her from shedding the tears that had built up behind her eyes, even though she wasn't sure what the tears were for.

Timi soon returned from his run and Preye looked at him with red-hot eyes. The flake formed from the drips of salty water was stuck underneath her eyes. The tears welled up again and she walked out of the hotel room without a word and with no destination in mind.

After walking for a while and the tears had dried up, she broke into a run until she noticed that the sun was receding and the streets were drying up. So she returned to her husband on their last honeymoon night, unsure of how to describe the adrenaline pumping all through her body.

Timi had guessed what might have transpired after he checked his phone and saw that Banky had called. She accused him and she wished she could slap him when the first word out of his mouth wasn't *sorry*.

'I can explain, darling. Of course, Banky wouldn't want to discuss such things with you. Anyhow, you don't have to believe me.' He shrugged. 'My responsibility is to tell you what I know. Believe whatever you want to about Kevin. He's dead anyway, so it doesn't matter. I thought you deserved to know the truth.'

'You expect me to believe you?'

'You tell me. Did you marry someone you can't believe? What is our marriage worth if you don't trust me?' Timi asked kneeling on one leg as he grasped her hands. 'I love you more every day. Maybe I shouldn't have broken the news to you. Let's forget about someone that's dead. This is our marriage and nothing should come between us. Let's focus on creating our family. Just think, next year at this time, we might be parents,' Timi gushed. Their future as parents was the one thing he could count on to motivate his wife. It worked.

Preye's dreams of having a lovely family were within reach. She guided him up off his knees and he kissed her, slowly at first, until it became passionate and he led her to bed as the sun set on their honeymoon. His hands started caressing her body and she complained that she wasn't feeling well enough, but he insisted they ended their honeymoon making love. She was sadly happy the honeymoon was almost over, and they could return to a normal schedule.

Her body hadn't reacted well to his insatiable libido.

CHAPTER TWELVE

Timi had arranged for a chartered car with a driver to pick them up from Murtala Mohammed Airport in Lagos. Preye's eyes widened and her mouth was agape when the driver led them to the sleek black Mercedes AMG SUV. Immediately she hopped in, she explored the inside of the car and slowly stroked the leather of the seat in a caress that felt like it shouldn't end.

'This is a rather fancy transport for the ride home, Mr Coker,' Preye smiled as she spoke. Timi was pleased that she liked it; it was his way to keep the magic alive and to help erase the problems from the honeymoon. Arriving home together as man and wife was the true start of their lives together.

'I thought of it as a way of extending our honeymoon. With you, I can't see the honeymoon ever ending,' he replied, placing his hand on her thigh.

'I'm all for that, but there will be a lot coming our way in the next few weeks. Let's start organising our new life together.' She pushed back his hand and arrested it. 'There will be plenty of time for that later.' He withdrew his hand and asked the driver to increase the volume of the music. Preye liked the song, so she didn't mind that they weren't talking. The turbo-charged engine manoeuvred around the several potholes along the road without breaking a beat, and roared on silently.

They were approaching her flat or their flat to be more precise. Preye had moved most of her belongings that she didn't use frequently to the spare bedroom which also served as a min-office. She had planned to decide what to do with them once it was time to move into their new home. There was a lot of back-breaking work ahead of her to sift through those belongings. They were filled with memories of good and bad times. It was time to say a final goodbye to Kevin. There were decorative items in her flat that she had chosen with Kevin and she'd simply have to let them go.

Timi retrieved the keys from his pocket. His eyes twinkled with a mischievous grin, which was a sign that there was a surprise up his sleeves. Preye held her breath as she wondered what he could have in store for her behind the door. He swung it open to reveal an array of cardboard moving boxes. They were taped shut and labelled. The boxes were ready to be transferred to their new home.

'Did you have the entire flat packed while we were away?' she asked. This one ranked tops as the most surprising of all the surprises he had concocted.

'I did, and I can't tell if you're filled with joy or horror,' he said hesitantly. He hoped it was the former. He knew it was a gamble, taking on the task of packing for her, but he was sure she'd eventually come round even if she didn't initially like it. She was a control freak in so many ways and this was a first step at chiselling away her control. Preye had been independent for so long and it wasn't going to be easy for her to yield autonomy. Timi knew he was the one to make that happen.

'I'm shocked. Let me process this for a quick minute.'

She walked through the maze of boxes that included the vinyl music collection that was gifted to her by Kevin. She didn't even own a record player, but she liked having them around. There were two words scribbled on the box – 'records' and 'donate.' She felt a tug at her heartstrings, thinking that Timi should have asked her what she wanted to do with the records rather than assume she wanted to give them away.

She was relieved when she entered the kitchen and noticed the dishes and utensils were expertly packed along with the small appliances. She had dreaded the time she'd have had to box-up the items in the kitchen. She took a deep breath and chose to respond positively. She knew he didn't have any bad intentions and accepting the surprise would make their first day back smooth. She turned to find him right behind her. 'You've done me a favour and I'm grateful.'

'You are very welcome. I was hoping you wouldn't go all sensitive on my. Sometimes, one never knows how to please you. Thanks for appreciating it,' he said. 'I saved your office for you to pack.' Timi knew what there because he routinely went through her desk. Before deciding to pop the marriage question, he had snooped around to be sure she didn't have any damaging secrets. On days that she was at Roadrunners, he had searched to see that he wasn't missing anything major.

'My wardrobe office, you mean,' Preye chuckled. 'That room is filled with more clothes than office documents.' She was looking forward to having a dedicated office in their new home. They planned to share the space, which would require them to blend styles, but Preye knew they were up for the challenge. 'I'll tackle my desk tomorrow before going back to work on Monday. Lola and Aisha are coming over to help and you can go spend time with your buddies.'

'Are you kicking me out already?' he teased

'No, but if you want to stick around while my friends and I gossip as we stroll down our memory lanes, you're welcome,' she said. She doubted he'd accept the offer. Someday, she hoped he'd get to appreciate Lola as she did. Both her friends were spectacular women who wanted nothing more than for her to be happy.

'I'll give Malik a ring. I haven't played with his children for some time. We'd better hurry in getting our own family started so that they can play with them.'

Timi dragged their suitcases into the bedroom and dropped them on the bed.

*

'Aisha, I haven't touched those boxes on the top shelf for quite a while because I'm too tall to reach them,' Preye joked.

Lola and Aisha were helping her pack up her desk and closet. The items they were going through echoed times of happiness and sadness, depending on which phase of life Preye was at the time. The three friends laughed a lot, recalling their countless trends and events. Lola had committed the most fashion-don'ts.

'Have you ever heard of a stepladder, *Omo* girl?' Lola teased. 'They make them for people like you. I think you get carried away and overestimate yourself because you have tall friends. That doesn't make you tall.' She shook her head at Preye.

'With friends like you, a stepladder is a waste of money,' Preye cooed. 'Happy?'

'Are you going to tell us about your honeymoon?' Aisha asked with a mischievous glint in her eyes.

'It was blissful. There were a few bumps on the road, but everything was resolved. Isn't that what marriage is all about?' Preye asked. The question was meant to be rhetorical, but Aisha didn't take it that way.

'If you're talking about having a misunderstanding on your honeymoon, mine wasn't like that. Maybe during the first year of our marriage, I can say we had those bumps, but that's where it ended. Come to think of it, we're rolling into our twelfth year and we rarely argue about anything. Sometimes I find it boring though.'

'You're a true unicorn, Aisha. Bode and I had a lame excuse

for a honeymoon. If I'm honest, I made a mess of the whole thing. Remember we went to Amsterdam and I should have guessed the moment he went to the red light district by himself. He came back with some sex toys and I was up for the thrill initially.' She waved her hands. 'Anyway, we splurged on room service for meals and any time we weren't having sex, we were arguing, which I guess was a predictor of how our marriage would go,' Lola said. She got three packs of crisps from her bag, offering one each to Preye and Aisha.

Aisha brought out a box that Preye stared intently at. It was filled with love notes from Kevin. He had gone for an internship programme in New York after they had been dating for about a year and sent her a letter nearly every week for six months, until he came back to the country.

Trying to avoid getting teary and ruin the afternoon, Preye put the letters away. The girls noticed the label on the box and didn't say a word when Preye set it aside.

Lola noticed that the mood was turning sombre, so she tried to inject the much-needed humour. She opened the box labelled pictures and flipped through several pictures until she found one of herself when she had been going through her *Grace Jones* phase. There was one that she had gone for a haircut and came back with a bald head. Preye had called it edgy, while Aisha had called it bold.

They friends laughed so much until they cried as they relived times that life hadn't been so serious. They concluded that it was proof that together, they could survive most circumstances.

Aisha checked her watch and patted her growing belly. 'I have to be home to take over from Adamu. If I leave him alone with Ashe for too long, they would get into all kinds of mischief. If this child is a boy, I'll be sorely outnumbered,' Aisha stressed as she started getting ready to leave.

'Aren't you going to find out the sex of the baby?' Preye

queried.

'No, not this time around. Adamu and I want to be surprised, and Ashe doesn't want a baby at all.' Aisha laughed. 'He changes his mind every day. He was into having a sister for a while. Who knows what tomorrow will bring? Every step is so precious, Preye. I can't wait for you to join the motherhood club.'

'I'm so looking forward to it too. I'm planning to load up on fertility drugs and home pregnancy test kits. I know I'll want to urinate on a stick every month.' Preye laughed, but she wasn't kidding. Nothing was standing in her way, and God knew she was having plenty of sex.

*

Tobi Abass and the crew at Beta bought Preye a welcome-back canvas painting on which was a silhouette of a couple, with the inscription of '...A better life ahead!' Preye loved it and told them it would remind her that she was supported by a great team at Beta.

It was exciting settling back on the Boomers account. She had fresh eyes and new ideas after being away for a couple of weeks.

'I love your idea for the Boomers artistes to take volunteering a step further. By sponsoring specific neighbourhoods or needy children, they'll have tangible results,' Tobi said as he packed his bunch of paper to leave Preye's office.

'We'll get testimonials from real individuals and I'm sure that will endear them to a lot of people. That should get them some positive media attention.'

A few minutes after Tobi left, she glanced at her phone and noticed that Timi had called her. She thought about returning his call, but immediately discarded the thought. She was experiencing a work high that felt a lot like an adrenaline rush.

She loved her work and her output always fuelled her confidence and gave her a sense of meaning. Burying herself into the stack of documents on her table helped to take her mind off her disappointment at the onset of her monthly period.

She had prayed and had been hopeful that she'd get pregnant this first month. But now, her stomach was cramping from menstrual pain and she needed to get her mind focused, away from the pain. She used to have extreme menstrual pains and bleeding before she had fibroids removed from her system over ten years ago. Her period had been bearable since then and she hoped this pain wasn't a sign of another episode. Her face was like a wrinkled piece of cotton when Tobi's head pushed back into her office.

'Hey boss,' Tobi called out from the door. 'Are you okay?' She nodded. 'Your husband called my phone, asking to speak to you. I told him you were busy playing catch-up, and I'd let you know he called. So, there, I've told you.' Tobi was wary of Timi because he had picked up on Timi's air of arrogance and possessiveness.

Preye asked the two employees about to enter her office to give her five minutes, so she could make a phone call.

'Hey, Mr Coker. It's your wife.' She tried the cheerful approach. The line was silent at the other end, but she could hear his breathing. She was familiar with the sound and predicted that the vein on his neck must be throbbing.

'Where have you been? I've called you three times. Tobi only gave me a terse response. I know you're in the office, so what are you playing at?' Timi expected changes after the wedding, but having his wife ignore his calls wasn't one of them. He worried that she was sick or probably on a date with someone she wouldn't be able to explain. Not answering his calls was unacceptable to him.

'I've been having a busy and very productive morning. I

haven't been here for some time, and before that, my head wasn't in the game. At work, Beta needs my undivided attention. Great news came through on the Boomers account and the last thing I was concerned with was answering personal phone calls. That's what I was playing at.' Preye tried to keep her voice flat. She could easily take out her pain on him, but she pounded out her emotions by trying to bore her fist into her desk. It did nothing to relieve her aching stomach and back.

'I'm not just any personal phone call woman. I'm your husband, unless you've forgotten already,' he said, with a slightly less angry tone.

'Beta is a part of me that is not going anywhere. You knew this before you married me. If you're going to keep reacting this way, I'm going to push back.' She surprised herself that she stood her ground firmly.

'Are you threatening to leave me already?' he asked. He hesitated to make Preye feel guilty.

'God, no. We're adults, and I expect we can work this out, along with the hundreds of other times we will disagree. This company may not be your priority, but it is mine and you need to appreciate that.'

'I'll pick you up at five fifteen,' he declared.

'Can you make it six? I'm sure you can use that time to tidy up some work at your end,' she replied.

'In the spirit of compromise, I'll be there at five thirty.' He hung up.An hour later, Preye received a delivery of red roses. *Typical Timi*, she thought as she savoured the delightful fragrance of the roses.

CHAPTER THIRTEEN

Their new four-bedroom house in Regalia Court was finally completed and ready to be moved into after three weeks. Timi assumed Preye would come to agree with him that living there was the right choice, while Preye longed for a neighbourhood around Ikeja more than ever before. The house was far from everywhere she wanted to go – church, her mother's, friends', the supermarket, office and where the Roadrunners met. Even all of her favourite running trails were far away.

Regalia Court was located on an untarred road, where new housing developments were springing up, causing lots of noise and pollution that made running near impossible. *Okada* riders lined the stretch of tarred road leading to the estate which had been tanned by the residue of dirt stuck to tires coming and going. The potholes were like oval-shaped children's swimming pools deprived of water. The earthen streets had been made dry by the blasting of the sun and the estate roads were nothing more than a monochrome spread of thin tar. Gravel, sand and wood debris, evidence of unfinished building business, were littered in different corners of the estate. All the houses were new and most were empty.

The four-bedroom terrace house was larger than any other house they could afford anywhere else but it had little character and looked like a piece from a Lego production line, with its flat roof and standardisation to the other houses. It was coated brown on the outside, probably to hide the dust that would eventually powder the walls if the roads were left in their current states. The front door was a heavy fireproof structure of green colour, the windows were huge and the floor was tiled with granite. Apart from the living room, there was a bedroom downstairs which Timi said would serve as the children's playroom. There was a bathroom adjoining the playroom. Preye consoled herself that the kitchen was big and equipped with modern appliances. The yard was also spacious, although it looked out at a paper factory. Isolation was the biggest drawback of the new house and Preye felt the only way they could fill up the house and make it worth living was to have a set of triplets soonest.

Timi's mother had pitched in with the landscaping while Tonye had helped with remodelling the house. The first couple of weeks after their honeymoon, Preye threw herself into decorating the home she didn't want. There were always workmen in the house; carpenters chiselling at wood work, electricians relaying cables, plumbers fixing leakages and delivery men dropping off pieces of furniture and decoration.

Three weeks after moving into Regalia Court, they still slept in the guest room because the white upholstered bed Preye ordered for their room hadn't been delivered.

She was surprised to wake up to an empty house on Saturday morning. Timi had gone out with the Lexus – the only car they now shared between them, since he sold his car to raise additional funds for the house. He hadn't told her he'd be going out and she felt stranded and alone, until she found herself a book to read after unpacking one of the boxes that hadn't been opened. He later sent her a text message that he was attending a meeting with a client at Lagos Island Club.

The same thing happened on Sunday. Timi left the house before she woke up. She had assumed that he'd want to spend the day with her since he had been away almost all day yesterday. She had been discussing with him about finding a church to attend in the neighbourhood, but they hadn't been able to reach an agreement.

She was left frustrated and helpless as she was stuck at home. But she felt it would be unfair to complain as it would seem like she was complaining because it was her car. Sharing one car hadn't been a problem when they were living at Ojodu as it had been easy to get cabs or walk to the roads.

On both occasions that he left her at home, he had come back with pieces of furnishings for the house and his kind gestures made it difficult for Preye to express her displeasure. But it would have been less exasperating if he had told her his plans ahead of time.

It was Friday again and they were going home together. Preye hoped that she wouldn't spend the weekend alone, like the last time.

As they neared the turn off the expressway, she chipped in her thought. 'Can we stop somewhere for dinner?' she asked. Timi had closed early and picked her up from her office. He looked especially sharp with his new sunglasses and haircut.

'I bought you a house with a gourmet kitchen, yet you keep asking us to eat out. Do you think it's intended for decoration or show-off? You could try using that kitchen more,' Timi responded sarcastically.

'I haven't got the time to go to the market. Have you noticed that the fridge is not stocked? I don't have the hang of this area yet and I don't know where to go for grocery shopping. Maybe next week. This week has been quite tedious. I can ask one of the ladies at the office to help with shopping again. Or I can try to find Agboju Market tomorrow. It shouldn't be too far from the house.'

'Wow! This whole speech just to avoid cooking? Okay, from

now on, no more eating out until our finances improve. Even Friday dinners have to be at home. We'll save money if we cook more and I can't think of a better way to end my week.' Timi reached over and patted her thigh.

She smiled. 'Cooking together is a fantastic idea. I had no idea you would want to cook. Have you been learning some culinary tricks behind me?'

His laughter was hysterical. 'Oh, Preye, you're so cute. I have zero interest in slaving over a hot cooker. You're the woman, I wouldn't dream of depriving you of that task.' He squeezed her hand. 'I suppose because your father wasn't around to make such demands, you don't consider feeding me a priority. Right?'

'Timi, that's an insult!' she fumed, unamused.

'How is a fact an insult?' He didn't wait for her response. 'Anyway, I know how much you want to become a better cook and I'll leave it up to you.' He couldn't believe his wife hadn't learnt from watching his mother wait on his father. He had presented her with the perfect example and she was slow to get the point. 'And if you want to pull some feminist come-back on me, I'll stop the car and you can walk home,' he joked. 'But of course, you know I wouldn't do that to my woman.'

She nodded in silence and persuaded herself that he didn't know the reference to her father was insulting. It was indeed a fact, but she was nonetheless confused. *Dinner wasn't a significant issue*, she concluded. She'd be spending the entire weekend with him and it wasn't worth an argument.

*

Timi eventually pulled up at an eatery to get some takeaway meals, since he didn't want to dine out. They had paid a lot for the dining table which had been delivered the previous day with some other furniture items. He believed they should be getting their money's worth from the house by using the kitchen more.

'As they sat to eat their meal, he cracked open a bottle of wine to christen the new dining table.

'Hopefully, we'll soon have a highchair sitting at the end of the table,' Preye cooed. 'Or probably two, if we're lucky with twins.'

'Are you trying to tell me something?' he asked excitedly.

'Unfortunately, no, but it hasn't been long, and if nothing happens in a few months, I'll make a doctor's appointment. In the meantime, we keep trying. Tonight will be the first night on our new bed. Did you remember to pick up the sheets that I asked the shop owner to reserve for me at the store? They were specially ordered.' Preye munched on her fried yam and took a swig of wine.

'I did, and it wasn't easy because you purchased them with your bank card. It was the card you keep with your last name, Banigo.' Timi's posture stiffened and he put down his fork. 'It was embarrassing to explain that my wife still has her accounts in her maiden name. It's the last time that's going to happen because this weekend, we'll work out which of your official documents need updating, to avoid any future confusion.' Timi looked up and saw her look of disgust. 'Don't fight me on this. It has to be this way because we're married now and I handle the finances. It's for the best.'

'No it's not. It's feels like I'm relinquishing control of everything to you. You can't make decisions like this unilaterally without a reasonable discussion. Even this house. You knew I'd never agreed to it. You keep springing these irrational surprise on me and expect me to obey like I'm your child or one random servant. I'm an accomplished woman in my own right and I'm a human being. I don't intend to pack my brains because I'm married. Is that what you want?' She pushed her plate aside and rushed to the visitor's bathroom, locking the door behind her.

He felt an overwhelming desire to be in control, but it was proving difficult. He couldn't understand Preye's obstinacy. *If someone wants to take some responsibilities off my plate, I'd be thrilled,* he thought. She was acting like a child and he found himself looking at a locked door. He felt powerless. 'You're getting too emotional over a small technicality. It's just a name on a couple of documents. This is marriage.' He continuously pounded on the door. 'Grow up and open the door, Preye.'

'If it's just a technicality, then why don't you relax and allow me to keep my name and my financial independence?' It struck her that she shouldn't have to ask his permission. She was looking ahead at life under his control and didn't like it. She had never had a panic attack in her life but she felt a cluster of bulbs flashing in her stomach and it seemed her heart would burst out through her skin. She took a deep breath to steady her heart beat. It was then that the tears started flowing. She felt the accomplishments that she had worked hard for draining from her body.

Timi's pleas continued from the other side of the bathroom door for what seemed like hours. She wasn't going to get away with her hysterics and he'd do anything to get her out to start acting her part. Once she calmed down, they could return to something that resembled a marriage. He needed to pull out all the stops. When Preye didn't respond to his pleas to open the door, he got a cushion from one of the sofas and sat against the bathroom door until he dozed off.

Preye opened the box labelled towels and made herself a bed in the bathtub. She nestled in and rocked herself to sleep as she ran out of tears. She hoped the sun would peek through the window, and she'd be next to her husband in bed because it had all been a nightmare. But she woke up with her cheek against the cold porcelain and realised the previous night hadn't been a dream.

She pulled herself out of the tub and began to put the towels back in the box. She'd deal with hanging them properly later. The box of pregnancy test kits caught her eyes, and she remembered her ultimate goal of starting a family. Despite all the facts that told her she wasn't at a prime age for getting pregnant, she hadn't anticipated that she wouldn't be pregnant in her first month of having continuous, intensive sex.

She sighed and thought she should spend the weekend trying to make things more tolerable with her husband. If Timi wasn't willing to compromise, her marriage might prove insufferable. She needed to take on the responsibility of making her marriage work and even become blissful. She swiped a tube of lipstick across her mouth, rinsed the sleep out of her bloodshot brown eyes and tried to open the door after unlocking it. The door wouldn't budge because something was blocking it from the other side. She heard a groan as she continued to push.

She finally succeeded at opening the door and Timi's soothing voice greeted her. 'Sweetheart.' He was knelt on the floor. And in his hand, he held a white flag, made from a handkerchief which he attached to a wooden spoon. 'I was willing to lie on the cold floor for as long as it took. I was only metres away, and it was more than I could endure to be separated from you. At night, of course.' Timi chuckled. 'Let's push our problems aside and think of how to make this house our home. I love you, my darling wife and I only want the best for us.' He waved his flag. He was shirtless and his muscles glowed. It was hard for her to resist him. 'I surrender my heart to you.'

Once again, he made a sharp turn from the raging storm of the previous night and showered her with affection. She accepted his words, although there was no apology or solution presented. It was always more of the same machoism. This time it had started with bed sheets.

What next? She asked herself.

*

Preye lounged under the awning canopy in the yard, reading one of her motivational books – *The Thread in the Broken Needle*. She was seated on one of the four rattan chairs and table under a circular parasol that provided shade. She was about to take a sip of the orange juice she had placed on the table as a call came through from her mother.

'Mum, I'm sorry I should have called you,' she said out before Miriam got a chance to accuse her of not calling. 'You won't believe how busy I've been.' Miriam spared no pleasantries, but asked Preye when Preye would come visiting. 'Realistically, I won't see you until the christening, unless I can convince Timi otherwise. He'd have to drop me at your place after work during the week, which may not be convenient.'

'I believe it's always convenient to see your mother. Your husband should agree because he's got a mother himself, who is a lovely woman by the way. I spent a lot of time with her at the reception and she thinks you're grand,' Miriam said. 'Have you found a new church now? I haven't seen you in church too.' Miriam switched from one thing to the other. 'Why don't you and Timi come visiting?'

'We haven't even had time to go church hunting. I don't think I want to change church. I've been super-busy with unpacking and arranging this massive house. I'll ask Timi if we can make church tomorrow. I've missed you guys and I need God more than ever now,' Preye said. She had said that before she realised her comment may lead to all kinds of questions from her mother.

'We all need God all the time. I hope everything is okay with you both,' Miriam asked. 'Or is there something you want to share?' Miriam hoped her daughter would announce that she was pregnant.

'There's been a lot of changes in my life in the past few months. Moving and marriage have left me almost breathless. I think the church will help me put everything in perspective. Just pray for us.'

Preye saw Timi walking towards her with a tray of snacks. He had been treating her like a princess since their argument the previous weekend. 'If we don't make church tomorrow, I'll call you during the week. Anyhow, I'll see you at Tamara's christening.'

'I'm praying for you. Say hello to Timi.'

Timi handed her a plate of fresh fruit and cheese. 'You have to keep your strength up because I know you've been feeling tired lately. Can I refill your drink?' He was aware that she had been speaking to her mother. 'I would have loved to say hello to your mum.' Miriam Banigo wasn't exactly Timi's favourite person because she never really warmed up to him, but she had a strong influence on Preye and he resolved to keep her as an ally.

'I'm hoping we can go to church tomorrow.' Preye told Timi, but guessing the answer, she quickly added. 'We'll see her at Tamara's christening. Why are you spoiling me this Saturday morning?' she teased, pulling up her sunglasses to look into his eyes.

'Only the best for you, Mrs Coker. Hmm, do you feel like talking PR or is work-talk prohibited on the weekend?'

She shook her head wildly. 'No, no. Work-talk is never prohibited. I love it that you're going all professional with me. What's up?' she asked.

He pulled up a chair beside her and took out a yellow writing pad. 'We've spoken in the past about me venturing out on my own after gaining experience at Mason Bridge. Thanks for your support and the example you've set with Beta, I believe I'm ready,' he announced confidently.

She was surprised. 'This is a lot sooner than I anticipated. I hope you know your contract with Mason Bridge prevents you from taking any of their clients for the next three years. PR is a referral-based business. Do you think your name recognition will get you enough new clients to break even within the next couple of years?'

'Way to rain on my parade,' he smiled and slightly nudged her. 'I already thought of that. I know it will take me time to develop clients, but we have time. You said business is booming at Beta, so we don't have to worry about money in the short term,' he said confidently. 'Besides, my dad will be sending some clients my way.'

'Beta is still growing, and everything extra is being put back into the business to foster growth. Let me put pen to paper and see how this is going to work cost-wise.' She put her sunglasses on the table and started crunching numbers on the writing pad Timi handed over.

Starting cost for a new public relations firm was a big factor to consider, but he reminded her that his parents could always pitch in. She thought Timi should be thinking about how to repay his parents for the extra money they gave him for the house, rather than collecting more. But she reckoned that he was their only child and they probably didn't have any other thing or person to spend their wealth on, which made her wonder about the wisdom in amassing wealth in the first place. Looking at the numbers on the writing pad, Timi's start-up idea seemed doable to her, until he opened his mouth to make a request.

'Now that we know it's financially feasible, I have another favour to ask. Can you go through your clients' list and throw a few clients my way?'

'Excuse me!' Shocked, she pushed herself up. 'Beta doesn't

belong to me fully, you know.' He didn't budge but rather focused his eyes on her. 'Okay, let me talk to Tobi. I can't do anything without his consent and I'm not making any promises,' she said flatly.

'Are you choosing that weasel, Tobi over your husband?'

'No, I'm following the rules of the business charter Tobi and I signed. And by the way, he is not a weasel. He's my partner and friend.' She picked her sunglasses from the table, wore it and stared ahead of her at nothing in particular. It was enough to let him know that the discussion was over. Beta meant too much to her and she refused to risk anything where it was concerned.

Timi found himself up against a wall and he didn't like it.

*

Preye pulled the soft cotton sheet over her head before she opened her eyes to the tiny ray of light filtering through the window. It was Monday morning and she was excited to begin the work week in the real world.

The weekend had gone without any incident and she was disappointed that apart from her mother, none of her friends or family members had called to say they would drop by to see her. She couldn't blame them. The three-hour traffic she experienced getting home from work on the last Friday of the month, attributed to the Redeemed Camp meeting was enough to discourage anyone from making that trip.

On a regular day, it still took her close to two hours to travel home, because of the bad roads. She seemed to be cut off from the rest of her world any time she was at her big empty home. She reckoned Timi loved the fact that no one could drop by their house randomly.

He was already dressed and having his coffee in the kitchen

when she stepped out of the bath to get ready for the day.

She walked to her new closet and threw open the doors. She was faced with what looked like an ice cream parlour. Her coloured clothes were hung neatly and her fitted suits were nowhere to be seen. She couldn't find her favourite black loafers with silver grommets.

'Timi!' she yelled. 'What happened to my clothes?' She felt violated as she struggled to understand what her husband was trying to achieve. She whipped her head around to find him standing casually in the doorway, staring at her with a smirk on his face.

'Good morning, Sweetheart.'

CHAPTER FOURTEEN

'I'll be ready in five minutes, Mum,' Preye called out from the bathroom at her mother's house where she had spent the night. It was the day of Tamara's christening.

'We have plenty of time,' Miriam Banigo responded. 'Erefa, Donald, and the baby just left their house and service doesn't begin until eleven. We may have time to stop by the banquet venue to check on the flowers, which Tonye should have done, but I want to double-check.'

It was the first night Preye would spend away from Timi since the wedding. He was to meet her at the church, and he had promised not to be late. Although it didn't matter much if he wasn't on time because they didn't have any role to play, other than to be present. The honour of godparents had been given to Donald's sister and her husband. Preye viewed the choice as a referendum on her marriage and the fact that she didn't have a child yet. She prayed fervently that the children would come, even if it was one. She believed if they had children, she could steer her marriage from the fragility it was currently hanging on.

Timi's outbursts were getting more frequent. He always wanted things his way and anytime Preye stood up to him, she had to bear the brunt of his temper. He called her names and chucked insults at her in subtle ways that left her imagining if they were intentional or accidental. Since the first time he alluded to her father's abandonment, he had found ways to continue chipping in snide remarks about how dysfunctional her upbringing must have been and how unlikely she was prepared for motherhood with the way she was committed to Beta.

On an occasion that she and Tobi returned late to the office because of a delayed meeting, Timi had made allusion to a probability that she must have slept her way up and turned to Christianity after achieving her career goal. And since then, whenever he was in a foul mood about her work, he called her *ashewo*. The first time that happened, she had told him off and warned him never to use that word for her. The telling-off had worked for a while until another day Preye left the house on a Saturday morning before Timi woke up.

Preye was weary of the hot and cold game Timi played and was never quite sure about his mood or what would cause a tirade, so she had decided to pick her fights and let him have his way as much as it didn't threaten her peace of mind, which had become fragile since they moved to Regalia Court. He chose to express his love for her with the same intensity that she experienced his nastiness. He still showered her with gifts and the surprises she sometimes wasn't sure how to respond to. He assured her he loved her as often as he didn't, and it was as if she needed to work hard to earn his kindness. Yet, his charming exterior remained intact and kept those facets of their relationship hidden from everyone around them.

All things hidden had a way of being revealed eventually. It was like a drip that filled a bucket before long. Despite their challenges, she was optimistic that he'd soften once they had children he could concentrate on.

The wardrobe disaster had been over a month and they had been enjoying some relative bliss. She had been shocked to find her newly unpacked closet arranged according to Timi's taste. She had learned that her favourite clothes weren't thrown in the bin, but been boxed away until they could build a larger closet.

Timi was working with a contractor to remodel the bedroom with a walk-in closet, which was an intended surprise for Preye. He had turned it around and made her feel stupid about thinking that he binned her clothes.

No matter how bad she thought his actions were, he followed them up with a romantic or considerate gesture. Preye thought of her marriage as a scale. They both had a way of throwing it out of balance and then adjusting it back to even.

She came out with a cream-coloured A-line dress that accentuated her curves. The high neck made it modest enough for both Timi and the church. Most importantly, it made her feel good. 'I'm ready. How do I look?' she asked her mother as she twirled.

'Stunning as always and well-rested. You slept really deep because you were snoring away as if you didn't care if the world came to an end,' Miriam said.

'You must be confused,' Preye replied with a smile. 'I don't snore anymore. Timi says I make a small murmur, but he has never described it as a snore.'

'Maybe you've not been sleeping soundly with him next to you,' Miriam said flatly.

'Sounds like you think I'm not comfortable sleeping with my husband. I can assure you that's not the case,' Preye said defensively.

'I didn't say that. You've always snored as far as I can remember and yesterday reminded me of when you were living at home. Maybe your husband wants to make you feel good. Although I don't think anyone should be ashamed of snoring.' Miriam tickled Preye. 'Let's get going. The cab is here.'

Miriam felt Preye was unnecessarily edgy and she didn't understand why. She told herself she'd find some time to visit the couple. She hadn't visited because she didn't want to be described as the intrusive mother-in-law and was waiting for them to invite her over. Preye grabbed her present for Tamara, and they were off to the cab.

*

Timi pulled into the church parking lot just as the service was about to start. He knew Preye would have arrived and hopefully have saved a seat for him. He hoped the church service wouldn't drag for too long. He already dreaded spending almost the whole day with the Banigo family. He knew Erefa and Miriam liked him to a point and Tonye didn't care much for him. It was Preye's father he was concerned about spending time with, in case the big man decided to show up. They had only met at the wedding and hadn't exchanged much except for a quick father-in-law and son-in-law embrace. Timi wasn't sure what Mr Banigo thought about him; fathers tended to be hyper-protective of their girls.

He parked the car and strode towards the church. Spending the night at home without Preye had given him a taste of the bachelorhood he left behind. He had invited Martin over to the house to spend some time, so that meant drinking and reliving old memories. Martin and Timi had been a good team when Timi was single and hitting the clubs. There was hardly a night they were out that at least one of them didn't take a woman home. Meeting and dating Preye had caused that part of his life to cease to exist and life had become even more boring since they got married. Martin reminded him of how much fun was still out there on the streets.

After Martin left, Timi had cleared up and gone to bed. But each time he closed his eyes, his mind had strayed to conflicting thoughts that focused his eyes on the white ceiling. He had thought about how successful Preye was, so much so that nobody noticed how hard he was working; he had thought about the times he wished he could fix a padlock on her beautiful lips to stop her from making so much sense; and he had wondered why she wouldn't beg him to make love to her like some other women he had been with. As if on a sequenced cue, the pictures of his numerous ex-girlfriends had seeped into his myriad thoughts, some looking sexier than Preye. Then he had wondered if his monogamous life was worth it. His mind had whirled around a complex carousel of beautiful and ugly actions and intents in his past and future. Curling up into his favourite sleeping position had proved futile as his brain chose to keep dancing around. Finally, he had succumbed to the last thought he could make sense of, by pushing himself up to place a call to Tina Alli.

Timi shook his head to rid himself of the warm feelings from his tryst and his impure thoughts, before entering the church.

'Darling, you can sit here,' Preye removed her bag from the saved seat beside her. 'How was your time out with Martin?'

'We retired early. Sips and bits, nothing major. I missed you,' he whispered back. Preye's eyes danced. 'Is your dad here?'

Preye shook her head. The anointing and official christening had already started. One thing Timi and Preye agreed on was that they wanted badly to be standing where Donald and Erefa were standing with their babies. A family without children was something neither of them wanted.

After the service and exchange of pleasantries with other church members, Miriam and Preye joined Tonye on the drive to the banquet venue, with Timi driving behind them. Preye was ruminating on whether Timi would make an issue out of not joining him after the church service.

'I haven't seen you in church since you got married. Did you enjoy the service?' Miriam commented. 'You grew up in the church and I hope you haven't forgotten that important part of your life. To me, the church is my north star. It guides me in the good times and the …'

'Have you noticed that I live on the other side of the city now?' Preye interrupted her mother with a sarcastic whine. 'It's not realistic for me to come every Sunday. Travelling to work during the week already wears me out and there's only one car between me and Timi. God knows I miss this church and He is always by my side whether I come to church or not. I'll try to come down any time I can, but for now, I have to look for a church closer to home.'

The conversation was unsettling for Preye and she had to fight back tears and avoid the emotions building up in her. Timi hadn't mentioned church since they moved to Regalia Court. She had initially thought they would resume church after they were well settled in their new home, but she soon realised that Timi's concept of church was different from hers. For him, church was where you went to because it was Sunday or you needed desperate help; for Preye, it was a place to refresh and connect with God and people.

Moreover, Timi usually used the car over the weekend and she hadn't found a church in their neighbourhood. She made a mental note to ask the family that lived next to them if they attended a nearby church. She had seen them usually dressed up and going out on Sundays.

'Have you thought to search online?' Tonye asked.

'So people go to church now based on online referrals?' Preye looked at Tonye incredulously.

'By the time you go to ten churches, you should be able to decide on one,' Tonye laughed. Preye hissed.

'It's better than not attending church at all,' Miriam finished off. She pursed her lips as she thought of asking Preye a question about Timi, but decided against it because of Tonye.

*

'My turn.' Preye held her arms out to receive Tamara. The baby was being passed around the family members like a piece of Holy Communion bread. 'She gets more beautiful every time I look at her, Erefa. Don't you want to spend every moment of the day watching her grow?' Preye laughed.

'Don't laugh. If I'm not sleeping, that's pretty much what I do and when I do sleep, I dream of her,' Erefa confirmed.

Donald chimed in. 'It's pathetic, but true. I do the same thing any time I'm home. The whole thing is a bit unfair because now that I have a daughter, I want to be home twice as much. Unfortunately, I have to work twice as hard to keep her in diapers.'

'Nappies are cheap. The older they get, the more expensive they become. Our daughters are almost three and already they're developing an eye for fashion,' one of Preye's cousins chipped in, jokingly.

Timi saw a chance to add to the conversation 'I'm looking forward to fatherhood and one of the best parts will be watching Preye become an adorable mother. She is by far the most nurturing woman I know.'

'This mother hen has watched out for me for as long as I can remember.' Erefa shoved her finger into Preye's side. 'More so, she nurtured Beta to be the envy of many that it is today, so I'm sure she'll do better with a child. It'll be interesting to see how much time she takes off before going back to work,' Erefa teased.

The others split off into different conversations and Miriam pulled Preye aside to make her say hello to someone.

'I'm sure she'll resume part-time once she has a taste of motherhood. Beta will take a back seat to family,' Timi stated.

Erefa was amused. 'That woman,' she said pointing to Miriam. 'She raised us as a single parent, and she's never stopped working, so I'm sure my sister will figure a way to balance work and family. You're married to a strong woman.' She nodded in Preye's direction.

Timi smiled and changed the subject. He predicted that Preye would try working from home and eventually decide that being a wife and mother should be her priorities. She could sell her share of the company to Tobi or someone else if he didn't have the cash on hand. People would line up to own a stake in Beta, which had become the darling of the local PR scene. It would be like the name change that she initially resisted. She'd come around to his way of thinking and enjoy home-life with him and the children. It wouldn't be much different from the household Timi grew up in, which was perfection in his eyes.

'Am I interrupting?' Preye asked, walking back to Timi's side.

'Not at all, sis,' Erefa answered. 'Your husband was just telling me you would stop working once the children start coming and I assured him you're the superwoman with nine lives.'

Preye looked surprised. Timi was in an uncomfortable situation, but he had been there before and hadn't been fazed. He could manage Preye but didn't want to look bad in front of Erefa.

'That's putting the cart before the horse, don't you think, Timi? We're not even pregnant yet.'

'I suppose it's your choice, but seeing you with Tamara made me think you'll be obsessed with motherhood. You're very capable and you'll do whatever your heart tells you,' Timi said, with a smile on his face. He hated having to please his wife's family.

'Hmm.' Preye nodded sarcastically before diving into a conversation with Erefa.

Timi felt he was getting in the way of the two sisters, so he moved along to chat with other people he didn't know well or care about.

*

Timi hadn't pulled out of the parking lot before Preye brought up his conversation with Erefa. 'You told Erefa that I get to decide if I would work from home.' It was more of a question than a statement. 'I got the feeling you were trying to impress my sister,' Preye concluded.

'What made you think that?' he asked.

'I know you. You're my husband.'

'Since you know me so well, you don't need an answer. I didn't want to get into a deep conversation in front of her. It's our family and it's personal.'

'Erefa is family and I shouldn't have to tell you that. My sisters are no less my family because I'm now married. I can be a fabulous wife and mum and still work at my company. Tobi has been busy building a family for years and it hasn't impacted the business negatively. I have no reason to believe I can't have a business and run a family. Even your mum has her own business.'

'Preye, I'll be starting my firm and one of us has to stay home.' Timi turned onto the freeway and sped up. 'And by the way, my mum's office is two blocks away from the house and you know she practically runs her business from home.'

'You're doing it again,' she said quietly. She didn't have the energy nor the resolve to raise her voice to match Timi's.

'Doing what?' he asked, his aggravation seeping to the surface. The vein in his neck was throbbing.

She didn't like that he had temper flare-ups and he seemed to be set on the course now. It was especially troubling in a speeding car. 'You're making decisions for us without consulting me. And stop comparing me to your mum.'

'Who brought my mum into this discussion? You!' He

chuckled. 'My love, this is marriage, and you signed up for it. You were successful at being single and it turns out that you're lousy in marriage. There are times you have to yield control and this is one of those times. What I say should matter to you. Now, I'm done talking so I can concentrate on the road.'

If she uttered another word he'd simply shut her up. She didn't want the argument escalating while he was driving. He was putting his finger on the scale again and tipping their relationship out of balance and she was displeased.

CHAPTER FIFTEEN

'Lola, I'm heading home for the weekend. Tell me you have something devastatingly exciting going on,' Preye teased. 'I live vicariously since moving out to nowhere.' Handbag in hand, she had stopped by Lola's office to have a casual chat before closing for the day. She kicked off her heels and took a seat on a soft chair next to Lola's desk.

'I wish I've got something for you. If you think a trip to the mall with Zara is exciting, then you're worse off than I thought,' Lola said, pitching her shoes on the floor next to Preye's.

'I might just be worse than that you know,' Preye chuckled. 'I was busy praying that I wanted to live in my own house. That prayer was answered before I realised I didn't specify the location. So I'm stuck in a big house I don't fancy. I don't think I'll ever love it. It's so isolated,' she sighed and swallowed the emotions that could easily open her tap of tears if not replaced with a dose of positivity. 'Well, the good thing is Timi brings me coffee in bed most mornings. And this weekend, we're going to look for a church we can attend in the area. It's just...' Before Preye could finish, her phone beeped. 'Timi is waiting downstairs. We'll talk more next week.' She sprang up and hurriedly picked her handbag without waiting for Lola to get up.

Before Preye switched to praising Timi, Lola had heard the tenseness in-between her words and she had clearly heard much more than what Preye had said. But Lola wasn't sure if it was a

169

shout of 'help me' or 'leave me alone'. She had wanted to embrace Preye before Timi's unwanted call interrupted the moment and set Preye bolting off.

'Call me.' With a look of tender concern and a hope of seeing through the storm brewing inside Preye's head, Lola's eyes and voice followed Preye as she left.

'See you on Monday.' Preye yelled back, walking towards the elevator.

She was exhausted with a cramp in her side, accompanied by a bout of work exhaustion, so she napped during the ride home. It was a quiet trip and Timi didn't mind. The silence gave him the room to think about his plans to spend some quality time with Tina.

He had met Tina twice already, and she was filling the emotional and sexual gap that Preye had brought into their marriage. It was ironic that Tina's subservience helped him overlook Preye's irritating recalcitrance and birthed a relative peace in his home.

As soon as they got in, Preye changed into her pyjamas and went to lie down on the sofa. There was no plan or discussion about having dinner and Timi went into the kitchen to make himself a bowl of *garri* and peanuts. By the time he returned to the living room, she had dozed off.

She woke up the next morning, still feeling exhausted. Timi suggested she might be pregnant, but she argued that the prospect was slim. She recognised the pain as a prelude to her period which she was expecting in a couple of days. This pain had only resurrected after her wedding and she wondered why.

Timi insisted that she might be pregnant and suggested that taking a test would be the right thing to do. She managed to drag herself to the toilet and urinated on a pregnancy test stick.

'Good job, Mine. Give it to me, let me read the results for a change. Perhaps I'll have better luck than you've had,' he cajoled. He took the stick from her hand before she could protest.

She was still in her pyjamas while Timi was freshly showered, wearing his favourite pair of faded denim trousers and a new t-shirt, as if he was going out. It seemed to her that her husband liked to shine when she was down in the dumps. It was as if he enjoyed being better than she was; looking better, feeling better, and acting more capable. She was about to lay her head on the pillow, but she heard his voice.

'Oh my good Lord! Mine, we did it. Preye Coker, you're pregnant. It's a clear sign. We're having a baby,' he screamed.

She felt an overwhelming surge of strength and bounded off the sofa into his arms. She kissed him and he responded with such passion that she started peeling off her clothes. Taken over by the euphoria of finding out that she was pregnant, she fell into bed with her husband. Her cramps magically disappeared and they ended up having unhindered sex.

He was ready to roll over afterwards, but she was still in an explosive state filled with warm thoughts of a range of possibilities about the baby; she felt like jumping up to dance, to shout, to run and to share the good news with anyone who would rejoice with her, especially her mother.

'What are we doing? We should be celebrating over a tub of ice cream, not making love,' she bustled. 'We'll have plenty of time to celebrate this way, I assure you, darling. First thing Monday morning, I'll call the doctor. Let's not share the news until I'm a bit farther along. Should we find out the sex ahead of time? I think yes, because it will help in planning the nursery.' She was talking a mile a minute. Timi was amused at first, but then insisted that she calmed down. 'I will, I will. I have to watch my blood pressure because every breath I take for the next nine months will be shared with this little one.' She patted her taut belly.

Timi shook his head and switched to his typical smirk any time he was up to some mischief. It was as if he was in on a joke that she was unaware of. He sat up and put his arms on her shoulders as he looked into her eyes. 'You're not pregnant, Preye. It was a prank. I just wanted to make you feel better and get you off the sofa so we could begin enjoying the weekend. Then you came on to me and I thought, this is working better than I could have imagined.'

She couldn't cool the firestorm surging through her body as her eyes turned black. 'You used a non-existent pregnancy to have sex with me! You're no better than a common rapist.' Her body vibrated and she visualised pushing Timi onto the bed and forcing a pillow over his head to stifle life out of his body. That way, he'd stop trying to make a fool of her with the stupid grin on his face.

As if reading her thoughts, he jumped off the bed and pointed his finger at her. His neck vein was pulsating. 'First of all, I'm your husband, so I can't rape you. I wasn't forceful. And if this hadn't happened, you wouldn't even have been keen on making love. For that, you should be ashamed of yourself. Secondly, I was joking. I was trying to make you feel better and cheer you up because the mood around here was gloomy. If you think I went too far, that's sad. But on the brighter side, you're up and you enjoyed it.' He bolted out of the room and slammed the door behind him. Since she didn't want him around, he'd go to Tina's where there would be no friction or accusations.

Preye was angry, sad, and a little embarrassed that she had allowed herself to get duped. She wished she could disappear and not have to see her husband for a very long time. Every time something came up with him that hurt her to the core, she thought it couldn't get worse. She believed their relationship had finally hit rock bottom. *Once you hit bottom, it is time to push up and see the light again, because there should be a silver lining somewhere,* she thought, trying to assure herself.

There had been so many incidents – the many times he left her stranded at home; the time he said she lacked home training because she broke a coffee mug; the time he called her gullible for believing something Lola said, the time he kept her waiting at the office till 8.40p.m because he forgot to tell her he had a meeting and then accusing her of hanging out with another woman's husband, because Tobi had waited with her; the time he left her to bring in from the car, all the groceries she brought home because he was too tired to get himself up; the times he stopped her from going to see her friends because he suddenly wanted to take her out, and the several times he called her *ashewo*. She couldn't recall everything, but she recalled that he had brought her to this house, knowing that she wouldn't want it. Now the fake pregnancy announcement!

It has to be rock bottom, right? Preye wondered, sighing. She felt helpless as she sat in the bedroom alone, waiting for the long, dreary day to turn to night so that the darkness would envelope her to a safe place.

*

She woke the next morning to a single petal of rose and a note on the pillow next to her. The scent of brewing coffee and bananas wafted through the air.

My Love,

I realise now that you didn't appreciate my joke. I'm sorry, but I'm sure you know I didn't mean to hurt you. I've made breakfast for you. We promised to visit my parents today, so I've gone, but don't feel obliged to come.

Love, Timi.

She dragged in a deep breath and pulled herself out of bed. She looked in the mirror to see her face which was blotchy from the long hours of crying. He had asked for forgiveness and said sorry, which he rarely did. He rarely apologised; instead, he'd try to cover up his gaffes. A note and a single rose made a difference. There was a chance they had reached rock bottom and it was time to spring up and enjoy the light.

She was optimistic.

She helped herself to the banana pancakes he had made and contemplated what to do next. She hadn't been to see the Cokers since after the wedding and she'd have liked to have gone with Timi, especially because his mum had helped with the house.

After musing for about an hour, she decided to order a cab from the taxi application on her phone, with a ray of hope that she'd get some succour at the Cokers.

It took over twenty minutes for the cab to arrive, but the traffic was light and she soon arrived at her in-law's front door.

'What a pleasant surprise,' Ife Coker's smile synced with her eyes and was welcoming. She wore a rose-coloured blouse on a pleated khaki skirt that made her look much bigger than she was. She called out to Timi and Wale. 'Timi mentioned you might not come. I understand that the distance can be discouraging. Make yourself comfortable, darling.' She excused herself and went into the kitchen.

Timi came from the kitchen and pulled Preye up to embrace her. She hadn't been in a good frame of mind and hadn't bothered to dress appropriately for a visit to the in-laws. She wore black leggings and a Roadrunners t-shirt. She was a bit of a mess and miraculously, Timi didn't make a snide comment.

'Look at that, Wale. Preye showed up to make things right with Timi. That is just how it should be,' Ife told her husband in the kitchen as she shut the door behind her. 'She's recovered from her tantrum and accepted Timi's apology.'

'Good thing, because sleeping on the sofa is no place for the man of the house. I don't think we ever went to bed so angry that I chose the sofa.' Wale followed his wife back to the living room to join Timi and Preye.

Her in-laws' conversation hadn't been meant for Preye to hear, but she did. It seemed Timi had framed the event differently and painted her as the one to blame. The sad part of it was that he believed he was in the clear and that Preye had overreacted. She settled on the sofa with Timi.

He pulled her in tight and tugged her hair down to cover her birthmark. 'I'm so glad you came. Does this mean we can put the unpleasantness behind us?' he asked privately. He knew Preye couldn't hold out on him for long and he had been happy when she expectedly showed up. It meant he could still predict his wife. He was pleased with himself.

'I'm emotionally exhausted, and we can't go into that right now. We still have to talk and make sure things improve. For now, let's enjoy our visit,' Preye responded, without looking at him.

Wale and Timi led the conversation and like Ife, Preye agreed with most of what they said. Timi mentioned that he was leaving Mason Bridge and he'd be starting Timi's Communications. He tactfully told his parents that he'd be counting on their financial support. Wale offered immediately, to Ife's delight and Timi's relief.

Timi thought it was good for Preye to see how unconditionally his parents loved and supported him. They were his cheerleaders and he wanted his wife to join the squad. He firmly believed that the more time spent with his family and friends, the more Preye would learn what a good marriage required. Preye's friends and family wanted her to hold on to too many parts of the life she had lived while single.

Before they left, Ife packed a bowl of *efo-riro* and handed it over to Preye. 'This is his favourite. He'll easily forget what your offence was,' Ife advised. Preye couldn't be bothered to defend herself and simply collected the soup after thanking Ife.

Preye broke the awkward silence on the way home. 'Timi, you left a note, saying you were sorry. Are you really sorry? Because, it seems like you've painted me as the devil to your parents. Do you realise the cruelty of your actions? I can't see the end of this emotional rollercoaster in sight and I wish it would just stop now, so I can get off.'

'I can't wave a magic wand and stop your rollercoaster from doing a merry-go-round. You've become unnecessarily emotional and sensitive and it's hard to predict your reactions. Was this aspect of your personality intentionally hidden before our marriage?' he asked. He paused for a moment and resumed to stop her from responding. 'I've thought about this and my mum agrees. Perhaps you should see a therapist.'

Preye's head splintered into hundreds of tiny bulbs. She stared at him in disbelief. 'You and your mum want me to see a therapist,' she repeated. She wanted to shake her head, but it felt too heavy. 'I'm not sure I understand. How did your mother get into the conversation?'

He ignored the question about his mother. 'I don't see the harm.' His voice was icy and he felt like his eyes would dislodge from their sockets as he focused hard on the road.

She drew in a long breath to slow down her rapid burst of heartbeats. 'But she doesn't think you need a therapist?' A lot of names surfaced to her mind that she could use to describe Ife Coker and Timi. 'What exactly have you told them about me, by the way? I don't go crying to my mum about any incident we have, yet your mother knows enough about us to suggest I go for therapy.' Her head finally shook of its own volition. 'Does that sound fair to you?'

'I'm not the one whose body shakes from having mere discussions,' he accused, pressing his hands on the steering. He tried to fathom why she had to always start a tornado from everything he said. A long reverberating silence followed as he drove on.

As he pulled into Regalia Court, she experienced an epiphany. All of the problems in their promising marriage were being blamed on her. As far as he was concerned, he had done nothing wrong and it was her emotional instability that caused their problems. She could start a new round of arguments, but her mind went back to those few moments when she thought she was pregnant; it had been sheer bliss. And like a drug addict needing a fix, she needed that feeling back. She'd do anything to feel that bliss again, and she started by remaining quiet, with a silent prayer to God.

CHAPTER SIXTEEN

Timi woke up earlier than Preye to start on his tasks and get ready for his co-worker who was to pick him up. He had a load of documents to go through and he decided Preye deserved the extra hour of sleep. He knew Preye was better suited for most of the documents he needed to review since she had been through the process before. He sorted out the documents at the dining table, took out the ones he felt were not important and left the rest for Preye.

He'd be handing in his notice at Mason Bridge today, and he had prepared to look his best in his midnight blue suit and brown loafers. He knew a lot of his colleagues envied him once they found out he was married to Preye Banigo, the enigmatic lady behind Beta. Some of them had hailed him for his prowess at winning his trophy wife, while others couldn't bring themselves to acknowledge that fact. Marrying Preye had added a few springs to his feet and boosted his conviction that he could get anything he wanted if he set his mind on it.

If all went well at work today as he expected, he'd give Malik a ring and ask him out for a drink, knowing that Malik wouldn't mind the short notice. Malik had a good relationship with his wife and the kids; enough to have some freedom when he needed it. It was a tip Malik had shared with Timi - Keep the wife happy and she'll give you enough rope as long as you don't betray her trust.

It was two weeks after the visit to his parent's home and there had been an awkward coldness between Timi and Preye for a few days until Preye elicited an apology from him before she returned to the bedroom.

His phone buzzed at the delivery of a text message and he checked to read that his pick-up car had arrived. He switched on the coffee machine and left a stuffed teddy on the table for Preye beside the documents. He expected her to appreciate it as his wish for her to have a baby soon, and if she didn't, he'd deal with it later. Knowing how sensitive she had become, he guessed she might find it offensive, but he left it behind anyway. He winked at the bear and walked out of the house.

Shortly after, Preye's hand reached over for him and realised he wasn't there. The smell of coffee jogged her memory that he had told her he'd leave early. She stepped out of bed, grabbed her silk robe and padded into the kitchen.

'Jesus Christ!' she exclaimed at the sight of the stuffed bear. The mother bear was cradling a baby bear. It felt like Timi was rubbing in the fact that months had gone by and she hadn't conceived. Again, she asked herself if he was being deliberately cruel or she was the one overreacting. She threw the stuffed animal in the bin and continued with her morning routine while trying to focus on some positive thoughts.

Her body craved to be at Beta or Roadrunners more than ever, because of the adrenaline boost they gave her. Before leaving for work, she jammed her running clothes and trainers into a duffle bag.

*

Tobi popped his head into Preye's office. 'I didn't realise you were here. A few of our applicants came in for interviews today. I would have invited you to join if I knew you were in the office.'

'What position are we interviewing for? I should know that if I wasn't so self-consumed,' Preye said apologetically. A mound of unopened mails sat in the centre of her desk.

'Janet in Accounting Department is going on a one-year study leave and we need someone to take up the slot for just a year. None of the candidates interviewed was promising, and I wish we could clone Janet. If you recall correctly, you and I did horribly in maths while at uni. It's beyond me how we've been able to get this company where it is today.'

'Oh my God! That reminds me, I have lunch with my dad today. He's helping me sort out my accounts.' Preye opened her diary. She was meeting Harry Banigo at Dada's Restaurant, about three streets away from her office. She had chosen the place because of its huge tables, so they could spread out their documents. 'Timi is stepping out on his own and we'll be relying solely on my income for a bit,' Preye said. She ducked her head under her table and changed into her trainers so she could walk to the restaurant.

'That shouldn't be a problem. You're always watching your spending and Beta is in good shape if you need anything. Speaking of good shape, Preye, as your friend, I think I'm in a position to ask, are you in good shape? We miss you at Roadrunners, especially the fun-runs and you weren't around for the last charity run. You never used to miss them, and now we don't see you at all. I hope you don't have an injury I don't know about?' Tobi asked. His round empathic face was always a comfort.

'No, but thanks for asking. Travelling from that part of the world is something else. And people would actually think I live in Lagos too,' she joked. 'Most times I simply lack the will to leave the house because of the roads and traffic,' she continued. 'I'm sorry, I know I've dropped a lot of load on your laps. I'm still trying to adjust to being married and we're also working on starting a family. There's a lot on my plate and…' She didn't finish the sentence. 'You're no stranger, Tobi. I must confess, it's a struggle.'

Tobi patted her hand. 'Of course. Just remember that I'm always here for you, professionally or personally.'

'You, Mr Abass are an amazing friend. Please tell everyone at Roadrunners that I'm working my way back and I'll be at the next fun-run for sure,' she said as she got up to herald Tobi out of her office.

She was always amazed at the level of support she received from Tobi. And she was more determined than ever to continue working after she had children. She wanted to be an example of a woman who was successful at living a balanced and fulfilled life. She quickly made a call to one of the clients before picking up her bag. She bumped into Lola as she was walking towards the lift.

'Whoa, stranger. Where are you off to in such a hurry?' Lola asked, holding a takeaway lunch in her hands.

'I'm off to meet my dad for lunch. I'm running late but we'll chat soon. You look great, Lola. Have you lost weight?' Preye asked while still walking away.

'A little. I met someone who makes me happy, and I'm doing less stress-eating,' Lola purred. She expected the comment to stop Preye in her tracks, but it didn't.

'Great, Omo girl. Keep it up.' Preye responded, absentmindedly. She was checking in with Timi with a short text message.

Before Lola could say anything else, the lift arrived and Preye stepped in. She later realised she hadn't listened to a thing Lola said. But as she had told Tobi, there was a lot on her plate.

On top of all the craziness in her life, she still experienced intermittent pain in her lower abdomen. It throbbed and stopped and then picked up again. It was the familiar pain of the fibroid episodes she had suffered in the past; not enough to keep her down permanently, but enough to be a bother.

Preye burst through the door of Dada's Restaurant and spotted her father sitting at a table beside a huge window. He had already ordered two bottles of malt drink and with a pen in hand, he was rifling through papers that Preye had sent to him the previous week.

'I hope I'm not too late.' She added an apologising and hugged her father before taking a seat.

'I know you have a business to run and I appreciate that you could take the time to come,' Harry Banigo said, as he removed his reading glasses to take a good look at his daughter before they ordered light lunch. 'The last time I saw you was at the wedding and in the pictures you sent. Thank you for those. They are really lovely. How's Timi?'

Harry had asked Preye if they could meet up for lunch. That was how they met most times, even before the girls started moving out of Miriam's house. None of them had really wanted to fraternise with Harry's other family, since they were never sure if the current one was the last, and Harry didn't want to come to Miriam's house. Preye had taken the opportunity of their lunch date to ask him to help review her accounts. Harry had qualified as an accountant before veering into the world of car dealership.

'Timi is fine,' she said curtly. 'That's why I need to know where I am with money now. He's starting a PR consultancy and I need to support him, but I need to see where I stand personally to know how much I can spend on his venture and still keep the house running. And I'm not intending to take any cash out from Beta.'

They started on their lunch. Harry picked his glasses from the table and put them back on. 'Sweetheart, I don't know what you did in the past four months, but you're in a bad financial shape with cash.'

Preye thought her father's financial skills were rusty. 'How?'

'You've built a good wall between your accounts and those of Beta. I give you credit for that, but the accounts in the name of Preye Banigo-Coker is almost empty. And you also have some dues piling up.' Harry leaned back and allowed Preye to absorb what she had just been told. 'Why are you looking at me like that? Are you surprised?'

'Tell me in plain figures.'

'Looking three months ahead with your outstanding bills paid off against your potential income, your cash balance will just be plus minus a million.'

Preye shook her head to reject Harry's position. 'It can't be possible is what it is. I'm as careful as I've ever been. The last time I spent real money was for the wedding and you know that was a modest one. I haven't done any big spending since then. Timi practically pays for everything,' she said with a slight tremor in her voice.

'If not you, then maybe your husband has made some large purchases in recent times. Most of the expenses are for pricy office equipment, furniture and supplies. Has Timi rented an office space and furnished it?'

She was shocked. Yes, she had indicated that she'd help in Timi's business venture, but she thought the conversation only just started. She hadn't taken so much notice of the financial records after he blended their accounts and what she just heard from her father was inexcusable. She was embarrassed that her father was the one to call her attention to the financial mess. She was supposed to be the responsible Banigo child; the one that the others looked up to. She resolved to have a closed-door conversation with her husband. But, she couldn't bring herself to talk ill about him to her father.

In a soft voice to hide her fury, she explained that Timi must have mixed things up and she'd sort it out with him. She explained that the new office set-up was for Timi and they still needed Harry's help to properly set out the accounting side before the business started. Harry assured her he'd help with whatever was required of him.

The silence between them as they ate their meals was heavy. As the waiter cleared the table, Harry made small talk by asking about Preye's sisters and Miriam. He also told her he'd be travelling to Germany the following week for a business meeting to discuss dealership rights for a shoe brand.

'Shoes?' she queried. 'From Germany?'

'Yes, my dear. Their shoes are rock solid. If you still pray, this is the time I need your prayers, because I want this deal to scale through. The exchange rate is killing my car business and I've actually lost interest in selling second-hand,' Harry explained. 'I'm hoping to be the sole distributors of the shoe brand in Nigeria, so that gives me an edge. They are men's shoes though. I think I should send you a pair for your husband. What size does he wear?'

'Timi?' she asked. 'Don't bother about him.' She wasn't exactly pleased with Timi and she didn't think he deserved a shoe of any kind right now. Her phone beeped with an alert. She checked and realised she needed to get back to the office to review the proposal on her table, so she could make final updates to get it sent off to the client before the close of business. She brought the conversation to a close. 'But thanks for asking. 'Thanks for your help. I think we're getting on well. Should I settle the bill?'

He made a face at her. 'I'm not poor and I haven't spent a fraction of what I should have spent on you if I had been around when you were growing up. So I appreciate that I can make myself useful sometimes.'

Father and daughter embraced before Preye scurried back to

her office. The receptionist told her Lola had left for a meeting and might not get back to the office before close of business. Preye was relieved for that message as she didn't want to explain herself to Lola or anyone else in case they noticed how frantic she was. She had never thought she'd see the day that she wouldn't want to see Lola. She sat down in her swivel chair and called Timi's phone.

'Well, hello, Mrs Coker. I was just thinking about you. What's up?' Timi asked in his most lively voice.

'Were you going to tell me about your spending spree? You've spent all the cash in our account and I only just found out,' she stammered. She wished she could call him all sorts of names, yet she was afraid he might get madder than her.

'Calm down. I'll pay it back once I get some money from my dad. I made deposits for all the things I'll need for the office. I can't afford to be cheap. No harm, no foul. For your information, it's our money and you know it went for a good cause. I resigned today and I feel like celebrating my new adventure. My colleagues here have been highly supportive, unlike you. Since you're so furious at me, I'll give you time to cool off, so I'll be home late. I'll meet up Malik after work.' And probably shack up with Tina afterwards, he thought, before he clicked the red button on his phone.

Preye didn't like being told to calm down, especially knowing that she was right. And she didn't like that Timi got the last word in this instance, but she was helpless. She felt desperate when communication broke down. She decided going for a five kilometre run after work will help bring her mind back on track. She was relieved she had packed her running gear and especially now that there was no hurry to meet Timi at home.

CHAPTER SEVENTEEN

Feeling like a ten-ton weight had been lifted off his shoulders, Timi walked into Rukkees Joint in Yaba, where he had agreed to meet with his friends. It was the bar where Timi was gradually becoming more regular, hanging out with Martin. Barely lit with dim-coloured lights, it was filled with mostly young professionals, going by the loose ties most of the men wore on their monochrome shirts with rolled up sleeves. The patrons were either seated, bent over half-filled glasses of drinks or standing at different places cradling their cups. A few others were ensconced at random spots to jiggle their bodies to the music. Clattered voices of laughing, bragging, back-slapping, waiter-beckoning and arguing filled the air to compete with the loud serenading music which very few paid attention to.

Timi was here to celebrate. Working at Mason Bridge provided him with experience and paid the bills, but working for someone else didn't make sense to him. He liked being the decision maker and he was remarkably confident that he'd hit it big.

Growing up, his parents had consistently told him he was the greatest and could achieve anything he wanted to; they had also praised him at every turn, except the one time they fell out when his father sacked him. As an only child, he had never needed to share the spotlight with anyone and that was what working for other people had foisted on him.

'I've done it, Bro. I gave my notice at Mason Bridge today, so it's time to celebrate.' Timi waved down the waiter and ordered a bottle of champagne and some bottles of beer.

'Congratulations. That takes some serious guts and I don't know if I have what it takes. That's the problem with working at a bank. You're not quite sure what you can do with your life once you quit,' Malik responded ruefully. 'How does Preye feel about your big move?'

There was a long pause followed by a sigh, before Timi answered. 'She's fine with it, except that right now her emotions are out of control. I'm going out of my way to make things work, but she goes off at the slightest thing.'

'Sounds like hormones. Is she pregnant?' Malik asked.

'No, and I think that's part of the problem. I'm supportive and I tell her to be patient because I have no doubt we'll eventually have children. I'm trying to be the best husband I can be, but she's so used to doing things her way and ordering people around as a boss. Thank your stars you married Penny when she was younger.' Timi wanted Malik to be on his side. 'It's not an easy job to bend an oak tree.'

'Give it time, man. Penny and I had our rough patch initially. I simply decided to play the fool until she simmered down. I think you're lucky to have Preye and this phase will pass soon.' He patted Timi on the back. 'Let's not talk about wife matters. Let's just drink to new beginnings.' Malik tipped his glass to Timi's. 'To the latest MD in town.'

Timi's head was floating as he visualised himself swivelling in the leather chair he had ordered. 'Absolutely. To the latest genius who is about to shake the scene.'

Martin eventually showed up. With Martin in the mix, things were sure to get out of hand. Being single and unmarried, he often led Malik and Timi to precarious turfs. Timi enjoyed spending time with his friends, especially when they didn't judge him. The three friends chatted about politics, the economy and other random topics that crossed their minds.

Malik left earlier as he always did, leaving Timi and Martin at the bar. Timi was especially raucous because he was celebrating his professional independence. He did like Martin and switched to beers after they finished the bottle of champagne. He was soon tipsy enough to get flirtatious with the lady who had been dancing alone beside him and beckoning with her twinkling eyes. Preye drifted into his mind for some time until after his third bottle of beer when thoughts of her vanished along with his good judgement.

He finally gave in to the mixture of testosterone and endorphins surging from his head to his veins and ended up having sex with the lady at the back of Martin's car.

*

Preye stepped out of the shower and put jasmine lotion all over her body because. It was Timi's favourite scent and she hoped she could turn the page after her annoyance with him about their finances but she wanted to turn the page. He had promised to reimburse the account once he received funds from his parents. She convinced herself that it made sense. Timi should have been a solicitor because he had a way of turning things around to his favour.

As she towel-dried her hair and slipped into her silk robe, she realised he was later than she had thought he'd be.

After closing from work, she had gone for a run for about forty five minutes and rushed back home so she wouldn't keep him waiting, after trying to reach him on the phone. But he hadn't been at home.

The wheat flour she had prepared for dinner was keeping warm in the cooler. She was tired and equally starving, but she didn't want to eat all by herself in case she started and he chose that time to walk in.

She poured herself a glass of non-alcoholic wine and went to sit at the dining table before she checked her phone for messages from her husband. He hadn't called since they last spoke five hours ago. Five hours. It was unlike him. She wished she knew a method of tracking his device as he had for her. It was silly that as an adult, she had someone tracking her whereabouts, but it wasn't worth resisting. Another argument was the last thing she needed. She flipped through the mails piled on the dining table and winced when she noticed a lot of unpaid bills in Timi's name. It wasn't a surprise; it was a pain. She had never given it much thought before marriage, but their organisational skills were vastly different. She was used to paying her bills when they came in and she had never missed a payment.

He wasn't exactly a slob, but he never hung up his jacket, and his clothes were usually scattered on the bedroom floor. Preye grabbed his black jacket, one out of so many, which was draped over the dining chair, so she could take it upstairs. She instinctively read a business card that fell out of the pocket. The pink business card didn't have any business description; just a name – Tina Alli, and a telephone number.

Preye flipped the card over. *You're the best. Let's do it again* was scribbled under the drawing of a heart shape. The words echoed loudly in Preye's ears and she dropped the card in horror. *Could the card be for Timi? Could he be cheating with this Tina? No! Maybe it's for someone else.* Her heart was racy as she picked the card again, unable to block the thoughts from her mind. But she remembered the several times he had been unable to reasonably explain where he was or what he was doing and when he wouldn't pick her calls the few times she had to call him. Like now!

Not for the first time, Preye wondered why he married her.

She knew he could have had his way with any other lady if he had wanted to. He only needed to switch on his enchanting smile and make himself seem uninterested to keep a fool like her glued on him. One for accepting responsibility, she tried to search deep in her heart to find out how she could have contributed to the way her relationship was swerving, but she hit a brick wall and retreated.

She placed the card on the dining table, sat down and poured another glass of wine. She kept looking at the card on the table. She bit her lips when the thought of calling the number on the card filtered into her mind. Unable to concentrate on anything else, she kept tapping the table with her nails, waiting for Timi to come home. She called his phone again, and again, but the calls went directly to voicemail as before.

If he answered, she had no idea what she'd say anyway, so it was just as well he didn't answer. After an hour and the bottle of wine was empty, she felt bloated and dozed off at the table.

*

Timi got home some minutes after midnight and tapped Preye. 'Did someone spike your wine? It looks like you had a bit too much to drink,' he gloated. He ignored the business card which was hard to miss. 'Come on, let's get you to bed.'

'I don't want to go to bed. I want to talk,' she said in a groggy voice. She wiped her face to wake up properly. 'Who is Tina Alli?'

'What about Tina?' He didn't hide his familiarity with the name as he picked up the card, smiling and turning it over in his hand. 'So you went through my coat pockets?'

'Since it's no secret, then you shouldn't mind telling me who she is and why she drew a heart on her pink card.' Preye ripped the card from his hand and slapped it down on the table. 'Are

you having an affair or was it just some cheap one-night-stand?'
She expected to hear a well-crafted lie.

'I've known her from way back, even before I met you and
we've remained friends. There's nothing more to it unless you
want to make it a big deal.' He twitched his upper lip to create a
callous smirk.

'Are you having an affair with her?' She shut her eyes to wait
for a direct yes or no response.

'I've told you what I have to tell you, or will you feel better
if I told you yes?'

'Oh, my God. So you don't deny it. Why did you marry me
if you weren't going to honour our wedding vows?' She tried to
still herself, but her body resisted and instead went into a
feverish shiver.

'Preye, you're getting overly emotional again. We can revisit
this topic later, but for now, I'm going to tuck you into bed.' He
practically dragged her up the stairs. Although she was mad and
would have resisted, she felt too tired and unwell to even
continue the argument. As much as she wanted to remain awake
to process what was going on in their marriage, she fell asleep
within minutes of closing her eyes. The last thing she
remembered was his warm stinking body snuggled up next to
her.

It was a sickening feeling.

*

Timi sat at the kitchen table after brewing coffee. Preye would
surely sleep for an extra hour or longer if he had any luck. She
was beautiful, with a hot body, gorgeous hair, hypnotic eyes, and
she was smart. He had known she was the one for him the
moment he laid eyes on her.
Unfortunately, she wasn't acting like a wife was supposed to. He

needed to find a way to turn her around. He hated being challenged and that was what drew him to Tina. Tina was compliant and practically adored him. She had just finished university and was looking for a job. Whenever he gave her money, she cherished it and made him feel like a king. Unlike Preye.

He had always gone out of his way to impress his wife, but it seemed being married made her less impressionable. It was her strong-headedness and financial independence that was robbing them of the joy they deserved in their marriage and he felt he needed to find a way to keep her separated from the bad influences in her life, to make her his ideal wife. If she became pregnant, maybe she'd slow down at work and stay more at home. *And why wasn't she pregnant by the way?* he wondered. He knew he wasn't the sterile one because he had gotten multiple girls pregnant in the past.

Preye's phone beeped on the countertop. He had learnt the access pin by looking over her shoulder. He had resisted monitoring her phone activity up until now, but he decided it was time for drastic measures. She needed help becoming the perfect wife and being the husband, it was his responsibility to make that happen. He ran upstairs to check on her and found her snoring. He returned to pour himself another cup of coffee.

With her phone in his hand, he scrolled through her recent calls and texts. He deleted anything he thought unnecessary for her to see. It would be too obvious that he had been tampering with her device if he deleted all of Lola' calls, so he just thinned them out. He did the same with calls from Aisha and her sister Tonye. Erefa was too busy with the baby to call much. The text messages gave him an insight into what Preye was telling her friends and how they responded. He read the group chat with Lola and Aisha, and found it troubling.

Lola: Remember Cassidy's Monday's 6. Tradition. Don't

miss.

Aisha: Cassidy's every Mon. *No chng just cuz you r hitched.*

Lola: Need a ride?

Lola: Where R U.

Lola: Really? U suck.

Aisha: Call me. I'm worried No show?

Lola: Does your husband have you tied up to the bed.

Lola: Sorry I'm drunk but 4 taking you out there, Timi is …. fill in the dots.

Lola: That's bcos Aisha *sez* I shouldn't say anything negative.

Lola: Aisha won't say but she's starting to think something is not right too.

Aisha: Call me

Lola: Which one of us. I'm right here. It's P *dt's* missing in action. Call me. Love u.

The text messaging between friends went on and on. It seemed one of them had something to say every day. He wasn't surprised about Lola's comments; he already knew she was a bad influence on Preye, but Preye wouldn't heed his advice to sack her.

Aisha: Spa day again, girls? Adamu and Ashe are going to his mum's. I'm eight months in so it has to be Saturday 9/8.
Lola: Count me in.
Preye: I'll be there. Details? I NEED A BREAK.

On reading Preye's response, he wanted to throw the phone at the wall. She hadn't cleared the plans with him. Worse was her declaration in capital letters that she needed a break. He was running out of time but there was a voice message from Lola from the previous night.

'Preye, it's me. Now I know something's wrong. Is it Timi? Of course it's Timi. Please ring me and tell me how I can help. I want to tell you about Sammy. He's the man I'm dating. Funny, I met him at the market. He's a soldier, if you can believe that. But he's a nice man. I can't even talk to

you at work anymore. What's up, Omo girl?'

Timi heard Preye making her way down the hall. He raised his index finger to delete the calls and voicemail and threw the phone on the counter and started humming a song.

Preye stood at the door, looking at him expectantly, hoping he'd say something about last night. But he didn't. Instead he poured a cup of coffee, added some milk and pushed it to her.

She collected it and sat beside him. She'd play along with him just to have some peace of mind. 'Thanks.' She took a sip. 'We need some foodstuff. I'm going to the market later today, so let me know what you want me to buy,' she said in a soft voice.

He casually looked up and nodded his head. If they had been playing a game, he was sure he was winning; she had likely realised the problems in their marriage were due to her overly emotional state. Her inability to adapt was causing their divide, and hopefully, she was ready to change.

*

Preye was tired as she drove to the Mile 2 market. The pains in her side and abdomen had only subsided a little. She had avoided starting a quarrel with Timi because she lacked the energy. It was easier to go along with his way of doing things and hope that their relationship would improve once they started a family.

Her options seemed limited because she didn't want Timi to leave her the way her dad had left her mum. Maybe she needed to slow down. Her mother and her siblings repeatedly told her that she was like Miriam in so many ways, especially with her doggedness. And she couldn't help wondering if it was her mother's inflexibility that chased her father away.

She started to think that this was how most marriages were – happy on the outside, with a trapped woman inside. That was how she felt – trapped!

'Hello, Mum,' Preye answered. The phone had started ringing just as she arrived at the parking lot. 'Nice surprise. I'm at the market, getting ready to fill the freezer for the week.'

'Just wait until you have little ones. Doing the weekly shopping is near impossible with toddlers tugging at your skirt,' Miriam said. 'Speaking of little ones, any news?'

'No, but I'm going to see the doctor soon. Those pains I used to have back then seem to have come back. I've been sick off and on,' Preye replied. 'The only problem is you're not here to comfort me.' She tried to joke to hide her pain.

'Your husband should be doing a better job at that. Let me know if you want me to come over. And don't put off going to see the doctor with the excuse that you're busy with work,' Miriam advised. 'Tell me how your first eight months of marriage have been. Don't be surprised that I'm ticking the calendar for you. I was crazy in love with your father during that first year and he couldn't get his hands off me after I had you.'

'Mum! I can do without the details. We are doing alright. It's just that being far away makes me feel like I've been cut off from everyone. I've been busy at the office too. Timi is trying to set up his own business and I get drawn into that also. But we're fine. We have busy schedules. It's fine,' Preye said, hoping it was enough to satisfy her mother.

'Not the glowing description I'd hoped for. You and Timi looked madly in love the last time I saw you. What happened?'

'Nothing. Like I said, it's fine. We'll soon come for a visit. I'd love to talk some more, but I have to get into the market and get this chore over with.'

Preye hated lying to her mother, but she didn't want to pull anyone else into her turmoil. It was temporary and it wouldn't be fair to trigger an alarm on issues that she couldn't even explain.

CHAPTER EIGHTEEN

Her pain subsided over the next few weeks, but Preye still needed to see the doctor to find out why she hadn't conceived. Timi had found a way to slot fertility issues into their conversations almost every day, hovering on the edge of accusing her, but she resisted biting his bait. She was merely going through the motions with him and he was walking on eggshells, expecting her to erupt at any moment.

His non-denial of cheating with Tina had been a turning point for her and she'd probably never be able to look at him the same way. As always, he had tried to romance her out of it, but each attempt to sweep her off her feet had been politely declined.

She had missed several group runs she used to lead for Roadrunners because she couldn't make the trip down to Ikeja on weekends, and she couldn't organise any run during the week because Timi insisted on picking her up from work since they shared only one car. She couldn't have her fun runs anymore because of the atmospheric dust in and around her neighbourhood.

She felt as if she was living her life in front of a dam that was threatening to break.

She skipped the lift and ran up to her office. The stairs were her only form of exercise without Roadrunners and her fun runs. Bounding up the stairs two at a time, she scared Tobi when she nearly knocked him over on the stairs.

'Going my way?' Tobi jested as she slowed down. 'You saved me a trip to your office which was going to be my first stop. Lagos Illuminated is getting a community service medal for the volunteer work their employees did with painting the streets. It's the best PR they've ever gotten and their MD is thrilled. I assume you'd want to be there. I'll drive.'

Preye walked with Tobi as she caught her breath. 'I'm going to leave that one to you. I'm feeling a bit unwell.'

'Seriously, Preye. This is your baby. It's your idea yielding tangible results. You normally rock this stuff and I know the MD would love to see you there. He needs someone by his side to make him look good.'

'Have you seen my office?' Preye smiled. 'My inbox is overflowing. Lola loves going out into the field. Ask her.'

'Lola isn't here for a few days. She's on leave. She said she's going on a romantic escape with Sammy. Everybody knows about Sammy now. Your friend can hardly keep anything to herself. But I don't blame her. He seems to be a good guy, unlike some of the men she's dated.'

Preye felt a pang of guilt because she didn't know about Lola's new boyfriend, yet Tobi and others knew. She recalled Lola had mentioned him, but she hadn't paid much attention. It seemed to Preye that she was failing at all fronts with a growing pile of disappointments - at home, at work and even with her best friend.

When they reached the fifth floor, Preye and Tobi turned to different directions towards their offices.

'Oh, Preye,' Tobi called out and she turned around. 'I think Lola is in the office. Her light is on. Just in case you want to drop in on her before she leaves.' Tobi winked. He cared about Preye and she could push him away, but Lola was a different story.

'Thanks, Tobi.'

Preye changed her course and walked towards Lola's office. She never felt anything but joy and pleasant anticipation anytime she walked towards Lola's office. Now, she bore a sense of dread because she was afraid Lola would see into her sad soul. She could lie about Timi and her marriage to just about anyone, but not Lola.

Preye heard Lola humming to an old familiar tune of Evelyn Champagne King's *I'm in love* and she hummed with her.

Lola straightened up from looking into her drawers. 'Mrs Coker! This is a surprise. I'm trying to get out of here because Sammy has a few days off and he's taking me away.'

'I heard about him. Tobi says he's a great guy, which means something, coming from big brother Tobi. My life has been bonkers and I'm sorry that I haven't been around to hear the good news,' Preye apologised.

Lola stared straight at Preye to wear down the barricade of aloofness behind Preye's eyes. 'You were around, I told you about him, but you didn't hear me. I called at least a dozen times and never got a reply. I've tried catching up with you in the office, but you're never around.' She edged close to Preye. 'Even at the time you were busy starting this business, you had the time to listen then, but now it's different and I'm worried.'

Preye hated keeping things from Lola, but if she opened up a little, everything would come flooding out. 'Don't worry, I'm good, everything is good. It's the stress of living on the other side of town, but Timi and I have settled into a comfortable groove. Apart from that, I've been having some painful episodes and…'

'Aisha says you haven't been to Roadrunners,' Lola interrupted. Her phone beeped and she checked that it was Sammy.

'Are the two of you gossiping about me again?' Preye snapped and threw her hands on her hips.

'No! We're just two good friends who are concerned and trying to figure out what is wrong with you.'

Preye insisted again that she was fine, and Lola still refused to buy it. But Lola was in a hurry to leave. She reminded Preye about their upcoming school reunion the following weekend and threatened that if Preye didn't come with them, she and Aisha would camp out on her front steps until she opened up. Preye didn't doubt that Lola would pull such a stunt, so she promised to be there.

They hugged goodbye before Lola breezed off to meet Sammy. Preye hadn't felt so comforted in a long time as much as when she was in Lola's soft arms. It was perhaps the first time that Lola was the first to stop hugging.

Lola looked deep into Preye's eyes and sensed the tension behind the brave front. 'I'm here for you, *Omo* girl. I love you.'

'I love you too. Have an amazing time and send pictures.'

Lola had a few minutes before hopping into Sammy's car, and she called Aisha to tell her about the encounter with Preye. Aisha complained that Lola and Preye had caused her to cancel their spa day and she had suspected Preye wouldn't have showed up anyway. She told Lola her scheduled caesarean section was a few days after the reunion because she didn't want to miss the show.

Aisha mentioned she had left a message for Preye, but Preye hadn't responded. At school, they had been tagged The Three Musketeers, and whatever was happening with Preye was of concern to both Aisha and Lola. There had never been secrets between them before. She assured Lola she'd try to dash down to Preye's office before the office closed.

On returning to her office, Preye dropped her head on the desk behind the closed door. If she didn't go for the reunion, her friends would probably realise what a sham her life was becoming, unless she could pull it together.

It had been close to an hour since she got to work and she hadn't received a ring from Timi. She practically counted down the minutes until her phone rang after about ten minutes. 'Hello, I'm here, safe and busy working,' she said in a monotone voice, after picking Timi's call.

Timi said he was going back home to pick some documents he forgot. He had a meeting with his lawyer today. Preye pictured him in the car, devising ways to make her life miserable. 'I think I'll keep the name as Timi's Communications. I can visualise it on letterhead and on the centre page of The Guardian. What do you think?' His voice was enthusiastic.

She had told him what she felt; that it wasn't catchy enough. But now, she thought it was perfect for a narcissistic husband. 'Sounds very good. Oh, I have my school reunion coming up and I'll be going. The flyer should be somewhere on the desk with the date and time.'

'Let me guess. You're going with Lola and Aisha,' he said, with an attitude.

'Yes,' Preye said flatly.

'I'll drive you and pick you up,' Timi said, before hanging up.

With a trembling chin, Preye slammed her phone down on the table and allowed a gale of hot tears to stream down her face.

*

With a stroke of luck, Preye was able to convince Timi that it made sense for her to go to the reunion from her mother's house if she closed early from work and since it was Friday, Timi could use the car. When he agreed without putting up a fight, she thought he probably had plans with Tina or some other women with little or no scruples. She left the office at 2.00p.m and Lola picked her up from Miriam's flat.

Preye and Lola arrived at Araba Halls in Victoria Island for the reunion and stayed in the car to freshen up their make-up before entering the hall. Lola wore a black jumpsuit with flared legs, a plunging neckline, and a gold belt. A pair of red loafers and gold hoop earrings finished off her look, which she pulled off fabulously. Lola didn't wear heels much because the men she dated were usually shorter than her. Sammy was an exception at six feet three inches.

Preye wore a fitted red halter-neck lace dress on gold stiletto sandals – a look Timi would abhor. She had moved some of her clothes to her mother's house because she feared Timi may toss them out or rip them off one day. Her short dress and her perfect hairdo should disguise her pain and portray how easy-going her life was. She hoped Lola couldn't see beyond her mask.

The two friends walked into the reunion venue which was filled with people they hadn't seen in over fifteen years. The hall was well lit with crystal chandeliers spiralling from the high ceilings. The setting could have passed for a wedding reception, except that there were no high chairs for the bride and groom. Round tables were well laid out with gold chiavari chairs, and topped with brown and cream table clothes. A backdrop of artificial silk flowers was set up in a corner and people milled around it to take turns for pictures. There was an open bar, and right beside it was a table of exotic fruits banquet depicting the Regency University logo. The music boomed thunderously and it was difficult to hold a reasonable conversation in low tones, so the voices gabbled over one another like torrential rainfall.

Canapés and drinks were being served round by waiters and Lola picked a glass of red wine, while Preye went with a malt drink. They introduced themselves to anyone who cared to ask and joined casual conversations wherever possible as they looked around for a vacant table.

They eventually found their way to a table for four. Lola put her bag on one of the extra chairs, to reserve a space for Aisha. 'Look around you, I'm rocking the hell out of this look and so are you. We're the hottest babes here. If you manage to put a smile on that face, you might even be approachable. What happened? Did Timi knock out your front teeth so you can't smile?' Lola raised her voice to joke.

Preye jabbed Lola in the arm. 'Timi has never laid a hand on me. Don't make a joke of domestic violence. That's a serious issue affecting a lot of homes these days.'

As the words flowed from Preye's mouth, she wondered if she wasn't going through a form of violence with her torturous life. Unlike with most domestic violence victims, her own scars were not physical. They were well hidden, etched deep down her soul and scarring the depth of her whole being. She drew a deep breath as she reckoned that after a cocktail or two, Lola would delve further into her private life. She was confident that she could deal with the mess she had created and as Timi told her, she was responsible for it.

Pausing on their chatter, Preye and Lola followed everyone's head to watch a lady breeze into the hall. She was an embodiment of *bling* - everything about her shouted *notice me*. She moved gracefully amongst the crowd, cheering and smiling and greeting everyone along her path as if she was the appointed hostess. Lola ogled and asked Preye if she knew the lady. Preye shook her head, grinding her lips. They went back to their small talk about the antics Zara had been pulling on Sammy.

They soon realised the bling lady was coming in their direction. Her figure-flattering evening gown sauntered with her as she landed in front of Lola and Preye. The lady patted Lola on the shoulder, and acknowledged Preye cheerfully. She had beautiful lively eyes and she was all smiles. She introduced herself as a businesswoman and said she remembered Lola, although she couldn't remember Lola's name. Lola and Preye introduced themselves in return. The bling lady told them she got married a year after she left the university and had five children. She casually mentioned her husband's name and Preye recognised that he was a famous politician who was also in the gubernatorial race. The lady paused, waiting for them to respond to the latest information about being a potential first lady.

Lola wasn't in the mood to play any superficial game, so she started turning her back to the lady, but changed her mind.

'Nice to meet you again. We are both single,' Lola mockingly retorted, then turned her back, leaving Preye to face the lady. The lady's face dropped. She summed Preye up with her eyes, shrugged and retreated elegantly without saying a word.

'That was uncalled for,' Preye admonished Lola. 'Although I enjoyed that look of surrender on her face. And by the way, I'm not single,' she laughed.

'Well, sorry Mrs Coker. That was the only thing I could think of to get that snob off you. You should thank me.'

Tobi Abass walked in then and waved at them. They waved back and he took a detour from walking towards them and soon found himself a crowd to mingle with.

Preye saw someone she knew and delved into her handbag to pick some business cards before she excused herself to greet him. She was soon dragged into conversations with other people, while Lola stayed on at the table, so they wouldn't lose their seats. Lola nodded at people in the distance and swayed to the music. A man she dated in her second year came to say hello to her. He told Lola he couldn't stay because his wife was also at the reunion, explaining that his wife was an alumnus too, but of another class. He ordered another glass of wine for Lola and gave her his business card. Lola was grateful to see him leave.

Preye returned and the two friends resumed their light talk as if they hadn't been interrupted.

As Lola started on her third glass of wine, people whispered and turned their heads to look at the owner of the distended belly who wore a yellow silky dress that was draped smoothly over her shoulders and stopped just below her thighs to reveal her shapely leg. It was Aisha. She walked down the hall, nodding randomly with a warm smile that lit her eyes and a constant slight wave of her right hand like that of the British Queen.

Immediately she got to Lola and Preye, she dropped into the chair reserved for her before emitting a gale of air from her lungs as if she had been holding her breath under water. 'Babes, *how you dey*? You look fab.' Aisha blew a kiss.

'You as well, Aisha. Like you always do,' Preye's eyes sparkled with pleasure.

'You lie! I'm as big as a house.' Aisha turned Lola's chin towards her with her long elegant hand. '*Omo* girl, time to switch to water for a bit. Drinking more alcohol than water makes you look older that me.' Aisha raised her index finger to Lola to scold her. It was a sign between the three friends to signify that they weren't pleased. Aisha had a way of calming Lola. The two had grown especially close when Lola moved in with Aisha after Lola's divorce. She possessed a gentle touch that worked with Lola like magic.

Lola went to get a glass of water and Aisha turned to Preye. 'It's been like forever. The last time I saw you, I was this short.' She raised her hand to the height of the table. I'm sure Lola would have told you that we're worried about you, because you've simply disappeared. You're still gone, even though you're sitting right in front of me.'

'I'm here. You and Lola are overreacting. I'm married and maybe it's taking longer than expected to get well settled, but I'm fine,' Preye insisted.

'This is for you, not me.' Lola handed the water to Aisha. 'Has Preye said she's fine yet?'

Preye stared daggers at Lola and walked out. Her friends

predictably followed. The trio sat on a bench outside watching a slight drizzle that started as if it had been cued for them, but they were shielded by an extended canopy, although it didn't stop Preye from getting wet. Her tears had started to fall; the dam behind the stoic frame had finally given way.

Aisha put her arm around Preye. 'It was a valiant effort, but Lola and I knew you were dying inside. Your skin is sallow and your eyes are vacant. What's up?'

Preye sniffled. 'Do I look that bad? I thought my makeup did the trick.'

'*Omo* girl, the bags under your eyes are over-packed,' Lola joked.

'I know how the two of you felt before I got married. I overheard your private conversation on the stairs the night of my wedding.' Preye collected herself and for the first time, she said out loud what she had been thinking since the honeymoon. 'I shouldn't have married Timi.' Once she started, it was as if she had needed to have an open-heart surgery by emitting the poison she had swallowed as she recounted how miserable she had been in her marriage with Timi's high-handedness, the insults, the cruel pranks, his financial recklessness and the Tina issue.

After what felt like a long confession for purgation, Preye felt lighter, knowing she no longer needed to hide behind a veil of marital joy or fulfilment. Now that she had poured everything out in the open, she didn't need to put on a brave face even though she felt stronger.

Aisha and Lola didn't say, *I told you so*. Instead, they offered their unconditional support to their friend. Lola ranted that she could drive to Preye's house to beat Timi black and blue, but Aisha glared at her to shut her up.

Aisha told Preye she didn't have to take all the rubbish Timi was dishing out. 'You may think you're coping, but I'm concerned about your mental health. This is not a healthy relationship and it's not doing you any good. Something has to give.'

'You can't go back to that house,' Lola insisted. 'Tell him you need a few days away to do some thinking. Actually, you don't need to give him any reason. Let's see if he'd come looking for you if you disappear. I stayed with Aisha when things got bad in my marriage. It saved my life and Zara's too. I want to pay it forward. Stay with me. You can bunk with Zara. She'd love it. I know Aisha's place is bigger but you can't go there. So that Adamu doesn't start thinking that all of Aisha's friends are liabilities that always need to be rescued from their husbands,' Lola concluded.

They smiled at Lola's attempt to make light of the situation.

'It's a good idea. Although, I would have offered, but I'm having this baby in less than two weeks. I doubt I'd make the best hostess,' Aisha apologised. 'And I'm sure you know this has nothing to do with Adamu.'

'No, I don't need to leave. Not yet. I'll be fine,' Preye said.

'I'm starting to hate the word, fine. That's nonsense. I'll go to your mum if you don't stay with me for a few days. I'll embarrass you. You know how easy it is for me to do that.' Lola wasn't to be messed with when she was protecting loved ones.

'Okay, but I'm sure my mum suspects too. Like the two of you.' Preye sighed. 'I wish I had told her earlier, but I didn't want to admit that I couldn't manage my own marriage. I feel like a failure. That is what I feel like. A failure,' she sniffed and swallowed her sobs. 'I agree with you Lola. Staying around Timi makes me lose all sense of self-confidence. I can go home and pack a bag, but I want to go alone. I know …' Preye was cut off by Lola, who told her they were scared for her safety and volunteered to go with her. 'I hear you, but Timi isn't going to be physically violent. He's a coward at heart.'

Unrelenting, Lola pinched her nose at Preye. 'You're just too naïve for your own good. And Aisha is too *ajebo* to tell you the way it is.'

The rain intensified and with her legs exposed, Preye was already feeling cold. She got up, prompting the others to follow suit. They ran back inside to join the party.

Preye's dam had broken and she had survived. She felt empowered to save herself; she'd no longer be a victim to Timi Coker's controlling ways.

CHAPTER NINETEEN

She stood before the door and tried to collect her thoughts before entering the house. For too long, she had been blaming everything negative on herself; she didn't recognise the woman she was becoming. Her confidence was deteriorating and she had failed to find satisfaction, regardless of where she turned. Running had become a chore and work at Beta had become unexciting, unlike what it used to be. She put her hand on the door handle and walked inside.

Timi was in a towel. His perfect abdominal muscles glistened. 'You're early. How did you get home?'

'I took a cab. I won't be here long, so if you have a date, don't change plans for me. Maybe the date has already started, and she's still in the shower. If that's the case, tell her to throw on a towel because I have to grab a few things from the bathroom.' She removed her shoes.

'What are you talking about? There's no one in the shower. Where are you going?' he asked as he looked her up and down. Her dress, in his opinion, was inappropriate and not something he would have let her out of the house wearing. There was little doubt Preye knew that, and it had something to do with why she wore it.

'I'm going to Lola's for a few days to save myself from having a nervous breakdown. You've been putting me through hell and I need a break. Or let me put it this way, I've become too sensitive and I've been putting myself through hell. Because it's never you, it's me, I accept. But I can't stay with you until I work things through in my mind.'

She braced herself from letting emotions take over. Timi had kept accusing her of being too sensitive. *Who wouldn't be, if subjected to emotional torture every day?* She squeezed her hands so tightly that her fingernails nearly tore into the skin on her palm.

'You went to your reunion dressed like this? You know what you look like? *Ashewo!* How are you different from those girls lining the streets? Anyway, I don't believe you're going to Lola's. Maybe you picked up your old uni crush. You're pathetic, Preye.' The tightening of his face and the anger from his eyes betrayed his need to dominate and be revered.

She wanted to find a padlock to keep his mouth shut forever. Instead she remained calm and walked past him towards the stairs, her shoes in her hands. Although she betrayed no emotion, her mind was in a flurry, not knowing what to expect from him. 'Believe what you want. I am going to Lola's and don't bother coming after me,' she warned. She was surprised at how easy the words flowed from her mouth.

He snickered. 'It doesn't work that way. You're my wife and I have the right to be anywhere you are. Mine, you took the vows to love me forever. You can't blame everything on me. I've told you, you need professional help.'

She walked into the bedroom and threw clothes into her cabin suitcase. She couldn't get away from Regalia Court fast enough. The smell of Timi made her sick; it wasn't the cologne or the soap he used; it was his natural smell. His looming presence was like a dark cloud hanging over her and refusing to move. She wasn't sure what she'd accomplish by leaving, but she knew it was a step towards freedom. It was something she needed to do, to be herself.

Next, she went into the bathroom with Timi following

closely behind her. She got her make-up bag and threw in her electric toothbrush before reaching for the charger.

Timi grabbed her forearm. 'You can't leave me without a charger. That's mine, anyway.'

She snapped her arm back. 'Fine, I'll buy a new charger.'

'Planning on a shopping spree? Don't go spending money we don't have,' he mocked.

She remembered her father commending her on creating a solid wall between her finances and those of Beta. Thank God, Timi couldn't touch that money. In the past few weeks, she had talked herself out of the thought of asking Tobi if she could get some money to buy another car, just so she could determine her own schedule without disturbing Timi. 'I'll call in a couple of days. If I come back, it's going to be on my terms.' She wheeled her suitcase towards the front door.

'Preye,' he called before she could walk out the door.

'I can't be talked out of this. What?' Preye replied.

'This drama bullshit is unbecoming and it makes you look desperate. I've been meaning to talk to you about divorce because I can't put up with your emotional instability anymore. Now, I've told you. Since you want to leave, I guess it works out fine for both of us. Go crying to your friends if it makes you happy, but I'm calling your bluff. Keep walking.'

Preye did keep walking, to the cab that was waiting to take her to Lola's house.

Timi closed the door behind her and kicked the dining table before going to the refrigerator to grab a drink. Under no circumstances was she going to get the last word in this debacle. She was going to find the world cold and lonely without him, and soon she'd realise that marriage to him wasn't so bad. He was sure she'd soon be longing to come back to her spacious home in Regalia Court.

*

She didn't cry during the over one hour ride to Lola's home, as she had expected she might. She was all tapped out and unable to shed a drop of moisture. Divorce was a surprise coming from Timi because she hadn't realised her marriage was that fragile. It had crumbled before her eyes and now she was looking at starting over as a divorced woman. She'd need strength to help her face he world. And she needed to rebuild her confidence before tackling that new reality. The cab arrived at Lola's apartment building.

She paid the driver and walked towards freedom, even if it was for a few days.

Lola pulled open the door as Preye walked up the stairs, dragging her suitcase. Zara ran out to help Preye with her things. Zara was thrilled to be sharing her room with her favourite auntie. Preye felt deeply loved and welcome, much more than she had ever felt anytime she walked into the house she shared with Timi at Regalia Court.

'Thank God you're here. I was going to send Sammy over to get you. What happened with the husband?' Lola asked after Zara ran to her room to get it ready for her sleepover with Preye. It was way past Zara's bedtime, but the little girl had pleaded to be allowed to stay up late when she was told Preye was coming over.

'He asked for a divorce.' Preye laughed at herself until a pang of embarrassment came over her as she told Lola about her husband's last minute request for divorce. That was probably his intention. Not only would she have to admit that her marriage had failed, she also had to admit that it was his idea to end it. It was a failure she'd have to carry around for the rest of her life; the scar of a failed marriage like her mum's.

'You can stay here for as long as you want. If Aisha hadn't taken us in, Zara and I would have been on the streets. At least you don't have a child with him yet,' Lola said.

The comment stung like a dagger through Preye's heart. Lola covered her mouth as soon as the comment passed her lips; it wasn't the time or place to bring it up. Preye thought her failure to conceive was the central issue of her marriage collapsing. She was heartbroken, and Timi had used that to make her feel inadequate. The regrets and self-blame came flooding back and she couldn't help but second guess herself. Lola could see Preye's despair and came to her aid.

'I'm sorry, I shouldn't have said that. You know that hurts me as much as it hurts you. I feel like a stupid cow now, and you should take me to task for it or smack me. You're too nice, though. What you need to do is get busy and stay busy. Roadrunners misses you, and so do your friends and family. Then we have Beta, your masterpiece that needs you back at the controls. The Preye I knew never stopped moving, and it's time you get moving again.' Lola stomped her foot on the floor for effect.

It wasn't the first time Lola would make Preye her project. After Kevin died, Lola had been determined to pull Preye out of her grief by getting her to go out and suggesting she dipped her toes into the dating pool too soon. Lola was the architect of her last two catastrophic relationships before Timi. Eventually, Preye had met Timi organically at the Roadrunner's office, at a time she thought she couldn't handle any more dating dramas.

'I'll reconnect as soon as I'm ready. I just need a few days to chill,' Preye responded in a lifeless voice. She wasn't keen on facing anyone just yet; not even people at work.

Lola sighed. She didn't like not getting her way, and it was at times like this that Preye saw a tiny glimpse of why Lola's relationships tended to fizzle. However, Lola was getting better at listening to the other side of the argument and not pushing so hard.

'I get it. I'll give you a couple of days to relax, but after that, you have to take the steps to reach for the things that make you happy.'

'Deal. I'll call Tobi in the morning to let him know I'll be off for a couple of days. Now I think I have a date with a certain little girl,' Preye switched the topic with a smile. 'We're going to experiment with my make-up. I have some samples in my bag, and we're going to have some fun.'

'Oh, God. You're going to spoil Zara,' Lola phone beeped. 'That's Sammy. I'll go downstairs to say hello to him. Or maybe we would go for a quick bite, now that you're here and you can keep an eye on Zara.'

Preye rolled her eyes at Lola mischievously. 'It's past ten. Are you sure you can do with only a bite?' she teased. 'And by the way, hope you're not planning to turn me into the baby-sitter. I don't trust you.'

'You never know. How else do you want to pay for my rescue service?' Lola chirped. 'I'll see you in the morning if you're asleep by the time I return.'

*

Timi lay in bed, considering his next move in the drama Preye was orchestrating. It was drama he hadn't expected in their short marriage. He had thought once they got married, they would start having children straight away and live a life similar to his parents'. Her inability to conceive had made matters worse.

The signs that Preye wouldn't easily adhere to his image of a good marriage had been there when they were dating, but he had thought they would overcome it in time. She saw his gentle nudging about her wardrobe, career and friends as attempts to control her, yet they were meant for her good. What married woman dresses provocatively for any man other than her husband? It sends the wrong signals to the wrong men. What kind of woman chooses a career over children and the man she vowed to care for? What type of woman spends time with friends who have questionable morals? There was no one else to channel his questions to, but himself.

She wouldn't want to hear anything he was thinking. He knew she'd bring up his infidelity and claim that she'd never cheat because it was against her Christian faith. He had seen no alternative to seeking comfort with other women. She had forced his hand in that regard. She was frigid and becoming more so by the day.

He concluded that she'd weigh her options and come running back when she had proved her point. He was sure she couldn't really walk out of their marriage.

As he dwelt on his thoughts, his consciousness gradually declined and gave way to a sound sleep.

CHAPTER TWENTY

'Preye, is that you in the flesh?' Papa James exclaimed. He had been with Roadrunners from the beginning and was one of the oldest runners, at sixty-eight years of age. 'Excuse me. I should call you Mrs Coker. Congratulations by the way. I haven't seen you since you got married. I hope it's not a year yet?'

Preye was using a bench to stretch. It was the place the Roadrunners met for their mid-week group run. 'Keep calling me Preye, Papa James. You'll be shocked that I still use Banigo sometimes. It's a thing with my generation, I know. We moved to Festac, and I'm afraid I used that as my excuse to ignore running. Aisha was helping while I'm away, but she's got a baby due any day now. Will you do me a favour sir?'

'What's that?' Papa James asked.

'Please, let your friends know that I'm back and we've got some exciting events lined up. Roadrunners will be stronger than ever. I'm going to form some new groups and increase our outreach efforts. Many people are looking for running partners and don't know we exist. Please, I want you to invite more of your friends along so they can enjoy your level of fitness too,' Preye pleaded. My office will be helping out on campaign to push us out more and we'll be updating our logo and getting new t-shirts going.'

Papa James had joined Roadrunners with two of his widowed friends as an opportunity to keep fit, but more

217

especially to fraternise with the younger generation that made up Roadrunners. He had stopped coming when one of the other two died in a road accident. After many visits by some of the runners, he had resumed a few weeks after Preye's wedding.

Preye hooked up with a few runners to keep pace. She felt a sense of euphoria after the first two kilometres. It was a feeling she only got from running and never realised how much she had missed it. She slowed at the turnabout and was joined by Tobi Abass. They started brisk-walking together because Tobi had a hard time chatting while running. 'It's great seeing you back with the Roadrunners. No one can match your high spirits. It motivates those of us who are... um ... less athletically inclined.' Tobi caught his breath and smiled.

She slapped him on the back. 'You put more effort in than most. We started this club to have fun and not compare prowess. Enough about running. How are things at work?' she asked.

'Looking good,' he responded and nodded his head. 'You've been missed for sure, but Lola tells me that your situation might be changing.'

'I see gossip is still allowed at work,' Preye said with a tone of sarcasm.

'Come on, Boss. We're all friends, and we've been worried about you. You look better today than I've seen you in months. You were so tense last week that I thought you were going to snap.'

'Was it that noticeable?' she asked. She had thought her charade worked well.

'Yeah, I tried saying something, but it's never easy telling a woman that her make-up doesn't cover everything,' he chuckled, and Preye did too. 'My wife and daughters have taught me a thing or two in that regard. So some of us look beyond the surface.'

Back at the Roadrunners headquarters, Preye reviewed the planned activities with one of the volunteers. The lymphoma charity run was approaching and she needed to get sponsors lined up. She contacted the same people every year, and they expected a personal note from her. She acknowledged that they were gradually building a loyal base of patrons. And she didn't plan on disappointing them. It was important to her to carry on the tradition towards finding a cure for cancer, someday. Working for the greater good made her feel warm inside; the opposite of the way Timi had made her feel in the past months.

*

On Thursday, Lola made coffee early so she and Preye could have a cup before leaving together for work. The previous day, Lola had bought a few clothes for Preye, commenting that she was due for an independence-day wardrobe.

Preye gathered her hair up and wore one of the clothes – an olive green skirt suit with a frontal side slit. She felt mischievous and exhilarated that Timi would swear if he saw her.

The duo took off together after the school bus picked Zara up. Preye went right to her office, and saw a card and a beautiful bouquet of wildflowers on her desk. She knew immediately that they weren't from Timi.

To Our Fearless Leader

Hugs

– The Beta Crew –

She turned around to find Tobi and Lola standing by the door to her office, smiling. 'Thank you both. It's just what I need to keep me steady on the right foot.' She looked at Lola. 'Will you set up a general meeting at your convenience? I have something I want to say to the amazing people working here. I should be giving the flowers and not receiving them,' she said, dipping her head into the flowers to inhale the fragrance.

'I'll get on that. Everyone knows you haven't been at full capacity and their generosity and hard work is a testament that you hire right.'

Tobi chipped in. 'What's the meeting about?' He waved down as Preye took a reflective posture with her head lifted up and finger tapping her lips. 'Never mind. Lola, over to you then.'

Although the company was doing well, Preye knew she had been mentally disconnected. But she vowed that it wouldn't happen again. Since the formation of the company, she and Tobi hadn't taken much of a salary increase, but that would temporarily change now, until she could get on solid footing. A young company needed to have visible strong leadership, which required her to be self-confident. She had allowed Timi to take that from her, and it may take time to rebuild it.

Ahead of the meeting, she had a brief catch-up with Tobi to pour out her thoughts about the projects on her mind. Away from walking on ice, she had spent the past few days reflecting and dipping into her creative depth.

The staff meeting was scheduled for 3.00p.m and she approached the boardroom with the optimistic outlook she was known for. She thanked everyone individually and told them about the exciting projects ahead. The employees were motivated, and their concerns were put to rest after her renewed commitment. She promised a return to her open-door policy and invited employees to come to her if they had any issues, so they could work on solutions together. She opened up the meeting for questions and invited Tobi to answer some of the questions. After the meeting, she felt as if she had reclaimed an important piece of her life.

She was eating lunch at her desk when her phone rang. Timi's name appeared on the screen. 'Hello.' There was no tone to her voice as she answered the call.

'Hi, Preye. I haven't heard from you and I wanted to make sure you were okay and you've been getting to work alright. You know I turned off the tracking app, so I don't know your whereabouts,' His words were refrained unlike the commanding stance she was used to. 'And I wanted to know if I should drop your car.'

His voice made her wince. She didn't know if it was a feeling of missing him or one of repulsion. 'Is that all?' she asked coldly.

'Yes. It's quiet here and I miss you. I hope you'll come home soon. Any idea what day that that might be?' he asked cautiously.

'No. I'm getting together with my sisters at my mum's house tomorrow night. You'll see me when you see me. In the meantime, don't worry about me. I can survive without the car, thanks for asking. I was perfectly capable before you entered my life. I'm busy now, so I have to go and I'm sure you would be busy with your divorce plans too. Take care.' She hanged up before he could say anything else. She shook her head to rid herself of any thoughts of him. She desperately needed to keep moving forward.

*

Tonye was surprised to find Preye in Miriam Banigo's kitchen when she walked in, carrying a pack of pizza.

'She's alive!' Tonye mocked Preye. 'I heard you were coming but I wasn't going to believe it until I saw you with my eyes. Timi unhooked the handcuffs, I assume,' she said flippantly. She had never seen Timi acting anything but loving towards Preye, but she had sensed that something was off about him from day one.

The Banigo girls had a tradition of meeting up at Miriam's house once in two months. Preye hadn't attended any of the meet-up since her wedding, except for the time she stayed over for Tamara's christening about four months ago.

'Tonye,' Miriam drawled Tonye's name. 'That's not a nice thing to say.' She gave Tonye a berating stare before heading for the kitchen.

'She's right, Mum.' Preye lifted her hand in Tonye's defence 'I'm staying at Lola's for a few days and yes, it has something to do with Timi. I don't want tonight to be about piling the insults on him. I've had enough of that with Lola, so I prefer to just enjoy your company,' Preye pleaded. It was unlikely that the main subject wouldn't be Timi, but at least she had tried.

Erefa walked in with Tamara napping on her shoulder. 'Preye, I've never been happier to see you. Talking on the phone can never compare with this physical contact. You've missed.' She rubbed her body against her two sisters before laying the baby on one of the sofas. 'I know your regular excuse is that you live far away, so to what do we owe the honour of your presence tonight?'

'It doesn't need to be a special occasion for me to want to get together with my family. Unless the rules have changed,' Preye shot back.

Miriam walked back in. 'Girls, as guests in my home, please leave the sarcastic comments at the door.' She embraced Erefa.

It didn't take long for the sisters to act as if they saw each other every day. They had dinner and flowed effortless into an evening filled with banters and jokes. The Banigo girls had a close relationship since they had needed to rely on one another when growing up. Looking back, they realised it had made them more creative and taught them the importance of hard work and money. In their family, time and maturity had softened the hard edges of their childhood.

Erefa looked at her watch. 'It's almost ten and I have to get Tamara home to her bed. We made it almost the entire night without talking about Timi. How is he?'

Preye took a deep breath. 'Things aren't going well, and I am spending a few days with Lola to figure myself out. He asked for a divorce,' she paused. 'I don't know if he meant it but if he did, it's all good, I'm not going to stop him.'

The others gasped in unison. Preye gave scant details and said she'd fill them in later. The truth was that she didn't know how to describe her relationship with Timi without sounding petty. Their issues seemed like every day squabbles, yet they left her feeling hopeless. She was finally feeling mentally strong and didn't want to get moody by talking much about him.

*

Timi had Malik over for dinner to ask for his help on how to get out of the hole he was in with Preye. He was honest with Malik about all that had been going on since they got married and he confessed that he was at a loss on how to relate with his wife without her taking offence.

'I can't advise you from experience, Timi. If I pulled half of the stuff you told me on Penny, she'd walk out and never return,' Malik said. 'I was in the dark about the issues you had with Preye. But why would you buy a house without her input? That's way beyond your mandate, Bro. When you announced it at the wedding, I thought she had seen it before and expressed her interest.'

Timi sighed. 'I wanted to protect her and provide for her like a husband should. I haven't talked about our problems because I'll be too embarrassed. I believe what happens in a marriage should stay between the couple. She is the type to make me sound like a monster and blame it all on me, which isn't true. I admit that allowing her to find out about Tina was inexcusable, but you know how it is. She is even accusing me of being controlling. Can you blame me for wanting to keep an eye on my beautiful wife?'

Malik shook his head. 'You have to be on your absolute best behaviour if she comes back. She has a right to be sensitive if you've betrayed her trust on more than one occasion. I know you're a good man. Show that side of you to your wife. The word divorce should never have been spoken. And now it's on the table for discussion. I don't envy you, man.'

Usually, Timi tried to make up for their disagreements with gifts or flowers. This time, he knew needed more than that to convince Preye to come back to him. He was never going to agree to be *besties* with Lola, but he'd do almost anything else to have his wife back.

*

The following week, Preye was in high spirits as she went to see her mother. Miriam was praying and on her knees when Preye let herself in. She made herself comfortable on the sofa opposite Miriam and waited. A few seconds passed before Preye decided to bow her head to join her mother in prayer.

The past week away from her home and her husband had given Preye a sense of liveliness and the freedom to be herself, the way she remembered – focused, fashionable, affable and productive. She had gone to her old church for the first time since she got married; she had gone out to dinner with Aisha, Lola and Sammy, where Lola officially introduced Sammy to Preye and Aisha as the enemies to contend with if he went out of line; she had done a two kilometre run twice with the Roadrunners; she had visited Tobi's house for lunch with his family; and she had taken Zara to a games centre.

She couldn't remember the last time she felt like no one was watching her from behind and expecting her to slip up or fall down.

She had also spent some time to reflect on her marriage and

her future, but she hadn't been able to come to any conclusion that didn't include a family of her own. She didn't think she could continue to endure her marriage, yet she knew unless a miracle happened as she had been praying, she couldn't count on Timi to change. She wasn't sure if he'd go ahead with the divorce, but she knew if he did, she wasn't ready for it.

Anytime she thought about the prospect of divorce, she acknowledged that Lola was much more mature than her and she respected Lola the more, for how Lola had been able to cope with her husband's abandonment and with caring for Zara as a single mother. Preye knew she wasn't that strong or detached enough not to care about what people say and she wasn't ready to face up to having a failed marriage like Miriam. That would be proving Timi right.

But she didn't know what to do. She felt like a tangled spool of thread. The little, untangled part was where she was free to be herself and enjoy her inner peace with boundless energy and opportunities. The tangled part was her marriage that seemed like a mirage; a mass of unending turmoil that got worse as she tried to untangle it.

Miriam ended the prayer and gave Preye a warm embrace before they both sat facing each other. 'Don't you want anything to drink?' Miriam asked.

'Maybe I do. What about you?' Preye responded, flailing her hands. Miriam shrugged indifferently. Preye went to the fridge and found a bottle of non-alcoholic wine. There was always that one bottle in Miriam's fridge for an unexpected visitor. 'I hope we're sharing this, because I can't finish it,' Preye said, before she opened the wine. Miriam nodded and got two glasses from the show glass cabinet. 'And I hope you have soup for me to take to Lola's house. She knows I'm here. Otherwise, she'll throw me out.'

'My heart is joyful anytime I see you. Don't worry, I'll pack some soup for you.' Miriam responded cheerfully as Preye served the wine.

They started on the wine and Preye asked Miriam about her shop, which opened a floodgate of gossip as Miriam talked about her funny customers who asked for repeat credit purchases without settling their existing debts. Miriam asked about Preye's work and commented that Preye looked more relaxed than she had looked the previous week.

'So, Mother, you said we had something to talk about. I hope it's nothing serious.' Preye asked as soon as she reckoned they had talked enough about insignificant matters.

Miriam sighed and cleared her throat before speaking. 'I wanted us to talk about you and Timi. I didn't probe so much the last time because your sisters were here. This is the third week and I'm concerned that if you stay out for too long, it may be difficult for you to reconcile. What exactly is the matter?'

Preye released a breath along with some tension from within her. 'I don't know how to explain it without making him look like the devil, but I know it's not all his fault. We just don't seem to agree on anything and almost everything I do gets him annoyed. I think he's also having an affair.' She shook her head. 'Did I make a mistake, Mum?'

'I don't think you made a mistake. Every marriage will have its own challenges, especially in its first five years. I believe if you can survive this phase, things will work out eventually. But you can't work it out by running away. That's not how to solve a problem.' Miriam guessed Timi may be difficult, but she didn't think that was enough to break Preye's marriage. She thought that if only Preye's generation could learn some endurance, their marriages would last longer.

'He's having an affair. He's tired of the marriage and he's asked for a divorce.' Preye raised her shoulders in resignation. 'These past days I've spent with Lola have been one of my happiest moments since I married him. The only way I can describe my husband is that he enjoys bullying me. The painful part is that I think he's not even aware of it. And I'm afraid of what it's turning me into. I've actually felt like killing him to end the insults. Would you believe that of me? Now I understand what may have happened to those women reported to have killed their husbands. It's hell, Mum.'

She couldn't bring herself to tell Miriam that Timi once referred to Miriam as an irresponsible mother and a failure. Nor could she talk about the other days: the day he abused her that she lacked parental training; the day he said she was good-for-nothing over a burnt pot of soup; the day he couldn't deny that he was having an affair; and the day he called her barren.

'Does he beat you?' Miriam asked, unsure what the distant look on Preye's face implied.

'He dares not.' Preye shook her head. 'How can that even cross your mind? Am I his child?'

Miriam opened her hands enquiringly. 'Then I don't see why you can't resolve things. If I left when your father went on with his affairs, I wouldn't have had the three of you. Even at that, he was the one that left, not me. I'm not saying what your husband did is okay, don't get me wrong. But you have to fight for your marriage and your family. You're a strong girl and if you set your mind to it, you will overcome these challenges. You didn't come this far to give up.'

Preye didn't know how to explain to her mother that her relationship with Timi was like a bestselling book that nobody could read; glossy on the cover and desirable to many. But on the inside, someone had scribbled rubbish on the texts so that no one would notice how meaningless the content had become from the cover. She wasn't sure who was scribbling the rubbish between Timi and herself, but she was sure the goal was to make the book useless. How does one erase the rubbish to make the texts legible again and salvage the book to serve its purpose? It may not be impossible, but it would be difficult; extremely difficult.

She closed her eyes and a tear dropped as she wished she had a genie that would teleport her to marital bliss.

CHAPTER TWENTY ONE

One week after visiting her mother, Preye returned to Regalia Court; the home she never wanted. She let herself in, to find Timi at the kitchen table, wading through several payment invoices. Something Preye had never seen him do. There were some sealed envelopes in a neat pile and he had a spreadsheet open on his laptop. He started to stand to embrace her but quickly sat down again, not wanting to overwhelm her since he didn't know her state of mind.

'I came back because my things are here and I still live here. I know the house is in your name, so I'll move out to give you your space. From now on, pay your bills without getting into my account.' Preye raised her hand as Timi started to speak. 'Not this time please. I was a shell of myself the last time you saw me, but now I'm stronger. I'm working my way back to the woman I was before you met me. I've given it some thoughts and I'm happy with your divorce proposal.' She walked towards the stairs, then turned back. 'One more thing. I love my birthmark. My mother always told me it's a kiss from God, and I'm no longer going to hide it.' She left for the bedroom without waiting for a response.

The silence in the house was unsettling as Preye unpacked her bag. No clothes were scattered across the floor and the drawers were all closed. Timi had been busy. Without turning from the task at hand, she sensed him in the room.

'I don't want a divorce.' His voice was gentle. 'I want a second chance to prove myself to you and then you can decide if this marriage is worth saving. I love you, Preye Banigo and I agree, that sexy birthmark of yours makes you special. I know you'll be a fabulous mother and I want to share the experience with you,' he finished softly, like a child found with a box of candies he shouldn't have.

'That's quite a mouthful. I can't share a bed with you, right now or in the days to come, if that is your intention,' she replied flatly.

He was encouraged. She had used the words 'right now,' which gave a window of probability. That was all he needed. Paying off the his bills was of no concern to him as his parents still provided a reliable financial safety net, but he didn't mention it.

'I'll use the guest room for as long as you need me to. I'll be around as much or as little as you like, so let me know any time you need your space. Take the car to work. I've not found an office yet. And if I have to go somewhere, I'll figure it out.'

'No surprises. I now know that you used those acts to keep me off balance.' Her lips curled up. She had a hard time pretending that she hated him.

'I'm sorry that I made you feel that way. You set the pace from now on, but know that I'm here to lean on, if you need me. I'll let you enjoy breakfast in peace tomorrow, and I'll be here when you return from work, unless you have plans.'

'No plans. Thanks for the space. Have you narrowed down your search for an office yet?' she asked. Since she was going to live under the same room with him, she needed to maintain a level of cordiality.

'I have a few to look at this weekend. I've already started working from home using the guest room. It still needs tidying, but I'll get on it tomorrow,' he said.

'I know what it takes to get a company off the ground. I might have some spare time this weekend to check out some properties with you,' Preye volunteered. She was trying to remain cordial to normalise things in a situation that was far from normal.

'That will be fantastic,' he gushed.

'No promises. I'll see how I feel,' she responded.

He nodded his head and got busy transforming the guest room into his micro-apartment until he was invited back to the bedroom. He planned to call Malik's wife, Penny the following day and ask her about things he could do that would be subtle, but effective to win his wife back. It was a given that Malik would have told Penny about what was happening in the Cokers' marriage, and like her husband, he believed she'd be happy to help.

*

'Good Morning. It's Timi. I'm sure Malik would have mentioned that we're not exactly in a good shape at home. I need some advice,' Timi said in a subdued voice.

'I guess this has something to do with your lovely wife. Malik mentioned you asked for a divorce, which you didn't exactly want,' Penny said loudly, against her children's noise in the background. 'It sounds like you have to make some changes that to get back in her good books.'

'I take it you and Malik share everything,' he said shyly. If he didn't want Preye back so badly, he'd have done anything to avoid being told off by anyone.

'We do, and there are times that feelings get hurt, but in the long run, we work out our differences. I have an idea of what guys can be up to when they think they can get away with stuff. Malik knows I don't bluff and there are some things he dares not try with me. Enough about us. What exactly do you need help with?' she asked.

'In the past, if things were going badly, I used to come up with some very romantic ideas that Preye couldn't help but appreciate. Now she thinks I've been using all that to scam her and cover up the real issues. If those things won't work, what do you suggest? The point is I've run out of ideas.'

Penny went on to tell him to do small things that meant a lot to Preye. 'Pick up her favourite item from the grocery shop, recreate your first date or the time you first shared a kiss. Be kind, and focus on sincerely pleasing her, not just because you want her back. I hope this is not coming too late though. If she allows you, try to listen to her more and let her be herself.' Penny rounded up by telling Timi to get to know his wife better, because it seemed he had been self-centred and hadn't dedicated time to understand his wife. She reiterated smaller gestures that could prove Timi was attentive to Preye's real needs.

Timi thanked Penny before hanging up, feeling confident that he could win Preye's heart again. He didn't quite agree with Penny that he was self-centred, but he had held himself back from arguing with her. Patience wasn't exactly his strong suit, but he'd give Penny's advice a try by going gently at his wife. Maybe he rushed her before, and perhaps his goals would be the same, but his methods would be different now.

*

Preye rolled over in bed and felt the weight of the empty, quiet house. She opened her eyes and didn't see a huge bouquet of roses or cards. She breathed a sigh of relief that Timi hadn't used his regular trick of assaulting her with flowers, although that had worked for some time. She had fallen for his antics over and over again, as she always thought there was a degree of sincerity behind his actions. She hated that about herself and now felt like she had thrown herself at him as if she was starved of affection. She vowed to keep it as part of her past and never let her guard down in future.

She walked barefoot into the kitchen. The coffee was made, and her favourite mug was sitting next to the pot. Timi had been up, as he had laid out her favourite newspaper and opened it to the business section, which was the only part she took the time to read. She tried to think of the right word for the gestures. After she sat down and poured her coffee, the word, thoughtful, came to her mind and she smiled.

As she got dressed to go out, she was a bit apprehensive that he'd push his luck and wander by, but luckily he didn't. It was either he had left the house or locked himself up in the guest room because she didn't run into him. She resisted the urge to check up on him before she left the house.

She climbed into her car and nearly hopped out on seeing how clean the car was. She thought it was the wrong vehicle. There were no fast food cartons on the floor or sweaty gym clothes on the backseat. When she started the car, she noticed that it was filled with petrol. And on the seat next to her was a sprig of lavender. It was her favourite scent. She had told Timi about it, but she hadn't thought he heard her then as he had given her roses more often than not. She drove to work, feeling surprisingly positive.

She called Timi from her office around noon. 'I'm calling to say thank you for this morning, for cleaning the car and for the lavender.'

'I love you, Mine. That's what you get when you're all I can think about. I'm glad you made it to work safely. You'll be exhausted by the time you come back, so I thought I'd roast a chicken for dinner and we can watch a movie on the sofa.' Preye was silent. The bells ringing in her head were putting her on caution. 'Are you there? I'm sorry if I pushed you. Don't worry about watching a movie. Will you eat my roast chicken though?' he asked cautiously.

'Since when did you know how to roast a chicken?' she asked in a measured tone.

'You don't think I could get the resources if I wanted to tackle a project in the kitchen?' he cooed into the phone. 'Well, I'm here with my mum, learning the ropes,' he confessed.

'Hmm, I should have guessed. Say hello to her for me,' Preye responded. She was about to hang up, but Timi slipped in a final comment.

'I love you.' Timi hung up.

The surge of activities in her stomach pushed a smile to her face.

*

Dinner with Timi in their kitchen, eating slightly overcooked chicken was what Preye had imagined their married life should have been. She hadn't expected a perfect marriage, just a peaceful one, but it seemed there was something about their relationship that repelled peace.

The kitchen wasn't cold and antiseptic as it had felt before; Timi had arranged scented candles. They joked about his failure in the kitchen and enjoyed the ice cream he had bought for dessert. They both agreed she was a better fit in the kitchen when she could make the time for it. She was relaxed and he subtly tried to persuade her to spend more time on domestic chores.

He admitted to himself that he owed a big thank you to Penny. If things kept progressing, Preye would be back in his arms in no time. Since Preye returned home a week ago, he had taken responsibility for preparing dinner. Preye had told him not to bother, but he had insisted that it was the least he could do since he hadn't started full time work.

They washed the dishes together and enjoyed a few flirtatious moments. Physical attraction had never been a problem between them, except for his daily demands for sex, any time he was in the mood and sometimes even twice a day. She found his muscular frame more attractive than ever, especially because he had been spending more time working out at the gym. She had equally kept fit from her running rounds. She had been lucky not to have put on weight in her adolescent years and when girls were packing on the pounds at university, she had been losing them.

Despite the wonderful evening they just shared, she insisted they stayed in their separate rooms. To elongate the night, he persuaded her to watch a horror film with him. Later, he confessed he had chosen the film in the hopes that she wouldn't want to sleep alone. She didn't mind the trickery since he was upright about it, and she teased him to try harder another time. He reached out to kiss her, but she turned her cheek to him.

The next night went even better. They ate out after viewing several office spaces for Timi's new business venture. Preye chose the restaurant and Timi agreed without hesitation. To Preye, it felt like they were starting over, which was the only way real reconciliation was possible.

She had felt re-energised from staying at Lola's. Just saying her problems out loud had made them easier to confront on getting back home. At Lola's house, she had reflected that her marriage had reached the lowest it could, so the only way to go would be up if Timi joined her to rise towards the light by embracing the opportunity to rebuild their relationship on mutual respect. Lola had been expectedly doubtful and still didn't believe Timi could change.

Three weeks after returning from Lola's, Preye walked in

with the groceries she had picked up on the way home.

There had been no unpleasant incidents and Timi had been at his best, attending to her needs as if her opinions mattered. She didn't fully allow herself to trust him yet because she wasn't sure if it was for real or a mere act before he reverted to his old self. They still kept to their separate sleeping rooms, but they were talking more than they used to and were growing close again.

'I hope you're in the mood for spicy Thai curry.' Preye had attended a cooking class with Timi the weekend before. It was something she had wanted to do for years.

'I'm always up for your cooking, sweetheart.' Timi held her hands and looked pleadingly into her eyes. 'I miss you. I miss your warm body next to mine. I haven't enjoyed a good night of sleep since …' he left the sentence hanging. 'Please, I'd like to ask for a favour. Can I come back to the bedroom?' He led her to the sofa. 'I love you and I'm ready to start a family with you. It's not easy if we're in separate beds.'

She laughed and playfully rubbed his afro hair with her hand. 'I'm having a hard time believing the past weeks were real. There has been so much turbulence before that and I don't want to bring a child into that world.'

'That world is behind us, Mine,' he promised. He wanted to share a bed with his wife again. Now that he was aware of her triggers, he could avoid them. It was blissful when she was compliant like she had been in recent weeks.

'Forget dinner, let's go to bed,' she said with a wry smile and pulled up to him.

He scooped her in his hands and carried her to the bedroom. Before joining her in bed, he took his phone out of his pocket. There was a message waiting for him from Tina.

CHAPTER TWENTY TWO

Preye wore a loose-fitting floral dress to the office. Timi loved the outfit, although he wasn't the reason she wore the flowery dress. Her abdomen was cramping and she couldn't wear anything that constricted her belly. Since she tested for pregnancy every month, she knew she wasn't pregnant and hoped the pain would pass.

The pains and heavy bleeding had gradually started creeping up on her since her first period after she her wedding married. She figured it had to do with having sex and stopping her birth control pills which her doctor had prescribed after having myomectomy for her fibroids. She usually went through her period with a good dose of painkillers, while wearing tampons and super pads simultaneously, but the pain seemed to have worsened, spreading to her back and causing her more discomfort.

'Boss,' Tobi said when he stepped into her office. 'Quarterly reports are in. Want a peek?'

'Sure. I'll take a look at some point today. I'm spending all day behind this desk, so I'll definitely get to it. I have a load of paperwork to deal with,' Preye responded. The pain was manageable as long as she didn't try to change her position.

'Are you okay? Normally, you can't wait to see the figures. Spoiler alert, they're spectacular,' Tobi said happily.

'That's great news. And I'm fine. The staff will be thrilled if they can get the annual bonus we've been promising. Life at home is great but I'm feeling a bit under the weather. Nothing to worry about. Timi has been at his best and I couldn't ask for more. If I knew getting away would work with him, I would have done that the day after our honeymoon.' Preye chuckled and winked at Tobi.

'If you say so. But if you need anything, call me. I'm on your side dear. It's great seeing that big smile back on your face,' Tobi replied, not amused at her attempt to joke. He wore a tender look of concern on his face.

She made it through the day and managed to drive home, although she had considered asking Lola or Tobi to drive her. By the time she left the office, her left leg had started cramping too. Her period had gotten heavier and she had changed her pads four times.

She had started experiencing heavy periods accompanied by pains, shortly after she met Kevin. Her condition had grown worse over the years until she saw a doctor who diagnosed her with uterine fibroids after an abdominal ultra-sound scan. When there was no abatement after about a year of treatment with medications, the doctor had suggested myomectomy. Preye's mother hadn't consented to the surgery; as far as Miriam could remember, no one in the family had ever had a surgery and Preye shouldn't be the first.

One day, Preye fainted at work and had to be rushed to the hospital. Her heavy periods had made her anaemic. That was when both mother and daughter agreed to have the fibroids removed. After the surgery, the doctor had hinted that there was no guarantee that the fibroids wouldn't return and that in very rare circumstances, it affected the uterus which might then have to be removed. Preye knew she'd never agree to that option. She preferred to endure the excruciating pain rather than decrease her chances of having children someday. Even as a youngster, she had seen women without children being referred to as empty shells. She had decided no one would be able to pin that label on her and had contented herself with the pills to help regulate her hormones.

It seemed like the doctor's prediction was right and the fibroids had returned, because the pain she felt now was familiar. She prayed she wouldn't have to get her uterus removed. Having children was more important to her than ever, now that she was married.

These thoughts crowded Preye's mind and seemed to increase the pain she felt. She was relieved that the freeway exit close to her house was in sight.

Timi was aware of her cramps and was waiting for her in the driveway when she arrived home. 'I've drawn a warm bath for you,' he said, helping her out of the car.

'Thanks. Let's hope it brings relief. The bleeding has gotten worse and I'm running a fever,' she explained weakly.

'I'm here for you, Mine. Maybe we should go see the doctor if you don't feel better after a bath,' he volunteered. 'I can ask Mum to book an appointment for us. I think it's time you went to register with our family hospital. We can ask for a female gynaecologist to be assigned to you.'

'No need to change doctors now. My doctor knows my history and I'm comfortable with him.' she countered. 'I'll wait until tomorrow and I'll go see him if I don't feel better. I just hope he doesn't refer me to the General Hospital again.'

It was after she removed her dress that she noticed it was already stained. She shed her soaked underwear and pad into the bin and managed to insert a tampon before she made her way into the warm bath. Timi had placed lit scented candles in the bathroom and she felt the exhaustion oozing out of her as her body loosened up to the relaxing atmosphere, heightened by the slow music he just turned on. She was grateful they were on good terms again and had moved beyond their misunderstanding.

There had been a lot going on in Timi's mind before Preye got back from work. He hadn't met Preye's doctor yet, but he didn't trust that the doctor would have her best interest at heart. He didn't like the fact that his wife had to open herself up to another male under whatever guise. He feared that her doctor may now try to convince her to take out her womb or ovaries without exhausting practical options. He didn't want his wife to suffer and he also wanted her to have his children. Although they had never talked about adoption, he knew that wasn't an option for him because his parents would never agree. He was afraid it could become a choice for Preye if she started talking to Lola about having children.

Without Preye's knowledge, he had been busy researching options for treating fibroid. He had listened to a recurring programme on the radio about a doctor who talked authoritatively on helping patients get relief from endometriosis pain, using a new surgical procedure. If Preye wouldn't go to his family hospital, he'd try to convince her to see the new doctor; it was worth a shot. Her last surgery had been at the General Hospital and he didn't trust the doctors there either.

After making sure she was settled in the bath, he went to his laptop to look up the details of the doctor on the radio show. It took him less than ten minutes. The difficult part would be to convince Preye to trust him on this.

Preye was near tears when he returned to the bathroom. 'What if this is it? What if having children isn't in the cards for me? Will you still love me?' She stepped out of the bath with his help and put on her pink terry robe.

'I dream of someday having a family, but without you, it means nothing.' He had a good feeling that she'd agree to his suggestion. 'Have you heard of Saint Mary's Hospital?' She shook her head to indicate *no*. 'I guessed as much. It's a big hospital, not so far from us. They have a doctor who is using a new technique that can get rid of pain caused by fibroids while preserving a woman's fertility. I'll see if I can get an early appointment. The doctor's name is Dr Natasha, but she goes by Dr Tash. You haven't heard about her?' She shook her head again. 'She hosts a fertility show on radio.' Timi trod softly. 'I think we should try a second opinion.'

'I'll try anything non-invasive, but let me see my doctor first. Although I've not seen him for close to three years now. I'm not in a hurry yet, but I wish I didn't have so much pain and discomfort.'

'I agree with you.' Reluctantly, he decided not to argue with her when he remembered that her clinic was somewhere close to her old house and he realised he could use the distance as an excuse to change doctors if it came to that. Once she was settled on the bed, he went to the medicine box in the kitchen cabinet and got a heat patch and analgesic for her. She felt safe in his capable hands and fell asleep.

The following day was no better. Preye wiggled in pain, took doses of analgesic throughout the day and slept as much as she could. She didn't notice that Timi went out for about two hours.

By Monday morning, she was ready to go with any suggestion to ease her pain.

*

'I have a good feeling she'd be able to help us. Is the pain any better now?' Timi asked.

Sitting in a stark white office at Saint Mary's Hospital in Satellite Town, they waited for Dr Tash. They had gone through some registration requirements at the reception and the nurse had taken Preye's vitals. Preye could only nod. She hadn't eaten much solid food since her episode started and was a little sapped of energy.

Built in the late 1990s, the hospital was still a landmark edifice, occupying a contemporary seven-storey building sitting on a little less than three acres. On each floor were different sections including Paediatrics, Obstetrics & Gynaecology, Urology, Neurology and Accidents & Emergency. It was the prime specialist hospital in the area covering the Festac, Okoko and Satellite Town axis of Lagos.

The grounds had a big car park with a towering masquerade tree in the centre, providing ample refreshing shade when the sun was scorching. The frontage canopy was made of brick and the floor was tiled with a variety of marble and ceramic. Most people felt welcome any time they stepped inside the reception which looked more like a hotel than a place where sick people sought relief. The ambience was made more pleasant by the warm purple walls, huge flower vases, the regularly freshened-air and the lively smiles of the many nurses that scampered back and forth. A water dispenser crowned with disposable plastic cups stood in a corner of the reception and regularly reminded visitors that they were thirsty, even though they hadn't realised it before they entered the hospital.

'Mr and Mrs Coker.' When she came in, the pretty diminutive doctor gave them a firm handshake with a smile that assured them they were in the right place. 'You sounded quite urgent on the phone. How may I help you?' Dr Tash was one of the senior consultant gynaecologists. Her office was devoid of any decoration. Apart from the table, chairs and a sofa, there was just an examination bed, a shelf, a computer and some medical equipment in different parts of the room.

'I've listened to your programme on the radio and I must say, you're doing a great job. As you can see, my wife is in a lot of pain. She's been like this all through the weekend. It's fibroid issues and she's had a surgery in the past. She's been bleeding heavily too, but it has subsided now. I believe you can help us.'

Preye was comforted that Timi took charge, but she wished Lola or her mother was present too. She felt the women would understand best, especially her mother who knew her history with the menstrual episodes before she had the myomectomy. Although she had been told that fibroids could grow back or lead to scar tissues, she hadn't thought that could happen in her case. She had ignored her doctor's advice to have an ultrasound to check her uterus after five years because the doctor had told her that removing her uterus couldn't be ruled out.

With her left hand supporting her head on the doctor's table and her right hand clutching her lower tummy, Preye prayed silently that this doctor would have some good news for her.

Dr Tash pulled up her chair to the side of the table to get closer to Preye and gently lifted her head. 'You'll be fine. Do you have an idea of when this started?' she asked.

Preye recounted how the pain had started about ten years earlier. Since she knew the doctor would ask about her medical history, she went on without waiting for any prodding and explained the events that led to her surgery and how the pain stopped afterwards. She told the doctor that the pain and heavy periods had started again immediately after her marriage and she had been using heat patches. When asked about their sex life, she was embarrassed to admit that it had been more pain than pleasure at the beginning, but that it was now better.

Dr Tash continued with the questioning as she examined Preye for body temperature and blood pressure. She soothed Preye and helped her to the adjustable bed to examine her stomach.

The doctor's face was impassive as she gently pressed Preye's stomach in different areas. After the examination, Dr Tash told Preye she'd be given some medicines for pain palliation and iron therapy. She made some notes in the file in front of her and asked Preye what time she'd be available for a scan. Timi responded before Preye could talk.

'She can have it today if there's a slot. I can't bear to see her in such pain. Will she need surgery, Doctor?'

'I can assure you the pain will subside. You need to stop using the heat patches because of the bleeding. We need the scan to decide what the lasting solution will be,' Dr Tash replied with empathy and shook her head. 'I can't be sure if she'll need to have surgery, until we have the results back.' She wrote some more on the file. 'Mrs Coker, if you're okay, you can have the scan done today and I'll see you next week.' She reached for her desk calendar. 'Let's see. Next Monday at ten in the morning should be fine. Does that work for you?'

Preye nodded. 'Yes, that's fine.'

Dr Tash continued writing. 'You'll also need to give some blood samples, so we can conduct a comprehensive test. We need to check your blood count too.' She walked them to the reception to wait for the scan and medication. She gave the file to a nurse and promised to see them the following week.

*

Preye didn't bother to go to work for the rest of the week. She simply lacked the energy to face the traffic and long drive to the office. She'd have loved to see her mother or sisters, but it required the same effort to do so as well. Instead, she called Tobi to explain her state to him and he advised her to get as much rest as possible, assuring her she could count on him to run the office effectively.

She ran through her diary and painfully switched on a smile to make her scheduled calls to clients. She also got Lola and Aisha on a video call. She asked how Aisha was healing from the caesarean section and congratulated her on the birth of the baby again. Lola got everyone laughing when she started talking about how little Zara was torturing Sammy with childish pranks. Preye was close to laughter-tears by the time she ended the call.

Timi was at her beck and call all through and only went out when it was important. He also found time to go on a date with Tina. He attempted to cook a couple of days and brought home takeaways for Preye the other days. For the first time in their relationship, Timi did most of the talking, filling her in on his office plans and how the property search was progressing. He lamented he hadn't thought that getting an office space could be that difficult.

They were back to see Dr Tash on Monday morning. She enquired from Preye how she was feeling and Preye responded that she was much better than the last time they were at the hospital. The bleeding and pain had subsided substantially since the previous visit.

Dr Tash read through the file in front of her before addressing the couple. 'Your blood test shows that you're anaemic. We can start working on that immediately. Here's your scan result.' She pushed the file forward so Preye and Timi could have a look as she illustrated. 'As we suspected, you have multiple fibroids.' She pointed her pen to four dots on the print-out. 'The biggest one is nine centimetres here and it may grow further. There are different things we can do. The safest one will be to wait for the fibroids to degenerate, but that still leaves you with the pains and bleeding and there's also a probability that they may not degenerate as quickly as you'd like. Unfortunately, you will need to consider another surgery for the bleeding to stop.' She waited for a reaction, but none was forthcoming from either Preye or Timi, so she continued. 'Since you're still considering having children, hysterectomy and fibroid embolization will not be appropriate for you and …'

'What does that mean?' Preye interrupted.

'Sorry, it's a procedure to shrink the fibroids by blocking off the arteries that feed them blood. That's about the least invasive. Hysterectomy is about the most common permanent solution, but we don't want to remove your uterus, do we?' Dr Tash looked at Preye for affirmation.

Preye sighed in exasperation. 'Where does that leave me then? Is there a way to avoid surgery?'

'There are medications that can be effective. The challenge is they will likely affect your fertility, so unless you've decided you no longer want children, you shouldn't take them. You also can't use them for too long, because they might have some long term effect and in your case, they may not work after some time. The reason is because you have both serious pain and heavy bleeding. The medications may treat one or the other, which sets you back to square one after a while. I'm afraid another myomectomy appears to be the best bet for now. Once you've healed, I suggest you start fertility treatments immediately. There's always a chance that the fibroids will grow again after a while, until you're menopausal or have your uterus removed.'

Timi tried to think of what to do, but he had to stop his brain from freezing, in reaction to what the doctor just said. His heart pounded against his chest and he took a deep breath before he talked. 'How soon can the surgery be done?' he asked.

'Can you give me some time to think about this?' Preye asked before the doctor responded. Her physical pain was subdued by her pain of apprehension.

'Definitely,' Dr Tash replied. 'If you do decide, we have an opening for surgery on Friday evening fortunately and I can get the team together. I'll give you some medications before the surgery and you'll spend a couple of days here afterwards. If not this Friday, then it would be a two to three weeks' wait and until after your next period.' She got up. 'Can you excuse me please? I need to see a patient in the ward. I should be back in a few minutes, if that's okay.'

Immediately Dr Tash left the room, Preye turned to Timi. 'I think she knows what she's talking about. But I was just thinking, maybe I should go back to the General Hospital since I had the first surgery there. At least now I know they don't have to remove my womb,' she opined.

Timi held her hand. 'Think about the distance to Ikeja. More so, you can enjoy a better service here. We're not poor, we can afford it. I've done the research and maybe you should check the hospital's website too. Apart from the hospital's testimonial, there's a rave about Dr Tash on social media. I think it's simply a miracle that they have a slot this early. But in the end, it's your decision because it's your body. Although this hospital will be more convenient and I can be with you all through. I simply can't bear to see you in pains. I love you and I'm sure you'll be a wonderful mom to our children.'

'Let's sleep over this. We can get back to Dr Tash tomorrow, but we can ask her to give me the prescription, in case we decide to go along with it.'

A million tasks piled up in Preye's mind, but she didn't know which one to do first. Maybe she should ask for Aisha's opinion, since Aisha just had a baby. She shook her head to dismiss that thought.

'I should call my mum. I also need to check in with the office. I've not been working actively for a while now and I don't want Tobi to think I'm abusing my privilege. And I wanted to go see Aisha and her baby,' Preye said. She was so worried about friends, family and work that she forgot she was in pain. She saw the look of disbelief on Timi's face. 'I know I'm not making sense. It feels rushed. I didn't think I would need to do a fibroid surgery again. I thought I was over it.'

Timi sighed. He wanted to shake some sense into her. He had faith in Dr Tash and wanted to get things done with no outside influence. He knew Lola would be against the plan for no other reason than it was Timi's idea. 'I only want the best for you. Like I said, it's your decision and I don't want to keep repeating that. I hope next month, you won't go through the same incident. And I think the earlier you do it, the earlier we can start focusing on fertility options. It's your …'

'My choice. I know. Don't say it again.' She kept on thinking about what other options she could explore while Timi was thinking about not wasting time.

By the time Dr Tash returned to her office, Timi and Preye had decided to go ahead with the surgery on Friday.

Dr Tash ushered them into another office where she gave them some forms to fill and informed them about the risks associated with the surgery, the extreme of which might be death. Preye half-listened as she completed the forms. She knew the risk recitation was no different from flight attendants' safety advice in a flying aeroplane; it was mere medical protocol.

*

Preye went to the office briefly the following day. She informed Tobi and Lola about her decision to have the surgery and they scolded her for coming to the office. Lola volunteered to come with her to the hospital, but she assured Lola that Timi was up to the task. She was able to complete some of her tasks and compiled a list of the outstanding tasks. Tobi came by to discuss the documents and cheques she needed to sign. Before she left the office, she had a meeting with Lola and Tobi, where she gave Tobi a brief handover note, assigning most of her outstanding tasks to Lola. On her way home, she called her mother to tell her she'd drop by.

Miriam was shocked to see Preye looking ashen, without makeup, and not particularly looking chic as she usually did.

Preye felt comforted when her mother embraced her, and couldn't explain why she burst into tears. After she gathered herself, she expressed how much she had missed everyone and went on to talk about her scheduled surgery. She felt very relaxed and it didn't take her long to doze off on the sofa. By the time she woke up, Miriam had made fish pepper soup and some *nkwobi* for her to take home. Before Preye left, Miriam prayed with her. Preye felt quite refreshed, although she was still a bit weak.

CHAPTER TWENTY THREE

Preye tried to do some positive self-talk as she was wheeled into the operating room. She felt was woozy even before the anaesthesiologist started working his magic with the potent drugs. She felt Timi holding her hand tight and then the release of his grip. The light centred above her shone over her face like an energised moon. By the time the anaesthetic mask descended, the light had gradually blurred into a blackness that nudged her to sleep. She was asked to count down from ten but she didn't remember a single number.

At the waiting room, Timi sent a text to Tina, that he might be able to spend the night with her, so she should be ready for him. He watched the television in the hospital waiting room for a while until he fell asleep. As he woke up, he looked around before checking the time. It was 7.13p.m. Preye had gone into the theatre at just before 4.00p.m and according to Dr Tash, it was about a two-hour procedure, so they should have been done.

Timi went to the counter. 'My wife, Preye Coker had a surgery this evening. Is she out? Which room is she in?' he asked the nurse. 'I dozed off in the waiting room, so maybe there was a call for me. Do you have an update? I'm sorry, I didn't know I slept that deeply.'

'Dr Tash was out a while ago, but she went back in almost immediately. They are still in the theatre. I'm sure she'll be out soon.' The nurse looked down at her chart.

Timi checked the watch on his wrist again and saw the nurse's name on her work tag. He touched her hand. 'I'm sorry if I sounded agitated, Stella. I love my wife and I can't afford anything to go wrong. Do these surgeries last this long? I hope everything is alright.'

'I understand sir. I'll let you know as soon as I have any information for you. Please relax and hope for the best,' she assured him as she briskly walked away from the nurse's station.

Timi's phone had been vibrating while he was asleep. He checked his phone. Tina, Miriam and Lola had called. Tina had also sent a text that she was waiting, so he returned her call. 'Hey, I dozed off,' he whispered.

'You said you'd keep me posted. This waiting game sucks,' Tina complained. 'Are you still coming?'

'Well, I thought I could make it, but they're not done yet. I have to be here for my wife. Hold on a little longer, I'll let you know as soon as I can get out.'

'Is that a when or if? Is she alright, though?' Tina asked.

'I'm sure she's alright. I'm waiting to see her. I have to go now.' Timi hurriedly cut short the call as he saw the nurse approach. He was disappointed when she told him that the doctor would be out to see him soon and went back to her desk.

He jumped up immediately he saw Dr Tash come out. She asked him to come into her office and sensing the urgency in her voice, despite her calmness, he hurried behind her. He had barely entered the office before the doctor faced him and took a deep breath before explaining that there had been some complications with the surgery. 'Your wife lost a lot of blood during the surgery and her blood sugar was low. Since she said she still wants to have children, the medical team had to make the tough decision not to remove her uterus. She's receiving blood transfusion now and hopefully she'll soon be out and you'll be able to see her.'

He felt cold and hot simultaneously, while his head swelled. Strength oozed out of his body and he dropped into the chair as he struggled with what to say or do next. 'But, will she be alright?' he stammered.

'We can only hope for the best,' she responded impassively and patted his hand. 'I need to get back now. I'll see you once she's in the clear.' She left the room and held the door open for him to follow.

He was back in the waiting room and pacing when his phone rang. It was Miriam. He ignored the call until it rang repeatedly and he closed his eyes to think about what he should tell Preye's mother. He didn't want anyone to make him feel he couldn't take care of his wife. The phone rang again and this time he picked it. 'Hello ma, I'm sorry I was sleeping.'

'How is Preye? How did the surgery go? I hope she's alright and recovering now?' Miriam didn't spare any pleasantries.

Timi didn't like to be questioned like this. 'I'm still at the hospital, waiting for them to be done. The doctor said there was a bit of complication, but everything is under control. Preye is fine.'

'What complication? Are you sure they are telling you the truth?' Miriam asked anxiously and muttered something Timi couldn't hear.

'Preye is fine. I just spoke with the doctor. I'll call you immediately she's out, so you can speak with her. Don't worry ma.' He liked to think he was in control and felt Miriam should understand that too.

'Okay, I'll call you again. Thank you.'

He sighed as Miriam ended the call. He was about to call his mother, but Tina's call came through. He ignored her and went on to call Ife to explain the situation. Ife commended him and told him she was sure he could handle the situation and asked him to let her know if he needed her to do anything.

A short while later, Preye was wheeled out of the theatre to the recovery room, with some nurses swarming her like vultures. Stella came to Timi and informed him that he could see his wife. 'Let me know if I can help you with anything, Mr Coker,' she offered.

'You're an angel, Stella. Thank you for your help. She's likely to be here for a couple of days, so whatever you can do to make my wife comfortable will be well appreciated. She means the world to me.'

'Your wife is fortunate to have you,' Stella commented.

He cautiously walked into the room to find a nurse by Preye's bed. The nurse held a chart book and was making notes as she checked the drips and devices surrounding Preye. 'How is she doing?' Timi asked as he peeped over Preye's still figure on the bed.

'She wife will soon wake up. It's good that you're here.'

'Thank you.' He sat down to hold Preye's hand. She looked very pale and helpless. He couldn't help comparing how she looked now to the time he first set his eyes on her and he wished she'd just get up and come home with him so she could look beautiful again.

Preye opened her eyes slowly. Her eyelids were heavy and it took an effort to get them to open fully as she tried to take in her surroundings. Her sight was blurred and she felt nauseous. She tried to speak and sit up at the same time, but she was too weak to even lift her finger. Her body was hurting and it seemed like there was a flow of hot fluid running inside her body. She felt the warmth of Timi's strokes on her hand and she turned to look at him, while the nurse touched her shoulder.

'Mrs Coker, can you hear me?' the nurse asked. Preye nodded. 'You're in the hospital and you've just had a surgery. Your husband is here. Can you talk?'

Preye nodded and spoke faintly. 'Yes Timi. Where's my mum?'

Timi was shocked and annoyed at Preye's question. The least he expected was for her to appreciate that he was by her side, but he contained himself. 'She called earlier. I'll call her back and tell her you're out. Maybe she'll visit tomorrow.'

'Are you hurting?' the nurse asked. Preye nodded and pointed at her tummy. 'That's okay. I'm just going to take your vitals now. It may hurt a little as you try to move, but I'll give you some medicines. The pain will ease out gradually.' The nurse went about her tasks and explained how each of the contraptions attached to Preye's body would help her recover.

Timi sent a text to Miriam that Preye was now awake. He stroked her face. 'I'm here with you, Mine. You'll be fine.'

*

Timi had jettisoned spending the night with Tina and gone home straight to sleep after they moved Preye to the ward.

He planned to impress Preye with his looks, so he took his time to shave, get dressed and spray his favourite perfume. He made himself a breakfast of French toast and coffee, and made some calls before heading to the hospital.

On the way, he stopped at the florist to pick up a bouquet of sunflowers, hoping to lift Preye's spirits. He was surprised when the receptionist directed him to Dr Tash's office, instead of the ward where his wife was.

'Good morning, Mr Coker.' Dr Tash got up to speak with him. Her face betrayed no emotion, contrary to the smile Timi was expecting. 'I wanted to give you an update before you see your wife.'

His entire body tensed and it seemed the floor under him was about to open up, sending his mind on a high alert. 'What's happening? Can you tell me what's going on here? Is my wife okay?' he ranted.

The momentary flash of sympathy on the doctor's face heightened his anxiety. 'She's alive. I told you yesterday that she lost a lot of blood during the surgery and we had to give her blood. In the process, the supply of blood to her kidneys was compromised, so we needed to have some tests done. I'm sorry to tell you, she's suffered acute kidney injury.'

'What?' He banged the table. His brain was spinning at an uncontrollable speed. 'What does that mean?'

The doctor stilled, but continued. 'She hasn't urinated since yesterday, which means her kidneys are not processing the waste from her body. Unfortunately, this can lead to further complications. We will reassess the kidney functions and keep monitoring her. We'll run some more tests to find out possible causes and determine our next course of action. In the meantime, we have to place her on haemodialysis to get toxins out of her body. I have scheduled a nephrologist to see her tomorrow. Please come with me. She's been moved to intensive care.'

Dr Tash left him at the door where Preye was lying. There were more drips, tubes and machines than the ones in the recovering room. They were intricately interwoven, most of them leading in and out of Preye's body; a dialysis machine was connected to her elbow and an oxygen mask was strapped to her face. Her eyes were fixed on the doctor who was reading an image from the film in his hands, and the nurse standing beside him. The eyes were hollow and tired as if life would go out of them anytime soon. The doctor checked the monitor and made some notes.

Timi was transfixed.

The doctor put the film in a folder and pulled Timi to the corner. 'Good afternoon, Mr Coker. I am Dr David. I believe you've seen Dr Tash. Good thing you're here. Your wife just woke up. Do you want me to tell her why she's here or you would want to do that?' The doctor whispered. Timi shook his head and nudged the doctor to go ahead. He hadn't yet come to terms with everything Dr Tash told him and felt ill-equipped to explain to Preye. 'Mrs Coker, can you hear me?' Preye nodded and the doctor continued talking to her slowly. 'You had a surgery yesterday.' She nodded again. 'There was a little problem, but we're trying to correct it. We need to support you to breathe properly and filter waste out of your body, so we don't have more problems. Has the pain reduced?' With great effort, Preye shook her head to indicate *no*. Both the doctor and nurse made some notes. 'You'll get some more medications to help relieve your pain.'

Timi eventually found his way to Preye's side. The only place he could safely touch was her head, so he gently rubbed his hand over her head to soothe her. He didn't have any word to say to his wife as he slipped into the chair beside the bed after the doctor left the room.

Preye was still sleeping and Timi had dozed off on the chair when Lola and Miriam came in, stealthily. He woke up to the gentle tap of Miriam on his shoulders.

It was obvious there was no love lost between Lola and Timi, but they remained cordial as Timi tried his best to respond to their questions about Preye's health status. He was relieved that Miriam had taken the initiative to come, but didn't like the intrusion that Lola presented. His mind subconsciously went to work on how to stop Lola from coming to see Preye. After Miriam got over the shock of seeing her daughter in her vulnerable state and shedding some silent tears, she knelt beside the bed and prayed under her breath.

Preye woke and slept intermittently after Miriam and Lola left. Timi told her about their visit and that Miriam had prayed for her, hoping that would give her some comfort. Instead, he saw a tear at the corner of her right eye. It wasn't long after, that she dozed off again. He had to go out and back to the room to make calls and to update his parents. He told his father that he'd need assistance with some funds to settle the hospital bills, to which his father responded in the affirmative.

He was getting frustrated, not knowing what to do and what was expected of him. He hadn't expected that he'd be unable to communicate with his wife, and merely sit and watch her lying helplessly on the bed was beginning to annoy him; he hadn't expected he'd have to abandon everything he was doing to stay at the hospital; he hadn't expected that his plan towards building his business to gain financial independence would be interrupted; he hadn't expected to be helpless; the only thing he had expected was for Preye to come back home to rely on him to help her recover.

He stood up expectantly when a nurse came in. She told him that some of the test results would be ready by the next day and advised him to get some rest himself.

On his way out, he called Tina to tell her he was on his way to see her. He needed someone to make him feel good.

CHAPTER TWENTY FOUR

'Yes Malik, I'll be fine. Thanks for checking,' Timi said tersely, as he ended the call.

Since he had spent all day at the hospital yesterday, he decided to get as much work done as he could. He had interviewed someone for the role of personal assistant last week and had scheduled two other interviews tomorrow, but he decided to cancel them since he wasn't sure what the next few days would look like. Instead, he'd hire the one he already interviewed, especially since the applicant had been recommended by Martin. He needed to get things moving for his new office as soon as possible.

His phone beeped. He hissed as he discovered that it was Tina's text, complaining that he had left without informing her. He thought it was high time he gave Tina the rules of the game – she should recognise that he was a married man with responsibilities. He switched off his phone to avoid further distractions, knowing fully well that she'd likely call him. He searched through Preye's laptop and got a sample of an employment letter to adapt for his proposed employee, Bruce Elliot. The thought crossed his mind that he could now access Preye's clients' details if he wanted to. He emailed the letter of employment and added a note that he expected Bruce to respond before the end of the day, if he wanted to resume the following Monday.

It was almost noon by the time Timi got to the hospital. He was surprised to find Miriam at the reception, on her way out to get some food. Miriam had gotten to the hospital early in the morning to avoid rush-hour traffic. She had prayed for Preye and was encouraged that Preye had nodded to her prayers and smiled.

Timi greeted Miriam politely, but was inwardly seething with rage, annoyed that Miriam wanted to steal first place with his wife. Apart from the doctors, no one should get to see his wife before him.

'Thank you for coming, ma. I hope she knew you were there?' he asked Miriam.

'Oh yes. We prayed together. You shouldn't thank me. Have you forgotten she's my daughter? I hope you're also resting.' Miriam sighed. 'Now that you're here, maybe I can leave.'

'Definitely. Let me get you a cab.' They started walking towards the exit.

'Did they tell you when she'd be okay, like when she can be discharged?' Miriam inquired in almost a whisper. 'I don't like seeing her like that. I pray God sees her through.'

There was a bustle of activities behind them with multiple nurses and doctors running towards the ICU direction. Timi shook his head, wondering. 'I hope it's not …'

'No, it can't be for Preye, she responded well to me,' Miriam assured him. 'This is a big hospital. Thank you for taking care of her.' She patted him on the arm with confidence. 'We need to be optimistic. She'll be out soon, I'm sure.'

They said their goodbyes and Timi went back into the hospital after the cab taking Miriam home left.

He broke out into a smile on sighting Stella, but the smile was stifled by his racing heart when she directed him to the waiting room, explaining that there were doctors in Preye's room. He paced in the waiting room for some time, then went back to ask the nurse if everything was okay. Stella's response that the doctors were giving Preye a check-up did nothing to assuage his anxiety.

It seemed like a long dreary day before Stella called Timi to go into Preye's room. Only Dr Tash and another nurse were with her. Timi looked around to see what had changed, but Preye was still embroiled with monitors and tubes. He looked at Dr Tash, questioningly.

'You may want to sit, Mr Coker,' Dr Tash advised.

He had to keep his voice low to avoid startling Preye. 'No, I don't want to sit. Please can you tell me what the hell is going on?' High tension wires sparked through the entire organs in his body. His eyes were focused on the doctor, but he couldn't see a thing.

'Mr Coker, your wife slipped into a coma. It's the body manifesting the injury to the organs. We're trying all we can to put everything under control.'

'You must be joking. Every time I leave, it's like something else goes wrong. Do you want me to pack up my life?' He dropped into the chair and buried his head in his hands.

'We are doing everything we can, but there are some things nature does for itself. Uremic encephalopathy is …'

'When will she slip out of the coma?' The doctor's words were like a pinch of bitter powder in his throat that he wished he could spit out. His life had been turned upside down by a surgery that was supposed to be a simple procedure. Sure, the risks had been explained to them, but not in his wildest imagination would he have thought Preye would be in this condition.

'I can't say for sure. We are working out a treatment plan and we'll continue to test for brain function.'

He sighed. 'So what do I do now?' He was subdued. A tear slid down from his left eye.

'We'll see how she responds to treatment, while she's on life support. She has brain activity and it's only her body that will be unresponsive for now. There have been cases where patients recover with only a headache, but we never can tell until she wakes up. She's stable now, so there's nothing you can do but to wait.'

And he waited. But with no single flutter of an eyelid or finger from Preye, he left after about two hours. On his way out, he saw Stella at the nurses' station and he asked to speak with her. 'My wife means the world to me and I want to do all I can to protect her.' He paused and soaked in the look of empathy on Stella's face. 'Preye is estranged from her family and some of her friends.' He waved his hand. 'It's a long story, but you know how people like to pretend they care when they actually don't. You'll be doing my wife a service by limiting her visitors. What I mean is no one should be allowed to see her unless I give express approval. She's been through so much these past few days and I'm sure you wouldn't want to add to our trauma,' he concluded.

In her few years of nursing, Stella had witnessed a lot of family dramas play out at patients' bedsides and she understood how traumatic it could be for some. The hospital management had a duty of care to patients and usually restricted visitors who may cause harm or disruption. In some rare cases, the hospital invited the security operatives to send away such unwanted visitors as a last resort.

'I quite understand, Mr Coker. I know how it is with some families and I'm sure your wife will have them back in her life when she's ready. I will alert the nurses and other staff on duty of your wishes. If there is a problem, come right to me and I'll handle the situation.' Stella blushed under his intense gaze. He came across as a knight in shining armour, going to great lengths to protect his love.

*

The following day, it was Dr David with Preye. He introduced himself to Timi and informed Timi that Preye was still in a coma. Although her body had been reactive, they needed the response to be consistent and specific. 'We need her to regain consciousness to know …'

'I hope there's no damage to her brain,' Timi interrupted the doctor. He had spent all night researching comas on the internet and he wasn't any wiser because of all the medical jargons used. The only thing he knew was that brain damage could make a person vegetative.

'The brain is very sensitive, but we have to hope for the best. As she improves, we may be able to get her off life support and hope she wakes up soon. She's currently not aware of her surroundings.'

Timi slapped his face with his two hands. 'Am I going to come here every day and do nothing? Isn't there something I can do? I need my wife back, please.'

'Your presence here will be therapeutic. Although it may seem frustrating that she's not responding, you just need to keep at it.'

So he sat there, staring at his helpless wife for most of the day without any indication that she was alive. It wasn't only Preye that was helpless; he felt helpless too, and hopeless. Right now, he'd do anything to have her back the way she was, even without the hope of having children. He cursed the fibroids that had brought her so much pain.

He could do nothing else but watch.

*

On the third day of being comatose, Preye heard the doctor

discussing her with the nurse, but she didn't know why she was the topic of discussion because she couldn't hear clearly what was being said. She also didn't know where she was or why she was there. She didn't want to bother them because she was too tired and rather satisfied with where she was. If she wanted to talk to them, she'd have to open her eyes and that required too much effort. She didn't make the effort before the face appeared to her. The doctor came to her bed and examined the drip. Initially, she couldn't tell who it was, but she eventually remembered his name. It was Kevin. Kevin was taking care of her; he always liked to fuss over her. That was one of the reasons everyone loved him.

She remembered…

*

…Preye was in the sitting room with Tonye when Kevin came in with a pack of fruits and vegetables. He never came to the house empty-handed, no matter how small the item was. *'My girl, how you dey?'* he asked.

'Not so good,' she responded tersely. Preye didn't get up; she was still brooding over her boss's rejection of a presentation she had made at the office.

Kevin dropped the items on the centre table. 'You thought the question was for you? Sorry. Tonye, *na you I dey ask*. How was your day? What have you been up to?'

Tonye's face lit up and she got up to embrace Kevin, as Preye hissed and smiled. 'It's getting better and I'm hopeful. I went for a first stage interview, but I wasn't so lucky. And someone here has been complaining to me about her boss not appreciating her work. Can you imagine that?'

'Don't mind her, she's spoilt,' he responded heartily to Tonye, but went to Preye and shoved his index finger into her side to tickle her. She responded by jumping up and wagging her finger at him. Tonye took the items to the kitchen. Kevin and Preye exchanged a kiss before Tonye returned. 'Don't get too excited. I need to say hello to someone that will be happy to see me. Before she finds me here, where is she?'

'Where else?' Preye pointed to the kitchen and Kevin darted off to see Preye's mother. A few minutes later, he was out with Tonye and headed towards the door. 'Where are you two off to?' she queried.

'To give you space, so you can cool off,' Tonye jeered and exchanged a wink with Kevin. Preye parted the curtain to watch them drive off in Kevin's old Toyota and blamed herself for sulking about her job.

Miriam came into the living room to praise Kevin's thoughtfulness. She had been trying to cut the meat to add to the stew, but the knife was blunt and she had been struggling with it before Kevin came in. He had volunteered to go to a shop nearby, with Tonye to get a knife sharpener. Preye said she didn't know the knife was bad and Miriam responded sarcastically that only people who cooked would know if a knife still worked. Kevin and Tonye came back with a new set of five kitchen knives instead of the sharpener.

He went to Preye after Tonye vamoosed to the kitchen. 'Tell me, what happened at work?' Preye tried to dismiss it, but he insisted. With some input from her manager, she had worked tirelessly for two days to produce an audio-visual presentation to pitch for a client, only for her to get feedback that the director had ditched it.

'Is that the only thing that happened to you today?' he probed further.

Preye thought for a moment. 'Well, not exactly.' She had an idea of what he was driving at. 'I got the star-word for the month's puzzle which earned me free lunch. I gave the cleaner five grand to help with her daughter's school fees. I've helped Tonye review her CV and ...'

'Come here,' he beckoned. He stroked her nose. 'And from all of these, the only thing you chose to dwell on is your ditched presentation. What if I add to that and tell you you're beautiful and you have a one-in-a-million beauty spot,' he concluded by stroking her birthmark. She smiled.

He always knew how to make her smile...

*

Dr David saw a smile form on Preye's face. It was the type of smile that disappeared before it could spread across the face; the type that failed to connect with the soul. Her eyes flicked open; there was no blink, no warmth, only a robotic gaze bereft of life. The doctor leaned down to look into her eyes, but their eyes didn't meet as Preye was staring at an invisible object on the ceiling. The doctor watched until she shut her eyes again.

She wasn't out of coma yet.

CHAPTER TWENTY FIVE

'Any change this morning?' Timi asked Titi, the ICU nurse who was in the room with Preye.

'No, but she's stable and she opened her eyes yesterday.'

'I have a few conference calls to make and I was wondering if I can do that from here. I only need to set up my laptop. Will that disturb her?' Timi asked.

'No. If anything, the sound of your voice will be stimulating to her,' Titi replied. She checked one of the monitors in the room and showed Timi a buzzer, telling him to call if he needed anything or if he noticed any movement with Preye.

Timi studied the nurse and thought to himself that she was beautiful. He also noted that she was quite young and wasn't wearing any ring. *She seems quite impressionable*, he told himself.

He waited for her to leave the room before he powered up his laptop. His phone beeped. It was a message from Tina, *'Ds is what u missed last night.'* She attached a picture of herself wearing a revealing negligee. He whistled involuntarily and placed a call to her. 'T baby, why are you doing this?' he paused to listen. 'Yes, I miss you too, but it's been tough the past couple of days. I can't exactly leave my wife alone at a time like this,' he paused again. 'Yes my PA will sort out the office.' He paused and laughed. 'Not fair, Tina. The thought of you naked in bed when I can't be there is torture.'

He put down his phone and started researching some internet sites on his laptop. After a while, he went to use the visitors' toilet and chatted briefly with the nurses. He returned to the room and brushed Preye's cheek, but she didn't respond. He planted a kiss on her forehead. 'Mine, it's time for you to come back home. I don't know how much longer I can live without you.'

He called his father and expressed his feelings of frustration. 'Dad, it's rare that I'm without options. I've always been able to get myself out of a jam, but right now, I don't think I've ever felt more useless,' he whined.

'Don't say that, son. You're not in any way useless. This situation can be overwhelming for anyone. Did you get the money I transferred to you?' Wale Coker paused and Timi responded that he had gotten the money. 'Seriously, this is one of those times when you have to step back and wait until Preye comes back to you. Are you sure your mother and I can't come to the hospital? The least we can do is provide support.'

'No. It's quiet around here and I think she should have it that way. The distance will also be too much on you. The doctor is hopeful that she'd recover soon, but they aren't sure what the outcome will be. The stress has me pushed to the limit and I'm not sure how much more I can take. I love her and I can't lose her,' Timi said through tears.

'We'll pray, Timi. But you need to be strong for her and yourself too.'

'I'm trying. I'll try.'

'Okay, son. Keep us informed. Your mum says hello.' Wale Coker ended the call.

*

…Preye wanted to open her eyes when she heard Kevin's sobs. It puzzled her that he was crying; he was the strong one, always caring for other people. And he was caring for her now. *Was he crying because she didn't want to get up?* She wanted to get up to soothe his tears, but pain racked her body and it was easier for her to remain as she was. He had told her he missed her after her surgery and that he wasn't going to leave her bedside until she smiled at him.

Everyone in the big recovery room loved him because he always brought treats whenever he came visiting and he'd go to each patient's bed to say hello before he settled down with her. The Sunday after her surgery, he had even come with a small choir band after church to have a worship service.

He came to see her every day at the hospital and told her he valued her more than anything and would want them to get married once she was well enough. He got on his knees the day she was discharged from the hospital and proposed to her. He said her hospitalisation had made him realise that he needed to appreciate and prioritise the most important things in his life. The other patients waited for her to say yes before they applauded them. They picked a date to start planning the wedding when she recovered well enough.

Then Kevin got sick. She remembered now, why he was crying. It had started with a fever and he had initially been treated for malaria. But he only got worse. He couldn't sleep at night and was always tired. The doctors later said he had lymphoma and it would be a miracle if he survived. They got into a serious discussion about postponing the wedding. She didn't want to postpone the wedding, believing that he'd recover soon. But Kevin insisted that he couldn't tie her down, not knowing what would happen to him.

It was then he started sobbing…

*

'Maybe you should try to call him, because I've been calling him since the last time I went to the hospital. You know he likes you a little, *as you responsible pass me*,' Lola ranted to Aisha as Tobi opened her office door and waved. She waved back for him to hold on. 'Even Preye's mother said she hasn't been able to talk to her. I just want to hear her voice.'

Aisha promised Lola that she'd give Timi a call.

'What's up? How is Preye?' Tobi asked. He had also tried to call Timi twice, but his calls had gone to his voicemail, with no response. If anyone would know, it was Lola.

'I still haven't been able to get hold of her. And that stupid apology of a man wouldn't pick my calls,' she moaned.

'That's your friend's husband,' Tobi rebuked her, although he shared her sentiment.

'*Abeg*,' Lola dismissed him. 'I don't know if she's still in the hospital or if she's been discharged. If it wasn't for the distance …' she hissed without finishing the sentence.

'Why don't you take the day off tomorrow? Call Aisha back and see if she can go with you. Take a drive down to the hospital. It's better if we know how she's faring, rather than brooding over Timi's attitude.'

'You had to mention his name.' She hissed again and gave Tobi the evil eye before he left for his office.

She worked through the piles of documents on her desk. She had always been restless and liked to be on the move. But since Preye got married, Lola had been picking up bits and pieces of Preye's tasks. Now that Preye was sick, Lola was saddled with a whole bunch of paperwork and research activities. She had thought Preye had it easy working from the office most of the time; she knew better now. She needed to conduct a focus group research, but she needed to identify the prospects first. Before, Preye would have researched the group and given her the list to contact them. Lola sighed and shook her head. *Never envy someone else's position.* She had made good progress today, getting eighteen names, but she needed seven more. Her phone rang. It was Aisha.

'Yes, *Omo* girl.' Lola smiled, grateful for the distraction from her paperwork.

'He didn't pick my call too,' Aisha announced despairingly. 'I also called with Adamu's phone, but it was the same.'

'It's not like you're surprised anyway,' Lola sighed. 'Should we take a drive to the hospital tomorrow? If she's been discharged, we can go to the house. If you're with me, he won't lock us out.'

'Okay, let me ask the nanny if she can look after Ashe too. I'll call you back,' Aisha promised.

'Yeah, I need to check with Sammy too. *Chai!* I didn't have to check with anyone when there was no boyfriend o,' Lola lamented. She ended the call and placed a call to Sammy. 'Boyfriend, *how you dey?*' Sammy whispered back into the phone, that he needed to excuse himself from a meeting. As soon as he was in the clear, Lola continued. 'Sorry to interrupt. I'm thinking of going to see Preye with Aisha. Can we do dinner tomorrow instead of lunch?' She held her breath, guessing what would be going through Sammy's mind. He always teased her about her level of unpredictability. Sammy agreed and asked if there was any other thing he could do regarding Preye. 'I'll be happy if you'd arrange a chopper for us. It's the traffic on that road that wearies me.'

She blew a kiss into the phone before ending the call.

*

Timi got through to his new personal assistant when he called Bruce a second time. 'Do you understand me, Bruce? You were supposed to send me the reviewed lease as soon as you received it. I don't want to hear your nonsense excuses.' His voice was booming.

'I don't know what to tell you. I'm sure I emailed it this morning. I'll send it again. You should be receiving it as we speak,' Bruce replied nervously.

'If you can't handle the job, tell me and I'll get someone who can. If I lose the chance to rent that space, I'll fire you on the spot. You can expect to hear from me at any time and I expect you to answer. I don't understand why your phone rang out the first time I called.' Timi disconnected the call. But the phone rang immediately. 'What?' he barked into the phone.

'I'm sorry, I wanted to ask about your wife,' Bruce said cautiously.

'Mind your own business and get your work done,' Timi growled and disconnected the call again. He went back to his laptop to start browsing for souvenirs for his office's grand opening. Thankfully, he had paid for the essential furniture items way back.

Dr David entered Preye's room. 'How are you holding up?' he asked Timi.

'I'm trying to remain optimistic. The nurse said my vibes might be picked up by Preye, although that's hard to believe. She hasn't moved a muscle.'

'She's not exactly in a vegetative state, so there's hope. The only thing you can do now is to try some form of stimulation. You might try reading to her. Does she have a favourite author or a section of any newspaper that she likes reading? Try reading it. It's better than sitting around and feeling like you can't do anything.'

Dr David left after examining Preye and Timi thought about what he could read to his wife. She used to read motivational books but she had suddenly stopped because he had continually teased her that most of the authors were toying with peoples' minds and didn't exactly practise the theories they preached. He picked up the business section of the *Daily Mirror* newspaper and began to read. He felt a little silly, talking to someone that didn't respond, but he did it, anyway. He was reading about trends in the stock market, which he didn't find interesting.

His eyes landed on a small article in the *Comings and Goings* section. Timi excitedly gripped Preye's bed and started to recite the short blurb, jumping to where his name featured. 'Timi Coker will be opening a PR firm in the next few months. Timi's Communications will be the first solo journey for Coker, formerly of Mason Bridge and husband of the PR industry hotshot, Preye Banigo.'

Preye didn't react.

Timi crumpled up the paper and tossed it in the bin. He was frustrated that the reading garnered no reaction from her. He was also annoyed because the article made it sound as if he was riding on the coat-tails of his wife. And she was referred to by her maiden name.

At the nurses' station, Stella checked in with the nurse on duty when she arrived back on shift. She wanted to make sure Timi's instruction to keep visitors away from Preye was obeyed. Timi usually showered Stella and her co-workers with compliments. He was beyond sweet to the nursing staff and on the verge of being flirtatious with Stella. He found that many times, this strategy worked with young women.

CHAPTER TWENTY SIX

Titi checked the bags of clear liquid hanging over Preye's bed. Each one had a tube running to a different vein. 'No change. Is there anything I can do for you, Mr Coker? The caregiver is too often overlooked in such a situation.'

He shook his head. 'Don't worry about me. I just want a sign that she's making an attempt to wake up. I can't stand to hear that there's no change because it puts me in a limbo.' He raked his fingers through his thick afro hair. 'Thanks for caring, though. I can't thank you and the other nurses enough. When I see your smiles every day, it gives me hope. I learnt some people came yesterday and tried to barge in. I know it's not easy turning them away, but I assure you it's for the best.'

'We know Mrs Coker's health is most important right now. The receptionist said a particular Ms Bello has been the most persistent, calling every day. She was the one who came yesterday, accompanied by another lady and they tried to sneak in. They've been warned that if they tried that again, we'll call the security guards to escort them out of the building,' Titi assured, pleased to prove that the hospital staff were efficient.

Timi smiled. 'I heard about that. That's the same lady Preye was thinking of giving the sack before she came for the surgery. She shouldn't be allowed near my wife at all.' Timi didn't want Lola anywhere near Preye. If anyone could stimulate his wife to consciousness, it was him. He knew all the buttons that triggered

275

her to life.

Once Titi left the room, Timi opened his laptop and started perusing audiobooks, so he could try reading to Preye. He received an instant message from Tina.

'Hey – a quick bite? You need to eat. Come to my place and we can do a takeaway.'

He typed his response. *Afraid to leave because the bitches are circling this place like vultures. I'm only hungry for you but I have to be with Preye for now. Send pics.*

As if Tina had been waiting for the cue, numerous pictures landed on Timi's phone in a jiffy. They were nothing like having sex with Tina, but they were close enough to send him to the toilet. He returned to Preye's side with a kind of smile that could infuse life into anyone around him.

He picked the novel he had brought with him and started reading to Preye. The story was about a female athlete who retrained to get back into competitive sports after her legs got broken in an accident. Timi hoped Preye could hear and get motivated with the come-back story.

After reading two chapters, he leaned in and spoke directly to Preye. 'Do you find this reading interesting in any way? You know how much I hate reading and it would be a waste if you didn't hear a word of what I'm saying.' He squeezed her hand and continued to read. His voice showed little enthusiasm for the subject. If he were a teacher, the students would easily doze off or find an excuse to leave his class. He looked up from the book again. 'You left me once. Are you pulling that on me again? I want you to wake up and come back. This is one drama I don't need at this point in my life. The new business will be our future and I can't do it without your support and industry connections.'

*

...All around her, Preye saw only darkness as she turned full circle. The biggest mystery was how she descended into the unending tunnel. She wondered which way led outside or if there was a way at all. The tunnel was lonely. And except for the occasional echoes that came out from the void, there was no one with her. She wondered where everyone had gone, especially her mother. She thought perhaps she had done something terrible to her family before night fell. Did she send them away or were they trapped somewhere in their own dark tunnels? She wanted the gentle touch of her mother, Miriam Banigo.

Preye remembered that Miriam had never been overly affectionate because she was always too busy. The few times she did caress her daughter's cheek or the birthmark on her neck, the feeling was powerful, and it was just what Preye craved while trapped in the black tunnel. Instead, it was her father, Harry Banigo who came out of the shadows and pleaded for forgiveness for leaving the children behind; for not tucking her into bed; for not dropping her off in school; for not helping with her homework and for not running with her.

After Harry didn't return home, Preye had cried every day, asking Miriam to bring their father home. Miriam had tried to explain that Harry wouldn't be coming back and that their marriage was a mistake that shouldn't have happened. Preye hadn't understood then; the only thing she had known was that her father loved her and he'd never desert her. Miriam had said her father forgot the way back home, so every time they went to church, Preye prayed that God should show her daddy the way and bring him home safely.

A lot of things had begun to change when Harry left. Miriam had needed to work harder and had been seldom at home, so Preye had been left to take care of her sisters. Preye had responded to the stress at home by randomly getting angry, lashing out and getting into fights at school. Any time she got a bad report from school, her mother would punished her by telling her to run around the house five times. One day, Erefa, out of pity for Preye, advised her to start running anytime she got angry instead of lashing out, since that was her punishment anyway. So Preye had started running to replace her outbursts.

Her two sisters finally emerged from the shadows, crying as they ran towards Preye. She petted them, hoping their mother would come back home on time, to give them food. When her mother didn't come on time, Preye went to soak *garri* for the three of them and added two cubes of sugar for each person, which was the instruction her mother had given her. Initially, Tonye refused to drink the *garri,* but later joined when she realised that Preye wouldn't pet her. Preye invited Harry to join her, but he shook his head and urged them to go ahead. #As usual, her mother rushed in after they had finished eating and encircled them away from Harry. He looked on and pleaded with Miriam to release the children.

Preye wanted to run back to embrace her father, but her arms hurt as she tried to raise them. A strong wind suddenly blew and almost knocked her down. The wind calmed and a beautiful lady wearing high heels stepped out from the void to drag her father away…

*

Timi decided to spend the night at the hospital, hoping that his readings would have touched Preye's heart enough to give her the will to live. He wanted to be around and be the first to welcome her back to life. He had only gone out briefly to hand over the signed lease agreement to the estate agent. He had become a favourite of the nurses so they changed the chair in Preye's room to a reclining one and gave him some pillows.

Every twenty minutes, Preye's blood pressure cuff expanded,

so updates could be sent to the nurse's station. The intermittent sounds from the machines and the heart monitor were comforting to him in some bizarre way, once he got used to them; the hissing and buzzing reminded him that his wife was still alive.

While he slept, nurses kept vigil. Titi peeked into Preye's room and returned to the charge desk. She spoke in a hushed tone, which the other nurses were well accustomed to. 'Timi Coker is fast asleep next to his wife's bed. His devotion is inspiring, and I wish I could find a man like that for myself. When that woman wakes up, he'll be elated. I hope she appreciates him.'

A nurse nodded in agreement. 'He hasn't left her side except for a few hours today and he's protecting her from those nasty people that call themselves her family and friends. I had the pleasure of meeting that Lola Bello and walking her out the other day. The cheek of it,' she made a face.

'You can't trust anyone in this world,' Titi agreed and went on with her notes.

'But I felt sorry for the mother and sister when they left disappointed yesterday. I think he should let the mother see her at the least. Everybody can't be against his wife just like that. Or what do you think?' another nurse asked curiously.

'I think we owe a duty of care to our clients,' Titi replied matter-of-factly. The other nurses nodded agreeably. 'I'm glad we agree on that. No one from Mrs Coker's family or her friends should get near her unless Mr Coker directs otherwise,' she concluded.

She went into the room, looked at the monitor and saw no change in Preye's condition. She handed over to the night nurse.

*

Timi went to the hospital cafeteria and came back with a mug of coffee. The smell of coffee flashed like a light and pushed Preye out of the darkness. She lifted her face to see where the smell was coming from and the smell took her down the path to the past.

*

…Two gentlemen, one holding a cup of coffee, had just walked into the room where she was busy with Aisha, arranging enlightenment fliers that they planned on distributing in the neighbourhood. She had started the Roadrunners Club to raise awareness about the cancer that caused Kevin Murphy's death. And having had a couple of failed relationships afterwards, she had chosen to fill her life with something meaningful.

The one holding the cup of coffee was Timi and he had come to join the club with his friend. Reflexively, Preye inhaled the smell covetously and smiled. He smiled back.

'Hello, I'm Timi Coker, I want to join Roadrunners, but I think you're interested in my coffee. Should I be concerned?' He wore khaki combats and a crisp white shirt, with brown loafers. It looked as if he was walking through the park during his lunch hour.

Preye met his eyes and widened her smile. 'A sign-up sheet is on the bench. We're about to begin a 1K loop around the park but you're not dressed for it. Perhaps you…'

Timi interrupted Preye. 'My friend is Malik,' he said and Malik shook Preye's hand. 'Can I offer you my coffee?' he insisted, pushing the mug towards her and spilling the coffee in the process. She said, *no*, thanks. 'Okay, I tried.' She found his confidence enchanting. 'We only came to register today. You can give us the guidelines and we'll come back.'

After they registered and were about leaving, Timi offered

her the coffee again. 'Are you sure you'll survive without this?' He challenged her with the soft smile that spread across his face.

She smiled...

*

Timi's eyes were set on Preye and he saw her lips curl into a slight smile. It was hardly noticeable, but he picked up on it and he shouted as he ran into the corridor. 'She moved, she just smiled!' he shouted as he grabbed Titi by the arm. 'She smiled, she moved her lips. I had just spilled coffee on my shirt, which is something I sometimes do. It's a joke between us. I'm sure she's alert and if you check her monitors, you'll see a change,' Timi gushed.

Titi asked the other nurse to get Dr David as she rushed after Timi into Preye's room. She used a stethoscope to examine Preye and began to analyse her readouts. Preye's smile had gone and she remained still. Titi called Preye's name twice to elicit a response, but Preye didn't flinch. Titi exerted some pressure on Preye's central upper chest with her fist in a rotatory fashion. Still there was no movement. Titi looked at Timi and shook her head; it was a sombre look.

Dr David walked briskly into the room. 'Did she show any sign of activity?' he asked, studying the monitors.

Titi pressed her lips. 'It was a reflexive movement. There has been no change.'

The doctor faced Timi. 'I know how anything you see will look hopeful. Sometimes, there's a motor function and it can appear...'

Timi interrupted him, exasperated. 'But I'm sure it was something about the coffee. She loves coffee. And she smiled. She definitely smiled.' His mind was dancing like a small kite struggling to find a way against the strong wind.

'I don't doubt it, but she's not conscious yet. Patients respond differently. Some may be able to open and close their eyes, even while unconscious. If you're sure it's the coffee, we can have some placed in the room. Does she have any special brand?'

Timi stared at them blandly. He was on the verge of a mental explosion, wondering why Preye would choose to make a fool of him. He was sure she had smiled. It was the smile she wore when she was pleased about something or someone. He spoke in a voice quieter than usual. 'Please, can I have the room alone with my wife?'

'Once she opens her eyes, we will start her on sensory stimulation,' Dr David said, to help Timi retain hope. He left, with Titi hurrying behind him.

Timi hurled his pen across the room and kicked the trash bin. He was furious that the nurse had thought he was seeing things, which made him feel incredibly stupid. 'Damn it, Preye. I know you can hear me and you're now telling yourself that I should calm down,' he raged as he paced back and forth. He was careful to contain his voice within the room, so he wouldn't get the attention of the nurses. 'You're lying half dead on that bed and you're still playing mind games with me. You still think you're smarter than me, right? Well, I've got news for you. You're not. Because if you're so great, you would get out of this bed. How long do you think I'm going to stick around for if you don't make an effort to come back to life? You might as well be dead right now.'

He collapsed on the chair next to the bed and wept uncontrollably. He figured that if she didn't make it, he could be blamed for her death. The wolves would devour him and his reputation. He cried some more and looked at Preye's chest rise and fall. She was alive and she had to stay that way.

After his tears dried, the guilt of spewing spiteful words at his helpless wife set in. He recognised that he had been taken over by negative emotions.

He kissed her hand. 'Look, I'm sorry. I was embarrassed and I snapped. I don't have any excuse and I need you here to keep me in line, Sweetheart. I'd be nothing without you by my side and life would lose its meaning. From the day I saw you in your Roadrunners' t-shirt, I knew you were someone special.' He paused to clasp his hand tightly on hers. 'You did that tight t-shirt justice and the twinkle in your eyes was captivating. I've been in love with you from that day and I haven't stopped loving you. No one beats your intelligence and kind heart, and your diligence. Seeing what you've done with Beta and how you've met every challenge with grace blew me away and still does till now.' He paused to see if there would be a response, but there was none. *Something has to work!*

'I haven't always made you proud, but I'm finally on the right track. Do you remember the office space we looked at, where the window was facing the trees? The one with the side entrance and safe parking. The offer was accepted. I've signed the lease and I am looking to make the payment this weekend. Hopefully, I can move in at the start of next month. You've got to be up and moving around by then because only you have the sense of style to decorate.'

Timi hoped that would make her proud and stir something inside her. He jiggled her bed softly, but she remained still. His efforts were futile.

*

Titi and a few other nurses were gathered at the nurse's station. 'I heard Mr Coker thought his wife had smiled,' Stella said to Titi.

'Yes o. You know how people feel about things like that. It

was hard to convince him that it meant nothing,' Titi replied, ploughing through files.

'If a man could will his wife back from the other side, it would be Mr Coker,' Stella added.

Another nurse looked over Stella's shoulder. 'Don't look. We have incoming friends and family of Mrs Coker. There are some new faces to contend with and the one that came the last time now has a baby with her.'

'I bet they're hoping to appeal to us with the baby,' Titi joked as the visitors approached the reception.

Aisha cradled Binta in her arms. Binta was Preye's goddaughter, so Aisha pleaded with the receptionist to at least allow them to see Preye. She maintained that a baby could only soothe Preye and in no way agitate her. Lola stood firmly beside Aisha, looking ahead towards the hospital wards as if Preye could walk past at any time. The receptionist told Aisha that a goddaughter wasn't considered family and that she should call before making the trip to the hospital again. Tonye and Miriam walked in too.

Lola started in a pleading voice. 'This is Preye's mother. Will you at least allow her to see her daughter? Is there any family bond that is stronger than that?'

The receptionist was courteously firm. 'Ma, with all due respect, this is a hospital and we are obliged to ensure that our clients' directives are followed regarding their welfare. Mrs Coker is not in a position to see anyone at this time.'

'I cannot figure out why you won't let me see my daughter. As far as I know, blood relatives are allowed to see a patient. She's my first daughter,' Miriam cried. A scarf which had all her grey hair tucked in and some strands sticking out, was tied round her head. Worrying about Preye's condition had taken a noticeable toll on her mother and it looked as if she was at her breaking point.

'Ma,' the receptionist addressed Lola again. 'We already informed Madam to call before coming to the hospital, rather than coming all the way. If the situation changes, we'll inform her. Coming around is not helpful to her daughter.'

'She is your patient's mother. Doesn't that count for something?' Lola queried, although she guessed what the response would be, but this was getting incredulous. Lola was holding herself from making a scene at the hospital, in order not to jeopardise the slim chance they still had.

'It does, but she's not registered as next of kin, ma.'

Stella walked past then and Tonye saw her. 'Mum, why don't you go to the nurse? Demand that you have the right to see your daughter,' Tonye suggested.

Miriam hurried to Stella and greeted Stella familiarly with a smile, reminding Stella that she had been to see Preye before, but now the receptionist was pretending that she had no right to see her daughter. Stella told her that Preye's condition was so delicate that Timi was the only person allowed to see her until further notice. She stated that Preye needed a state of complete calm and therefore, neither Miriam, nor any of the others could have access to her. Miriam returned to sit, dejected.

'We can't allow ourselves to be railroaded by Timi Coker. He's a monster, pure evil,' Tonye cried. 'I always knew there was something sinister about him. But sister was all over him.'

The others huddled around Miriam. 'I'll speak with Tobi tomorrow. I think he'd feel useful if I drop this one on his laps. If that doesn't work, Aisha, you're the lawyer,' Lola announced.

The receptionist heard Lola referring to Aisha as a lawyer and responded without looking up. 'Please come with an executed power of attorney by the client.'

'I can't believe this.' Tonye shook her head. 'I'll have to call Dad too. He usually knows what to do in such situations,' she added soberly.

'I would have called him, but his uncle is ill as well and your father has been attending to him,' Miriam told Tonye.

Miriam felt the weight of guilt pressing her down. Guilt that she had persuaded Preye to go back to Timi. She always had a bad feeling about Timi from the time Preye introduced him. She had ignored her intuition and even shut Tonye up when Tonye mentioned her reservations too. All she wanted then was for Preye to keep her marriage and start a family.

Admitting to herself that she had failed her daughter, Miriam didn't bother to contain the tears emitted from her eyes.

CHAPTER TWENTY SEVEN

… On the last day of her first semester at the university, all the first year students converged at the school auditorium for the valedictory service. The service started in the morning with an opening prayer and a rendition of two hymnals by the school choir, which caused most of the students to twitch restlessly. Before calling out names of students who won prizes, the vice chancellor gave a speech that no one listened to. For the students, the highlight of the programme was the performance of a dance-group that interpreted the beats of the instruments and the lyrics of the hip-hop song that was playing, as their bodies twisted in unison, like waves of water. The choreography was so sensually invigorating that the students began to twirl their bodies and participate in the activity happening on the stage, contrary to being mere spectators.

Once the service ended, it was time for heart-warming goodbyes and the students cheered and chattered for the few moments they had left. Most of the other girls in Preye's hostel already had their bags packed and they quickly went to meet their waiting parents in the car park. The ones who didn't go with their parents had collected gate passes to leave the campus by themselves. But Preye wasn't one of them. She didn't know how to get home by herself, so she had to wait for her mother. The other girls started leaving one after the other until there were just Preye and two other girls left, by noon. The two other girls, Aisha and Lola didn't want to leave Preye behind and they decided to keep her company until her mother arrived.

That was the beginning of their deep friendship as they shared details about their personal lives and aspirations without any inhibitions for the first time. They hadn't been close during the semester and Preye was touched that they could care so much as to wait with her.

It was about four o'clock and her mother had still not arrived, but the girls had to leave Preye reluctantly, so their parents wouldn't be worried. Preye already had tears in her eyes before the girls left. Lola and Aisha cried too as they parted ways. Preye went to stay with the hostel administrator to wait for her mother.

Until her mother came in about one hour later, apologising to her and the administrator, Preye had cried intermittently, wondering where her mother was and if her mother had abandoned her just like her father did...

Preye relived these flashbacks as she lay still on the bed in her hospital room. Her mind was consumed with a non-sequential and unrelated batter of past episodes, phantom events and sub-conscious reality.

…Preye didn't know why she was being drawn into the dark abyss again. She was too tired to fight. She tried raising her hands, but they felt like bricks and her legs wouldn't move too. She knew she needn't worry; her mother would always come for her, no matter how late, just like she did that day at the university, many years ago. She decided to enjoy her sleep and allow the darkness to pull her in. She didn't want to wake up until she was sure her mother had come for her...

*

Timi sat in his chair, staring at his laptop. It wasn't easy focusing on work when he was in a hospital room. The antiseptic surroundings were hardly suited to creative thinking. Titi came in with a cheerful bounce. She was starting to feel an affinity for the couple, especially for Timi. 'Hello, Mr Coker, how are you? I've been off for a few days, but I've been praying for your wife. I believe she'll come around soon,' Titi said, checking Preye's monitors and tubes. 'I try to leave this place behind when I go home, but some people just stay on my mind.'

Happy for the distraction to talk to a human, he shut his laptop and sipped on his coffee. 'Thank you for caring. This ordeal started with a simple procedure to reduce her pain and improve our chances of having children. I never imagined it would end up like this. I keep replaying the fiasco in my head and wondering if I could have done something different to change the outcome.'

'She had a good surgical team but sometimes these things happen and you can't explain them. Dr Tash is one of the best gynaecologists around. You shouldn't blame yourself. It was beyond anyone. Maybe you should speak with the doctors again,' she shrugged. 'Maybe just to assure yourself.'

'It seems like time is ticking out on me.' Timi mused. 'I spoke with Dr Tash yesterday, but there was no comfort in that discussion. She says if Preye doesn't open her eyes next week, then her chances of improvement are slim.'

Titi felt like patting him on the shoulder, but restrained herself. 'You must be hungry by now. Is there anything I can get you from the kitchen?' she asked, concerned that Timi may have been overlooking himself while caring for his wife.

'This is my second coffee. I'll be fine. I might pop out to the house later. I've been drowning in coffee every day to stay alert and to get another reaction from her. It's frustrating, you know.' He sighed. 'But since there's been no activity, I might as well catch up on my sleep. She doesn't need me keeping watch over her, since nothing I do matters.' Timi spoke in a gloomy voice.

Titi sensed his frustration and walked across the room to Preye's bed to lift her hand. 'Are you in there, Mrs Coker? Give us a sign darling. Your husband has been here round the clock waiting for you.' She noticed a tic in one of Preye's fingers. Timi saw it too and asked her to call the doctor, but she told him that it was just another reflex. He argued, pointing out that it was different this time because he had also noticed that her blood pressure ticked up slightly when her finger twitched.

Titi left and came back with Dr Tash. Dr Tash went to Preye's bed. 'Mrs Coker, it's Dr Tash here. We've been in this fight for a long time and I need you to keep up with me. If you can hear me, hold my hand, open your eyes, or wiggle your toes. Anything, just do something,' she paused. 'Your husband has been waiting for you.'

'She's not responding, Doctor. What does that mean?' Timi asked. The emotional roller coaster was getting to him and he was beginning to resent Preye for not waking up. It was getting harder to conceal his growing anger and to continue portraying himself as the doting husband.

Dr Tash sighed. 'Titi said she twitched again. That doesn't tell us much, unless it's followed by a response to stimulus. Let's wait and see if she'd do that again.' She looked straight into his eyes. 'You shouldn't be doing this alone. Have you considered pulling in some of her family?'

'No,' Timi said firmly. Dr Tash got the message and shrugged.

His impatience grew and his mood soured after the staff left him alone with Preye. Patience had never been his strength and he was being pushed to the limits. 'This is torture, Mine. When I married you, this wasn't in the agenda. If I had known, I would have waited a little longer, but you made me want you so much, I couldn't wait. If you could see yourself now, you wouldn't wish to marry you. It's been three weeks and I can already see the muscle tone in your legs starting to diminish. You're just a mess right now.' He emitted a sigh. He looked down at his phone and there was a message from Tina. 'The nurses recommend I take a break from the hospital. I think I should heed their advice,' he finished with a smile as he started calling Tina.

'T baby.' He hailed her. 'I'm sorry we have to cancel that getaway. There's been no change at my end, and as the loving husband, I don't think it would look right to abandon my helpless wife.' He giggled. Tina responded with disappointment that their plans had to be delayed. She suggested meeting at a bar for drinks, which Timi couldn't refuse. He promised to meet her in an hour.

He left Preye's room and told the nurses he was leaving to check on his house and would return later in the evening.

*

Tina walked towards the table with her high heels clicking and her straight blond Peruvian weave blowing in the slight breeze. Her soft curves were highlighted by her tight jeans and red crop top. She was the polar opposite of Preye; easy-going, with no bone of resistance in her petite frame. It suited Timi just fine. He didn't want anyone challenging his authority like his wife. She leaned in to land a peck on him, but he ducked by picking non-existent thread on his shirt. Yet, immediately she sat down, he nuzzled up to her in the dimly lit café.

You're late,' he accused.

'I deserve a pass, *abeg no give me yawa. I never try?*' The waiter brought her regular beer. 'I should be packing for the weekend-away as we planned. You said your wife wouldn't get in the way. Her needs keep coming before mine and it's not something I can deal with long-term. What does she have that I don't? If you keep placing me second, you won't like me if I start nagging.' She took a sip of the beer

Timi's eyes widened. He always had Tina under control, but it seemed something had triggered her. 'You're lucky I came out tonight. Preye being in the hospital and about as active as a houseplant is driving me crazy. I have to put up a show and be there if the worst happens. You knew I was married before we started, so don't start complaining.' He looked down at the menu blankly. He was annoyed that Tina was trying to challenge him and he wanted to snip her wings before she started flying. 'If you compare yourself to my wife, then you're number nothing. And you should feel happy with that because I didn't make you any false promise. Let's order so we can go back to your place. I need to get back to the hospital.'

'Why are you talking to me like I'm trash? Why can't you just pretend to be nice? If this is half as bad as you treat your wife, I don't blame her for leaving you,' Tina eyed him and hissed. She had been tolerant of Timi's many excesses because he was generous to her. But two days ago, she had met a guy who seemed to be very cultured and with more money than Timi. And she had decided she could walk away from Timi anytime now. She beckoned to the waiter.

'Come on, Tina. I don't treat you to nice things and splash money on you to get this bullshit in return. You're not exactly the type of woman a man takes home to meet his parents. That's just the type of girl you're not. So shut up and let's get on, I don't need you to add to my stress level right now.' Timi said flatly as he waved down the waiter. He was struggling to keep his voice down.

Tina tossed her napkin and stood up from the table. 'You're a bully, and don't tell me what type of girl I am. I'm Tina Alli and I have better things to do with my time than spend it with you. You should think about what type of man you are before telling me what type of girl I'm not. Have a nice life.' She turned on her spiked-heels and walked away.

His face froze in confusion and his mind went into a sudden pause. He opened his mouth but no words came out.

CHAPTER TWENTY EIGHT

Timi saw Tonye's car as he pulled into the hospital parking lot. The sight of the vehicle made his chest tighten. At least he was in the right place if he had a heart attack. Before heading for Preye's room, he grabbed the bible he had brought with him to read to Preye.

'Any update?' he asked Titi as he went to sit beside Preye on the bed.

Not much had changed except that someone took some time to brush Preye's hair; not that it made any difference to her appearance. As he looked at the cables and tubes hanging all around her, he couldn't help reflecting on what would happen if she refused to wake up or if she woke up in a vegetative state. He felt it was time he started considering his options. This was an expensive price to pay for love, even for Preye. If his father hadn't bailed him out, he wouldn't have been able to afford the hospital bills and may have had to call Tobi, Preye's partner to settle part of the bills from the company's purse.

'Preye, I've been told to read something from your favourite author, but I really couldn't figure out which of your books you'd like, since you didn't respond to the last one. You know I hate all those books, so I brought the bible.' He randomly flipped through the bible until he stopped on Ephesians 5:

Therefor be imitators of God as dear children. And walk in love, as Christ also has loved us and given Himself to us, an offering and a sacrifice to God for a sweet-smelling aroma. But fornication…

He stopped reading and looked at Preye. Her eyes were opened wide, staring straight ahead. He dropped the bible and put his hands on her shoulders to pull her in. 'Preye, you've come back to me. You can see me, please talk to me. I love you. Thanks for coming back to me and to…'

Preye's eyes closed and a blanket of darkness engulfed everything within her.

*

…She was behind the chasm. She heard the sound of feet clanking towards her and she started running in fear. A voice called out her name from behind her and she stopped running because she recognised the familiar voice, but she couldn't quite place who it was. The voice kept on talking, but it was muffled and she didn't understand why. She wanted to ask him to speak louder, but her lips were sealed with a tape. She wanted to pry the tape off, but she was tired from running and couldn't lift her hand to her mouth. She was about to run off again, but she heard the voice call Jesus and the blanket over her was completely removed. Preye stopped a second time, but a whirlwind of voices was coming at her, like cascading snow in an avalanche.

She retreated. The void embraced her, but she wanted to go back because she now remembered the voice from the confusion. She couldn't remember the name, but she knew he'd be angry if she ran away again. She had run away before and he had pleaded with her to come back. Her head hurt as she tried to recall his name, so she stopped trying, but she remembered that when she eventually said yes to his invitation, he had been overly excited, jamming his hands in a fist and wiggling his waist.

They went to Naana's Kitchen. It was a cosy restaurant and perfect for first dates. He listened intently as she told him about herself, her family, her company and how she started Roadrunners. He didn't have much to say about himself, except that he found her highly enchanting and hadn't been able to stop thinking about her since the day they met. He even teased her that she had charmed him. He showered compliments on her and told her she was naturally beautiful and didn't need to wear the tight dresses and jeans that she wore. He liked her hair long and asked her if she was using it to cover her birthmark, because he knew where she could have the birthmark removed. She laughed off his suggestions, simply happy that he had noticed the little details about her.

He wasn't like Kevin, but he treated her like a special person in his own way, springing up surprises and showering her with mementoes that made her suspend her analytical approach to life. He repeatedly assured her that he loved her and she loved him in return. He wasn't a strong Christian like she was, but he wanted to grow. He was a looker and a hunk of a man. No wonder he couldn't wait to have sex with her. She remembered the night they struggled over sex and it made her head hurt more. He had promised it wouldn't happen again and he had kept his word.

She knew Lola didn't exactly approve of Timi. Yes! His name came to her now. She heard Aisha and Lola gossiping about him before the wedding. *Is that why they were not with her in the abyss?* She heard Timi's voice again. It was faint, but sounded agitated, like he always sounded any time the veins in his neck were throbbing. Though his voice was muffled, it was unrelenting.

Preye wondered when her mother would come back from her shop…

*

Timi tried again and decided to read from 1st Peter 3.

Wives, in the same way submit yourselves to your own husbands so that,

297

if any of them do not believe the word, they may be won over without words by the behaviour of their wives, when they see the purity and reverence of your lives. Your beauty should not come from outward adornment, such as elaborate hairstyles and the wearing of gold jewellery or fine clothes.

He slammed down the book. 'Open your eyes again. I wish I could reset the clock so we can start afresh. It's time for us to rely on each other and each other alone. You're my rock and I need you back.'

He snapped his fingers beside her right ear and tried prying her eye open as a way of coaxing a response. It didn't work. He pulled his arm across the table which served as his makeshift desk. The laptop and some sheets of paper fell to the floor.

'Look what you made me do. Your pranks have caused me to lose my work and my temper. I've had enough of this nonsense.' He picked up his laptop which had survived the crash and threw most of the sheets of paper in the bin. 'I can't spend many more days like this because I need to get on with life. I need to go to work and make money to take care of us and try to repay my dad. He's the one that has been picking your bills and I need to stop that. The clock is ticking and I don't know how much time you've got left. I don't want to lose you, but I can't help you if you don't respond to me.' He grabbed her hand and kissed her on the head. It seemed colder than in the past. He sighed.

Preye heard the humming voice, but sleep was more comforting.

CHAPTER TWENTY NINE

Timi had been trying to reach Tina after she left him at the restaurant. He wasn't happy that he hadn't been able to give an appropriate response to her silly drama as it turned out that she was more like Preye than he had thought. He should have figured that, because all women were alike. Except, perhaps his mother, Ife Coker. He called Tina again and left a voicemail.

'Tina, you haven't taken my calls in two days. You know I need you in my life right now. You're the only one who understands my needs. I was testy the other night and deserved the poor treatment you gave me. Let me make it up to you. We can reschedule our holiday and I promise not to cancel, no matter what. I'll be your sex slave the entire time. Just call me.' If Tina agreed, he'd feel better if he could be the one to walk out on her.

He was by Preye's bed as he had been in recent days. He was expecting Dr David to come in to examine her and then discuss the next steps. He didn't know exactly what those steps would be, but he guessed decisions would have to be made in the not too distant future. Preye looked peaceful and at times it was easy for him to imagine she was sleeping and could wake up and fall into his arms. He was daydreaming about embracing her when Dr David walked in.

'Hello Mr Coker. We won't take long.' Dr David told Timi. He was accompanied by Titi. The doctor examined Preye while the nurse went about changing the drips and checking the tubes. Dr David dismissed Titi. He explained to Timi that the longer Preye lingered in her present state, the less chance she had of making a full recovery. She was living on life support and Timi had a choice about how long to wait until they removed the machines, if ever. She could go on for years in that state if he chose to continue with the breathing and feeding tubes. In that case, she'd be moved to a long-term care facility. The costs would be high and she'd continue to be Timi's responsibility.

'The electrodes monitoring her brain activity show that she's not brain dead. However, if she doesn't respond to physical stimuli in two days, her likelihood of full recovery is low. And if she does recover, it may be with reduced motor function and severe disability.'

'Are you saying I should pick a date for you to shut down her breathing?' Timi asked incredulously.

'It's something you need to start considering,' Dr David said quietly. He didn't meet Timi's eyes and he looked like he'd rather be somewhere else.

'That sounds like I'll be murdering my wife. I've been called a lot of things, Dr David, but a killer isn't one of them and I'd like to keep it that way,' Timi said, wiping a lone sweat from his brow.

'Have you thought about bringing her family into the discussion? I'm not sure how much longer you should keep holding them off if you don't want to be called a killer,' Dr David said passively. He rarely intervened in family matters, but this was bordering on fatality.

'Absolutely not,' Timi said without equivocation. 'I cannot stress that enough and I won't change my mind.' The doctor disagreed with Timi's approach but since he was the patient's husband, he had the legal authority to keep anyone away. The hospital wouldn't want to enter a court case on family rights.

'Can we have a review in one week please?' Timi released a weary burst of air from his lungs, unaware that tears were slowly streaming down his face.

Dr David lowered his head solemnly. 'It's protocol to invite other doctors for such reviews, so you should be prepared. We'll proceed from there.' He patted the weeping Timi on the shoulder. 'No judgment Mr Coker. This is an impossible situation.'

'Thank you Doctor,' Timi muttered.

*

The following day, Lola arrived at the hospital first thing in the morning. She knew where Timi parked his car and it wasn't there. She parked further away to wait for Tobi to arrive.

Tobi had found a way to get access to Preye by calling his associates and friends until he found someone who knew one of the hospital's directors. Lola had also informed Miriam Banigo that she could come to join them.

As soon as Tobi arrived, Lola led him through the sliding doors and informed him that there was a likelihood Timi wasn't in the building. Tobi responded that it was all good. 'For some reasons, this reminds me of *uni*,' he said with a naughty smile.

'I remember the time I was on the verge of being kicked out by the hostel administrator and you talked my way back in. You've always been a clever boy,' Lola said. I wonder why it didn't occur to me to snatch and marry you.' she teased Tobi, slinging her arm over his shoulders.

'Your loss! It's that big mouth of yours and your *fokifoki* eyes that were roving around, looking for big boys to date,' he smiled back at her. 'My mum wanted me to be a lawyer, but I couldn't resist the allure of PR and here we are.'

'Thank God for you and Preye. You guys gave me a chance

even though I didn't have seed money then,' Lola reminisced.

'Time to do Preye a good turn, so let's get down to it.'

It was during a shift change and only one of the two receptionists knew Lola. She was already geared to address Lola before Tobi spoke. 'I'm Tobi Abass. We are here to see Preye Coker. You should have instructions from one of the hospital's directors to allow me and Preye's parents have access to her. Do you want to check?' The receptionist asked them to wait and took her time to check on her desktop. She placed a call to the nurses' station to inform them that Preye had visitors. She waved Lola and Tobi in, inferring that Lola knew the way.

Titi was at the nurses' station, when they got there and she beamed a smile at them. In reality, the nurses had become concerned that Timi didn't allow anyone else to visit his wife. Lola didn't return Titi's smile, making a face at her instead. Tobi was about to repeat what he had told the receptionist, but Titi asked them to follow her, with a welcoming demeanour. Lola sent a text message to Miriam that she and Tobi were heading to Preye's room.

Tobi and Lola clasped hands when they got into Preye's room. They both gasped. Preye was almost unrecognisable with so many lines connecting her to fluids and machines. Lola thought the lines had grown from the last time she visited. After Titi left them in the room, they both remained speechless for a few seconds.

Once she recovered herself, Lola rushed to Preye's bedside. She grasped the part of Preye's hand that was without a line. '*Omo* girl. It's been a minute since we've had one of our sisters' sessions. I've missed you.' Lola's voice broke like sea waves nearing the shore as tears trickled down her face. Tobi, holding his lips tightly together, massaged Lola's shoulders from behind. 'I hear you're sleeping and you refuse to get up, which isn't like you at all. The Preye Banigo I know always has a million things happening at once and each one of them is handled with grace. Stop being lazy and get out of this bed because I will be so mad if you leave me,' Lola joked. 'You know how I am when I'm annoyed and you don't want to try that now.' There was no response from Preye. 'Remember I don't have problems with talking. If you don't get up, I will keep talking until I weary you enough to ask me to stop.' She looked at Tobi and shook her head. Tobi urged her to go on. 'I've told your mum we found a way in and she's on the way with the rest of the family. I think she may be able to get your dad to come over too. Tobi is here with me. He's been running the office as if he is Idi Amin. You don't want to leave Beta to him to run, I promise. I didn't know he could be so mean. Ah, yes, I've been getting most of the work that should come to your desk. I'm not enjoying it at all, I can tell you. I wanted to come here with Sammy. That guy is a wonder from God. After all my *waka about*, God has finally decided to bless me with a man that deserves me. You would have met him, if not for …'   She checked herself before she mentioned Timi. She wished she could curse him right now and tell Preye how he had barred them from seeing her.

Lola looked back at Tobi again and asked if he had anything to say. He told her to continue because he didn't think Lola would move aside for anyone, so she continued. 'Some of the nurses here have been terrible. They didn't allow us in to see you, when I came with Aisha. They thought I'd give up, but they're wrong.' Lola squeezed Preye's hand. 'You will be amazed to hear that I've started praying and I've joined a church.' She counted her fingers. 'Yes, I have gone to church four times now. I finally took your advice for once and I think there's something about God that calms me down. I now understand, but it's a gradual process for me. God and I have a pretty cool relationship now. *Haba,* you had to check yourself into a hospital to get me into church. You're pathetic.' Lola giggled and then started to pray silently.

…Preye felt overshadowed by the sunlight and felt a flow of energy go through her body. She wanted to raise her arms to shield her face from the ray of light, but she didn't have enough energy yet. She sensed the faint fragrance and tried unsuccessfully to sniffle to take it in. She remembered Lola. Yes, that was Lola's perfume.

She floated back to when Lola and Aisha waited for her at school and she was thankful that Lola was still waiting with her, but she wanted her mother. She was used to Lola talking endlessly and most times it was rubbish. Maybe that was why she couldn't understand the exact words Lola was saying to her; it was like listening while under water.

Lola suppressed an outburst of tears; she didn't want to let loose in the room. Without saying a word, she dragged Tobi along with her to the corridor. They met Miriam, Harry and Tonye marching towards Preye's room. Lola waved them ahead and told them she'd soon be back. Almost immediately, Timi stepped off the elevator and quickened his pace on sighting Preye's family heading towards her room. With Tobi behind her, Lola accosted Timi.

'The big lie is over, Timi Coker.' Lola had a look of disdain on her face. 'Even if the worst happens, Preye will know that she's loved. I don't know what you were trying to achieve by keeping us out, but whatever it is, you've failed.'

Timi was unflustered. 'Please move so I can go to my wife's room,' he said flatly.

'Otherwise what?' Lola challenged and hissed. 'Who exactly do you think you are? It's not your fault.' Lola refused to move.

It took Tobi's two hands to pull Lola back. 'Let me deal with this. There's no need to make a scene.' He faced Timi assertively. 'Talk to me.'

'Tobi, regardless of how you've pulled this off, I have every right to see my wife. I love her very much. I will appreciate it if you don't meddle in my family affairs.'

'No, I'm not meddling. Right now I've chosen to be Preye's cousin, so I'm family. If I were you, I'd pay attention to Timi's Communications because a new company requires some serious attention to grow. Don't forget, I'm the president of the PR Professionals Association and I have the ears of everyone that matters. It would be easy to start a rumour, you know. Based on the truth of course. You wouldn't be able to get your company out of the gate if you made an enemy of me or Beta. Tread lightly, Timi. Give the Banigos time with their daughter and that's not a request,' Tobi concluded, before folding his arms and standing tall.

'Are you threatening me?' Timi asked.

Tobi nodded. 'Yes, I guess I am. What do you want to do about it? And how does it feel to be on the receiving end? I've got your number, if we need you, I'll call you.'

'I'm going to let them spend time with Preye. Not because I have to, but because I'm a reasonable man. I want the best for my wife and there's no need to fight over her. I'm still her husband and nothing you or anyone else does is going to change that.' Timi wondered what excuse the nurses would give him for the infringement on his rights, but he soft-pedalled to avoid a scene. He waved them off and detoured back towards the elevator.

Tobi Abass got a glimpse into what Preye must have been dealing with and how easily she'd have allowed Timi to convince her that day was night and black was white. Tobi shook his head and thought Timi would be better suited for sales than PR.

Lola hissed and wrinkled her nose at his back before trailing Tobi back to Preye's room.

*

Miriam Banigo sat on the chair and pulled up to her daughter's bedside. Tonye and Harry joined hands at the corner of the room to allow Miriam speak. 'My dear sweet Preye,' Miriam spoke through tears. 'I would have been here sooner but, well, you know… I had trouble getting in. I prayed for God to watch over you, as did the rest of the family. I know you can hear my voice. I'm waiting to embrace you once you open your eyes and get up. Your daddy is here and Tonye too. Erefa couldn't come because of her baby, but you know she loves you too. I'm sorry if I've not been a good mother, but I'll change, I promise. I will be the best mother you want me to be. Just give me another chance.' Miriam couldn't hide her grief and she choked on her sobs so she allowed Tonye to take over while she composed herself.

'Big sis, you gave up so much to help me get to where I am. I was wayward and lost, but you always had the strength for both of us. You're in a dark place now, just like I was many years ago, so I guess it's my turn to pull you out. We are praying because we don't know what else to do. You're my inspiration and my hero and losing you is unacceptable. We have to grow old together as you promised, and you always keep your promises.' Tonye gasped for breath before she continued. 'Oh, did you know your friend Lola is a little crazy? I love that woman. I love you more. Please come back.'

…Preye felt the warmth of her mother's touch. She was happy now as she walked towards the light. She had been sure her mother would come for her and now that her mother was here with her, she needed to get up and follow her. She still felt drowsy and couldn't see her mother yet…

Lola and Tobi came back in. Miriam pushed Harry Banigo forward, to have a few words with Preye. Harry hesitated at first, but Miriam insisted. Regardless of their relationship, she always encouraged the father-daughter bond.

'I never imagined I'd ever see you this way. Of all the women in this family, you're the strongest, the all-star. That's saying a lot because you're all fantastic. I'm sorry I wasn't the father you needed or deserved. I wish I could have protected you,' Harry said. He cracked and could hardly continue. 'I've never stopped loving you, my angel. You were the one who encouraged me to grow up. I saw your success when you started running and it made me more determined to succeed too. If Preye can do it, so can I. That was my mantra. I love you.' Harry concluded. He placed his face in his hands; his tears didn't erupt onto the surface, rather they seeped into his veins to give him a hot fever, and he quaked as he re-joined hands with Tonye and Preye's friends.

They started praying silently.

Miriam grasped her daughter's hand. 'Enough of this, it's time to come back. By the grace of God, come back to us. I wish I could trade places with you, I would do it in an instant.' Miriam squeezed her daughter's hand and her heart skipped. 'Preye, your hand is getting colder and the colour is draining from your face. Please God, do something.'

The machines started beeping as the lines flattened. Titi and another nurse rushed in. Titi looked at the monitor and rushed out to get Dr Tash.

*

Preye sensed that Lola had left and wanted to fall asleep again, so she closed her eyes, but a familiar hand tapped on her shoulder. …

…It was the hostel administrator. 'Wake up, Preye, your mother is here.' …

Everyone in Preye's room, except the nurse, was holding hands and crying as the flat lines started to squiggle and the beeping tone changed.

Preye opened her eyes.

*

She could hear clearly and see what was happening around her. She could see all the people in the room, but she couldn't open her mouth. She didn't have the strength and the apparatus over her mouth, along with the tube down her throat made it impossible. She felt her hands when Miriam touched them but she wasn't able to move and she couldn't respond. She realised she was on a hospital bed and they were all there to see her. There was chaos around her bed.

'Her eyes are open,' Miriam yelled, the tears running down her face intensified.

Harry lunged forward to make sure Miriam wasn't merely imagining that Preye had opened her eyes. He wanted to have a look for himself. He got a look at Preye's tired but warm eyes before Tonye pushed him aside, with tears pricking her eyes. Tobi and Lola embraced each other.

Dr Tash charged into the room with Titi. There was increased brain activity and Preye's blood pressure was up. The latter had happened before, but this time it was more than a momentary blip. Everyone was giving their account of what had happened at the same time to the doctor.

Dr Tash spoke when she eventually calmed them down. 'Can everyone leave, please? Mum and Dad can stay.' The others dragged their heavy feet out of the room as the doctor checked Preye's vitals, prying open her eyes.

'Is she coming back? I knew she'd come back once we showed up. Please tell me how long until my daughter comes out of this horrid coma?' Miriam asked. Titi pulled Miriam back so Dr Tash could conduct her examination. Miriam tried to resist Titi and Harry had to peel her away from Preye's bed.

'Dr David is off-site but he's been called and I expect him within the hour.' Dr Tash exerted some force to Preye's feet and felt a reaction. 'Her response and sustained brain activity are a good sign, but I can't give a definitive outlook until Dr David comes and gives her a thorough examination,' Dr Tash paused. Preye was aware of her surroundings more than before, but her eye-opening burst of energy had taken a lot out of her. 'There's nothing more I can do until Dr David comes. He'll re-examine her breathing capabilities and might remove the mask and tubes so she can speak. I encourage you to keep talking to her since it worked before. Do you have any questions?' she asked.

'How soon do you think she'll be able to say a few words?' Miriam said.

The doctor shrugged her shoulders. 'I really can't say. I'm sorry I don't have more information. This is the most frustrating thing about treating coma patients. No two patients are alike and they recover at their own pace,' Dr Tash softened her voice. She left Harry and Miriam alone with Preye.

'Thank you for coming,' Miriam said to Harry. 'I know your uncle is in bad shape.'

'Everything is going wrong at the same time, but I have to be here for my daughter. Uncle would want it this way, knowing how he loves the girls. And he loves you too.' Harry dared to be chirpy. 'His cancer has been advancing for years, but like Preye, he is also a fighter. I hope he makes it through.'

'Harry Banigo, I've never seen you handle priorities so deftly. Preye will be proud,' Miriam said.

Preye wiggled her small toe, which her parents missed while they were talking. She was indeed proud of her father for his efforts at being more responsible towards his children. Now she knew she could move her digits and open her eyes with some concentrated effort.

Miriam perched next to Preye's bed and picked up her hand. It was warmer than it was when Preye had seemed to be drifting away. 'My daughter, I know you're listening to me now and you'd tell me not to wallow in regrets. You'd tell me that I did the best I could and that I'm a fabulous mother. That's the kind of girl you are, always worried about how everyone else is doing. As soon as you get out of here, we're going to have a long talk.' Miriam was referring to Timi, but like the others, she also avoided mentioning his name, unsure how Preye would respond. Preye was able to squeeze her mother's hand slightly. The movement would be imperceptible to anyone else, but a mother had instincts. Miriam knew her daughter was there and soaking in all the love that surrounded her.

*

Outside Preye's room, the joy was infectious as Tonye, Tobi and Lola couldn't stop talking. They could see the hugging and high fives exchanged by the nurses too.

'I knew Preye would respond to her mum. What next?' Lola asked, overpowering Tobi with another hug. She couldn't stay still or stop talking. Her mind was strung as if she had been injected with an overdose of sugar. 'We owe this to you for getting us in the door and that made all the difference. We should be having a champagne toast now, even though I've stopped drinking and Preye prefers boring sparkling wine. Next time I come, I'll stash a bottle in my bag.' Tobi and Tonye looked at Lola oddly. 'What? Can't you guys take a joke? Although, that's how we used to roll back in the days,' she said unapologetically.

'I love your energy, Lola, but let's not get kicked out. We worked too hard to get where we are,' Tobi reproved.

Timi sat in his car, helplessly fuming. He had come to the

hospital earlier and had gone to the charge nurse who informed him that the Banigos were still with Preye and that she had shown significant improvement. The nurse had advised him to check in on his wife, but he had excused himself under the pretext that he forgot something in the car. He had learnt they were waiting for Dr David to give a more accurate prognosis. He had been waiting for three hours, watching out for Dr David's car so he could go in with him to see his wife, but the doctor hadn't showed up yet.

With the belief that the worst was over, he decided to make better use of his time and take the rest of the day off from the hospital. Before he started the car, he placed a call to Tina to see if she had calmed down. 'T baby, *how you dey?'*

'*Nothing do me.* What can I do for you?' Tina responded curtly.

Timi fumbled to talk. '*Hey,* I was wondering if we …'

Tina cut him short. '*We wetin?* That Tina trash has moved on. She doesn't use this number anymore. Don't call her again. I shouldn't bother telling you, I should block your number instead. Stupid man.' She ended the call abruptly.

Timi banged the steering and knocked his head against it. *Why was he losing control over every woman he turned to?*

It was Friday and it was time for a boy's night!

*

With his fingers crossed, Timi had called Martin and Malik to hang out for a few drinks, not minding the long drive to their regular joint, Rukkees at Yaba. He had been happy when they both agreed, hoping they would be able to offer some advice on how he could take back control of his life. A night without having to look over his shoulder for Lola or the Banigos could do him some good.

After settling down with their bottles of beer, Timi thanked his friends for their support and kick-started the discussion. 'Good news, guys, Preye opened her eyes today and it's for real this time.' Malik and Martin leaped in excitement, almost knocking the table down as they congratulated him. 'Her situation has been like a nightmare for me. I've been going through a lot of stress and I just needed this night to cool off,' Timi said quietly, evoking sympathy from his friends.

Martin raised his glass. He was two beers ahead of the others as usual. 'You'll be of no use to her if you don't take care of yourself as well. Now that we're on the subject of taking care of yourself, has Tina been performing?'

When he met Tina, Timi had bragged to his friends about his beautiful and endearing conquest. Martin had hailed him, while Malik had told him off, warning that an affair was a complication Timi didn't need in his life. But Timi had chosen his path.

Malik slammed his drink down on the table and immediately got the attention of Martin and Timi. 'Tina? Really? Preye is lying in a coma and you feel the need to bring up a side chick?' Malik glared at Martin with scorching eyes. 'I'll stand up for the helpless woman in the hospital if no one else will. She deserves better.'

'Whoa, chill out, Malik,' Timi said. 'Don't jump all over Martin. You can see he's had a few drinks. I love Preye but she's turned my life upside down. Do you know how it feels to always go back home to an empty bed while dealing with this much stress? Besides, Preye has been rocking me the wrong way before this happened. She moved out of the house and I accepted her back, yet I can't seem to convince her what's best for her. I bought her a house and she complained about the location. I politely asked her not to dress so provocatively, and she took that as an insult. The list goes on. What else can a man do?' He shrugged.

Martin was drunk so he agreed with everything Timi said.

However, Malik challenged Timi and he thought he should have done that a long time ago. He had known about Timi's arrogance, but he had ignored it for the sake of friendship. He finally decided he'd be doing Timi a favour by calling out his flaws.

'You can start by not controlling every move she makes. She's a grown woman, capable of making her own choices. That girl built a thriving company from scratch, yet you think she can't decide what to wear. Give her some respect man. Why? Where does this controlling streak of yours come from?'

Timi was stunned that his friend of so many years was challenging him. He was tempted to upturn the table and walk out on his friends, but a part of him wanted to explain himself. 'I'm not the horrible person you're trying to make me out to be. I've never had to compromise for anyone and I liked it that way. Can you blame me?'

'No. Not being challenged sounds like a nice existence, but not a realistic way if you want to be in a successful marriage. Once Preye pulls through, she deserves some autonomy, respect and monogamy,' Malik advised.

Timi clenched his fists to suppress his anger, but he couldn't do anything about the pulsating veins in his neck. Malik wouldn't understand because everything came easily to him. He was married to a dutiful wife, wonderful children and an amazingly lucrative career. Timi realised neither of the men sitting on both sides of him could understand why he acted the way he did. And Malik was beginning to sound like Preye.

'Well, gentleman, this night has not turned out as I had planned. I wasn't looking for a therapy session. I was hoping for something a whole lot lighter, but here we are. I need my sleep and I have a long way to drive back, so I'll leave you to it,' Timi said, getting up. 'No hurt feelings, we're good.' He stretched out his hand to shake his friends.

Martin shook Timi's hand. He was too drunk to care much about the underlying message, but Malik understood clearly. Timi was set in his ways and didn't expect any challenge from even his friends; he was far too comfortable with himself, which was probably why he didn't have other long term friends. He liked playing people like puppets and if he was figured out, he cut ties.

'No problem, Timi. Penny asked me to say hello and we both miss Preye. Give her a squeeze from both of us,' Malik said.

'Yup.' Timi left for the comfort of his familiar house.

On getting home, the emptiness of the four-bedroom house drilled into his flesh and marked him with unseen wounds. He switched on the flat-screen television but he lacked the energy or enthusiasm to follow any programme and he flicked between channels. After a while of staring into space, he threw the television remote control at the wall. He set his gloomy eyes on the painting hanging on the wall. It was the wedding present from the Beta crew. He turned away but his eyes went back to the inscription on the painting – *Better lives ahead!* An invisible force pulled him from the sofa before persuading him to pry the painting from the wall and break the frame into pieces. The canvas stayed intact after his destructive act. Then he collapsed heavily on the sofa and released a volcanic torrent of tears. Without anyone to comfort him, he finally gave in to the heaviness of his heart and eyelids.

CHAPTER THIRTY

Timi woke up, feeling refreshed and ready to take back control of his life and his wife. He needed an ally.

He placed a call to one of Preye's nurses, Titi but he had to leave a message because she didn't answer the phone. He had collected her number one of those days she was chatting away. She called back a few minutes later.

'Thanks for calling me back. We missed you in Preye's room when you were off. Your level of care is beyond anything the others deliver,' Timi said. He had to walk a thin line between flirting with the nurse and remaining the devoted husband to Preye.

'Oh, if any of the nurses is acting inappropriately or providing mediocre service, you can report it to me confidentially,' Titi said with alacrity.

'No,' he responded. 'That was meant to be a compliment to you more than anything about the other nurses.'

'Thank you, Mr Coker. It's my job. Your devotion to your wife is touching. Once she's well enough, I'm sure she'd appreciate what an amazing husband she has. There's more hope now that she's responding.'

'Yes, hope is the word. You know I've been away to attend to some urgent matters since yesterday while her family was with her,' Timi treaded cautiously.

'Yes, that. I heard they got a letter from one of our directors.

Although, I think it was a good thing the mother came around.'

'Yes, I chose to be reasonable in the end too. I just want to find out the status with my wife. I need to be sure the family is not pressuring Preye in my absence.'

'Pressuring, how?' Titi asked.

He wasn't sure how to respond initially. 'Well, I don't know. You know they were not essentially on good terms. But Preye may have forgotten due to her state and they may be feeding her with some nonsense that will trigger her off again. They may want to destroy our beautiful home without her realising it. They can play dirty,' he said.

'Don't worry. I'll watch out for them and make sure they're not alone with her. I think they'll be here today. We're observing Mrs Coker and we would likely move her anytime from now. You should come once you're free, Mr Coker. This is when you need to be by her side,' Titi suggested.

He wasn't too pleased that the Banigos were still hovering around. He wasn't ready to share his wife's moments with them. 'I'm still a bit busy, but I should be there tomorrow. If there's any way you can tell Preye I love her, please do. Thanks a lot, I'm going to give you a glowing recommendation and I'll be sure my comments get to the top.'

'Mrs Coker is lucky to have you,' Titi said shyly.

'No, I'm the lucky one. I can tell your boyfriend is lucky too.' Timi laughed and ended the call. Flattery with someone as naive as Titi worked every time.

He called his parents to update them. 'Mum, I'm calling to share the good news about Preye,' he said.

'Has her condition improved? I have put you on speaker so your father can hear too,' Ife Coker said.

'She has made some improvements, but the Banigos are trying to put me on the side-lines. I've given them enough space. Now, I think it's time to do what's best for my wife,' he told his parents.

'You have our support no matter what. We know you'll always do the right thing. What do you say, Wale?' Ife asked her husband.

'I'm with you every step of the way. Don't doubt yourself for a second,' Wale added. 'Are you okay with money? I know the bills are mounting up, but you should concentrate on your wife's recovery. Let me know if there's anything I can help with.'

Timi explained his intentions to his parents and they told him it was a good decision. His parents' agreement with him gave him the confidence to move forward as he wished.

*

Harry and Miriam were back in Dr David's office, waiting to hear about their daughter's current status. Tonye was with Preye, trying to weave Preye's thinning hair. The Banigos were happy that Preye had opened her eyes several times and her brain activity hadn't plummeted.

A nurse came by and told them that Dr David was still with a patient and would be running late. Miriam used the time to open up to Harry. She had to explain why she was overwhelmed with guilt regarding Preye's condition. 'Harry, you asked earlier how I was holding up and I said fine. I lied.'

'You've forgotten we were married. I knew you were lying, and I also knew you'd tell me about it, if you wanted to,' he said sympathetically. 'You feel the need to be strong for the girls, but you don't have to hold it up for me. You saw the way I cried.' He shrugged. 'What's bothering you?'

'I think I was the one who pushed the idea of this marriage on Preye. With our marriage turning out a mess, I should have known that walking down the aisle doesn't always lead everyone to a happily ever after. Preye has succeeded at everything she's tried in life. I thought marriage would be no different. In my old-fashioned belief I thought she needed a man to take care of her so that she wouldn't face the kind of snobbery I endured as a single mother. That was crazy thinking. She was doing fine by herself.' Miriam felt lighter through her sobs, as if the mass of muscles pressing against her heart had been removed.

Harry handed her his handkerchief. 'It's okay. No one expects you to be perfect. You gave her your opinion and she didn't walk down the aisle in shackles,' Harry said. 'Tonye and Erefa are happily married and if their unions do fall apart perchance, that won't be your fault. You raised the girls to be independent thinkers and they make their own decisions. Preye made hers too,' he paused. 'And since when did she live life by anyone else's rules?'

'I should have told her to take things easy with him when I noticed the red flags. But she wanted to have a family so badly, I didn't want to be accused of standing in her way of joy.' Miriam was contrite. 'I think I was selfish. Because I failed in my marriage, I always advise the girls that they should never quit their marriages. I shouldn't have asked her to go back to him,' she concluded, writhing inwardly with regret and hoping that there was a way she could go back in time and direct Preye through another path of life.

'Don't overestimate the influence you have over the girls. You didn't have a failed marriage. It was your stupid husband that walked out. Don't be so hard on yourself. If anyone should be blamed, don't you think I've walked through that road several times?' Harry tried to assure Miriam. He had his fair share of remorse etched on his heart. Oftentimes, that he thought about Miriam and his three girls, guilt ate at his insides like a tick leeching a dog, and he wished he could retrace his steps to fix the biggest mistake of his life. But the road to the remedy of his wrongdoing had been long shut and he was reconciled to the indelible pain of living with the regret forever.

Miriam rubbed her eyes. 'When did you grow up, Harry?' she teased.

'It's about time, don't you think? He tilted his head lightly.

Miriam was happy that she had allowed Harry maintain a relationship with the children at the time he reached out after their divorce. Now, she wondered how she'd have coped otherwise.

Dr David finally came in. He sat at his desk and opened Preye's considerably large file. 'How are the two of you holding up?'

'We're doing our best and hoping for good news,' Miriam said, while Harry nodded his head in agreement.

'I'm happy to share some with you,' the doctor answered. 'Your daughter is improving. I've checked her lung capacity and she can breathe on her own. We'll monitor that a bit more and get the breathing tube removed tomorrow. Maybe she'll have something to say. Talk to her to keep her eyes open longer and respond with blinks. She has to walk before she can run. Does that analogy make any sense to you?'

'Yes,' Harry replied. 'I guess I was hoping she'd just sit up and begin talking. I envisioned us walking out arm in arm in a week.'

'Unfortunately, a lot of movies have led us to believe that's possible. Her body has been asleep for weeks and it will need time to wake up. Think of her brain as a computer that needs a reboot.'

'Has Timi complained about our presence?' Miriam asked.

The doctor folded his arms across his chest. 'My job is to treat the patient. I don't get involved with those issues. If you have any concerns, we have people on staff including nurses who relate with the patients on that level. I'm sorry I can't help much in that regard.'

Miriam and Harry were disappointed, but they understood. Doctors couldn't afford to be distracted by legal issues and family differences.

'Can you tell us if Preye will fully recover? When she gets up, what kind of abilities will she still have?' Miriam asked.

'Will she walk, talk or even be able to feed herself? Will she require full-time care?' Harry added.

'We don't know if she recognises us. Will she remember things in her past?' Miriam picked up after Harry.

Dr David stared at Preye's parents and pleaded with them to slow down. 'I urge you to be optimistic but cautiously so. At this point, there's more we don't know than what we know. We're still monitoring and the medical staff will let me know if there is the slightest change. I wish I could answer your questions but right now, I cannot. Keep in mind that relapse is still a very real possibility.'

Miriam and Harry knew they weren't going to get anything else from Dr David. He was doing what he could and now it was a waiting game and trust in God. They were both exhausted as the left for the waiting room. There was no one else there and they sat beside each other.

'Who would have thought we'd be sharing a room after all these years?' Harry asked, looking for any means to douse the gravity of the situation.

Miriam laughed. 'You push your luck. If this is what you call sharing a room, then you've been too deprived. Unfortunately, my door is locked.'

'I need to charge my phone so I can call the only one that opens the door for me these days,' Harry's voice was mischievous and his eyes had a glint. He and Miriam had been good friends and open with each other. It was one of the reasons he had taken her for granted.

'Tell her I say hi,' Miriam teased.

*

Preye couldn't guess how long she had been in hospital, but she figured it wasn't one or two days, from what everyone around her said. Her entire body ached. She couldn't move, and going by the number of cables she was enmeshed in and the way the nurses whispered around her, hers was a serious case.

She had gotten accustomed to the sound of feet walking along the corridor; the cheerful chit-chat of the nurses; the smiles on the faces of her visitors; the continuous bleeping of the monitors and the antiseptic smell in her room. The activities around her were comforting. She felt euphoric as Tonye played with her hair, and she just wanted to lie in bed all day, except that her visitors kept urging her to stay awake. If she could open her mouth, the first thing she planned to say was to tell Tonye not to stop, especially now that she was massaging her feet.

'I should be nominated for the sister of the year award. Your nails were a mess and the cuticles needed trimming. Your nail beds have turned blue. I learnt it's because you were oxygen-deprived. The nurses said I couldn't give your nails a good coat of polish and I wasn't about to start a war by arguing with them. When you get out of here, we'll go to the spa, have lunch and have our nails done. Sis, doesn't that sound so grown up?' Preye's index finger moved and Tonye paused. 'That's the kind of response I get from Tamara. I'll take it, but you have to do better than that next time.'

The more her visitors talked, the easier it was for Preye to make sense of her existence. Her life was a jigsaw puzzle and she had all the pieces, but wasn't sure how to put them together yet. That part of recovery was coming along nicely and with all the love surrounding her, she liked the scene the puzzle depicted.

'There you go,' Tonye said, after she finished painting Preye's nails. 'I should open a pedicure bar, but don't get used to it. I expect you to be doing your hair and nails by yourself before long.'

*

Lola arrived in the afternoon and sailed into Preye's room, unrestrained. Tonye told Lola that the doctor had advised that Preye should to be talked into opening her eyes more and wiggling her fingers if possible. Lola boasted that she was the right woman for the job. Tonye took a break and went out to join her parents.

'*Omo* girl, it's me, your worst nightmare. I'm not going to feel sorry for you as you lie here, having everyone wait on you. Stop being lazy and open your eyes. For your information, we all have our lives to live, although I have to admit that living my life without you right now sucks. I'm in a new relationship and I can't even concentrate on the poor guy. You know how long I've been looking for a solid *bobo*, I finally got one and you're trying to mess it up. That's not you, Preye, you're not selfish. And if this hospital bed has made you that way, *I fit drag Sammy com arrest you, carry you go guardroom.'* She chuckled. 'But he's not like that. He's a gentleman. I don't know *wetin him find go do soldier work sef,'* Lola ranted on.

About five minutes later, Preye opened her eyes and slowly raised her index finger. Lola cried tears of joy; she knew Preye's gesture was intentional. Lola thought about calling out for the nurses, but she thought of her breakthrough with Preye as a personal conversation between intimate friends. She'd send out an alert when she and Preye were finished. Lola gave Preye the index finger right back. 'I knew you were listening. I miss you loads, *Omo* girl.'

Preye closed her eyes and tried to build up her energy while Lola kept chatting away. She opened her eyes again and typical

Lola wanted more than Preye was giving. She held a pen inches from Preye's face. 'Now that I know you're in there, let's get those eye muscles moving. See if you can track this pen,' Lola could have been a pet owner training her dog. It was silly but it worked as Preye began moving her eyes left and right. Lola let out a cheer, which of course prompted a nurse to rush in. It was Titi.

'Is Mrs Coker alright?' Titi asked, without waiting for an answer. 'Ma, you shouldn't be in here unaccompanied by a family member.'

'Did someone tell you I'm not her family member? *Ish,*' Lola dismissed Titi's statement. 'Preye has opened her eyes twice. She's been tracking this pen with her eyes and she was able to raise her index finger to me too. It was deliberate, it's a sort of sign between us.' Lola threw her hands on her hips and glared at meek Titi. 'My being here has only helped. Can you get Tonye from the waiting room? Let's see if we can do some more. Then, I'll be complying and I'm sure Preye would love to show her sister the progress she's made.'

'Mr Coker said you might present a problem. I'm going to have to report you to the charge nurse on duty,' Titi said.

'Oh, do that. And tell her I said hello. We have some friends in common,' Lola said.

Titi slowly walked away. As she moved down the corridor, she started dialling Timi's number

CHAPTER THIRTY ONE

The nurses on the long term care floor at Saint Mary's Hospital were frustrated about the power tussle over Preye Banigo and tried to insert some rules into her visitation schedule, but not before Titi got the entire day blocked out for Timi after the Banigos and Lola left.

Timi had invited his parents to see their daughter-in-law for the first time since the surgery. He wanted an entire day to see how much Preye had progressed. He was just about ready to have the Banigo family legally banned, which was in his rights as a husband. He had informed his family lawyer, who promised to draw up a draft for him. Until that was ready, he had to allow the Banigos family to see Preye.

He showed up in her room alone with some hot *dundun and akara* that he had gotten from the bus stop.

He made himself some coffee from the table and set himself to have his meal. 'Isn't this nice, darling? Breakfast together, just you and I, like the old days. I brought your favourite food to help with your sense of smell. I should thank you for responding and coming back to us. You're showing signs of progress and I hope you open those beautiful brown eyes for Mum and Dad.' When he finished, he picked up Preye's perfectly manicured hand and kissed it. 'This looks nice. I love your hands the way they are clean. Finally, someone decided to give my wife a well-deserved treat.'

Soon Wale and Ife arrived with a bouquet that included lilies, which went a long way to douse the smell of Timi's breakfast. Timi was thrilled to see his parents.

'I'm so glad you came and I'm sure Preye can feel the love and warmth you bring. She might be up to opening her eyes and lifting her hand, which will be her way of showing appreciation,' Timi said.

'She looks like she's taking a nap. I thought she'd look ghastly, but I was wrong. She's as beautiful as always. Just a little slimmer,' Ife said with a terse smile. She wore a red skirt and blouse set of floral print on red flat sandals. If Ife Coker loved anything about fashion, it was getting her outfit colours matched. 'Doesn't she look lovely, Wale?'

'Not bad for a girl on a hospital bed,' Wale said with a grin. 'What's the update?'

'She's making progress, but she has a long road ahead of her. Her doctors are cautiously optimistic, and I am too. They might get her off the vent today. It depends on how fast her recovery is. She might come home with me or I may have her moved to a long-term care facility and we'll re-evaluate at that time.'

Timi wanted to show his parents that there was some hope for his wife and he had everything planned. He had been told that she regularly opened her eyes to other visitors, and he hoped that she'd do the same for his parents.

He turned to Preye and spoke directly to her. 'Mine, my parents are here to see you. I know you can hear me. Could you just open your eyes, so you can see them? And let them know you're here with us.' He held his wife's hand.

'Let me sit with her. Maybe she'll respond to my touch. It may stir something inside of her,' Ife said, dragging the chair to Preye's bedside. Ife held Preye's hand and massaged it a bit, but there was no response. She got frustrated. 'Are you sure she's been responsive? She hasn't done a thing since we've been here.

I expected some form of reaction from her.'

'Give her a break.' Timi sensed his mother's disappointment. He was becoming irritated too. 'Mum, can you get Stella from the nurses' station? She may be able to tickle Preye,' Timi told his mother. He wanted some time alone with his father, and it was apparent his mother also needed a break from Preye.

'I need to use the toilet too. It was a long drive here.' Ife disappeared.

Timi collapsed in the chair. Wale walked over to comfort his stressed son. 'This can't be easy on you. No need to pretend you're stronger than you need to be. Now that your mother is gone, tell me your plans if Preye remains in limbo.'

'Now that there is visible brain activity, I no longer have to worry about removing her life support. The future, however, is unpredictable. I need to concentrate on my business at some point and I don't want the Banigos coming in to take over. As I told you, my lawyer is drawing up a permanent decree that gives me sole custody of Preye.'

Wale turned around sharply to face Timi. 'Custody? That word sounds like something you'd do to a child.'

'Indeed, Dad. I will be responsible for her needs and determine who is allowed to visit. This will be a permanent arrangement so I won't have to worry, and I can start focusing on Timi's Communications. Preye is the only person who can nullify the arrangement and I don't see that happening if she can't even open her eyes. It sounds cold and calculating but it's in the best interest of my wife,' Timi explained.

'When will the lawyer bring the documents? He'd need to get them stamped too.'

'Two weeks, three, max.' Timi strolled over to Preye and looked down at her motionless body.

'She's very lucky to have married you. Who knows what would have become of her if you hadn't come along.' Wale patted his son on the back.

Ife returned and told them Stella would be coming over soon. They talked briefly about Timi's Communications and his parents commended him for doing them proud as always.

*

'This has been a productive day, Preye,' Timi said sarcastically, after his parents left and he was alone with her. He lifted her limp hand and let it fall. 'My parents were overwhelmed by your performance. Maybe it's just me, but I think you became unresponsive to make me look like a fool in front of them. I hope you won't force me to do what I don't want to do. I want my wife back but without effort on your part, that's not going to happen.' He felt it was time to let Preye know the reality of her potential future. 'It seems like you want me to check you into a long term facility. If that's what you want, it's fine. I'll make sure your basic needs are met, but I can't promise much beyond that.' He started stroking her thick beautiful hair. 'Your sisters won't be around to take care of your hair and I doubt if your parents can foot the bill, anyway. Too bad, but that's the way it's going to be. I'm going to leave for the evening.'

He leaned down and kissed her cheek.

*

It was the desirable aroma of the *akara* that wafted through to Preye's senses and woke her up. She was trying to muster the energy to open her eyes when she heard the strange but familiar voice. It wasn't one of the voices that had been with her in the past couple of days. She remembered it was Timi after she caught the whiff of the coffee. He was talking to her about joining him for breakfast and the scene of the day they met

328

flashed in her mind …

*

…He had walked into Roadrunners office with a cup of aromatic coffee in his hand. She had been immediately attracted to him and she had tried hard to resist his charm, but he had broken down her defences with his thoughtfulness and advances. She remembered they had gotten married and he had bought her a beautiful house she didn't want. She knew she shouldn't have married him. But he had known how to get to her and no matter how much she tried, she hadn't been able to resist him until he cheated on her and...

The word, wife interrupted Preye's flashback. She heard Timi refer to her as his wife and it confused her. How could she still be his wife when she already left him? No! She couldn't be his wife. A flood of memories assaulted her senses and magnified her headache as she remembered several things that Timi had done to batter her self-esteem in many ways; ways she shuddered to recall. She was no longer his wife!

He kept talking, so she listened to him.

She heard his parents come in and she wanted to tell Ife to leash her son. When Ife touched her, she wished she had the energy to cringe, as she felt no kinship towards Ife. Preye liked Ife and it pained her that Ife had to plead for her to open her eyes, but she wasn't about to give Timi that satisfaction. He always had his way with her, but somehow, she knew that there was nothing he could do to her on her hospital bed. She heard them talk about her as if she was non-existent. She understood everything he said and she was going to fight to get up. The only thing she didn't understand was how she was still his wife. Timi eventually turned his back to leave her room and Preye slowly lifted her middle digit to give him the finger.

She needed the exercise.

CHAPTER THIRTY TWO

Lola was a little ahead of Miriam, who had sent a text that she was almost at the hospital. She stopped by at the toilet to apply some makeup and adjust her dress to look good for Preye's sake. She waved sarcastically as she walked past the nurse's station, swinging her hips as she headed for Preye's room.

'Good morning,' Lola greeted. Dr David was in the room with a nurse unfamiliar to Lola. 'How's she today?' Although the ventilator attached to Preye had been removed, she looked the same as she had looked two days ago, with a half-moon smile on her face.

'It's a good day. She's been making some sounds, but no words yet. Are her parents coming?' Dr David asked, just as Harry, Miriam and Tonye pushed themselves into the room. 'I'm going to have to ask that there is only one person per time, so you may need to take turns to stay in the room with her. I think she'll benefit from some quiet periods today. It's up to you to work it out.' Dr David picked up the chart book, studying it.

Even with her eyes shut, Preye could see the smiles of everyone around her and it infused her with some energy, assuring her that life was possible, so she mustered herself to open her eyes.

'Hello,' Preye said in a whisper. 'I want to say I'm sorry, but my head hurts.' Her words were soft, but audible enough for everyone to hear.

Everyone froze. And by the time they recovered, there wasn't a dry eye in the room, except for the doctor and nurse. Lola broke the spell first and she ran to throw her arms around Preye but she could only cradle the bed until the nurse pulled her back. Everyone started talking at the same time, thanking God and embracing one another.

The doctor whispered an instruction to the nurse as she slowly adjusted Preye's drip. He asked the visitors to calm down and told them they still needed to take turns to be in the room. After they left, Dr David asked Preye questions but she could only respond with head movements. He made some notes on the chart book before leaving the room with the nurse.

Outside Preye's room, everyone agreed Miriam should go first. Harry pleaded to stay with Miriam because he didn't know what he'd say to Preye by himself. He added his hand when Miriam clasped Preye's hand. 'Your words are music to my ears, but don't waste your energy apologising to any of us. Just get well. Your dad and I love you.'

It was Tonye's turn and she held Preye's hand. 'Don't ever do that to us again,' Tonye pleaded. 'I didn't realise you were such a vital part of my life until I almost lost you. I can't tell you how many times I picked up my phone to give you a ring. Suddenly, I needed advice on everything, from work to whether I should wear my blue or red trousers.'

Preye smiled. If she had the strength, she'd have told Tonye to trust her own instincts. Tonye was the smartest of them all, but the years of alcohol abuse had thrown her into self-doubt, such that she didn't recognise how smart she was. Although Preye thought she'd tell Tonye to toss the blue trousers to the bin because they had been out of fashion for almost a decade. Tonye was comforted by her sister's slight smile. 'Next time, I hope Erefa will be able to make it. If she can trust me with her baby, I'd stay behind. That baby is growing fast too.'

'Yes,' Preye whispered. She looked forward to seeing Erefa. Tonye left and ushered in Lola.

'Knowing you, you're looking for a way to worry about Beta while fighting for your life,' Lola babbled. '*Omo* girl, you know how you tell your Roadrunners that taking care of their bodies would yield long-term benefits. Well, think of yourself the same way now.' She picked up Preye's hand and gently drew a pass mark on it with one finger. 'If I never told you that you were a champion, I'm telling you now. You fight to win and you've won this.' Lola's voice cracked, but she pulled it together before it fell to pieces.

Preye smiled. Her day had started as her family and Lola made their way to her bedside, one at a time. She opened her eyes and smiled each time someone new came in. They made her happy by saturating her with warmth, and they were worth the effort.

Miriam had a few wrinkles that Preye hadn't noticed before. Harry's hair was almost entirely grey and everyone else looked generally exhausted, except Lola, who was dressed as if she was going for a client's meeting. Preye hated that she was such a nuisance and had caused her loved ones so much stress. That was why she wanted to apologise. She was happy in their presence, even though for the most part, she lay motionless.

She had dreamt about Kevin in her sleep and he had told her she needed to fight to stay alive. She was trying but she wasn't sure how much longer she could keep it up. The feeling of being tapped on the shoulder by Kevin was exhilarating. From the moment Preye and Kevin met, to the last time he squeezed her hand, it had been something unique. Dwelling alongside Kevin Murphy in the warm glowing light she had seen earlier seemed like nirvana and Preye preferred it to one more moment with Timi.

*

The nurses saw Timi walk in and they feared that a drama was about to play out. He had decided that keeping away was conceding victory to Lola and the Banigos. If they couldn't deal with him, then it should be their problem, not his. He resolved that he wouldn't leave the hospital until Preye opened her eyes. In the course of his restless night, he had convinced himself that it was because he wasn't around enough that he missed those important moments with Preye.

Lola and the Banigos had left for the waiting room, to give Preye a break to sleep, so no one accosted Timi as he approached Preye's room and there was no drama as the nurses had envisaged. When he got to the nurse's station and asked about his wife, they told him she was asleep. And they shared the good news that she had muttered a few words.

Preye slept as much as she was able to. The hospital was the worst place to sleep because nurses were constantly in and out of her room, checking vitals, taking blood samples and making sure she didn't died suddenly. She was able to move her fingers, but it took strength - the type she needed a year ago to run fifteen kilometres. Weakness dominated her body like she had never experienced before; it was as if an alien had taken over. She determined she'd fight to take back control as she heard the echo of Lola's words that she was a champion.

She heard footsteps coming down the corridor once again and she knew it was Timi by the scent of his perfume.

'I hear that you've talked today, Mine. Congratulations. Is today the day you show me what you've got?' Timi asked, stepping close to her bed.

There was no way Preye was going to open her eyes or move a muscle for him. She still hadn't been able to unravel how she was his wife. She intended to ask her mother or Lola when she had enough strength, but right now, she wouldn't give him what he asked. The smug satisfaction on Timi's face is what Preye would see if she opened her eyes.

'Until your family became involved, I was by your side nearly every moment, begging you to open your eyes and talk to me,' he said, looking intently at her. He was wearing faded jeans and a green t-shirt, one of Preye's favourite looks. 'Yet you refuse to spare me a blink.'

Stop! Preye thought in her fuzzy state. She wished she had a shield to protect herself. She felt his venom as his gaze lingered and she knew she'd be forced to deal with him if she chose to continue running from the light. He thought his disguise of love was enough to keep fooling her, but he was wrong. He still didn't understand that she wasn't his wife, and he persisted.

He smiled. 'Oh, I see your family has gotten to you and probably told you not to talk to me. They have filled your head with lies, but if you listen to me, I'll be able to explain everything. We have something special and sometimes people have a hard time getting that.'

She thought of what she'd say to him if she had the strength. *Since the day you met me, you've tried to mould me into the woman I am not. My clothes, friends, lifestyle and everything else weren't good enough for you. Even my birthmark. My confidence was destroyed to the point where I was unrecognisable to my family or myself. You tried to steal my financial independence and you cheated on me. I've left you Timi, I'm not your wife.* They were words Preye wished she could spew out, but he wasn't worth the effort.

So she retreated.

He continued to plead his case. He said he had been by her side since she lost consciousness and he deserved a chance to hear her voice and see her beautiful eyes. He assured her that their love was the only thing that mattered. Then he asked her why no other man had taken her to the altar if she was as successful as she made out. He said he was the only one that could love her the way she deserved and he informed her that he was the one paying her hospital bills even though he hadn't known that she was going to be such a liability.

He fluctuated between sweet and harsh words to get her to open her eyes. He threatened to abandon her forever if she didn't respond.

She wished she could yank his hand away as he placed it on hers to tell her he loved her. His touch felt cold and too much to bear. The other side where Kevin's gentle voice came from was where the light was warm, and it was in sight.

All Preye had to do was let go…

With the love radiating from her family when they were with her, Preye had felt there was so much good to keep fighting for. But it was only Timi Coker's face hovering over her now and she thought he might never go away. She felt him shaking her shoulder, repeatedly crying that he loved her. It was the same words that had kept her confused...

The machines went wild, the lines on the monitor flattened and the alarms shrieked. Timi jumped back, startled. A nurse burst in immediately as if she had been waiting by the door. She pushed Timi aside and said a doctor would be there soon. Lola and the Banigos heard the menacing chaos from the waiting room and rushed to Preye's room too. Dr David was already at the door and he told them they couldn't enter. They obeyed, filing out like automated beings, each in a different state of mystification.

… She passed the light and peeped into the abyss. She saw a path open up through the abyss. She felt the serenity and the urge to run into the unending bliss.

Her pulsating breaths became nothing more than slow shallow gasps as they gradually detached from her heart. The pain that lurked in her soul like an inferno began to chip away, to make way for a soothing coolness. Her sight blurred to a pitch of velvet black, but she could see Kevin walking away from her. He must have guessed that she couldn't see clearly, because his smooth melodic voice reached her soul and she followed the tune to find her way into the void ahead, using her hands on both sides to feel the smooth and shiny buttercups that lined the path.

She finally reached the edge of the void. She couldn't see anything, but she could hear the rustling of trees; the pure saturating laughter; the chirping birdsongs; the lyrics in the elegy, and the unending sound of nature. It was a peaceful place.

Preye stepped into the abyss to embrace the peace.

GLOSSARY

Abeg – Please.

Abeg no give me yawa, I never try – Please don't give me stress. Haven't I tried?

Adire – Native Nigerian tie and dye cotton fabric.

Ajebo – Sophisticated (slang)

Akara – Snack of fried beans-balls.

Ankara – Colourful cotton fabric.

Ashewo – A prostitute, slut or someone who exchanges sex for favours.

Bobo – Gentleman.

Chai – Rueful exclamation.

Dabi moseda – Someone like me.

Danfo – Public transport bus

Dey shark – Excites.

Dodo – Fried plantain.

Dundun – Snack of fried yam.

Efo-riro – Vegetable soup full of assorted meat parts

Fokifoki – Coveting.

Garri – Popular Nigerian cassava flour.

Haba – Really!

How now / How you dey – How are you?

I fit drag Sammy com arrest you, carry you go guardroom – I can bring Sammy to arrest you and take you to jail.

If to say na my papa get that kain money – If my father had that kind of money.

I no wan carry last for the dance – I don't want to take the last position in the dance competition.

It's P *dt's* missing in action. – It's Preye that's missing in action.

I wan go sleep abeg, work dey tomorrow – Please, I want to go to bed. There's work tomorrow.

Juju – A genre of Yoruba music.

338

Kente – Native Ghanaian thick colourful cotton fabric.

Na you I dey ask – I'm asking you.

Nkwobi – A delicacy dish of cow foot.

Nothing do me – Nothing is wrong with me.

Ofada – Nigerian-grown local rice.

Ogbologbo – Veteran of a negative type

Olowo ori mi – Pet title for husband.

Omo girl – Darling girl.

No chng just cuz you r hitched – Not changing just because you are hitched.

Sake of say she marry better person – Because she's married to a good person.

Sez – Says.

Shayo - Drunkard

Spray – Pasting money an entertainer's body as a show of appreciating the act

SU (abbreviation for Scripture Union) – A Christian spiritual movement.

Sushi – A dish of raw fish wrapped with rice and seaweed

Suya – Grilled peppered thin steak.

This one na nonsense - This is nonsense.

When you reach here – What are you doing here?

Wetin him find go do soldier work sef – Why did he become a soldier?

We wetin – We will do what?

When I never fast reach – When I'm not fast enough.

You be woman wrapper o – You're being controlled by a woman.

You know say I no send - You know that I don't care.

Zobo – Hibiscus flower drink

A NOTE FROM TAYO

Thank you for reading Peace in the Abyss. I hope you've enjoyed reading it. As you can imagine, I've had to live in the heads and hearts of the characters and writing this novel has been an emotional experience for me, because I see this play out in all spheres of society.

You may have been disappointed that this story didn't end in a happily ever after. Sadly so, some romance do end in tragedies.

I have seen too many strange bed-fellows trying to force relationships to work without addressing fundamental issues; I have seen loads of people getting married due to family, friends or societal pressures; I have seen a lot lose themselves to a relationship that should never have been; and I have seen some battered physically, others damaged emotionally and a few killed. I have seen concerned folks trying to reconcile couples who aren't willing to make the required changes. I have sat with a woman who wished she could kill her husband just so she could experience some peace. And in all of these, I can only ask why?

While Peace in the Abyss is entirely fictitious, I sincerely hope it stirs you to ponder on the quality of your relationships and those of people around you.

Whatever you feel about Peace in the Abyss and my other novels, I'd love to hear from you. Please drop me an email at info@tayoutomi.co.uk.

Printed in Great Britain
by Amazon

64607242R00208